Kay Brellend never imagined she would become a writer, certainly not a writer of novels inspired by her own family. Kay's Campbell Road series, set in the 'worst street in North London', follows the same Islington family covering the years between WW1 and WW2. The Campbell Road series of books has been an absorbing journey and she has learned much about the toughness and resilience of her ancestors: Kay feels pride in her roots in the worst street in north London.

Please visit her website www.kaybrellend.com for more information.

A SISTER'S BOND

Kay Brellend

piatkus

PIATKUS

First published in Great Britain in 2017 by Piatkus

1 3 5 7 9 10 8 6 4 2

A CIP catalogue record for this book is available from the British Library.

ISBN 978-0-349-41526-0

Typeset in Palatino by M Rules
Printed and bound in Great Britain by
Clays Ltd, St Ives plc

Papers used by Piatkus are from well-managed forests
and other responsible sources.

Piatkus
An imprint of
Little, Brown Book Group
Carmelite House
50 Victoria Embankment
London EC4Y 0DZ

An Hachette UK Company
www.hachette.co.uk

www.littlebrown.co.uk

Although Barratt's was a real confectioner in Wood Green, all the characters in the book and the events described are fictional. Any resemblance to real people or events is coincidental.

For Chantal, with love

Chapter One

November 1913, Wood Green, North London

'Ain't gonna do you no good, hiding under there. You might as well come out and take what's coming to yer.'

The threat in that drunken voice had the small boy slithering backwards on his bottom beneath the table. His wide blue eyes were glistening but he didn't weep. Alfie Bone had learned by now that his father, even when sober, wasn't moved by his tears. Alfie might howl and say he was sorry but his father wasn't given to pity.

Though his eyes were squeezed almost shut, Alfie could see in his line of vision five fidgeting fingers with potato mould beneath the ragged nails. Soon that hand would grab and hurt him.

Tommy Bone would have finished his shift down the market by midday then gone to the pub. Tommy rarely returned home before ten o'clock at night; even if his money ran out early, he'd hang around on a bar stool hoping to filch drinks off pals. But this evening he had returned hours earlier than usual, catching his son unawares.

As soon as he'd heard the key strike the lock Alfie had abandoned his supper of tea and bread and shot off the chair to wriggle beneath the table. He'd hugged himself into a small ball in his hiding place with his knees up against his chest and his nose pressed into them; even so he could smell the booze on his father's breath.

Alfie squeaked as his safety barrier was flung noisily aside. He felt the hot trickle against his inner thigh and clenched his bony buttocks in an attempt to stop wetting himself further. He knew he'd get a taste of his father's belt as well as a clouting for making that mess.

His father's corduroy-clad knees bent and a bristly face appeared, making Alfie shudder and soak himself.

'You dirty little git.' Tommy had seen the pool of urine and drew back his lips over tobacco-stained teeth. 'Ain't enough that you wet the bed regular ... you've started pissing on the floor 'n' all.' He snaked out a hand out to grab a hank of his son's fair hair and haul him up. Alfie levered his heels on the bare boards, jerking himself backwards out of reach, making his father roar in frustration.

'Leave him alone! I'll clean that up. Get yourself to bed, Dad. You're drunk and you've got to be up early in the morning for work.'

Tommy straightened up, slanting a glance over one shoulder at his eldest daughter. He'd not heard Olivia come in, so intent had he been on giving Alfie a thrashing. She had a challenging look in her eyes. But that wasn't unusual or unexpected.

Olivia was her mother's daughter: fine-boned and blonde-haired with the face of an angel, but delicate though she looked, she was tough and not at all frightened of him. Unlike the others, especially Alfie. Planting his fists on his hips, he stared narrow-eyed at his daughter. Olivia held her ground. She didn't even blink. Tommy looked her over, from her buttoned boots and long serge skirt to the small neat hat set atop a thickly coiled bun of fair hair. You'd have thought she had been out with her friends rather than working behind the counter of a rough-house caff. But that was his Livvie ... she kept up her standards, just like her mother had before her.

'Turn in, Dad, you can't stand up straight,' Olivia said when her father's eyelids began to flutter. Unbuttoning her coat, she hooked it on the back of the door then unpinned her hat. Taking her father's sleeve, she attempted to pull him towards the corridor.

Tommy roughly shook her off; shuffling his feet apart for balance, he stood there swaying. 'Don't you go ordering me about, miss,' he snarled. 'I'll get me rest after I've given that little bleeder a hiding.' Tommy's thick finger fiddled with the scarf knotted round his neck then stabbed repeatedly at the table. 'Broken a winder round at the Catholic Mission, ain't he? One of the nuns collared me in the pub and started asking fer money.' Tommy's lips were bloodless with rage. 'Been shown up good 'n' proper in front of me pals, and all on account of him!' Tommy's forefinger resumed jabbing. Having worked himself up again, he suddenly plunged one hand beneath the table to drag his son out. Olivia wrestled him back but he sent her to her knees with a sideways swipe.

Olivia now had a clear view of her seven-year-old brother and the sight of his chalky face and quaking limbs rekindled her courage, propelling her to her feet. She couldn't let her father sense her fear. His was the sort of character that fed on another's weakness. She'd always stood up to him and would continue to do so while she had breath left in her body to protect her siblings – especially Alfie. Their mother had never been able to protect him, but Olivia had … from the day he was born.

She dug in her skirt pocket and pulled out the wages she'd just received from the proprietor of Ward's eel and pie shop, tipping the coins on to the splintered tabletop. 'There, that should cover the damage to the window.' She looked and sounded quite calm but she was carefully watching her father's reaction. When he was seriously drunk, as now, it was difficult to know how he would react. He could blub sentimentally for his late wife or turn vicious and lash out at any of his kids, to try and ease the guilt that devoured him. But the coward took it out on his youngest child the most.

Tommy blinked, bleary-eyed, at the silver and copper. The sight of cash always had a sobering effect on him. His eldest daughter uncomplainingly handed over the majority of her wages but he knew she usually kept back some pennies that she was saving up. 'Ain't enough there for a new winder pane and your share of the kitty,' he growled.

'It'll have to be enough for now, 'cos it's all I've got. I'll speak to the Sisters and tell them we'll settle up the rest of what's owed next week.' Olivia started counting out her housekeeping, intending to put the rest back into her pocket to take to the Mission Hall.

Clumsily, Tommy Bone knocked aside his daughter's small hand and swept all the coins into his greedy palm. 'I'll speak to the nosy cows, and I'll tell 'em to send Brody round next time he's got an axe to grind.' Tommy hunched his shoulders into his donkey jacket. 'Sent a woman to do a man's job, and a nun at that!' He spat in disgust.

Olivia attempted to steady her father as he wobbled. Again

4

he disdained her help by shrugging her off before weaving towards the door under his own steam.

She knew that the window-pane money wouldn't get as far as the Mission, or Father Brody. It would stay in Tommy's pocket until spent on a pint, or a bet on the nags. But she was glad the sight of her wages had side-tracked him; he'd forgotten about Alfie, hiding under the table. Once she heard the bedroom door slam shut Olivia crouched down. She beckoned to her brother, giving him a reassuring smile. He crawled out on his hands and knees, snuffling and knuckling his damp eyes.

'Let's get those wet things off you,' Olivia said on a sigh, helping him to his feet. While Alfie peeled off his sodden trousers she got a towel from the cupboard by the side of the fireplace and proceeded to briskly dry off his scrawny buttocks and legs. He winced as she rubbed over a spot on his thigh that had a healing bruise on it. Olivia soothed him, her heart squeezing tight as she turned her brother round to dry his other side and saw another purple blotch, this time on his shoulder. She swallowed the anger rising in her throat that made her want to rush to her father's bedroom and bawl at him that he was a brute. She pressed her lips against her little brother's shoulder, kissing it better.

'I hate him!' Alfie croaked, clasping his sister's head close to his chest and starting to cry.

Olivia had heard that before, and not only from her brother. Her two sisters claimed to feel the same way. Olivia found it hard to like their father as well, but at seventeen she was learning life had a dark side and that the lines between love and hate and good and evil could be blurred. Heartache, and the never-ending struggle to scrape a living for your family, could knock all the decency out of folk. She'd seen girls she'd been friendly with at school turn into coarse tarts, hanging around the market place after dark looking for punters. Yet they'd been full of joy and hope just a few years ago. Even those kids, like her, who'd been raised hard and hungry had cherished dreams of a better future. Olivia wasn't giving up yet, even though those dreams seemed to shift further away from her every day.

'Stand still,' she said as Alfie attempted to wriggle free. 'You'll get chapped if you don't dry off properly.' She put aside the towel. 'Now find yourself some pants and a vest in the cupboard. I'll rinse these trousers through.' She fetched a tin bowl and began to wring the worst of the pee into it.

'If you wash 'em they won't dry by morning. Need 'em for school.' Alfie was pulling on his patched vest, trembling with the cold.

It was late November and the frost had shrouded every surface outside with silver. As she'd hurried home over icy ground Olivia had imagined a poet would be inspired to write verses about nature's sparkle. Now such flighty nonsense was forgotten.

'I'll rinse them. They'll smell else and you won't want your mates calling you names, will you?'

Blood stung Alfie's cheeks. He'd been called Piss Pants on numerous occasions after he'd wet the bed and the stink of the sheets had lingered on his skin.

Pulling up his clean pants, he nipped to the table to wolf down what was left of his bread and gulp his cold tea.

'Why didn't you get to bed on time, Alfie?' Olivia asked. 'You know it's best to be out of his way when he comes in.'

'He was back early. Anyhow, I had an errand to do for Mrs Cook so didn't get me tea on time,' Alfie explained. 'She asked me to fetch a bucket of coal from the corner shop. I took a few lumps off the top and put 'em in our scuttle.'

'If she finds out she won't ask you again,' his sister warned.

She didn't want Alfie to think she liked what he'd done, although she recalled doing similar things herself while still at school and wanting, in her own way, to help the family out with a bit of ducking and diving.

Lifting his empty plate, Alfie retrieved his earnings hidden under it. He knew that if his father had realised the coins were there he'd have taken them. He held out the two ha'pennies to his sister. 'You can have 'em,' he said magnanimously. 'Dad's taken all of yours.'

'Thanks.' Olivia took the money, paltry offering though it was. She was indeed broke now and she didn't want to have to dip too far into her small savings pot, hidden away to pay for a few Christmas treats for them all. Besides it wouldn't hurt her brother to contribute something if he'd been causing trouble. She fixed a jaundiced eye on Alfie. 'Did you break that window?'

'It was an accident. It did get broke but it weren't me done it,' Alfie stressed. 'I was in goal, but Wicksie booted the ball that put the glass out.' Alfie frowned. 'He blamed me and said it was my fault 'cos I should've saved it. Went way over me head, though.' Alfie looked ashamed not to have reached the shot although he was much younger and smaller than the boy he'd been playing football with.

Olivia ruffled his hair for comfort. Tearing up a rag she'd found in the cupboard, she dropped to her hands and knees, carefully keeping her skirt away from the puddle on the floor. She didn't want to be washing that too. 'Make yourself useful and tip that pee down the privy then fetch me some water in the bowl.' She started to mop the wet lino.

Alfie pulled on his battered boots then scooted off in his underwear. He returned, sloshing water. After putting down the bowl he stood at his sister's side, quaking with cold, his shoulders hunched to his ears and his arms wrapped about himself.

Olivia stopped scrubbing the floor, pushing her blonde fringe from her eyes with one wrist. She'd forgotten it was icy outside and regretted sending him out there half dressed. Sitting back on her heels, she dried her damp hands on her skirts then rubbed some warmth into his goose-pimpled limbs until he groaned a protest.

'Go on, get to bed now, I'll finish up here.' She gave him a little push towards the door. 'Jump in with Nancy and Maggie and snuggle up. I'll be along myself soon. I'm all in.'

The Bones had three rooms in the terraced house on Ranelagh Road that they called home. At one time they'd rented the whole property but they'd had to let the upstairs go when money got tight after Aggie Bone passed away. Their landlord had carved the hallway into two with a partition so the downstairs had its own doorway but all the occupants shared the square of corridor leading to the stairs. The family's accommodation now consisted of just a back parlour housing a cooking range, and two front rooms used to sleep in. Tommy had taken a bedroom to himself while his four children shared the other.

Several residents had come and gone upstairs. Some had disappeared during the night after getting behind with their rent. The landlord didn't tolerate arrears but he'd never needed to chase the Bone family. Tommy Bone did his duty by his family that far at least.

Olivia immersed the soiled trousers in the bowl, dunking them up and down a few times before leaving them to soak. She perched on the edge of a chair and let her head droop into her cupped palms. Now Alfie was safely in bed she gave way to a tiredness that wasn't wholly to do with her having rushed home after toiling for several hours washing pots and doling out pie and mash at the caff. The constant anxiety of looking out for her brother and sisters was sapping her strength. She'd managed to defuse things this evening, just as she had on previous occasions, but there was always tomorrow and the day after that to worry about.

Despite feeling ashamed for having such thoughts, Olivia often wished her father would abandon them to bunk up with a woman, leaving them all in peace. Of course, if he did they would suffer financially. She'd struggle to raise her school-age siblings without her father's contribution providing them with basic necessities. Mentally, Olivia balanced that disadvantage against the fact that if he wasn't around she'd be able to bring in more. At present she worked when certain he'd also be out, reasoning that if they were at home at the same time she could keep the peace.

Like Alfie, she had been caught out by Tommy's early return from the pub. Usually they were all, herself included, behind the closed bedroom door by the time he let himself in.

Tommy worked daytime shifts at Barratt's sweet factory and boosted his earnings by helping out at the weekends on a market stall. For all his faults, Tommy Bone wasn't a shirker. He liked to keep enough cash in his pocket for booze and bets and 'bacca.

Olivia started to wring out Alfie's trousers, continuing until her wrists and knuckles ached with the effort. She hung them over the mantel, pinned there by a heavy brass candlestick. Slow drips from the material hit the metal beneath, hissing quietly on the hot hob plate. Olivia shook the scuttle. Hearing Alfie's few purloined lumps of coal rattling at the bottom, she built up the fire in the hope the trousers would dry by the morning. After briskly rubbing her stiff fingers together she put the kettle on to boil for a cup of tea. It was all the supper she felt she could stomach.

'What's up, Livvie? Heard you come in a while ago. Thought you'd have come to bed by now.'

Olivia turned to see her sister Maggie entering the parlour, wrapped in her dressing gown. 'Heard Dad come in first though, didn't you?'

Maggie bit her lip and shrugged, looking sheepish.

'I'll be turning in in a minute, after I've had me tea,' Olivia said. 'Is Alfie getting off to sleep?'

'Nah ... he's just laying there snivelling, getting on me nerves. I got up 'cos I can't get back to sleep now he's woken me.'

Olivia made the tea but she didn't offer her sister a cup. Maggie was the next eldest child at almost fourteen and, although Olivia didn't expect her to stand up to their father in the way she did herself, she believed her sister capable of protecting their little brother more than she did. Maggie and Nancy had turned in, knowing that Alfie was out on his own. It wouldn't have hurt one of them to wait up for a short while for him to return from his errand then hurry him to bed.

Maggie sat down and cocked her head. 'What's got your goat? Ain't my fault Alfie's in Dad's bad books again. Broken a window, ain't he?'

'You knew about that?' Olivia put down her cup, surprised.

'Ricky Wicks told me. Didn't think the nuns would rat on him, though.' Maggie stifled a chuckle. 'Alfie just told me they collared Dad in the pub about it.'

'I'm going to bed now.' Olivia put the cup in the washing up bowl, feeling maddened that her sister could find anything amusing in what had happened.

'Ain't my fault Dad takes it out on Alfie, you know.' Maggie sounded huffy.

'Not saying it is, but our brother nearly got another hiding for something he didn't do. You can tell Ricky Wicks that I know he put the window out and in future he should hang around with kids his own age.'

'Tell him yerself,' Maggie answered back. She and Ricky were in the same class; she knew he liked her and that's why he'd let her little brother play football with him and his mates.

'Keep your voice down or you'll wake Dad up *then* you'll be sorry.' Olivia made an effort to subdue her annoyance. Picking up a stub of burning candle from the mantelshelf, she headed towards the door.

In the bedroom they all shared, the sound of her younger sister's snoring made Maggie chuckle. 'Nancy'll suck the paper off the wall, way she's going.'

'What's left of it,' Olivia muttered as she closed the door and put the candle on the floor next to her bed. The small room stank of damp and even in the dim light rags of wallpaper could be seen drooping by the ceiling.

''Ere, shift over, Nance,' Maggie hissed, climbing onto the double iron bedstead she shared with her eleven-year-old sister and Alfie. It groaned beneath her slight weight and Nancy rolled over, mumbling as she settled back to sleep.

Olivia sank onto the edge of the sagging mattress on her single bed, pushed against the opposite wall, and started to unbutton her boots. She eased them off her aching feet, flexing her toes in her woollen stockings. Quickly she took off her skirt and blouse, making sure to fold them neatly at the end of the bed before slipping on her dressing gown over her underclothes. The looming shadows of the wardrobe and nightstand made the room feel claustrophobic.

'Can I come in with you, Livvie?' Alfie called quietly into the darkness.

'Yeah ... come on.'

Olivia took off her dressing gown and wrapped him in it

11

then pulled the solitary blanket up over them both, doubling it back and over Alfie to give him extra warmth. She put her arms about him, cuddling him fiercely. 'Now go to sleep . . . your trousers'll be nice and dry in the morning.' She whispered that last comment, knowing he wouldn't want his sister Maggie to know he'd wet himself. If she knew then so would others; she kept nothing to herself . . . other than that her father was a bully. But then they all did that.

With a sigh Olivia leaned down to snuff out the candle flame.

Chapter Two

'How you doing then, Tommy?'

'Bearing up, mate ... bearing up.' Tommy Bone clapped Bill Morley on the shoulder in greeting then settled his cloth cap back on his head with a flourish. The two men carried on walking along Mayes Road towards Barratt's sweet factory where they worked. In fact Tommy had a thumping head after his Sunday drinking session but he'd never let on to anybody about how he felt. Even work colleagues he'd known for over a decade found him hard to fathom. He might have a drink and a chat with them but in reality he was a loner with no close friends. The only places anybody ever saw Tommy Bone were the factory, the pub, or hanging around the bookie's. It was well known that he was a widower with four kids but he could have been a bachelor because he was always seen on his own.

Tommy had got up for work as usual at a quarter to seven that morning. A shift at the sweet factory ran from eight in the morning to six-thirty at night and woe betide any latecomers or shirkers. The bosses expected strict timekeeping and, to be fair, they more or less stuck to the rules too.

His eldest daughter had already been up when Tommy appeared in the parlour, scratching his belly over his vest. Olivia had been lugging a basket of sheets out to the washhouse. Monday was washday and Livvie had a heavy task in front of her. Not only did she spend from early till late doing their washing and ironing, but she took in for the old girl next-door who had arthritic hands. As was his custom, Tommy didn't stop to help his eldest carry the washing basket, or to speak to her other than to grunt a 'mornin''. Neither did she receive a thank-you for the modest breakfast that she had prepared for him and left under a cloth, as she did every morning before he rose for work. He drank his tea and ate his bread and jam in silence, as usual, seated at the small parlour table.

Despite his hangover, and his run in with the nun that still made him seethe when he thought about it, Tommy was in a good frame of mind as he bowled along, arms swinging at his sides. He'd remembered that the new motor van was due for a run that morning, the latest addition to the company's transport that to date had comprised only horse-drawn vehicles. Tommy was hoping to get a crack at driving the van, being as he was one of Mr Barratt's most loyal employees. He was the only original staff member still with the firm since it had moved from Hoxton to spanking new premises in Wood Green.

At Hoxton, Tommy had been a sugar-boiler, manufacturing the 'stickjaw' toffee that kids loved. He'd started work there at thirteen but it had been before his time when George Barratt Senior had accidentally hit on a novel way of making his fortune. He'd over-boiled a batch of sugar being prepared for cake confectionery. The old skinflint hadn't wanted to waste it so had sold it on as kids' toffee. It had gone down a treat with customers so he carried on manufacturing sweets, becoming successful enough to afford to build a sprawling new factory in North London.

'Didn't see you down the pub last night,' Bill Morley said innocently as the two men carried on along the frosty street in the weak wintry dawn. 'Dick said you'd been in but left around half-eight. Didn't get down there meself till gone nine being as the missus burned me tea then come over all lovey-dovey to make up for it.' Bill bit his lip to subdue a smile. He'd heard from Dick Barnes, the pub landlord, that Tommy Bone had gone off in a rage after a nun tore him off a strip on account of his lad misbehaving.

Tommy would talk the hind leg off a donkey about his job and how far back he went with the firm's guvnors. But when it came to his home and his kids, he kept it all to himself. If it weren't for a woman who'd once rented rooms above the Boneses letting it be known that Tommy walloped his kids, nobody would know he paid them enough attention to discipline them.

Tommy plunged his hands into the pockets of his donkey jacket, aware that Bill was winding him up. 'You was in late Friday.' He'd changed the subject to one he knew Morley couldn't ignore, to get his own back. 'You'll get short wages for that. It ain't the first time, is it?'

'Was only ten minutes,' Bill protested. 'Weren't my fault anyhow. I'll have a word with Mr Black. He's all right.'

'He ain't the guv'nor.' Tommy's voice held contempt. 'You'll need to suck up to the organ grinder, not the oily rag.'

Tommy didn't like the way that Lucas Black was gaining influence in the company, though a lot of people thought it was good that the old hierarchy welcomed new blood and fresh ideas.

15

A posh boy Black might be, but he was sharp and fair-minded; he had put his weight behind getting the management to agree to a half-hour afternoon break for those working overtime until eight o'clock. That same week, though, he'd docked Tommy's wages for causing an accident. Several hundredweight of boxed sweets had tumbled off the back of a cart, narrowly missing a couple of factory girls who were passing by at the time. The spooked horses had bolted, adding to the chaos, and the drama of it kept everybody talking for weeks. Tommy hadn't liked that: he wanted to pick the topic of conversation, not be the butt of it.

Mr Barratt had kept out of the dispute, allowing his new manager to deal with the matter, and Tommy had lost half a week's pay. Some colleagues thought it wasn't punishment enough because it could have ended in disaster.

'If I say that me alarm clock don't work they'll have to let me off. Barratt's bought the bugger after all.' Bill burst out laughing as they turned in at the factory gates. Most people had muttered they'd sooner have had a plum pudding as a Christmas present than a heavy-handed reminder of their bosses' obsession with timekeeping.

A small crowd of men stood in the yard and Tommy speeded up as he saw they had congregated around the new vehicle.

He elbowed his way through to the front of the crowd to run one hand over the shiny coachwork of the pristine van. He glanced about for Mr Barratt, hoping he'd put in an appearance so Tommy could wheedle out of him the opportunity to learn to drive the motor. His eyes met Lucas Black's and the younger man gave him a faint smile and approached.

'Nice, isn't it ... but I reckon we'll be needing Dobbin for a while yet. At least until we know all the pros and cons.'

'You'll get further afield and supply more customers with

a motor, and this little beauty won't go lame on you neither.' Tommy crossed his arms over his chest, adopting a knowledge-able air.

'True enough, but a horse and cart won't need expensive maintenance.'

'They do if some silly sod stacks the wagon wrong and pallets of liquorice hit the deck, spooking the horses.'

Tommy swung about, looking for the big-mouthed joker, his scowl making it clear he didn't appreciate being ribbed in front of the man who'd bawled him out and lost him half a week's wages.

"Least with the nags you get a free bag of manure for your allotment,' another voice shouted from the back of the group.

'I'd keep that quiet . . . he'll dock it off yer wages,' Tommy said with a sarcastic inflexion in his voice.

He still only grudgingly accepted that he'd done wrong that day. In his opinion he'd not been careless . . . or still hungover; he'd been using his initiative to cram the cart because they were a driver down that week and the extra load still had to be got out.

When the factory first opened in Mayes Road, Tommy had started on the production line. As they expanded and a lot of women were taken on, he had sought a more masculine envir-onment in the growing transport department. That's where he'd stayed ever since. He'd worked with the horses and in the warehouse. He'd even had a go at learning signwriting so as to decorate the sides of the carts, but hadn't shown much skill at it. All in all, though, he liked to think he was the factory's most versatile and indispensable employee.

But there was one person who seemed to think differently.

'Right . . . that's enough standing around. Let's get some work done, shall we?' Lucas Black directed the order at the group of men but his eyes returned to Tommy, and he wasn't smiling now.

*

'Thanks, love.' Mrs Cook sniffed the crisply folded sheets and gave a loud exhalation. 'Love the smell of Sunlight soap, I do.'

'It's certainly nicer than that pong.' Olivia nodded her head in the direction of Barratt's sweet factory. Day and night, a pall of sickly liquorice seemed to hang over the neighbourhood. In the summer months it was even worse and could carry for miles on the breeze.

Mrs Cook wrinkled her nose in agreement and pulled a silver coin from her apron pocket. 'There you go ... a bob for your trouble. Would you do me best tablecloth with me sheets next week, Livvie? Had me grandkids over fer Sunday tea and Nora got beetroot on it. Want to get it all crisp 'n' clean fer Christmas Day.'

"Course I will,' Olivia said.

"Ere ... look ... see her?' Mrs Cook was nodding her head at somebody along the street. 'You stay clear of that one, love. She's up to no good.'

Olivia thought she recognised her and was racking her brains to recall why that was. The woman stopped at Olivia's own house and took a key from her bag.

'Oh ... yes, Mr Silver showed her upstairs last week. He's showed quite a few people around but I heard them grumbling about the rent he was asking.'

'Scandalous what those Jews get away with,' Mrs Cook snorted. 'I've been waiting for the privy out the back to be fixed for nigh on a month. A plumber ain't been near nor by. Stinks to high heaven it do ... and rats running about!'

Olivia was only half listening to Mrs Cook's complaints as she was more interested in meeting her new neighbour. 'I reckon she's moving in.'

Mrs Cook sucked her teeth. 'Take it from me, she's no good.'

Olivia gave Ethel's arm a farewell pat and hurried away, keen to say hello to the new neighbour. Mrs Cook was in her late sixties and thought most younger women were up to no good. Olivia had heard it whispered that it stemmed from her late husband having had a roving eye. Instead of leaving him, Ethel had blamed his 'fancy women' for his death from syphilis. Mrs Cook's two daughters lived close by but neither of them helped her out, saving her the shilling she gave to Olivia for delivering a pile of pressed laundry on Tuesday mornings. She had wondered if Ethel's daughters felt angry that their mother hadn't stood up to their philandering father.

'Are you moving in upstairs?' Olivia held out her hand for the newcomer to shake. 'I'm Olivia Bone and I think I spotted you with Mr Silver last week when he showed you round . . .'

'Ain't interested in who you are and what's it to you if I am moving in?' The woman looked Olivia up and down and sniffed in disdain.

Olivia withdrew her hand, narrowing her eyes. 'It's to do with me 'cos I live in there.' She pointed to the window that overlooked the street.

'Do you now?' the woman observed. 'Well, I live there.' She pointed up the stairs. 'Me name's Mrs Maisie Hunter, and that's all you need to know.'

'Yeah . . . it is,' Olivia said crossly. "Cos I wouldn't want to know any more about somebody as rude as you.'

'You cheeky, bleedin' madam . . .'

The woman stepped closer but Olivia was already out of reach. Not that she was shy of giving as good as she got, but there was somebody else who deserved a mouthful from her. And she wasn't going to miss the opportunity of nabbing him.

'Oi, Ricky Wicks! You wait there!'

Ricky had seen Alfie's sister coming purposefully towards him and, guessing what she wanted, had started jogging up the street. Olivia, no mean sprinter at school, hoisted her skirts and caught up with him by the corner, blocking his path.

'Got a bone to pick with you!' she burst out breathlessly, stabbing a finger close to his greasy nose. 'You broke a window round at the Mission and blamed my little brother for it.'

'Was his fault.' Ricky began glancing nervously about to see if any of his pals had spotted him being outstripped by a woman. 'Get out me way or I'll be late for school.'

'Maggie and Nancy left half an hour ago. You're already late for school so a few more minutes won't make much difference.'

Ricky attempted to fling off the hand gripping his arm but Olivia held on.

'Alfie didn't kick that ball, he was in goal and you know it,' she said. 'You stay away from him. And you can cough up five bob so I can take it round to the Sisters. If it's any more than that I'll make up the rest meself.' She held out an upturned palm.

'Ain't got five bob,' Ricky snorted. 'Ain't even got sixpence on me.' He swiped his runny nose with his knuckles.

'Best go back indoors and get it then or I'll knock and ask your dad for it.'

'What's goin' on here?' A stocky fellow of about nineteen had come up behind them, hunched into his donkey jacket.

It was a cold and damp morning and Olivia was wishing she'd put on her coat before venturing out with Mrs Cook's laundry.

'Your brother owes me five bob.' She didn't like Harry Wicks any more than she liked his kid brother. But she knew that

Harry liked her, just as she knew that Ricky was sweet on her sister Maggie.

'Five bob for what?' Harry's eyes slipped lecherously over Olivia's figure; beneath her thin white blouse her bosom was still heaving from her dash up the road. 'Bit young fer you, ain't he? You been meeting him up the alley?' Harry leered at her. 'You need a real man, Livvie, and I'd've give yer six bob to go up there with me.' He burst out laughing to see his younger brother blushing.

'Wouldn't meet you up the alley if you had six quid,' Olivia spat, backing away from the overpowering smell coming off him. Harry worked at the butcher's in the High Street and whenever she met him he stank of raw meat, even on his day off.

'Reckon you would meet me.' He drove one hand into his pocket and pulled out some coins. 'The best tarts down Finsbury Park don't charge no more'n six bob.'

Olivia resisted just grabbing the cash off his palm, wanting him to give it to her properly. 'Five bob, that's all I want. Your brother broke the window round at the Mission and he's blamed Alfie for it.'

'Take five bob then,' Harry taunted her. 'You can pay me it back in yer own way. But pay it back you will.'

Olivia picked up the half-crowns. 'He'll have to pay you back, 'cos you'll get nothing off me.' She set off for home at a brisk walk. She heard Ricky howl and knew that Harry had cuffed his brother but she carried on without a backward glance.

When she reached her door she was glad to see that Mrs Hunter had disappeared. She'd turned up without any belongings so Olivia guessed that a cart was due to arrive soon, possibly with more members of the family. She hoped they weren't all as obnoxious. Ethel Cook might be prejudiced against lone, middle-aged women but she had certainly got Maisie

Hunter right when she'd said Olivia should stay away from her! If that woman tried to give her father lip, it wouldn't surprise her if the two of them came to blows in the hallway.

*

'Is Sister Clare inside? I'd like to speak to her, please.'

'Come in now, won't you?' a lilting Irish voice invited her.

Olivia stepped into the Mission Hall. She knew that the nuns held a social gathering there on a Wednesday evening for the pensioners of the parish. Olivia had come along to hand over to Sister Clare the money for the broken window.

She had stood outside for some moments staring at the boarded-up opening, cursing beneath her breath that Ricky Wicks hadn't hit one of the smaller casements: it looked to be a sizeable pane of glass he'd smashed. She had put three shillings from her own savings to Harry Wicks's money and hoped it would be enough to cover the damage.

Olivia loitered in the narrow passageway while the plump black-clad figure of the nun disappeared into the meeting room. Through the square panes of glass set in the double-doors Olivia could spy some old folk drinking tea at a trestle table set sparingly with plates of biscuits. Open Bibles were visible too. Olivia smiled wryly; the nuns were keen to save souls in return for their meagre hospitality, it seemed.

Olivia had no truck with religion: she could quite clearly recall begging God ... any God ... to spare her mother's life; but he hadn't. He'd taken Aggie Bone not long after her eldest child's tenth birthday.

'Oh, hello there, nice to see you.' Sister Clare had slipped out of the door leading to a small kitchenette, wiping her fingers on a pinafore tied about her habit. She approached Olivia with outstretched hands and a smile on her face. She was one of the youngest nuns, perhaps around twenty-five, although it was hard to tell without seeing her hair. Olivia had always thought that a woman's age and beauty showed in her crowning glory rather than in her complexion. Her mother had been a lovely woman despite the lines on her face. Her hair, like Olivia's, had been a light honey colour and thick and wavy, and Aggie had also passed on to her daughter large eyes of a striking green.

Sister Clare was a nice young woman and always stopped and had a chat when Olivia bumped into her in the street. They had struck up an unlikely bond after the night her mother had died and the novice nun had turned up in the early hours of the morning, having heard from a neighbour that Mrs Bone wasn't expected to see another dawn. By the time she arrived Aggie had passed away. The Bones weren't Catholics and Tommy had made a point of making that known while holding the door open for the nun to leave. But Sister Clare had taken his churlishness graciously, saying that denomination didn't matter, she'd pray for them anyway because they were people who were grieving, and she was sorry for their loss.

Olivia had never forgotten her simple words of comfort, or her kindness, and considered Sister Clare one of life's good souls.

'I suppose you heard that my brother was involved in breaking the Mission window?' Olivia rolled her eyes, jerking her head in the direction of the damage.

'Afraid so. And I expect you heard that your father was cornered over it.' Sister Clare shook her head. 'Bad behaviour ... from one of mine, not one of yours,' she whispered. 'Sister Maria has little understanding or tact. The matter could have been handled better.'

Olivia smiled, appreciating the older woman's attitude. 'It

wasn't my brother who broke it.' She shrugged. 'No point in telling tales, though. The lads were playing football – it wasn't intentional.'

'I know ... boys will be boys.' Sister Clare squeezed Olivia's arm. 'How is your family? Your father's getting married again, isn't he?'

Olivia frowned. 'Dad? No ... why d'you think so?'

Sister Clare blushed in confusion. 'Sorry ... I just thought ... Oh, never mind me.'

'Why did you say that about Dad?' Olivia asked again. She could see that Sister Clare wished she'd not brought the subject up.

The nun waited until a couple of elderly ladies who'd come out of the meeting hall had left the building before she continued speaking.

'Sister Maria believed your father might have been belligerent over the broken window because she'd spotted him out walking arm-in-arm with a lady. She can be a bit overbearing so I can understand why he might not have wanted to stop and speak to her. Mr Bone seems a private sort of man.'

'A lady? Oh, she must be mistaken. Dad doesn't socialise much other than in the pub with his work pals. It couldn't have been him ... unless he was with my aunt Sybil. But they don't get on so it couldn't have been her if they seemed happy together. Besides she lives south of the water.'

Her mother's family hadn't visited them since Aggie had died. Olivia had come to the conclusion that Sybil and her husband blamed her father for his wife's death, and in a way she did too. On that horrible night Olivia had been roused from her bed by her mother, who was doubled up in pain. The pubs had been shut by that time but still Olivia had hammered on their doors, searching for her father. When she'd got back hours later, crying with fright, Tommy had been there. He'd been gripping his wife's hand while the local handywoman grunted and pulled at her mother underneath a covering sheet.

Olivia had been ordered to mind her little sisters, who'd been woken by the noise. Aggie's shrieks had been awful but it had been even worse when everything went quiet. Then her aunt's husband had turned up and for a while it seemed a fight would erupt in the street. Olivia could recall peeping from behind the curtain, almost blinded by tears, as her uncle Edward and her father started pushing and shoving each other. Maggie and Nancy had been huddled together on the mattress, sucking their thumbs, watching her with eyes that pleaded for reassurance. And she had given it although she recalled feeling frightened and furious at the men for even bothering to fight while her mother was slowly turning cold in a blood-stained bed along the landing.

'It wasn't in London ... Sister Maria was visiting her folks at the seaside in the summer.' Sister Clare had waited a while before saying any more. She felt awkward but had come to the decision that too much had been divulged already for her not to finish the tale. 'Sister Maria saw Mr Bone and his friend down by Clacton pier. I just jumped to the conclusion that he might be thinking of re-marrying, though I had no right to do so.' She frowned. 'Sister Maria wouldn't have mentioned that chance encounter when she confronted your father in the pub, but perhaps he thought that she would.'

'Right ... well, thanks for telling me,' Olivia murmured. Gathering her wits, she delved into a pocket and held out the assortment of silver coins. 'Hope that's enough to sort out the damage. 'Bye for now.'

She turned away and quickly went outside, struggling to make sense of what she'd heard. She hesitated at the corner, not wanting to go home before she'd mulled things over. There hadn't been a recent Barratt's works outing to Clacton that she could recall. Neither did her father have a woman that she knew of. But he did sometimes go off for a night or two without warning or explanation, leaving her to care for the others. Olivia had never questioned his welcome absences. In the past she'd always imagined he'd stayed the weekend at a pal's place, being too under the influence after a couple of nights of playing cards and drinking rum to make the journey back home.

If he did have a girlfriend, he wouldn't tell her, or anybody, about it. In the past she'd thought it would be a relief if her father moved in with a fancy woman and left them in peace. The possibility of this becoming a reality was now staring her in the face, and she was unsure she was strong enough to shoulder the burden of her younger siblings unaided. She loved Alfie, Maggie and Nancy even when they acted daft or selfish and drove her mad. But she'd harboured a dream of getting a proper job – perhaps in nursing. Then in time, God willing, she'd like to settle down with a man she loved and have her own children. None of that could happen while her sisters and brother still needed her, and Alfie had many years of schooling in front of him still.

A few nights ago Olivia had naturally jumped to the conclusion that her father's rage had been brought on by his son trying to keep secret that he'd broken the Mission Hall window.

Perhaps what had really infuriated Tommy Bone was that a secret of his own might soon be revealed.

Chapter Three

'What are you looking at me like that fer?' Tommy Bone had shifted beneath his daughter's vacant stare.

'What?'

'Give me that! Stop dawdling and get off home. You've plenty to do, getting things ready for tomorrow,' Tommy growled. Having snatched the package of food that his daughter was holding out to him, he turned his back on her. As he strode away he glanced over his shoulder, annoyed to see that Olivia was still by the factory gate. She'd seemed preoccupied for weeks and had loitered by him on occasion as though she wanted to say something but didn't know how to start. He knew his eldest wanted to get a better job. She deserved to as well: working in a dead-end caff was more the sort of thing for Maggie, who was shaping up to be lazy and useless. Olivia had brains and good looks and could easily capitalise on them. But Tommy needed Livvie where she was: looking after him and her siblings so he had time to do as he pleased. He didn't want his eldest daughter chasing a man or a career and leaving him in the lurch.

Tommy wove a path through the men loading carts with pallets in the front courtyard, merely grunting at those who called out to him to cheer up 'cos it was Christmas. On entering the premises he saw that Lucas Black was standing just inside the open doorway with his hands thrust into his pockets. 'Your dinner break's already finished, isn't it, Bone?'

'Forgot me grub this morning. Somebody just brought it up for me,' Tommy said, resenting the need to explain himself to this man. Tommy was forty-nine and Black was at least two decades his junior and an upstart as far as the older man was concerned. He didn't mind being brought up short by the proper governors, but not by this kid.

'Another ten minutes then, that's all, then get back to work. We've not packed up for Christmas just yet.'

'Yeah . . . chance'd be a fine thing,' Tommy muttered sourly.

Lucas was staring out of the open doorway. 'That's your daughter, is it?'

Tommy turned on his heel to look back the way he'd come. He then squinted suspiciously at his young boss. 'It is.'

'Does she want a job? We're short of packers.'

'She's got a job . . . looking after me,' Tommy retorted as he walked away.

'That's a bleedin' job in itself for the poor kid,' Bill Morley ribbed. He shifted along on the bench, making room for Tommy by the coke burners that were used to heat the sugar-boiling pans. Tommy gave Bill a glare. He didn't appreciate any talk about his family in public. He worked with these people and he might take a drink with them later, in the pub round in Coburg Road, being as it was Christmas Eve, but that was it. His private life was private even from Bill even though they might have a laugh and a joke together. He unpacked a piece of boiled bacon and a floury potato saved from yesterday's meal and put the food close enough to the burners to warm up.

Tommy started eating, keeping an eye on Black's broad back as he went out of the door. 'Time we got a longer break anyhow,' he muttered, through a mouthful of lukewarm meat.

'Time we got a proper bleedin' canteen as well,' came another voice from further along the bench. 'It's all right fer them, sitting up in the boardroom all nice 'n' cosy.'

'You could bring that up, Tom, couldn't you?' Bill Morley said, all innocence. 'You've got Mr Barratt's ear, ain't yer? You could ask if he'll build us our own canteen and give us a bit longer for our dinner breaks as a Christmas present to us all.'

'Canteen's already been brought up in strike action years ago. Didn't do no good banging on about it back then.' As far as Tommy was concerned he wasn't bothered where he ate; if they were going to stir up trouble he'd sooner make increased wages and overtime rates top of the agenda.

'If they can afford to shell out for new motors, I reckon they can put their hands in their pockets for a decent place for us to sit down and eat our food,' a woman called out, and gave the workbench a thump for emphasis.

'Wouldn't mind a proper apron to put on neither,' another female voice announced over the sound of machinery clanking in the background. The middle-aged woman pulled in disgust at the bit of makeshift sugar sacking tied round her waist. 'A uniform would save me clothes and me legs. A spill burned right through me skirt onto me thigh last week.' She whistled through her teeth. 'Did it bleedin' hurt!'

'One thing at a time,' Tommy said craftily. 'Go for it hammer 'n' tongs and we'll get nowt.' He carried on chewing. 'Last thing we all want is to push 'em into doing this, that and the

29

other then docking the cost off our summer share-out. I need that cash.'

'You're right about that, Tom,' Bill said seriously. 'We don't want the buggers taking our dividends back off us either. They might if we kick up too much.'

Tommy nodded, looking thoughtful. Five years ago the firm had turned into a limited company and shares were allocated to 'attentive and diligent' employees. Tommy had been one of those thus rewarded. A lot of those not so lucky had got quite narky about being overlooked.

The shares stayed with the company – no doubt so the recipients couldn't sell them and jack their jobs in – but dividends were paid to shareholders and the money had come in very handy to Tommy, especially in the years when profits soared and payouts were high.

'I don't want to lose me bonus neither,' the woman called out. She wiped her hands on her hessian pinafore and trotted over to the men. 'Don't you go causing no trouble, Tommy Bone. I need me September money. Always put it by fer Christmas, I do. Grandkids get treated out of it. Ain't even got enough left out of this year's for a booze-up with the old man later. And it's Christmas Eve!'

'All right … all right, Nelly, I heard yer.' Tommy gave the woman a scowl. Nelly Smith was well known for moaning her head off about working conditions, but when push came to shove she'd always shy away from losing a penny in wages.

'All gob, no do.' Bill jerked his head at Nelly as she went back to the boiling pans, out of earshot.

'Like most of 'em,' Tommy said bitterly. 'Want more – but want me 'n' you to risk our jobs getting it for 'em.' He stood up, wiping his greasy hands on his trousers. 'Best get back to work then before that jumped-up nob sees me and docks me pay.'

*

Olivia had turned her back on the factory and shifted to one side, leaning against a brick pillar, out of sight of the men loading up the boxes of sweets. She knew her father would be angry if he noticed her loitering about his workplace. He didn't like his kids anywhere near the factory, in case they were asked questions about him. But *she* had questions about him and she wished she could find the words to ask them because not knowing was driving her mad.

Ever since the nun had told her about her father being seen with a woman Olivia had not been able to put the matter from her mind. He was her dad and in her own way she cared about him and wanted him to be happy. If he had a girlfriend it was his own business but it would be nice to know how it might affect them all. If he were intending to marry in the future and bring their stepmother to live with them, perhaps it would not be a bad thing. He might mellow towards Alfie. Also it could give Olivia more time to herself and then her dreams of getting a good job could become reality. But the living space they had was already cramped. Should the upstairs rooms become vacant again they might be able to take them back, if her father's girlfriend paid her way. Olivia hoped that a bedroom of her own, or at most shared with just one of her siblings, wouldn't then be a pipe dream. She reined in her racing thoughts. If . . . if . . . if . . . was no bloody use; she needed some facts to go on.

She didn't want to go back to the Mission and quiz Sister Clare or Sister Maria over it as that would make it seem the matter held great significance for her, and although it did, she didn't want anybody else knowing that.

'Looking for work?'

Olivia's fierce concentration was rudely interrupted. She

whipped about, gazing up into a handsome face set with a pair of dark blue eyes.

'No ... no, I'm not. I was just on my way actually.' It was a dreary day, not much like Christmas at all, and Olivia hunched into her coat, hands in pockets.

'Don't go on my account.'

'I won't, don't worry,' she retorted, putting up her chin as she sensed the man's amusement. He was not the usual sort of worker to be seen hanging around the gates of the Barratt's factory. He was smartly dressed in a suit for a start, with a gold fob watch visible on his waistcoat and polished black brogues on his feet. She turned to walk on, feeling rather disconcerted by him. He had a confident air but it wasn't the sort of arrogance she was used to. Cocksure lads she could cope with, knowing as she did that they were often quite vulnerable underneath.

Swaggerers like Harry Wicks thought they owned the place yet had nothing much to crow about. This fellow wasn't a youth, though, and his posh way of speaking and air of privilege were foreign to a girl like her. He confused her, but she guessed he did have something to crow about.

'You're Tommy Bone's daughter, aren't you?'

'Who told you that?' Olivia swung back to face him.

'He did.'

Olivia looked past the young man to the factory building but her father had disappeared and wasn't witnessing this conversation.

'Well ... if you change your mind and want a job, come and see me in the New Year. We're hiring.'

'And who are you?' Olivia demanded to his broad back.

He pivoted on his heel, inclining his head by way of a lazy introduction and farewell. 'I'm Lucas Black. Ask your father about me.'

She gave him a quizzical look as though the idea that she might enquire after him was ridiculous. Then she turned and marched along Mayes Road towards home.

Olivia forced her thoughts away from Lucas Black, to what should be a wonderfully happy time of year. But Christmas Day always filled her with melancholy, and had done since her mother died. She never let on to her sisters and brother how she felt and every year she tried to take on Aggie's role and make their home an attractive place in which to celebrate and have a good meal. Aggie had always decked the parlour with greenery and put their best cloth and china and a vase of flowers on the table at dinnertime. She'd managed to fill a small stocking for her girls to share too, even if the majority of the contents was bruised fruit that her husband had brought home from his weekend shift in the market.

Olivia had already retrieved last year's decorations from the top of the wardrobe in their bedroom. She had left Nancy and Maggie giggling and wobbling about on their bed, attempting to string red and green paper chains against the wall by looping them over the branches of the gas lamps. Alfie had gone out earlier to find a few more sprigs of holly and ivy to decorate the parlour, to add to the conifer he'd brought in yesterday.

When she got back Olivia would join in their fun and try not to worry too much about her depleted savings pot. As soon as she got back to work after Christmas she would start squirrelling away a few coppers out of her wages for next year.

The day before their annual feast her father always gave her enough money to buy a chicken and a small plum pudding. He had done so before he'd gone off that morning and she imagined that distraction was probably to blame for him forgetting his parcel of food. Or had it been his mystery woman on his mind? Olivia wondered if he'd spend some of Christmas with her – whoever she was. Tommy always ate Christmas dinner with his kids but that apart he usually spent the time away from home, as was his custom the rest of the year too. Previously Olivia had believed him to be drinking with pals ... now she suspected he might not be.

With an exasperated mutter she told herself to buck up and forget the things she knew nothing about. She should concentrate instead on how to drive a hard bargain at the shops later. She knew she'd have to time her purchases just right. She couldn't leave it too late or everything would be sold out but neither must she go along to the butcher's at the height of the rush and compete with others in the queue for a plump bird at top price.

*

Olivia rounded the corner into their street and her heart sank when she saw Harry Wicks. She'd managed to avoid him since the incident with the broken window. She'd hoped he'd settled matters with his brother. But she could tell from the smug look on his chops that it wasn't going to be that easy.

'Just the gel I wanted to see,' Harry purred, dodging from side to side to block her path as Olivia tried to get past him on the pavement.

She stopped and stared at him with baleful green eyes. 'Get out of me way. I've got lots of things to do this afternoon.'

'Yeah ... and so have I 'cos I'm only on me dinner break.' He smirked. 'But one of those things you've gotta do is pay me back that five bob I give you to get them nuns off yer back.'

'Ask Ricky for it. He broke the bloody window.'

'He ain't got it though, has he?' Harry had come closer, forcing Olivia to back against a privet hedge to escape him.

'Tell you what ...' he leaned over her to whisper '... me mum's out at the moment Christmas shopping. Why don't you come in and I'll make you a cup o' tea? If you're nice to me we'll say no more about that five bob.' He started to barge her up his garden path. 'If you're *really* nice to me, I'll give you something pretty for Christmas. Fancy earrings ...' He breathed against her earlobe, giving it a suggestive lick.

Olivia turned her head as far away from him as possible; the reek of fatty minced beef seemed to spill out of every fibre of his clothes and sour his breath.

Carefully she removed her fingers from her coat pockets then suddenly punched him double-handed, full in the chest, to force him back so she could dash back onto the street.

'Fucking bitch!' he gasped, winded by Olivia's assault on his ribs. He was a stocky man but unfit. He grabbed a hank of her thick blonde hair before she reached the gate, knocking off her small hat and scattering a few hairpins on the ground. His other hand spitefully grabbed at her breast as he pulled her closer to his front door.

The pain in her head was making her eyes smart but Olivia managed to claw his cheek although prising his fingers from her scalp was impossible. Then suddenly Harry gave a grunt before sprawling on the ground.

'You all right?'

Olivia smeared away the tears of pain and humiliation misting her eyes, blinking at her saviour.

'Yeah ... thanks.' She recognised him as the fellow who lived upstairs. Or rather she imagined he lived upstairs. In the time that Maisie Hunter had been at the property, Olivia had seen this man only a handful of times. She couldn't be sure if it was his home or he was just visiting.

Harry lumbered to his feet, snarling, and took a swing at the newcomer. The fellow dodged aside and kneed him in the groin with the assurance of a seasoned fighter. As Harry folded over, clutching himself between the legs, the knee caught him hard under his chin, making his teeth clash together.

The next moment Olivia's rescuer had started steering her away towards her home.

Using the hedge for support Harry pulled himself upright and started bawling after them. Apart from lazily flicking two fingers at him, the other fellow ignored the insults.

When they got to the house he opened the door with his key and let them both into the hallway.

'Does he often bother you?'

Olivia shrugged and bit her lip, trying to tidy her loose blonde locks with the couple of pins that remained anchored there. A small frustrated sigh escaped her as she realised that her hat was still in the Wickses' front garden.

'I can deal with him – he's just an idiot.' She sniffed and gave her companion the once over. 'You Mrs Hunter's son? I've noticed you a few times, going in and out of the house.'

'Yeah . . . I'm Joe Hunter.'

Olivia held out her hand for him to shake. 'I'm Olivia Bone. Thanks for what you did. I was all right though. I would've got away on me own,' she added stoutly.

His subtle smile told her he didn't quite believe that. And in truth neither did Olivia. Harry had intended to drag her into his empty house. God knows what else might have happened to her if he'd managed to do that. She knew that as a last resort she would have screamed blue murder and found a poker to hit him with.

'We've not spoken before, have we?' Olivia said conversationally. 'I tried to be friendly to your mum but she didn't really want to know.' That was an understatement, she thought, remembering the woman's rudeness on the day she'd first moved in. Since then the only effort Maisie had made at neighbourliness was to bark out 'Mornin" if they met by chance in the passageway.

'She's quite shy,' Joe said, and started to laugh.

'Yeah ... and I'm Marie Lloyd,' Olivia retorted, but then she chuckled too. 'Is your dad moving in upstairs at some point?'

'No.'

It seemed Joe Hunter had nothing more to say about his father so she changed the subject. 'Not at work today then? Finished early for Christmas, have you?' Olivia wanted to carry on talking to Joe. Now that she was calmer she realised how grateful to him she felt. Harry Wicks was a nasty piece of work, known in the area for picking fights. But Joe Hunter had floored him with no trouble at all.

Previously she'd only got a fleeting look at her neighbour's son, from the window or as he was disappearing up the stairs. Now she could see that he was probably a few years or so older than she was, and he had a sort of rough attractiveness. He was very unlike that sophisticated fellow Lucas Black, who'd introduced himself to her outside the factory.

Nothing about Joe Hunter was refined. His voice was as coarse as his donkey jacket, worn open over a plain shirt and with a scarf knotted at his throat. But he had clean hands and nails, she noted, although they were a bit scuffed around the knuckles from having walloped Harry.

'Well?' he asked, amused by her inspection.

'You seem friendlier than your mum,' Olivia blurted, confused by his directness.

'And you seem friendlier than your dad,' he returned with a wry grimace.

'Have you spoken to him?' Her father usually made a point of keeping himself to himself. If he was drunk or in a particularly bad mood it was not unknown for him to ignore a neighbour's greeting or be downright abusive.

'Once or twice.' Joe laughed. 'Just a word or two. It's enough for him, I reckon.'

'Yeah . . . I know what you mean,' Olivia said wryly, thinking that they both had parents nursing chips on their shoulders. Her father's had been put there by his wife's death. Perhaps Mrs Hunter too had a tragedy eating away at her.

A silence developed between them in which Olivia began to feel awkward.

'Keep away from that troublemaker,' Joe said, his voice matter-of-fact. 'If he bothers you again, let me know.'

'I hope he's buggered off somewhere by now,' Olivia replied flatly. 'I've got to go back and get me hat, though. He knocked it flying when he pulled my hair. But I'm not losing it 'cos I only bought it a few months ago.' She had bartered with a market trader to secure the hat for two bob.

'I'll fetch it,' Joe said.

'No . . . honestly . . . you've done enough, thanks all the same. I can deal with that bully.'

'Not as well as I can.' He sounded adamant. 'What's his name?'

'Harry Wicks. Are you sure it's no trouble?' Olivia said, but Joe had already gone back out into the street.

'It was stuck under the hedge,' he said, when he returned a few minutes later. 'The coast's clear if you want to go out now. Wicks is nowhere to be seen.' He plonked the small velvet hat atop her blonde head with a grin then turned away and took the stairs two at a time. Halfway up he peered over the banisters. 'Merry Christmas,' he said before carrying on up.

'And to you too!' Olivia called.

She frowned at his sudden disappearance. She would have liked to talk to him some more. She thought she could get to like Joe Hunter. His light brown hair and hazel eyes were appealing. But she'd learned nothing much about him other than that he was Maisie Hunter's son and that he knew his mother was a difficult woman to get on with. He'd not even acknowledged Olivia's comment about his work.

She sensed there was something Joe Hunter didn't want her to know about him that went beyond most folks' need for privacy. She was slightly miffed too that he'd not flirted with her when she'd made it clear she liked him. Olivia wasn't conceited but she knew she was pretty because she'd been told so plenty of times and had been ogled by better fellows than Harry Wicks.

Letting herself into her home, Olivia was greeted by the fresh scent of pine needles and the sound of her sister and brother warbling 'Good King Wenceslas'. They were already in the festive spirit and enjoying themselves, and she was glad; but Heaven only knew what mood their father might be in when he returned. He'd doubtless go to the pub for a Christmas Eve drink so could return full of good cheer if they were lucky ... or maudlin and resentful if they weren't.

Olivia bucked herself up; she impressed on herself that it wasn't every day a girl made the acquaintance of two very different yet handsome fellows, so that must account for her unaccustomed pensiveness. Then to top it all she'd been assaulted by vile Harry Wicks. She took off her coat, about to hang it up when she noticed a clump of her fair hair stuck to the wool. She gave the sore spot on her scalp a brisk rub, hating Harry Wicks for what he'd done to her.

Alfie had heard her come in and rushed from the bedroom with sprigs of greenery in his small fist. 'Help me pin these up?' He waved the holly and ivy.

"Course,' Olivia said, lifting him and spinning him round. 'Know what day it is tomorrow?'

'Christmas!' he whooped.

'Yeah ... Christmas, and I reckon Santa's coming over our roof just for you, Alfie Bone.'

Chapter Four

'About done now, is it?'

Olivia closed the range door, having basted the chicken and potatoes. She could hear the impatience in her father's voice.

'Think it's almost there now, Dad. Stove's not coming up to heat so it's taken longer than it should.' She glanced at the scuttle; it was half full but she guessed that no matter how hungry her father was feeling he wouldn't want her using up more fuel on cooking the chicken and roast potatoes. That would leave next to nothing for tomorrow's fires.

Tommy prowled to and fro in the parlour then slumped down at the table, drumming his stained fingernails on the snowy white cloth. The table had already been laid for their Christmas feast. Aggie Bone's best china plates were accompanied by polished cutlery that only came out of the dresser once or twice a year.

Because their father was restless he was making them all feel ill at ease. Alfie was sitting quietly in a corner of the room with his knees drawn up to his chin. He was reading a comic but sliding wary glances at his dad from beneath his lashes. Maggie and Nancy were listlessly playing a game of cards on the rug. All the jollity of yesterday, decorating the house and singing carols, had evaporated now their father was home with them, waiting to do his duty and eat Christmas dinner with his family.

Olivia had poured off some of the chicken stock into a jug and was sprinkling into it some flour to thicken it into a gravy. While stirring she wished that on this of all days their father would relax and show them a softer side. He didn't have to be a tyrant to get obedience and respect from his children ... in fact his sustained cruelty had always had the reverse effect. Fear wasn't respect and submission wasn't obedience. But perhaps Tommy Bone thought differently because his parents, long deceased and unknown to their grandchildren, had been bullies too.

Olivia knew he was still hungover. The others had been asleep when he'd come home in the early hours. But Olivia had heard him drunkenly stumbling to bed and her heart had sunk, knowing that he would rise nursing a headache. She could tell from his bloodshot eyes and the fingers massaging his forehead that he was feeling rough. He had been the same last Christmas Day. But last year he had at least slept in the chair for most of the time, leaving them to their own devices, playing quietly so as not to wake him.

She pushed the jug to one side of the hob, determined that he wouldn't ruin their enjoyment. She would make an effort to get through Christmas dinner harmoniously. If he went out to his fancy woman or his pub pals afterwards then it would be a relief for everybody. 'While we're waiting we can open presents,' Olivia announced, turning about with a smile. 'I'll fetch them.'

She returned with the gifts she'd wrapped up in tissue paper and ribbon, handing them out. She'd wrapped one for herself too so they all had something to open. There was no surprise for her, of course, when she took the lace-edged hanky from its paper but nevertheless she held it up to show the others.

Nancy looked disappointed with her school pinafore but managed to say a gracious thank-you. Olivia knew her sister had wanted ballet shoes; she'd been hinting as much for months. But those were a luxury beyond Olivia's means. A school pinafore to replace her patched one was what Nancy needed, just as her brother Alfie needed a new school shirt as the collar and cuffs on his old one were frayed. He folded his present carefully as though the shirt were precious.

'Thanks, Livvie,' he said sweetly.

'What've you got, Mags?' Nancy asked, frowning at the scrap of leather her sister was turning over.

'A new purse,' Maggie replied, opening and closing the clasp. 'Wish I had something to put in it.'

'You will have soon enough,' Tommy interrupted. He'd watched his kids opening their presents with a certain amount of satisfaction even though he'd contributed nothing towards buying them. As far as he was concerned, he put food on the table, paid the rent – and that was his part done. 'You'll be out to work in a few months' time, miss. After you've handed over your wages on a Friday, you'll get back a few coppers to save in that.' Tommy stabbed a thick finger at Maggie's gift. 'So say thank you to your sister.' He crossed his arms over his chest. 'You'll bring home your school certificate by Easter, or I'll know why.'

Maggie mumbled her thanks and said that she needed the privy. She stood up and left the room.

'Open yours, Dad,' Olivia urged, wanting to see his reaction.

She'd thought long and hard about what to buy him that would put a smile on his face.

Tommy's stubby fingers pulled at the ribbon. 'Very nice,' he said gruffly and put the pewter cigarette box into his pocket. 'Check if dinner's done now, Livvie.'

Olivia rose with a sigh. He hadn't smiled but he'd seemed pleased enough to say thank you for the gift. She skewered the chicken thighs and the potatoes and thankfully it was all ready.

'While I dish this up fetch Mum's best vase, Alfie. There's a bit of greenery left over on the washstand to put in it and decorate the table.' Olivia went to the drawer and took out the photo of her mother and father taken on their wedding day. Their beautiful mother was seated, wearing a pretty pale dress, while her handsome husband stood proudly behind her chair. Once the photograph had taken pride of place on the sideboard but Tommy had accidentally knocked it to the floor in one of his rages. Now it resided in the drawer but Olivia often took it out to gaze on her mother's smiling face.

'I'll prop this against the vase when Alfie comes back.' Suddenly Olivia felt confident that the rest of the day would pass enjoyably.

Alfie had immediately gone on the errand. Having found the vase in the cupboard, he arranged the holly and the ivy and carefully proceeded to carry the filled vase towards the table while Olivia started taking the chicken from the oven. 'Will you carve at the table, Dad?' she called over her shoulder.

As Alfie came level with the door Maggie opened it, catching her brother's arm and making him drop the vase.

'You clumsy little git!' Tommy roared as glass shattered at his feet. 'That was my Aggie's favourite. You should never have touched it!' He threw down the carving knife and fork he'd picked up. Swiping out at Alfie he caught his son on the shoulder, knocking him into Olivia. She dropped the chicken she'd been carrying towards the table, saving her brother from falling against the hot stove.

Tommy bellowed louder as the dinner was spoiled. 'You're a useless bleeder! Should never have been born!' His face contorted in rage, he tried to hit Alfie again but Olivia rushed forward to stop him. Her father's palm stung her cheek, knocking her head sideways and making her stagger. With tears smarting in her eyes she turned back to confront him, straightening her slumped shoulders. Blood was trickling from her split lip but she didn't flinch as she gave him a blazing, hate-filled gaze.

She could tell that he was in two minds about whether to carry on his rampage or storm out. One thing she knew for sure: he wouldn't apologise even though she could tell he was sorry for what he'd done. His lips were pressed together and writhing as though fighting to contain what he wanted to say.

Tommy ripped his coat off the peg on the back of the door. He turned to face his four white-faced children.

'Get this lot cleaned up by the time I'm back or you'll all be for it,' he snarled, slamming the door behind him.

And even with him gone they obeyed, clearing up the mess without speaking although Nancy and Alfie were crying and shaking as they bent to pick up shards of glass.

'It was your bloody fault.' Maggie suddenly rounded on Alfie. 'You *are* a clumsy git, like Dad said.' She felt guilty for having been the one to crash the door into her brother, making him drop their mum's best vase. She knew if she hadn't been in a mood over her father telling her she'd got to hand over all of her wages when she started work, she would have stayed in the parlour. Then none of this would have happened.

Even though her head was throbbing from the blow she'd

taken Olivia had been trying to rescue some chicken from the floor so there was something for them to eat for Christmas dinner. 'Now you wait a minute!' She banged down the dish. 'None of it was Alfie's fault. He was doing what I asked him to do. Accidents happen.'

'It's Dad's fault! I hate him!' Nancy shouted tearfully. 'And *you* knocked into Alfie.' She pointed at Maggie and the two girls started arguing loudly. Only Olivia, closer to the door, heard the knock upon it. She opened it carefully, peering around the edge.

'You all right in there?' Joe Hunter asked.

Olivia was too stunned by the unexpected sight of him to speak for a moment. She'd seen his mother go out that morning and had thought nobody was in upstairs. 'Yes ... we're fine, thanks ... just dropped something, that's all.' Her voice was faint but she was determined not to appear embarrassed.

Joe put his palm flat against the door as though to open it and glance inside but Olivia pushed against it, her eyes daring him to try. 'What's happened to you?' he asked very quietly.

'An accident ... I told you,' she returned sharply.

'You've got blood on your face. Just saw your father go out. He didn't look too happy.'

Olivia was aware that her brother and sisters were now listening inside the room. She quickly stepped into the hall and pulled the door closed behind her, to prevent them from hearing too much. She swiped her cuff over the bloody lip and raised her eyes to Joe. They were still moist with tears from the sting of her father's hand.

'It's none of your business what's gone on and I'd prefer it if you left us alone.'

'And if I don't?'

'And if you don't ... ' She'd been about to return a threat but the fight went out of her suddenly. She turned her head away as fresh tears sprang to her eyes. 'You'll just make things worse . . . for all of us,' Olivia said hoarsely. 'What are you doing here anyway? If you're looking for your mum, I saw her go out this morning.'

'I know . . . she's gone away for a few days. I'm not looking for her.' He pulled from his coat pocket a small box of chocolates and handed them over. 'For you and your brother and sisters for Christmas. Nothing to it. Just being neighbourly,' he said before letting himself out into the street.

He'd looked smart, she realised, dressed in a tailored jacket and trousers. She glanced at the gift she had received, the first in seven years that she hadn't bought for herself so she had something to open on Christmas Day.

Chapter Five

'Why aren't you at school?'

Olivia had just finished her early shift at the caff. It was mid-January and the weather was perishing. She had got soaked in a sleety cloudburst while hurrying home with a bag of groceries, and felt cold and hungry and in need of a warming drink and a bit of toast and jam. Her boss was a tightwad who made his staff pay for a pie, even if eaten while they worked.

On leaving the house that morning, not long after her father, she'd given the kids their usual instructions to get their break-fasts then get going. She felt irritated to see once she got in that her sister hadn't done as she was told. Olivia had noticed that Maggie was getting defiant and skipping off school lately for any little excuse.

Maggie rubbed her belly. 'Don't feel well, Livvie,' she moaned. 'Was that last bit of boiled bacon we used up off, d'you think?'

'I feel all right and the others haven't complained,' Olivia returned shortly. 'Where's Alfie and Nancy? Did they get off to school—' Olivia broke off as somebody hammered on their door.

'Open up, I know yer in there. I saw you come in, you trouble-making cow!'

Olivia pulled open the door and planted her hands on her slender hips, facing Maisie Hunter. 'What's your problem then?'

'That's my problem!' Maisie waved a piece of paper in Olivia's face before thrusting it against her chest. 'And I know you did it, you little bitch.'

Olivia snatched the paper. It seemed to have nothing on it, then she turned it over and saw the message printed on the other side.

She felt her complexion heating up but there was a throb of amusement too. 'It's nothing to do with me. If you want to entertain gentlemen upstairs then that's your lookout. If Mr Silver finds out you'll probably be out on your ear, though.'

'You saying you didn't stick this on that lamppost?' Mrs Hunter jabbed one rigid finger towards the street.

'I'd like to have the time to bother with stupid stuff like that!' Olivia slammed shut the door, ignoring the hammering on the panels and the coarse threats. Eventually she heard her neighbour stomp off.

'What the bloody hell was that all about?' Maggie demanded, momentarily forgetting her aching abdomen.

'Don't swear. If Dad hears you, you'll be for it.' Livvie bit her lip. 'Somebody's stuck a note on the lamppost outside calling Maisie Hunter a prossie.'

Maggie's eyes popped. 'Who'd do a thing like that?' she snorted. 'I know she's horrible, but . . .'

Olivia shrugged although she had a good idea who might be responsible. She'd given Mrs Cook her washing as usual last

Tuesday morning and cut her off short when she'd started on again about Mrs Hunter being an old bag. Maisie Hunter was unpleasant but her son wasn't, and Olivia owed him a favour and her thanks for the box of chocolates he'd given her. After he'd gone on Christmas Day she'd realised how rude she'd been. She'd not seen him since even though she'd looked out for him. Thankfully she'd not clapped eyes on Harry Wicks either.

'Any more tea in that pot?' Olivia asked.

'Might get a half cup out of it,' Maggie sighed. 'I'm going back to bed. Me guts are killing me.'

'If you feel better this afternoon you'd better go into school for an hour or two. Dad'll wallop you for missing a whole day.'

'I'm leaving school soon anyhow,' Maggie answered. 'Gonna get a job at Barratt's.'

'Dad won't let you work where he does. I've had a word with Mrs Kendall . . . '

'Ain't going into Kendall's laundry!' Maggie retorted. 'Time I'm fifteen me hands'll be chapped and swollen.'

'Won't hurt you to start there until you can find something else.'

Maggie pulled a face that conveyed better than words would have how she felt about her job prospects. Carrying her tea, she slouched towards the bedroom.

Olivia had been pouring out a mug of lukewarm tea for herself but suddenly put down the pot. She'd seen a smear of blood on the seat her sister had used. Taking Maggie's arm, she turned her about. 'You'd best take off your skirt and clean yourself up. You've started your monthlies by the look of things.' She felt mean now for thinking that her sister had been malingering.

'No . . . can't be . . . it's horrible!' Maggie twisted round to see the stain on her clothes, wrinkling her nose.

'Best get used to it, like the rest of us,' Olivia said flatly. 'Find some clean bloomers and some rags as well. I'll fetch some water in and sponge your skirt.'

*

'What can I get you, sir?'

'Pie, mash and plenty of liquor, please, miss.'

'Coming right up, Mr Hunter,' Olivia said, mimicking a posh voice.

She'd been surprised and pleased to see Joe entering the caff. She had never seen him in there before, but it was possible he had been in on her day off. She worked irregular part-time shifts. The weekends were when the men were most generous with their tips after rolling out of the taverns all merry and bright. To take advantage of it she'd sometimes do overtime until late then rush home to try and beat her father back from the pub. Thankfully, it wasn't unusual for the landlord of his local to feel amiable and allow regulars to have after-hours lock-ins on a Saturday night. Sometimes she'd do a Sunday shift as well if she could manage it.

'Know him, do you?' Ivy Ward whispered, slanting a side-long glance at Joe while stacking crockery at a vacant table. 'I like the look of him.'

'Yeah . . . I know him,' Olivia replied, and left it at that as she went to fetch the order. Her married colleague liked the look of practically every man under thirty who came in for a meal. On coming out of the hot, clamorous kitchen balancing a full dinner plate Olivia felt a stab of annoyance. Ivy had propped a hip against the wall close to Joe's table and was chatting to him.

Olivia put his dinner before him, smiling stiffly. She was aware of Joe's eyes on her rather than the golden-crusted pie and mound of mash floating in a moat of parsley gravy. Most hungry men had their knives and forks at the ready when their meal was served but he was still lounging back in his chair. Olivia went to serve at another table. Ivy had seen a customer waiting yet had carried on flirting with Joe, rather than taking the order. Olivia decided to leave them to it but ten minutes later Joe caught her eye.

'Did you cook that? It weren't half bad.' He smacked his lips, standing up.

Olivia straightened from polishing off a stained tabletop, pushing her blonde fringe away from her eyes with damp fingers. 'No ... Danny cooks. The rest of us chop the eels and vegetables then serve and wash up,' she answered.

'You've got the short straw then.'

'Not 'alf,' Olivia replied with feeling. It was hard work, too, slicing through the tough and slimy eel skin and cutting the fish into pieces for boiling. Then there were mountains of spuds and stock vegetables to peel and parsley to chop finely for the liquor. 'Not been in here before?' she asked.

Joe shook his head. He pulled some cash from his pocket and counted out coins onto the table then gave her a sixpence tip. Olivia was more used to receiving pennies and thrupenny bits if she was lucky. She pocketed it with a murmur of thanks.

'Just came in today 'cos I found out you worked here,' he said.

'Oh? Have you got something to say to me?' Olivia's mind went straight back to the day his mother had called her a bitch. It had been weeks ago and she hadn't caught more than a few glimpses of Maisie Hunter since. The woman had gone out with a suitcase one afternoon shortly after their altercation and hadn't returned for a week. If Joe had just found out she'd had a run-in with his mother and had turned up to have a go at her ... well, at the very least he'd get his sixpence thrown back at him because Olivia had done nothing wrong!

'I've got something to ask. Two things actually.' Joe smiled.

'Ask away,' Olivia invited, cocking her head defiantly. She was aware that Ivy was watching them both from the counter.

'What time do you finish, and do you fancy going to the flicks later on?'

That took Olivia aback. She wasn't planning on doing over-time later but she rarely went out on the spur of the moment. She had become used to finding out her father's plans before making her own in case he started on Alfie in her absence. Sometimes she would take in a matinee with an old school friend when she knew she could snatch an hour to herself, and the kids were safely out of the way. But there was more making her hesitate to accept his invitation than just family concerns.

'It's taken you a while to ask me out, hasn't it? I haven't spoken to you since Christmas.'

'I got the impression you wanted me to leave you alone then so I thought I'd wait a while before coming to see you. How have you been?'

'Fine, thanks.' Olivia knew this wasn't a general pleasantry, he wanted to know if her father had been on the rampage again. He'd known how her lip had been cut on Christmas morning.

'Yes . . . no?' Joe prompted, tilting his head to catch her eyes. 'I don't want to tread on anybody's toes. If you've got a boyfriend, just say.'

'I haven't.' Olivia noticed that her boss was glaring at her because the tables were filling up again with customers. Ivy had been galvanised into action and was just emerging from the kitchen with a steaming plate in each hand.

'I've got to go. We're always busy Saturday afternoon.' Olivia took out her notepad and a pencil from her apron pocket and approached a table of three labourers, who looked to have recently clocked off work at the railway yard. She could smell the tar about them.

'Call by your house about seven o'clock?' Joe suggested lightly.

'If you want.' She sounded blasé but her heart was hammering and she could barely concentrate on writing down the navvies' order.

'Nice gel like you shouldn't get mixed up with the likes o' him,' one of the men purred after Joe had gone out of the door. 'I'm more your sort, duckie.' He stroked the back of her thigh over her serge skirt.

Olivia whacked her notepad against his hand, making his pals guffaw. She was used to beery-breathed fellows coming in at dinnertime, acting randy.

'Don't mind him.' The oldest of the group hung back as his pals paid up and left, having gobbled down their dinners. 'Ale's oiled his tongue. But he's right about Joe Hunter.'

Olivia immediately stopped stacking up their used plates and frowned at him.

'Man like that's best avoided by decent young ladies. But you never heard a word against him off me, right?' He patted her arm in a fatherly way and ferreted in the pocket of his dirty trousers for a thrupenny bit tip before leaving.

*

At a quarter to seven Olivia was peeping from behind the curtain to see if Joe Hunter had arrived. She needn't have worried about her father being around. Tommy hadn't returned, which meant he'd probably earned enough at the market to keep him out until last orders. Maggie and Nancy had gone off up the road to see their friends. Only Alfie was in; his best pal had gone to visit his nan so he had nobody to play with. Since the business with the broken window Ricky Wicks hadn't asked Alfie to have any more games of football.

'Are you going out, Livvie?' Her brother tried to sound brave rather than plaintive at the idea of being left on his own on a cold Saturday evening.

Olivia put down her hairbrush. 'No ... I'm just trying to tidy myself up a bit, that's all.' She twisted the thick golden tress securely into a neat coil and pinned it at the nape of her neck.

'Who's that then?' Alfie asked as there was a bang on the door.

Olivia felt butterflies circle inside her stomach, despite half expecting the knock. 'Go and see, will you?' she said lightly.

'Man come to see you, Livvie.' Alfie frowned at them from under his fair brows.

'Can't make it after all,' Olivia said. 'I'd've let you know if I could've got in touch with you.' Joe was dressed in a suit and wore polished shoes rather than heavy boots. She could see he'd made an effort to look smart.

'Could've gone upstairs and asked my mum where to find me, if you really wanted to know,' he said ruefully.

'She'd not tell me. In fact, I bet you'll be in trouble for asking me out.' Olivia gave him a challenging stare. 'Maisie doesn't like me.'

He shrugged. 'Doesn't matter. I do.'

'I'm stopping in with Alfie. Nobody else is home.' Olivia shrugged in apology.

Joe looked at the lad but Alfie kept his eyes down, digging his toe into a crack in the lino. 'Fancy a trip to the flicks, mate?'

The glimmer of a disbelieving smile touched Alfie's mouth. 'Who? Me?'

'Yeah ... *Ivanhoe*'s showing, if you fancy it.'

55

Alfie nodded vigorously before remembering to look to his sister for permission.

Joe beckoned Olivia. 'Come on ... just a couple of hours. We've got a few things to talk about.'

*

They emerged from the cinema into a foggy evening with air so cold it made their throats feel raw. As Alfie ran ahead, practising his swordplay against an imaginary foe, Olivia and Joe walked briskly behind.

'Reckon he enjoyed seeing that.'

'He did. Thanks for taking us both,' Olivia said warmly. 'Thanks too for the chocolates you got us at Christmas.'

'Nice, were they?'

'Lovely!' she exclaimed. 'Not that I got to sample many, what with the gannets around.' She smiled fondly, remembering the look of delight on her sisters' and brother's faces as they'd eaten chocolates after dinner. Their Christmas dinner, in the end, had consisted mainly of roast potatoes and plum pudding as most of the chicken had glass shards embedded in it. But the most wonderful thing had been that their father hadn't returned home until Boxing Day evening. He'd come in and not mentioned a word about any of it although the mark on Olivia's face was quite visible.

'How old is your brother?' asked Joe.

'Seven. I don't like leaving him at home on his own,' she said defensively.

Joe put up his hands in mock surrender. 'Didn't say a word.'

'Sorry ... didn't mean to jump down your throat,' she mumbled.

Joe took her hand, slipping it through the crook of his arm, and that first innocent contact made Olivia think back to what the fellow in the caff had said about avoiding the likes of Joe Hunter. Yet of all the fellows she'd gone out with – admittedly there had been very few and mostly they'd been school pals – he seemed the nicest.

Joe had insisted on paying the cinema admission fee, but not in a brash way. He'd slipped her brother the money and let him run to the kiosk and get tickets for them all.

'Want a cup of tea and a bite to eat? There's a Corner House a short walk from here.'

'Only if you let me pay for the treat.'

'Righto,' Joe said with a grin. 'In that case, I'll have a steak dinner.'

'Glutton!' She tutted. 'You had pie and mash earlier.'

'Growing lad, me.'

'How old are you?' Olivia asked.

'Twenty. What about you?'

'Almost seventeen and a half,' Olivia answered. 'I thought at first you lived upstairs with Maisie. You don't, though, do you?' She cocked her head, keen to hear his reply.

'Nope.'

'Where then?'

'Islington.'

'Do you have a job over that way?'

'Yeah.'

As the silence lengthened Olivia asked, 'Is it a secret what you do?' She watched his expression.

'Only to the police.'

Olivia's pace faltered, forcing him to slow down then turn to face her.

'Is that a joke?'

'No. Nobody yet told you to stay away from me?' He gave

her a direct, mocking look that told her he already knew the answer to that.

She felt a guilty flush steal into her cheeks.

'Who was it?' he asked.

'Don't know what you mean.' Olivia called to her brother, putting out her hand for him to hold.

'Your dad?' Joe guessed.

'If my dad knew I'd gone out with somebody in trouble with the police he'd . . . '

'He'd what?'

'Go mad.' Olivia knew she'd taste the back of Tommy's hand, and this time he'd mean to hit her. She didn't want Joe getting involved. She remembered how easily he'd floored Harry Wicks for manhandling her, and she didn't want any more fights breaking out because of her.

'Fair enough, anyway,' Joe said. 'I'd go mad too if it was my daughter knocking about with a wrong 'un. But he doesn't have to worry. I'm not in trouble with the police.'

'Because you're crafty enough to keep a step ahead of them?' Olivia guessed.

'Something like that. Has Harry Wicks bothered you again?'

'No, I've seen nothing of him at all.'

Joe gave a satisfied nod.

'Have you seen anything of him?' Olivia asked suspiciously. She wondered if he had run into Harry at some time and given him another thumping.

'No, I've not seen him either,' he said, smiling.

'We going in there?'

They'd stopped outside the Corner House and Alfie was agog with excitement at the idea of having something to eat in a proper caff.

'Special treat. Just a cup of tea and a bun though,' Olivia said, hoping she'd brought enough cash with her. She'd boasted about paying for them all, and she would.

The Corner House was crowded but they managed to find a table close to the window.

'Fog's getting worse,' Olivia said, gazing into the street and guessing it to be close to ten o'clock. An omnibus went by with headlights on. She was hoping Joe wouldn't carry on their conversation now her brother was listening. She needn't have worried about that. It seemed he'd picked up on her concern and they chatted about *Ivanhoe* and the prickly cinema seats while they ate currant buns and drank their teas.

Olivia was feeling quite subdued when they strolled home. She'd enjoyed her night out with Joe but there was a side to him she couldn't quite fathom. As they turned the corner into Ranelagh Road she spotted her father as he passed under a street lamp. Her heart sank at the sight of him lumbering towards them. She'd hoped he'd be out until almost eleven, giving her and Alfie a chance to turn in. She knew there was no way of avoiding him; in a moment he would look up and spot them through the misty air. Alfie had seen his father too. Olivia felt his fingers tighten on hers and heard his anxious gasp.

'Oi! What you two doing out this time o' night?'

Tommy increased his pace, stumbling from side to side on the pavement before coming to a swaying halt before them. 'Where've you been then?' he slurred, narrowed eyes fixed on Joe Hunter.

'Hello, Mr Bone. We've been to see *Ivanhoe* at the flicks.'

'Weren't talking to you,' Tommy began to say, jabbing a stubby finger against Joe's suit jacket. He turned his attention to his daughter. 'Yer brother should be in bed!'

Olivia felt her father's fingers bite into her arm, shaking it in punishment for keeping Alfie out late. He made to whack the boy round the back of the head but Joe grabbed his hand short of its target.

'If you want to beef about it better do it with me. It was my idea to take your son out.'

Tommy wrenched himself free so forcefully that he teetered backwards and landed on his posterior. He rolled off the kerb, banging his head on the way.

Joe crouched down and turned the snoring man's bristly chin towards him. 'He's all right. Just knocked himself out for a while.' He looked at Alfie's white, frightened face. 'Best get your brother indoors.'

Olivia nodded, ushering the boy inside, feeling angry and humiliated by her father's boorish behaviour. She had taken Alfie out before at the weekend and come back at this time without Tommy saying a word. Her father had acted belligerently just to show off in front of another man. But this time it had backfired on him.

'Get Alfie settled down,' she told Maggie, who was seated at the kitchen table eating toast and dripping for supper. 'Dad's stumbled over outside. I'll just help him in.' Olivia watched her brother and sister go into the bedroom then hurried back into the street. Joe had hoisted Tommy onto his shoulder. Her father was still snoring and the sound gave her some relief. With any luck he'd be out for the count till the morning.

'This way,' Olivia said in a whisper as Joe entered their home. She quickly showed him where Tommy's bedroom was.

With little care for his burden, Joe tipped Tommy off his shoulder and onto his back like a sack of coal, making Olivia gasp. She held her breath, hoping the jolting wouldn't waken her father.

'With any luck he won't even remember meeting us outside when he surfaces in the morning.'

Olivia nodded, her eyes wide. She peered at her father's forehead, noticing the egg-like contusion where he'd whacked himself. 'Thanks for your help.'

'Any time. He hits you, doesn't he?'

Olivia opened her father's bedroom door and led the way back into the parlour. 'You'd better go. Thanks for taking us out.'

'You didn't answer me,' Joe said.

'My father believes in disciplining his kids,' Olivia said stiffly. She didn't know why she felt so loyal to a man who terrorised his youngest child and lashed out at the others whenever it suited him, but she did. Blood was thicker than water she supposed.

Joe took out a scrap of paper from a pocket and found a pencil in another. He scribbled something on it. 'If you need me, that's where I am. Take it!' He thrust the paper at her.

As Olivia pocketed it he raised his hand, brushing his thumb across her pale cheek.

'Hard life you've got, I reckon, Olivia Bone.'

She choked back a sour laugh. 'I get by, thanks all the same for your concern.' The last thing she wanted off him was pity.

Joe walked to the door. 'Don't forget. Any trouble off your old man or that fellow along the road and this is where you'll find me.'

'I've looked after myself and the others since my mum died. I was only ten years old at the time so reckon I can carry on doing so.' Olivia crumpled the paper in her fist and chucked it in the scuttle for fire-lighting.

Joe shrugged, his hazel eyes flickering over her body in a way that made her burn. And then he was gone.

Chapter Six

Olivia was inspecting a blouse in Chapel Street market in Islington when she thought she caught a glimpse of a person she'd not seen in a very long while.

"Ere . . . you 'aving this or not?' the stallholder yelled after her as she hurried away. Cursing, the fellow picked up the pretty embroidered scrap and folded it.

'Ruby?' Olivia called hesitantly as she started to weave through the crowds to catch up with her quarry. If it *was* her cousin up ahead, Ruby had changed a good deal. From the young woman's gaudy clothes she reckoned that Mrs Cook would say she should steer clear of her because she *knew her sort*.

Halfway across the road Olivia put on a spurt and tapped the woman on the shoulder.

For a moment Ruby scowled at her then a glimmer of recognition lightened her expression. 'Bloomin' heck! Is it you, Livvie?' She looked Olivia up and down from her neatly coiffed blonde bun to her shiny black shoes.

Olivia smiled although she found it hard to conceal her shock. She'd last seen Ruby at a Christmas party held at their nan's house. Olivia had been ten years old and her cousin Ruby would have been twelve. Even at that young age Ruby had been pretty ... and she'd known it. *A right little madam,* Olivia's mother had called her sister Sybil's platinum-haired only child. Sybil had since had a son but the stuck-up daughter she'd reared seemed to have disappeared. This Ruby was a stranger; her hair was a mess of brassy curls, trailing beneath a flashy feathered hat, and her complexion was coated in powder and rouge. A scarlet cupid's bow had been painted on her mouth and the overall impression given was that Ruby Wright was world-weary at nineteen years old.

'Surprised you recognised me, ain't yer?' Ruby said with a wry inflexion in her voice.

'Been such a long time, hasn't it?' Olivia replied tactfully. Her cousin knew she looked like a tart then. 'How's your mum and dad and Mickey? Not seen any of you in an age.'

'Yeah ... we're all right,' Ruby said evasively, crossing her arms over her chest. 'What about your lot? How's the gels and little Alfie?'

'Maggie's leaving school soon. Nancy's daydreaming about being a ballerina. Alfie's seven now.' The two young women fell silent. No mention was made of Tommy Bone. But then he was the reason that her mother's family no longer kept in touch with any of them. Tommy had been an outcast since the day his wife died.

'You're a long way from home. What are you doing this side of the water?' Olivia asked amiably.

'Oh ... we're not in Bermondsey now.' Ruby wrinkled her nose. 'We've upped sticks to Islington.' She seemed reluctant to say any more although it seemed the move wasn't to her liking. 'Well nice to see you, Livvie ... best get on.' She lifted her shopping bag. 'Told Mum I'd get these spuds home to her in time for tea.'

'Hold on a mo'!' Olivia caught Ruby's elbow as she stepped away. After so many years of silence between their families she'd like a better reunion with her cousin than a five-minute conversation in the street. She could remember some good times for the two families with everybody together at Christmas, singing around her late granddad's old piano. The children would eat sausage rolls and drink pop while the adults got merry on brown ale. The memories of those times with her mother were precious to Olivia and she liked to dwell on them.

About a year after Agatha Bone was laid to rest their nan had died. Tommy hadn't been invited to the funeral. Olivia had wondered if the shock of her daughter's death had caused the old woman to go downhill so soon afterwards. Previously her nan had seemed to be in robust health despite having lived alone for years. Olivia had wondered too if the others in the family would hate Tommy even more now, thinking that he had shortened Nan's life.

'It's smashing to see you, Ruby. Fancy going in there for a cuppa? We can have a proper catch-up.' Olivia pointed to a caff set behind some market stalls. She had so many questions to ask about the Wrights; questions that her father wouldn't even listen to, let alone answer. But perhaps her cousin Ruby could fill in some of the gaps.

'Ain't got a farthing left on me after buying this veg.' Ruby shook her shopping bag, looking embarrassed. 'Sorry.'

'Don't worry about that. I've got enough to treat you to a cup of tea.' Before Ruby could change her mind Olivia took her arm firmly and steered her towards the Greengage Café.

Inside it was bustling with people and raucous shouts from

one side of the room to the other greeted the arrival of the two young blondes.

'Oi, oi!' one fellow called to his mate. 'Looks like trouble's arrived.'

'You can shut up, Riley McGoogan,' Ruby replied and led Olivia towards a table. 'Don't mind them,' she said. 'They're just showing off.'

'Know them, do you?' Olivia had been to Chapel Street market before but had never used the café. If she'd realised it was a rough house for costermongers and the like she'd have suggested they go elsewhere. But it seemed that her cousin was quite at home amongst such people.

'Neighbours,' Ruby briefly explained. 'Salt of the earth most of 'em. But some need slappin' down.' She waved a hand at the pot-bellied fellow in a dirty apron who was ambling over to take their order. 'We'll have two teas, Les.'

'Coming up, Rube.' Les gave her a wink.

'Surprised I know blokes like this, aren't you?' Ruby challenged her cousin.

'*I* know blokes like this,' Olivia returned stoutly, adding by way of explanation, 'I work in a pie and mash shop and get me best tips off customers arrived straight from the pub.'

Ruby snorted a laugh. 'Well . . . who'd've thought it? I always reckoned you'd end up being a nurse. It was what you wanted, wasn't it? Or I had you down for nabbing a rich husband.'

Olivia detected a hint of malice in her cousin's voice but ignored it. 'I thought the same about you. We all have our dreams, don't we?'

Ruby gave a sigh. 'Yeah. Don't take long for 'em to turn to ashes, though.' She looked at Olivia's bare fingers. 'Got a boyfriend?'

Joe Hunter had sprung to mind but Olivia pushed thoughts

of him away and shook her head. 'How about you, Ruby? Anybody special in your life?'

Her cousin gave a dry laugh. 'Couple of fellers I've liked over the years ... but nothing come of it.'

They broke off talking as the proprietor put down their teas and seemed in no hurry to go away.

Quickly Olivia took out her purse, thinking he was waiting to be paid.

'On me, love,' Les said magnanimously. 'Introduce us then.' He gave Ruby's arm a nudge.

'This is me cousin Olivia and mind yer manners around her, 'cos she's from the posh side of North London.'

'Are you, love?' Les asked, sounding interested.

'Hardly call where I live in Wood Green posh!' Olivia choked back a laugh.

'Bet it's better than the Bunk though, eh, Ruby?' Les smirked.

'Anywhere's better'n the Bunk,' Ruby muttered. 'Go on then, sling yer hook,' she continued, waving him away. 'So where was we?' she said. 'Oh, yeah, talking about blokes. I can't believe you've not hooked yourself a fiancé. You're even prettier than I remember.'

'You too,' Olivia said gamely.

'I'm off fellers and sticking by Mum and Mickey fer now,' Ruby said. 'They need me putting in the kitty since Dad's run out on us.'

Olivia put down her cup, frowning. 'Sorry ... I didn't realise.' Her uncle Ed had always seemed rather a quiet man and curiosity got the better of Olivia. 'Did he go off with someone?'

'Gawd knows. Mum won't speak about him. Ain't seen him in donkey's years. Don't want to neither.' Ruby took a big gulp of her tea then stared into the cup. 'We've hit hard times,' she admitted quietly. 'If that's what you want to know.'

'Is that why you moved?' Olivia asked gently, aware of her cousin's defensiveness.

'We hung on as long as we could in Bermondsey then got evicted. That bastard of a landlord wouldn't give us no more credit. He knew we'd had rotten luck but it didn't make a bit of difference to him.'

'People like that make me sick,' Olivia said heatedly.

'Me 'n' all,' Ruby agreed.

'Did you come over here to find work?'

'We heard about a place in Islington that rented rooms out really cheap, that's why we left South London. Mum chars and works in a rag shop and I do waitressing up West. I turn me hand to pulling pints in the local pub to bring in a bit extra as well, if I can get a shift.'

Olivia squeezed her cousin's fingers. 'It's a bloody hard life, isn't it?'

'I know some worse off'n us round our way,' Ruby said valiantly.

'Does your mum ever speak about us Bones?'

Ruby shook her head. 'I don't suppose your dad ever mentions us Wrights either.'

'Perhaps eventually they might forget all the bitter memories if we keep meeting up with one another,' Olivia said. 'I really missed visiting Nan after Mum died.'

'She missed seeing all of you. She told me once she'd have liked to have you kids round for tea but she wouldn't ask because of how she felt about your dad.'

The knowledge that her grandmother hadn't carelessly turned her back on them all was balm to Olivia's aching heart. She realised she should have defied her father's command that they stay away from her mother's people. She should have just gone round to see her nan on her own; but she'd been younger then, too timid, and it was too late now.

'Gotta get home. Mum'll wonder where the bloody hell I've got to. Thanks for the tea, Livvie.'

'Thank him,' Olivia reminded Ruby with a wry glance at the proprietor.

Outside the caff the two young women embraced. 'I'm heading off that way.' Ruby jerked her head to the left, setting the feathers on her fancy hat dancing.

'Can we meet up again? I won't come round yours if you'd rather I didn't.' Olivia gazed enquiringly at her cousin.

''Course,' Ruby said. 'Meet you here outside the Greengage next week, same time, if you like?'

The women embraced again then Ruby headed off with a wave. Olivia stood watching her for a moment, feeling elated and sure that something rather important had just taken place. She turned towards the bus stop to catch her ride home but had barely taken more than a few paces when her arm was gripped in firm fingers.

'Have you been looking for me?'

Olivia spun about and felt her heart drum madly as she gazed into Joe Hunter's narrowed eyes.

'Oh ... hello. No, I'm not looking for you. Why would you think that?' she blurted out breathlessly.

'You're in Islington and I told you to come and find me here if you needed me.'

Olivia twisted her arm free. 'I don't need you, thanks. I was looking to buy a nice blouse in Chapel Street market, that's all that brought me here.'

'Right,' he said, tipping the peaked cap back on his head and fixing her with a hard stare. 'So you didn't come to see Ruby Wright either?'

'If I thought it was any of your business, I might tell you.' Olivia felt more composed now that the surprise of seeing him had evaporated. Her green eyes narrowed suspiciously. 'How do you know her?' Olivia had already guessed that Ruby was popular with the men in the neighbourhood. The idea that her cousin might be a good-time girl didn't put Olivia off wanting them to keep in touch. Ruby could have been backed into a corner before taking a wrong turning that had seemed to be the only way out.

'She lives over my way,' Joe replied. 'And my advice would be to stay away from her.'

'I didn't ask for your advice.'

He shrugged and gave her a tight smile. 'How've you been?'

'Fine, thank you. And you?'

He pulled a face. 'Your old man might be a drunk and a bully but he's brought you up polite.'

'That was my mum's doing,' Livvie returned, then bit her lip for having said too much.

'Been gone a while, has she?'

'Yes,' Olivia said hoarsely. 'Seems like forever.' She remembered then that his mother lived alone. 'How about your dad? Do you miss him?'

'Nah ... don't miss him one bit.'

'Is he dead?' Olivia asked.

'Could be. I'd say that somebody's swung for him by now. If not and he ever comes back, I'll kill him.'

Olivia was shocked by his callousness. She knew he'd not been bragging; he meant it. Tempted though she was to ask him to explain what the man had done to make Joe hate him, she held her tongue. Joe Hunter was the sort of man who'd want answers from her in return for any he gave. And she didn't trust him enough to tell him anything personal.

'I have to get home,' she told him 'The kids'll be in from school wanting their teas.' She craned her neck, glimpsing her bus on the horizon.

'How was your dad after that crack on the head?'

Olivia smiled wryly. 'He didn't say a word about it and neither did I. You were right: he didn't remember seeing us that night, or taking a tumble. He must've guessed he'd done something though 'cos he had a bruise on his forehead you couldn't miss.'

'Want to go out again?' Joe asked as she stepped towards the kerb ready to board the bus.

'I don't know . . . ' Olivia hesitated. 'It's awkward.'

'Doesn't have to be,' Joe said. 'Don't let him bully you into thinking it is or you'll be under his thumb, skivvying and nurse-maiding his kids, until you're too old to care about buying nice blouses anymore.' He stroked the backs of his fingers across her rosy cheek.

'I know what I'm doing!' Olivia got on the bus then turned to face him. 'Anyhow it's none of your business.'

'So you keep telling me.' He walked beside the bus as it started to pick up speed. 'Thing is, I reckon you are my business, Livvie Bone, and you should listen to what I say 'cos if you don't, you risk ending up sad and lonely.'

'What do you know about Ruby? Why do you want me to stay away from her?' Olivia demanded, hanging off the pole on the platform to gaze back at him.

Joe didn't answer her, simply raised one hand in farewell before turning away and disappearing into the crowd.

Olivia slipped onto a seat and stared sightlessly out of the window, a frown on her face. She realised that there was nothing particularly odd in him being aware she was acquainted with Ruby Wright. He'd seen them saying goodbye outside the Greengage Café and had been inquisitive about their relationship because Ruby was one of his neighbours. Olivia felt that the fewer people who knew about her and her cousin meeting up the better it would be. If her father found out she'd been seeing any of the Wrights against his wishes, he'd fly into a rage. And if she wasn't around to take the brunt of it then one of the others would.

Joe Hunter was a puzzle to her; he had so far treated her with kindness and respect and yet what she'd learned about him made her shy away from wanting to get to know him better.

He was honest; he liked her and wanted to take her out again yet he didn't attempt to hide things about himself that might put her off accepting his invitations. Despite being aware of all that, there was something about him she found undeniably attractive.

He was trouble, she impressed on herself, even if she didn't know exactly what that trouble amounted to. She got up to alight at Wood Green bus station, still mulling things over. People had warned her about him and taking everything into account she'd be a fool not to heed those warnings.

Chapter Seven

'Well? What did he say?' Bill Morley pushed away from where he'd been resting against a company cart gaily adorned with paintings of lozenges and toffees. He eagerly approached his pal, though he could tell from Tommy's thunderous expression that he wasn't about to hear happy tidings.

'He said: get back to work and get that load out on time or your pay'll be docked,' Tommy Bone replied through gritted teeth.

Tommy flung down onto the empty cart the roughly written list of things he'd wanted to raise with Mr Barratt. In fact, he'd never got to speak to the top man about any of their grievances over working conditions. Barratt was distancing himself from the workforce. He had passed a message down the line that any staff matters should be taken up with Lucas Black. So, reluctantly, that's what Tommy had done. He'd gone cap in hand to the young boss's office with the demands he and his colleagues had come up with, and got short shrift for his trouble.

Nelly Smith sidled out of the sugar-boiling building and bounded closer with her rough skirts held up free of her flying feet. 'Any news about getting a canteen?' She grinned optimistically.

'Nothing doing, that's the news,' Tommy snapped.

'Right lot of good that was then,' she huffed. 'It's high time us women got a rise even if you men don't. We work as hard, we deserve the same pay as you. Wish I'd gone and seen the guvnors meself. Could've reminded 'em about the factory gels over Bermondsey way what caused a rumpus for their bosses. We can do the same. See how they like that!'

'Feel free.' Tommy thrust the bit of paper at her bony chest. 'Good luck!'

Nelly screwed up the paper in her fist and flung the crumpled ball back at the cart. She stalked off, muttering, retying her sacking apron about her skinny waist.

'Never mind, mate,' Bill said, thumping Tommy on the back. 'Let's get this lot done then or I reckon the bugger will dock our pay. The missus wants a beef roast on Sunday when her sister's lot come over fer dinner. That'll cost, so I need a full pay packet.'

'It's getting late, we'll be clocking off in an hour. They don't want to pay a decent overtime rate so I ain't hanging around here fer a pittance.' Tommy crossed his arms defiantly and stared up at the window of his nemesis's office. He could see Lucas Black gazing down impassively onto the courtyard, hands in his pockets as though he didn't have a care in the world.

And he didn't! Tommy thought, feeling resentment boil within him. The lucky sod was a bachelor from a posh family who lived in a mansion in Hampstead. Lucas Black didn't have rent and kids and a nagging woman emptying his pockets every week.

Bill clapped Tommy on the back again to console him. He knew his colleague was seething at being ejected from Black's office but Tommy didn't help himself. He often came across as arrogant and unpleasant when talking to people, be they colleagues or guv'nors. His attitude had probably put Black's back up before he'd got out a word about negotiating a better pay deal.

But the list of grievances they'd all come up with was valid; working hours were too long and there was no real incentive to do overtime for a piddling reward. Meal breaks weren't long enough and the lack of a proper canteen where staff could sit and eat comfortably was something everybody moaned about. As was the absence of a uniform to protect bodies and clothing.

Loyalty was all very well but it was hard to maintain when the bosses were all doing very nicely thank you off the backs of those tired and grubby souls toiling away for them. Pulling the heavy machinery about by hand and staying clear of nasty scalds from boiling sugar was no easy or pleasant task.

'Bet they're all having a chinwag about me in there.' Tommy jerked his head towards the factory entrance as he humped boxes of toffees onto his shoulder then slid them into place on the cart. He could see a knot of men congregating by the gates, heads together while sliding glances his way.

A few minutes later one of the fellows sauntered over. Sam Linnet worked as a farrier at the factory and he'd also take the new van out when the regular driver was off. 'Any chance of a rise on the horizon?' He nodded at his pals by the gates. 'They're for coming out and I am too if you can drum up enough support from everybody else to make it worthwhile.'

'How about you and yer pals drumming up some support in your departments to help make it worthwhile?' Tommy returned acidly. He'd felt resentful when Linnet got the job he'd wanted, driving the van.

'Can't make it too obvious what we're doing – the manage-ment will fill strikers' jobs almost before we've set up a picket line, like they did before.'

'Risk we've all got to take, ain't it?' Tommy said, fists on his hips. He knew that Linnet was referring to the strike that had taken place when scores of people lost their jobs. But that had been over a decade ago and times had moved on. 'So ... you and that lot over there prepared to do a bit of agitating?'

'I'll go and speak to them.' Sam Linnet adjusted his waistcoat and strode off.

'All full of it but none of 'em's got the bottle to stick their heads above the parapet.' Tommy was watching the fellows dispersing. They slunk off, hands in pockets, heading back to the forge and the sheds and the stables. 'Mention the downside to going on strike to 'em and they scatter like rats.'

'True enough, Tom ... true enough,' Bill said soothingly. He'd stood at a distance watching proceedings. He felt more or less the same way as Linnet and his pals did: he'd not rock the boat if somebody else was already in the water and risking drowning. But Bill needed more money than he was earning at Barratt's and if he couldn't get it from a pay rise then he'd have to investigate other ways of boosting his income. His wife was constantly wanting new clothes and new furniture to show off to her sister.

After ten minutes of working together with nothing break-ing the quiet but their grunts, and the scrape of wood against wood as boxes were manoeuvred, Bill surfaced enough from his contemplation of money-making schemes to say, 'That'll do, I reckon, mate.' He looked at the pallets stacked high on the cart. He started to unwind the rope used to lash the load and unfold a tarpaulin.

'I'm finishing this lot.' Tommy pointed to the cartons still on the ground. 'Ain't waiting for another wagon to come round. I'm off home. I've got an early start down the market. And it pays better than this bleedin' does!' He hoisted another two boxes, wedging them this way and that to make space for them. 'Wants this lot out on time, so he said. Well, let's get it out on time fer 'im.' Tommy jerked his head at the office window. 'He's watching us up there, y'know. See him? Nosy git!'

'Some of the other gels on the boilers said they'd be prepared to go on strike and so will I . . . '

Nelly had come back out to speak to Tommy just as he was plonking two extra boxes on top of a high stack.

'Yer silly cow! You startled me!' he roared, losing his grip on the boxes. They slid sideways, toppling off the cart and hitting Nelly on the hip.

As she screamed in pain and fell to the ground the men at the gate came running over to help. And Lucas Black disappeared from where he'd been stationed up at the window.

'All right, Nelly?' Tommy had leaped down from the cart to crouch over the injured woman. He shook her shoulder as her eyelids fluttered and her thin face creased in pain.

'No, I ain't bleedin' all right!' she whimpered. She rubbed her sore thigh and wailed louder as she saw blood on her hand.

Lucas Black had pushed through the crowd of people to lean over Nelly.

'Reckon she needs 'ospital,' a woman shouted. 'Best fetch a doctor, sir.'

'What's happened? What's going on?' Numerous voices called out as other workers came streaming out of the factory. They all gawped at Tommy as word got around that he'd caused another accident. Some looked genuinely sorry for him, others privately pleased that the man with the big mouth had again landed himself in trouble.

'Morley . . . you go and fetch a doctor. The rest of you, back to work except for you, Mrs Crabbe.' Lucas Black beckoned one of Nelly's colleagues from the sugar-boiling room. 'Stay with Mrs Smith, please, until the doctor arrives.' He turned to Tommy, his face a mask of cold fury. 'You . . . go and wait in my office.'

'I was getting it out like you said . . . ' Tommy blustered in his own defence but was soon cut off.

'Get to my office. Now!' Black hadn't raised his voice but Tommy obeyed without any further objection. He stalked off towards the factory entrance, chin jutting belligerently.

'Clear these split boxes up, shall we, Mr Black?' A few of the men who'd been talking of striking sounded quite humble now as they scurried to and fro, collecting spilled confectionery and splintered wood.

*

Olivia spotted Harry Wicks hanging about by the privet hedge outside his house with some of his pals. Her first instinct was to go back inside and wait till he'd gone because she felt in no mood for a row with him. But she refused to hide. It was a sunny May morning with a breeze stirring her fair hair. She draped her cotton shawl across her shoulders and set off towards the corner shop at a steady pace and with her chin elevated.

'Where you going then, sweet Livvie?' Harry bawled.

'Shopping.' She wouldn't ignore him because that would just give him an excuse to call her stuck-up or something similar.

'Shopping, eh? Surprised you can afford to do that now yer old man's lost his job at Barratt's.'

That taunt so surprised Olivia that she almost stopped and turned to give him a mouthful, but she managed to take the information in her stride, carrying on despite their catcalls. Inwardly her mind was whirring and her heart was pounding with anxiety. Olivia had a dreadful suspicion there was truth behind Harry's spiteful taunt.

Her father had come in a few nights ago very late. Thankfully the others had been asleep but Olivia had heard him in the parlour staggering around. He normally got himself straight to bed when he was roaring drunk. She had crept to her bedroom door to listen, and heard him mumbling and weeping for his dead wife. He'd stumbled off to his room and the old iron bedstead creaked as he collapsed onto it. Soon afterwards she'd heard through the thin walls the rumbling of his snores. But Olivia had lain awake. Her father was a man of routine and if that changed Olivia grew worried.

The following morning he'd got up late, after the kids had gone to school. Olivia had asked him if he was feeling unwell; he never missed a factory shift.

He'd bawled at her to attend to her own business and leave him be. Then he'd gone out and come back hours later with peat covering his hands. The significance of that hadn't sunk in until today. He'd not explained why he'd not gone to Barratt's on a weekday morning and Olivia hadn't asked because it had never occurred to her that he might no longer work there. Her father had been employed at the factory for decades; indeed he'd often boasted that he was one of the longest-serving members of staff there. But no more it seemed.

Entering the grocer's, she bought the pot of fish paste and loaf of bread she needed for the kids' tea when they got in from school then hurried home, barely aware, in her agitated state, of the group of men leering at her and making lewd gestures.

Her father had been up with the lark that morning and gone out with his wrapped dinner in his pocket just as he had yesterday and the day before. But now Olivia realised he'd not been heading for Barratt's; instead he had been leaving the house and staying out all day to look for work. The significance of the loss of her father's regular wage suddenly hit home and Olivia turned cold.

She sank down at the table, nibbling at the side of her thumb while concentrating on how to go about things. She knew she mustn't sink into melancholy. Her father was a hard-working man ... but if he'd been sacked for some misdemeanour he'd not get a good reference from Barratt's. He was an unpleasant man, but since he had accidentally struck her at Christmas he seemed to have made an effort to curb his temper. He hadn't lashed out at any of them since then although it still took little for him to raise his voice. Olivia reckoned even he had been shocked by what he'd done that day. But it hadn't stopped him drinking.

Mentally Olivia did some arithmetic, working out how they might economise and at the same time increase their income. She knew she could ask for extra shifts at the pie and mash shop. Maggie would soon bring in some wages; at least ten shillings a week, Olivia reckoned, bucking herself up. But her father wouldn't let Maggie leave school until she'd achieved her Standard Seven for the Labour Certificate. He was a man who would never back down on what he'd said even if doing so might reap benefits for them all.

He'd made Olivia get to Standard Seven before allowing her to leave Elementary School at fourteen. It had been no hardship; in fact she would have liked to carry on her education and go to Secondary School. But she'd not been able to. Her father had wanted her out and earning as well as acting as his house-keeper, so that was that.

She wondered if he would tell them why he'd lost his job;

probably he would consider it to be none of his kids' concern. Whatever Tommy Bone had done, he'd never admit to being in the wrong.

*

'Never heard Dad come in last night,' Nancy said. She flicked over a page in her book, studying pictures of Anna Pavlova striking a pose as Giselle.

'Me neither,' Maggie said. 'With any luck he's gone away for a few days, like he does sometimes.'

'I expect he's been putting in some extra shifts on the market and stayed at a pal's house.' Olivia also knew he'd stayed out and she had risen that morning wondering if he'd been with his lady friend. Although it had been months since Sister Clare had told her that Tommy Bone had been spotted arm in arm with a woman, Olivia had not forgotten about it. She had just pushed it to the back of her mind as other, more pressing matters overtook her.

She poured tea into three mugs for the children. She'd have her own breakfast once they'd left for school. She handed them each a penny ha'penny for their meals. 'Don't go out at dinnertime,' she warned Maggie, wagging one finger at her. Her sister had been caught by her teacher, sneaking out of the school gates with Ricky Wicks to buy a ha'porth of chips rather than have a school dinner. Olivia knew that the spare penny then went into Maggie's pocket to be spent at the weekend. Luckily, Olivia had come face to face with Miss Elliott when walking past the school and been told about it. Thankfully no letter had arrived for Tommy, informing him of his daughter's conduct. Had it done so, Maggie wouldn't have been able to sit down for a week.

Alfie munched his toast and jam, the serene smile on his

80

berry-red mouth speaking for him. If his absent father never came back it would suit the boy down to the ground.

'Dunno why you're looking at that stupid stuff all the time. You're too clumsy to be a dancer.' Maggie flipped shut Nancy's book, making her younger sister swipe out at her.

'Better being clumsy than stupid like you,' Nancy sniped. 'You can't even pass your exams and you'll have to go back in the autumn and sit with us in our class. Dunce!'

'Come on, pick up your homework books and get going,' Olivia ordered. 'It's almost the end of term now.'

'Bloody good job too,' Maggie muttered, getting to her feet. 'Can't wait to leave this dump and get a job.'

Olivia called her back as the others went to put on their shoes. 'Nancy's right. Dad won't let you leave school unless you get your certificate, same as I had to. It's time you bucked your ideas up by getting a proper job and putting in the kitty.'

'I already put in the kitty from doing me errands at the weekend.'

'Fivepence isn't nearly enough and you know it – and if Dad finds out what you're up to, you'll be sorry.' Maggie scrubbed doorsteps over Muswell Hill and got fourpence a time. Out of that she gave up a penny a time. If their father knew she was holding back most of what she earned she'd be thrashed as much for lying as for hiding her earnings. She'd told him she got paid tuppence a step.

Maggie shrugged. 'Don't care whether I get me certificate or not. I'm not going back and he can't make me. And when I'm out working, I'll only put in the kitty what I can afford.'

'You reckon Dad'll take that, do you?' Olivia's forceful tone wiped the smugness off Maggie's face. 'Nancy gives up the same as you do and she's only earning a tanner winding wool at the draper's on Saturday.'

'That's her lookout,' Maggie said sullenly.

'You'd better take the laundry job,' Olivia warned her. 'And you'll hand over *all* your wages and I'll give you back what *I* can afford. Don't bother lying about your wages – I can easily check up on you.' She tipped up her sister's chin. 'You're not hard done by. I put all my earnings in except for ninepence. You can save up, same as me, if you want to have little luxuries.'

Maggie muttered beneath her breath and stomped off.

Once they'd all trooped away up the road Olivia sat down at the table and propped her elbows on it. She settled her chin on her fists and stared into space. Her father hadn't put anything in the pot for the rent and Mr Silver would be by later that evening to collect it.

A mound of laundry caught her eye and she stared dejectedly at the dirty linen ready to be hauled out to the washhouse. Joe Hunter's warning that she'd be a fool to carry on as she was, skivvying for her family, preyed on her mind. There was truth in what he'd said. But if she didn't care for the younger ones, who would? She couldn't abandon them.

The likelihood that her father had a woman seemed more remote as the days passed and nothing much changed. Yet Olivia wished it *were* true, and things *would* change. She had started to crave the freedom it would give her.

Before discovering he'd lost his job, she'd been tempted to ask her father about what Sister Clare had told her. But if there was to be an argument it seemed more important to tackle him over the loss of his factory work and how that would affect them all.

She'd heard him weeping again the other night for his wife. Olivia rarely got a glimpse of the softer side to her father's character. He might seem unfeeling but at heart he wasn't. He was just a man who'd been battered by life into uncontrollable bitterness. Sometimes when she looked at his haggard profile while he sat at the parlour table eating, or reading the news-paper, she felt a great sadness wash over her.

She pitied him because his children didn't like him ... and because he vainly tried to cover his own guilt and loneliness by being brash. And she pitied him because the one thing that he'd always had to be proud of – his long-term employment at Barratt's – had been taken from him. It was doubtless his own fault, and he doubtless knew it. She put a hand to her throat to touch her mother's silver locket as she often did when worrying about things. Her fingers passed to and fro over soft warm skin but the chain was missing. She jumped up and searched on the floor but there was no glint of metal under the table.

'What you doing? You'd best get that washing started on, hadn't yer? Day'll be gone ... '

Tommy Bone had come in, startling his daughter. Olivia shrugged. She'd not tell him about the locket in case it started him off. She'd probably find it in the bedroom later. She never took the locket off but it could've come loose while she slept. She shook the teapot to offer her father a cup of tea. She felt flustered, as though he might have guessed she'd been think-ing about him. He seemed in a reasonable mood, however. He started whistling while sluicing his hands in the water in the bowl. Olivia handed him a towel with a smile. With the kids out of the way it seemed the perfect opportunity to pluck up the courage to ask him about his job.

Tommy put a handful of coins onto the table. 'Rent money,' he said, and seemed on the point of slouching off to his bedroom.

'Want a cuppa?' Olivia hoped he'd stay so she could man-oeuvre the conversation round to Barratt's.

Tommy grunted acceptance, loosening his neckerchief and shrugging out of his jacket.

'Take a pew then,' Olivia said. 'I'll do a fresh brew.'

Tommy hung his coat over the back of a stickback chair then pulled it out from under the table and sat down. Jerking the *News of the World* from one of his coat pockets, he spread it out on the table in front of him.

'Have you lost your job at Barratt's, Dad?' Olivia blurted. She'd wanted to find a better way to approach him but the burning question had simply rolled off her tongue, surprising them both.

Tommy lifted his head and gazed at her in a peculiarly expressionless way as though he had difficulty understanding her. Olivia guessed that her audacity had shocked him and he was considering how to react. She fidgeted on the spot, unsure whether or not to apologise. But she had a right to know ... they all did.

'Didn't lose it ... didn't want it no more.' Tommy had spoken in a flat voice then turned his attention back to the racing pages pinned beneath his elbows. He started marking off favourites with a pencil. 'Gonna get that tea made then?'

Olivia quickly put the kettle on the hob grate. She moistened her lips. 'How we going to pay the bills then if you're not working?'

'Just give you the rent to pay the Jew, ain't I?' he barked, and eyed her from beneath his bristling eyebrows.

He'd got impatient with her but he hadn't stormed off and Olivia realised he knew as well as she did that they needed to speak about this.

'Have you picked up extra market shifts? Is that where you got the rent money?'

Tommy lounged back in the chair, plunging one hand into his pocket. He pulled out at least ten one-pound notes, waving them at her. 'I had a bit of luck on the gee-gees fer a change. Come in at good odds 'n' all they did.'

Olivia smiled although she didn't have much to smile about. One lucky win was nice, but the way her father was scrutinising the runners made her sure the money he'd gained would soon be lost.

'Didn't think you'd ever want to leave Barratt's. What turned you off your job after all this time, Dad?' Olivia's attempt to wheedle information from him worked; she almost got a sour smile from him.

'Not what ... *who.*' Tommy's jaw hardened as he recalled the way Lucas Black had dismissed him on the spot after the accident. He'd been paid up there and then and told to get off the premises.

'Thought you got on all right with the guv'nors.'

'I did ... till Lucas Black got put in charge.' Tommy pulled himself up short, snapping, 'That tea nearly ready? I'm parched. I'll have a biscuit 'n' all.'

Quickly Olivia shook the pot to hurry the brew along then poured it out into two cups. Her mind had flashed back to the day she'd taken her father's dinner to the factory for him. The handsome man who'd offered her a job had introduced himself as Lucas Black.

She found a few Digestives to put on a plate, pushing it towards him. 'The fellow you don't like offered me a job on Christmas Eve.'

Tommy took a bite of biscuit. He too was remembering the incident when Black had asked if Olivia was his daughter. He'd seen the glint in his boss's eyes and had known Lucas thought his Livvie pretty. Tommy watched her washing up crockery in the tin bowl. It tore at his guts that he'd hit her on Christmas morning because he loved her more than all his other kids put together. She reminded him so much of Aggie that sometimes it made him ache to look at her. It stabbed at his guts too that he hated his own son. Yet he knew he did, and couldn't stop himself although he knew he should. Every time he was around the boy he remembered the day he'd first seen him: a little naked scrap of flesh on the bed, flailing purple arms and legs and bawling his lungs out, while his mother bled to death beside him. If Alfie hadn't been born, Aggie would still be here.

Tommy stabbed the point of his pencil against the Newmarket runners while he gazed at Livvie, shaking washing-up water off her slender fingers; she had hands that appeared better suited to fine needlework than pulling machinery or boxes about.

But a seed of an idea was in his head– something that would involve hard work for her. She might look fragile but his Livvie was strong as an ox . . . just as Aggie had been. As youngsters growing up together, he and his sweetheart had lifted sacks of spuds at the weekends while helping their parents run their market stalls. A man's work Aggie could cope with; it had been women's work that had killed the only one he'd ever loved.

'I told you not to hang about outside the factory that day, didn't I?' Tommy poked a finger at Olivia. 'So . . . he spoke to you direct, did he, Lucas Black?'

Olivia nodded absently. She was working out how she could keep Alfie out of her father's way if she took on extra shifts at the pie and mash shop. There was always a chance that her brother might be able to park himself at an empty table and wait for her to finish work . . . 'I'll see if I can get some overtime. Maggie and Nancy will have to pull their weight with the cooking and cleaning here.'

Tommy shot to his feet. 'You just keep doing what you're doing till I tell you different,' he bawled. 'I'm still head of this house and don't you forget it.'

'I know you'll always work hard, Dad . . . just saying us kids can help out more'n we do.'

'Agree with you on that.' Tommy jutted his chin. 'Maggie needs a job now. Before the month's out I want her down the Labour Exchange with her certificate. And Nancy could do with taking her nose out of those books she reads and finding herself a few more errands. She can take on her sister's doorsteps for a start before somebody else gets hold of 'em when Maggie goes full-time.'

'And Alfie does chores for Mrs Cook.' Olivia took the opportunity to praise her brother.

'Won't hurt him to help, neither. Make sure he puts in the kitty all what he's given.' With that Tommy shoved aside his chair and bowled from the room. A few moments later Olivia heard the front door slam and she renewed her search for her locket.

Chapter Eight

Bill Morley had felt bad about Tommy getting the sack. His colleague had been very unlucky that day; if Nelly Smith hadn't crept up on the poor bloke unawares it was likely that Tommy would still be working at the factory. The woman's injuries hadn't been as severe as first imagined; Nelly had escaped with cuts and bruises, although from the racket she'd made everyone had thought she'd broken something. The doctor had patched her up pretty quickly. Nelly was still playing on it even though she'd not missed a day's wages.

A pay-out wasn't on the horizon since Lucas Black had enquired why she had been outside with the men loading the cart when she should have been inside working. Nelly hadn't had an answer ready for him. She certainly wasn't going to own up to conferring with Tommy Bone about strike action. Sympathy for her was dwindling amongst her colleagues, and increasing for Tommy. He'd had the gumption, after all, to tackle the management over issues that affected them all. And it was as much for that as for the accident that he'd lost his job, in Bill's opinion.

But Tommy had played into Black's hands that day by loading a cart too high for the second time. He'd already been warned he'd be dismissed if he caused another accident. It was obvious the young boss and Tommy would always clash heads.

Bill swigged moodily from his tankard. As the door opened he spied the fellow on his mind entering the pub.

'What you having, Tom? The usual?' Bill gave him a cheery wave. 'Pint of light 'n' bitter, is it?'

'Thanks, Bill.'

'Turned anything up yet in the way of permanent work?'

Tommy took a gulp from his glass as soon as the landlord slid the ale in front of him. He shook his head, smacking his lips. 'Got me market work keeping me going, though, so ain't unduly bothered.' He'd sooner lie and say everything was good as gold than have people pity him.

Bill wasn't fooled by Tommy's brave face. He'd been loading the cart as well but Tommy hadn't tried to drop him in it to ease the pressure on himself. He'd taken all the blame and never once thrown that in Bill's face. He reckoned that between the two of them they should be able to do something to square things up.

'Got something for you,' Bill whispered, and slipped a fistful of toffees into Tommy's hand.

Tommy pocketed them. 'Ain't that keen meself on stickjaw. But the kids'll soon scoff 'em.'

'A lot more where those come from ... if you get my drift?' Bill rumbled and gave a sly wink.

The slight smile on Tommy's face turned foxy. 'You saying what I think you're saying?'

'Reckon I am.'

'How d'you manage that?'

'Ask me no questions, I'll tell yer no lies.' Bill glanced about. 'Not in here anyhow, 'cos you never know who's earwigging.'

Tommy threw back his head and guffawed. 'Well, I never,' he said quietly. 'You've surprised me, Bill Morley. Didn't think you had it in yer.'

'I have, see, and I'll come round yours later and tell you what's on me mind. Bring a box of goodies with me. You can put 'em by for Christmas for your lad. Or sell 'em; it'll put something in yer pocket.'

'Ta, mate,' Tommy murmured and emptied his glass. 'Be indoors about ten o'clock if that ain't too late for you?' In fact, he'd be home sooner than that but he wanted it nice and dark because he didn't fancy the neighbours seeing anything they shouldn't. He didn't want his kids in the way either.

'Fine by me,' Bill said.

Over his years at the sweet factory Tommy Bone had contemplated having sticky fingers. But he was a logical man and knew on balance he'd be better off keeping his nose clean and hanging on to his job. But in his opinion he'd been unfairly dismissed and he'd deserved something more from the employer to whom he'd given so many years. As Tommy strode home he was smiling for the first time in days.

'In on yer own? Where's yer sisters?' Tommy had spotted his son as soon as he opened the parlour door.

Alfie had heard his father's key strike the lock and tried to scuttle into the bedroom before he entered.

'Livvie's at work still and Nancy and Maggie have gone to see their friends,' Alfie rattled off, his wide eyes darting nervously.

'Time they was indoors. School tomorrow,' Tommy said gruffly.

Alfie nodded, standing ramrod still so he didn't catch his father's attention.

'Go on, get yerself to bed, you little tyke.' Tommy jerked a thumb over his shoulder.

Alfie sidled past, keen to do as he was told.

Tommy called to his son to halt before the boy had taken more than a step along the corridor.

Alfie froze, eyes wide as saucers as his father approached him. As a fist came his way he gasped and ducked instinctively.

''Ere ... you like toffees, don't yer?' Tommy opened his fingers to show the sweets Bill had given him. He was trying to make an effort with his son, hard though it was even to be near him sometimes. 'I'll lose what teeth I've got left if I chew 'em.'

Alfie gawped at the gift, his jaw slackening.

'Don't want 'em?' Tommy barked.

'Do ... thanks.' Alfie snatched the toffees from his father's palm and trotted to his bedroom, a sob gathering in his throat.

*

'Me pal's coming round to see me so get yourself straight to bed.'

Olivia had just got in from work and had barely removed her hat when her father barked that command at her.

'A pal?' she echoed in puzzlement.

'Bill Morley from the factory,' Tommy curtly explained.

'Oh ... right.' Olivia tried not to sound too surprised. Her father rarely had visitors. She was glad to know somebody liked him enough to come and see him. 'Are the kids in bed?' Her father had got home before her and that always made her feel uneasy about what might have occurred in her absence.

'They are. And Maggie's had a hiding and she'll get another if I ever see her again with paint on her face.'

'What?' Olivia gasped as her father gripped her arm, giving it a shake.

'Using rouge . . . and she's been outside the house wearing it!' Tommy snapped. 'Caught her before she'd had a chance to wash it off. It's your job to teach yer sisters what they need to know about decent behaviour, and you'd better do it or you'll get the same as she did.' He thrust Olivia away from him. 'Apart from that I've told the gels to make sure they're in bed by half-past eight in future on a school night. You make 'em stick to it, or I will.'

'I'll speak to them.' Olivia would too because she didn't like Maggie taking such liberties when she was out at work, and leading Nancy astray into the bargain.

'Alfie turned in a while ago . . . ' Tommy broke off as he heard a knock at the door. 'That's me pal arrived.' He jerked his head, indicating to Olivia to get to bed.

She entered the bedroom quietly and was met by whispering voices.

'Who's that calling at this time of night, Livvie?' Maggie hissed.

She was sitting up in bed with the sheet pulled up to her chin. Nancy was lounging beside her with her book open and the light of the candle playing over illustrations of music-hall dancers.

Olivia hurried closer, scouring Maggie's face for signs of a bruise. 'Dad said he gave you a hiding for wearing make-up.'

'Was only a bit of rouge, that's all,' Maggie said sullenly. 'And he just whacked me round the legs and told me to get washed and get to bed.'

'Well, you were very lucky then that he had a visitor on his way or he would've belted you good and proper.' Her sister's attitude annoyed Olivia. If their father hadn't known

Bill Morley could turn up at any minute, he wouldn't have let things go so lightly and the others would have suffered as well. Mostly, though, Olivia was angry at herself. *She'd* bought the pot of rouge for her sisters, years ago. It had been used sparingly – just a dab – so they could dress up at home as ballerinas. It had been innocent fun; Olivia had enjoyed helping them put spots of colour on their cheeks and lips so they could pretend to be Sugar Plum Fairies. Olivia had always made sure they'd scrubbed their faces clean by the time their father arrived home. It had been the sort of fun that young girls everywhere loved to experience ... but she'd doubted Tommy Bone would see it that way.

And Olivia doubted it now. Maggie had gone out painted up, not because she and Nancy had been pretending to be ballerinas but because she'd wanted to look older than her fourteen years.

Olivia sat down on the edge of the mattress. 'Why were you back so late? What were you doing? You know to be home by half-past eight.'

'Nothing ... just larking about,' Maggie mumbled.

The room was too gloomy for Olivia to notice the furtive look that passed between her sisters but she did see that Nancy's jaw was moving rhythmically. 'What are you eating?'

Alfie had burrowed beneath the blanket on Olivia's bed but he sat up and held out his hand to display a single toffee. 'Dad give me some sweets. I shared 'em out and I saved you one, Livvie.'

Olivia went over to him. She unwrapped the sweet and popped it on her tongue, her heart soaring until it felt as though it too were in her mouth and sugar-coated. 'Dad gave you sweets, eh?' she said in between chews.

Alfie nodded, grinning. 'Does he like me now, Livvie?'

Olivia cuddled her brother in her arms, blinking away the

heat in her eyes. "Course he likes you. Now get yourself to sleep.'

As Alfie rolled himself in the blanket on her bed Olivia blew out the candle, making Nancy tut and snap shut her book.

But the two girls settled down quickly with only a few heavy sighs as they shifted to and fro, trying to find a comfortable spot on the creaking bedstead.

Olivia undressed in the dark, folding her clothes neatly as she always did and placing them at the bed's footboard. She sat on the edge of the mattress, listening to the rumble of male voices and some muted laughter coming from the parlour. The sound of her father enjoying himself made her mouth curve into a smile. If he was feeling less under pressure and more kindly towards his young son since he'd stopped working at the factory then he'd done the right thing in putting Barratt's behind him. Olivia wondered if another hand – perhaps her father's lady friend's – had been instrumental in persuading Tommy to make changes. If so, the sooner she became a fixture in his life, the better it would be for them all.

Olivia had been on her feet, rushing to and fro serving pie and mash dinners, since midday and it was now gone ten o'clock at night. Heavy-eyed, she opened her purse for the tips she'd received. The darkness didn't stop her counting her earnings. By size and weight alone she knew exactly how many thrupenny bits and coppers she'd received and tallied them up to one and tuppence-farthing. Having slid the money under her pillow she lay down and closed her eyes; immediately her little brother snuggled up to her and she patted his hand affectionately as it clasped her waist. In no time Olivia could hear Alfie softly snoring, his breath coming in warm puffs against her spine. Gently she disengaged herself from him and turned onto her back, gazing at shadows on the ceiling. She'd been so wrapped up in other things that she'd not thought much about her surprise meeting earlier in the week with Ruby in Islington . . . and with Joe Hunter too.

She felt under the pillow, ignoring the coins and drawing forth instead the scrap of paper she'd hidden there on the night Joe had helped her drunken father to bed. As soon as he'd gone she'd retrieved the scrap of sooty paper from the scuttle where she'd thrown it in a temper.

There was no light by which to read the address scribbled on the paper. It didn't matter anyway because she knew it off by heart. Joe Hunter lived at thirty Playford Road, Islington, and that's where she'd find him if she needed him.

But she didn't. Never would. The Bone family were turning a corner and had brighter days in front of them, she was sure.

*

'How's things round at yours, love?' Mrs Cook took her clean washing and smiled sympathetically at Olivia. 'You all right for the rent? Can lend you a couple o' bob if you want.'

'We're paid up to date, thanks.' Ethel's comment was all the proof Olivia needed that the woman knew about her father losing his job . . . or giving it up, as he called it. Having reflected on it Olivia found it hard to believe he would have done that even if he had clashed heads with Lucas Black. But it didn't matter; her father had been in a better mood lately. He seemed to be making a real effort with Alfie. The other day he'd read aloud some football scores from the paper to him, making his son blink in surprise. But Alfie was too intimidated to respond and had sunk to the floor, simply listening without comment. Finally, Tommy had tired of talking to himself. Folding the paper, he left the room.

'Who told you about Dad losing his job?' Olivia asked her neighbour.

'I know Nelly Smith's sister-in-law. I used to be an orderly over North Middlesex Hospital and Vi's still a nurse there. She told me about Nelly getting injured that day.'

'What day? Injured? How?' Olivia garbled.

'Oh, perhaps your dad didn't want you to know ... sorry. Best get on.' Mrs Cook turned away to hurry up her path. She'd said too much and didn't want to get on the wrong side of her churlish neighbour. The Bones and Cooks had been living next-door to one another for a long time yet still Ethel found Tommy hard to fathom. On the night Aggie had died she'd had her offer to help look after the three girls thrown back in her face. Ethel understood that people needed their privacy but Tommy could be downright rude.

'Was my dad involved in an accident at the factory?' Olivia caught Ethel's arm.

Mrs Cook gave a tiny nod, frowning.

Olivia was sharp; it didn't take her long to work out that if her father hadn't been hurt then he'd probably caused the accident. *Now* she knew why he'd lost his job.

'Was Nelly Smith in a bad way?' Olivia prayed to the Lord that the woman hadn't been.

'Don't believe so. Just a few boxes toppled over and caught her. Mountain out of a molehill, I expect.' Mrs Cook quickly changed the subject. 'How d'you get on with *her*? Got her claws into your dad yet, has she?' Ethel nudged Olivia's arm as Maisie Hunter came into view at the top of the street, swinging a shopping bag in each hand.

'She keeps herself to herself, but that suits all of us,' Olivia replied flatly. She'd not said anything to Mrs Cook about the incident when Maisie Hunter had called her a bitch. But now might be as good a time as any to bring it up. If Ethel had had something to do with spreading rumours then perhaps she'd think twice about doing it again.

'Actually I feel rather sorry for Maisie ... some stupid person stuck a notice on the lamppost calling her names. Whoever it was better hope her son doesn't hear of it 'cos he won't see the funny side even if it was a joke.'

'What did it say?' Mrs Cook was agog with interest. Olivia had to admit that if the woman was acting a part, she was convincing.

'It said she invited men to her room. Nobody goes upstairs in our house apart from Maisie and her son. I'd've seen them if they did.'

'You'd be asleep in bed, love, when she's getting up to all that.' Mrs Cook grimaced in disgust. 'I know her sort.' With that she marched indoors with her washing gripped under her arm.

Olivia shook her head and went to say hello to Joe's mother. Feeling affable, she thought she would mention that she and Alfie had gone to see a film with Maisie's son a while ago. The woman had been away again for several nights. Olivia had seen her go off with her suitcase. So to break the ice she asked if Maisie had taken a summer holiday.

'What's it to you if I have?' she snapped in response.

'Nothing ... just thought you might have been somewhere nice like the seaside as it's been so warm.' Olivia shrugged, disappointed that Maisie still seemed determined to be unfriendly. 'Forget I asked.' She started towards the front door but the other woman grabbed her by the elbow.

'Got something else to say to you, miss.'

Olivia shook her off. 'What's that?'

'Stay away from me son! I know he's been sniffing around

you. He's no good for a decent gel like you. Besides, he's got a wife.'

With that Maisie elbowed past and thrust her key into the lock. For a moment Olivia felt winded and quite unable to rouse herself from the shock of what she'd heard. Eventually she went indoors, thinking herself a gullible fool.

Others had told her Joe was no good. He'd told her so himself. And now she'd heard it from his mother. What further proof did she need that Joe Hunter was not the sort to get mixed up with? If she saw him again, she'd tell him exactly what she thought of him.

Chapter Nine

The pinprick of light wavered then disappeared. Tommy slunk forward, the palm of his hand scraped by gritty brick as he kept close to the wall for cover. A hiss reached his ears from the shadows, drawing him into an alley. He felt his elbow yanked and, striking a match, saw Bill Morley grinning at him, dangling a liquorice bootlace in front of his face.

'No toffees this time, mate, but how d'you fancy a few boxes of these?' Bill chuckled. 'Or perhaps you'd prefer a fag?' He pulled a sweet cigarette from his pocket and pretended to smoke it before sticking it into his mouth and eating it.

The match singed Tommy's fingers and he dropped it and struck another. Yesterday evening Bill had stopped by his house to give him a hushed message. They'd not talked for long out the front as Livvie had been hurrying towards them in the twilight, having finished work. But Tommy hadn't needed a lengthy explanation for why Bill wanted them to meet up at midnight the next day.

'That's enough chinwag. Let's go,' Tommy said, turning serious. He wanted to do the deed and get home.

Bill led the way towards the mouth of the alley. After glancing left and right, he started trotting towards the looming outlines of the factory buildings that dominated the skyline. Although the machinery had long since clanked to a halt, the sickly scent of cooked sugar hung heavy in the mild night air.

'Get over the top here,' Bill whispered, and gestured for Tommy to help him with the ladder lying ready by the wall.

Tommy had a feeling somebody else might be involved in this caper; he was becoming increasingly uneasy that he might not have got the full SP from Bill. He still didn't know how the man was getting access to the sweets before they were loaded. There was no way he would be able to put a few boxes aside for himself in full view of everybody in the yard. Bill had promised him everything was watertight but Tommy felt irritated with himself for not having asked more questions. He was usually cautious but in this case he'd let elation at the idea of getting one over on Lucas Black undermine his proper restraint. 'We got any help tonight?' Tommy asked, grabbing his accomplice's elbow.

'Nah ... just you 'n' me, Tom,' he replied. 'Now keep shtum and foot this ladder. When you see me at the top there, take the stuff off me. Make sure this bugger's secure, though. Don't want you causing no more accidents with boxes of sweets, now do we?'

'Hah bleedin' hah!' Tommy mumbled sourly, but he stamped his boot on the bottom rung, squinting up at Bill's wobbling rump as the man carefully climbed the ladder in the dark.

Within minutes Bill had disappeared over the top of the wall. Tommy wedged the ladder into the ground then nipped half-way up, waiting for his pal's head to pop into view. The minutes dragged by and Tommy was about to forget about keeping the ladder stable. He was tempted to hare straight to the top and peer over the wall, to see what was going on.

'Come on ... ain't got all night. D'you want this lot or not?'

Bill's mocking voice had Tommy bounding upwards to carefully take his cargo. He balanced a box on his head, steadying it with one hand while holding tight to the rail with the other and shimmying down. He repeated the exercise half a dozen times before Bill threw a leg over the wall. Sitting astride it, he caught his breath for a moment before scrambling down the steps to join his pal on the pavement.

'Could do with a handcart to shift 'em,' Bill wheezed, eyeing the stack.

'Bleedin' hell, you're not done in, are yer?' Tommy sounded disgusted. 'You're younger'n me 'n' all. He gave Bill's shoulder an encouraging thump as the other man planted his hands on his thighs and bent over to suck in air. 'Moon's coming out from behind them clouds, Bill. Come on ... let's shake a leg before we're spotted.'

'Just let me rest a mo ... ' he panted.

'You can manage 'em.' Tommy sounded exasperated. 'I'll stick three of 'em on your shoulder then you get going fast as you can.' He hoisted the boxes one on top of the other then, with a grunt of exertion, lifted them. Bill started off along the road, knees bowing beneath the weight.

Tommy, being the stronger of the two men, managed to manoeuvre the boxes onto his own shoulder by using the wall and some bodily gyrations.

On the day Lucas Black had sacked him he'd been told he'd never handle any more of Barratt's merchandise. Tommy set off home, chuckling beneath his breath.

There was a small shed out the back of the house that contained a scythe and a few other gardening tools. These were never used now Mr Silver had concreted over the back yard to install a bigger washhouse and outside privy. Tommy had the only key to the shed so he had a nice storage place for his stock while he found customers for his sweets. Far away from Wood Green, of course.

*

'The little git's wet the bed again, has he?'

Olivia hadn't heard her father come in, nor had she been expecting to see him in the middle of the afternoon. She whipped around to find him pointing at the bundle of sheets she'd plonked in the corner, ready to be taken to the washhouse. She'd been grateful for the fine weather, confident that her father would be none the wiser about Alfie's accident because she'd be able to rinse the linen then get it blown dry in the back yard.

'It's nothing ... only take a little while to do. Weren't Alfie made a mess anyhow. Maggie got blood on them from her monthlies. She's just started.' It was a lie that Olivia knew would shut her father up. He was embarrassed by women's stuff. She remembered being doubled up with cramps when she'd first started her periods. With no mum to ask, she'd flown to her father in horror on seeing the blood on her knickers, wondering if she was about to die in pain like Aggie. He had angrily marched her into next-door and asked Mrs Cook to speak to her, before he'd turned tail.

'You won't think it's nothing when you're still ironing at midnight,' Tommy said gruffly. He shook the teapot then put it down with a grimace. 'I'll have a cup of tea when you're ready.' He made to walk out then strode back to the parlour table.

'There.' He plonked down some silver coins. 'Sick of boiled

bacon and pease pudding every Sunday. Get something to roast this week.'

'Thanks, Dad, it'll make a nice change,' Olivia said, watching him carefully. She could see and smell the evidence now that he'd had a skinful; he'd probably returned home early to sleep it off. Tommy Bone was a big man: five foot ten and running to fat as he got older. He'd plenty of body to soak up the booze but as he approached fifty it seemed he couldn't take it like he used to. Drunk or not, though, the offer of a Sunday joint was extraordinary enough to make Olivia immediately wonder what might have prompted such generosity.

'Oh . . . and another thing,' Tommy said, crossing his arms over his chest. 'Get yourself down to the factory tomorrow for a job.'

'What?' Olivia had been bundling the washing into her arms but she dropped it and swung around to look at her father.

'You said you should help out more, and that's what you're gonna do from now on. Black offered you a job months ago. So you get along there and put yourself forward. You're in with a good chance as the guv'nor's already taken a shine to you.' Tommy's voice had turned harsh with authority.

When word got round there was a vacancy women would congregate at the factory gates hoping to be taken on; the company rarely needed to advertise for staff. As soon as Tommy had found out that Black had offered Olivia a job he'd known he had a chance of getting his foot back in the factory door. And Tommy did want his job back. It wasn't just for the regular pay, although that was a big part of it. He missed the routine and the status he'd enjoyed at Barratt's. Colleagues who'd barely spoken to him then now waved to him if they spotted him in the street. He felt as though he'd become a bit of a folk hero and knew he could capitalise on his unexpected popularity if he went back. And apart from all that he wanted to get even with Lucas Black.

The extra money he was bringing in from selling the buck-shee sweets was very handy but Tommy didn't like the set up. He was a loner and needed to control things. He wanted to be the one running the show, not acting as a sidekick. He didn't trust Bill to be smart enough to cover all his tracks; neither did he think that his pal was working alone in getting the boxes out of the factory. Tommy didn't fancy getting his collar felt because of somebody else's big mouth or carelessness. He was planning to tell Bill he'd had a change of heart and no longer wanted to be involved. Then once Livvie helped him ease his way back into Barratt's, he'd nose around to find out what had been going on and he'd be able to run his own show.

As the water in the copper started to steam Olivia automatic-ally plunged the dolly up and down on the bed sheets. But her mind was elsewhere. Her father's command that she start at the factory excited her once the shock had worn off. It certainly explained why he'd buttered her up by offering them a feast at the weekend. Perhaps he'd expected her to refuse to be pushed into full-time work; if so it proved he'd no more understanding of her than he had of the rest of his children. Tommy Bone might be their father and main provider but his interest in his kids had died when his wife did and only a resentful sense of duty kept him at home with them.

For some while Olivia had yearned to end the drudgery of a life that was ruled by routine tasks. When Joe Hunter had bluntly told her she was wasting her life she'd no longer been able to ignore what she already knew. The years were slipping by, taking her youth with them. She'd never begrudge giving up the money she earned so as to support the family, but she wanted more than a few coppers left in her pocket. She wanted to be able to afford some of the pretty things she gazed at in shop windows, things other girls easily bought from their wages. She'd like to banter with friends of her own age while eating cakes in a tearoom instead of refereeing her two younger sisters' bickering over bread and jam at the parlour table. And now that her father seemed more tolerant of Alfie, even giving him gifts of sweets, it seemed that that burden of anxiety was lightening, promising her more time to herself.

Olivia had always found the dark winter months the most depressing time of year; she'd spend days on end enclosed in the four walls of their home, only escaping to the pie and mash shop to don another apron and start skivvying again. She envied those smartly dressed young women who had proper jobs ... the ones she watched walking purposefully towards bus stops or underground stations, nattering with their companions. She was fed up of handling chilly, slimy eels in the pie and mash shop, then scrubbing her hands till they were sore to rid her skin of the fishy smell. She knew that factory work wasn't glamorous but it was a start ... a foundation stone for her future. It would be hard work, but Olivia had never been afraid of that.

As for Lucas Black having taken a shine to her, as her father said, and favouring her job application because of it ... she wasn't so sure about that. The meeting between them had been over six months ago and it was possible he'd forgotten all about her. But she hadn't forgotten him. She could quite clearly recall his dark blue eyes and lean, handsome face. But it was his confident attitude that had really stuck in her mind; he was privileged, she guessed, lucky in life, and that was something that would have stuck in her father's craw.

Olivia shaved Sunlight soap into the hot water, agitating it to a froth with the dolly while smiling to herself. Tommy had treated them to more sweets since he'd left Barratt's than ever he had while an employee. If he was attempting to make it up to his son for his past cruelty then it was a poor attempt in Olivia's opinion. But it was at least something and she was glad for small mercies. Tommy always gave Alfie the sweets to share out and her brother seemed to be less nervous now in his father's presence.

Impulsively she decided that once the sheets were pegged on the line and she'd smartened herself up, she'd head to the factory and try and secure the job before someone else did, or before her father sobered up and changed his mind about losing his housekeeper. Her sisters would need to pull their weight from now on and whether Maggie liked it or not she'd have to take the first job that came along, even if that meant taking the laundry work she hated.

'Nearly finished with that mangle, have yer?'

Olivia let go of the handle she'd been pushing round and turned about to see Maisie Hunter standing behind her with a basket of smalls.

'Rinsed these out upstairs,' the woman said gruffly. 'Just need to wring 'em.'

'Won't be long . . . got this last bit to do.' Olivia undulated her shoulders to ease the ache in them then put her weight behind the handle again, feeding the soaked cotton between the rollers. Maisie's rooms overlooked the back yard so the woman must have known the mangle was in use. Olivia knew that usually her neighbour would avoid coming down to the washhouse when anyone else was out the back, so that led her to think Maisie might have something on her chest that she wanted to get off it. They'd not spoken since the day the woman had warned her to stay away from her son because he was married.

'Give us a hand, would you?' Olivia held out the ends of a crumpled sheet and Maisie took them and helped her bring the sides of the linen together so it formed a folded square that would be easy to unravel and peg out on the line.

'Got a favour to ask you,' Maisie blurted.

'Oh?' Olivia took the wooden peg from between her teeth and snapped it onto the rope strung between two brick walls, anchoring the first corner of the sheet on the line as she did so. She slanted Maisie an enquiring look.

'Any chance you could put in a word for me with old Mr Silver? Ain't got me rent this week.'

'Don't see why he'll listen to me.' Olivia was surprised by the topic of conversation but carried on casually pushing wooden pegs right the way along the top of the sheet until it caught the breeze and flapped back at her.

'Silver's always telling me how you lot are never behind. Reckon he thinks the sun shines out of the Bone family's arses.' Maisie grimaced. 'The tightwad won't let me run a tab like the landlord did where I was before.'

'Where was that?' Olivia asked curiously.

'Don't matter where it was,' Maisie retorted, before remembering herself. She'd not get any help if she turned shirty. 'Sorry ... got things on me mind.'

'Me too.' Olivia smiled at her. 'What about your son, can't he loan you a bit?'

Maisie snorted. 'Ain't seen Joe and don't expect I will neither, now he knows I told you to give him the elbow.' She started running her washing through the mangle.

'I've not spoken to him about that.' Olivia frowned. 'I've not seen him in months. Anyway, there was nothing to it – we only went out once.'

Maisie dropped a wrung-out camisole into her washing basket then started on a nightdress. 'You've only gone out the once 'cos I warned him off. I told him straight I'd grass him up unless he stayed away from you.' She suddenly turned about, planting her hands on her hips. 'Fallen out with me own son over you, ain't I, and he was treating me to a few bob every time he come over. Anyhow, I thought you might like to do me a good turn back.'

Olivia gave a short laugh. 'You should have let us sort it out between us. I'd've sussed him out soon enough and told him to clear off back to his wife.'

'It's not just her . . . he's a . . . ' Maisie's voice tailed off and she pressed her lips together. 'You should be grateful to me.' She sounded belligerent. 'Your father'd take his belt to yer back if he found out what sort of man you was knocking around with.' She shook her head. 'Got enough on me plate without trouble off Tommy Bone adding to it.'

'What were you going to say?' Olivia asked quietly. 'You said he's a . . . ' She walked closer to Maisie. 'Your son's a what?'

'He's a pimp, that's what he is,' Maisie said hoarsely. 'Runs young gels for a living. Used to get me my clients too. There! Now you know. That poster on the lamppost weren't telling lies – I thought you might have found out about me past and wanted to rub it in. I moved here as much for a fresh start as anything so I don't want people gossiping.' Maisie looked uneasy at having divulged so much about herself. 'You're a nice gel, Livvie Bone, I know that now. I've seen how you look out for your younger ones and there ain't many gels your age would do it with such good grace. You've got a lovely face and a lovely nature and I'm just trying to help you stay that way.' The woman sniffed, embarrassed by what she'd said.

Olivia believed Maisie hadn't just been using flattery to get a favour but had meant every word of her praise. But what really shocked Olivia was what Maisie had freely told her about her own son.

Last time she'd seen Joe they'd parted rather frostily when she'd jumped on the bus. But he'd made it clear he'd like to see her again and she had been expecting him to turn up in the caff any day, pretending to fancy a pie and mash dinner. Now it had all fallen into place: once he knew his mother had spilled the beans about him, he'd realised he'd be flogging a dead horse trying to pull the wool over Olivia's eyes about the real reason for his interest in her.

'Thanks for telling me,' she said hoarsely.

"S'all right, got a daughter of me own,' Maisie muttered. 'Like I said, I trust you to keep this private.'

'I didn't know you had a daughter ... '

'No reason why you should. None of your business, is it?' Maisie cursed beneath her breath at having let her temper rise again. She swooped on her washing basket and strode towards the back door. 'I'll peg these out later when your sheets are dry.' On the threshold she blurted, 'Just put in a word for us, will you, with that bleedin' Jew? I'm only short by seven bob but he's talking of evicting me. Ain't asking no more'n that. And I reckon you owe me.'

'I reckon I do.' Olivia gave her a faint smile. She knew that Maisie really wanted her to settle up the overdue rent with Mr Silver. Nevertheless she said, 'Thanks for putting me straight about things. Oh, and before you disappear, got something to ask. I lost me mum's silver locket somewhere. The chain must've broken. Haven't found it lying about out here, have you?' Olivia had searched high and low for the necklace, and asked Alfie and the girls if they'd seen it. But they hadn't, and she feared it must have come off when she was outside the house. She hated the idea of never getting it back.

Maisie shook her head and disappeared. Olivia sighed and stood still for a moment, reflecting on what she'd learned about Joe. She felt her eyes smarting yet didn't know why she felt so upset. It wasn't as though they'd got properly acquainted and she thanked God for that! If they had she might have been joining those girls she recognised from school who now hung around the market place touting for business. How many of them had been approached, as she had, by a good-looking fellow, who seemed kind and generous enough to buy you chocolates and treat your kid brother to a night at the flicks. She too might have succumbed to sweet talk and promises and then discovered that all the charmer was really after was another mug to leech off.

If her father ever found out that she'd been associating with a man who lived off prostitutes ... and that Alfie had also been in his company ... Coldness washed over Olivia. She'd always stood up to Tommy but knew he'd be capable of knocking her black and blue before he put her out on the street with the toe of his boot. And there weren't many people who, knowing his reasons, would blame him for it.

So he mustn't ever know. Thankfully it seemed he had forgotten about the time he'd rolled home drunk on a foggy night and fallen over, cracking his head. Not once had he mentioned the incident, or having been put to bed by Joe Hunter.

*

'Have you any experience in factory work?'

'Mmm, no, but I learn fast.'

'So where are you working at present?'

'I'm doing part-time at a pie and mash shop.'

'The hours here aren't part-time. They're long and we expect strict time-keeping.'

'I know. I don't mind doing the shifts. I'd work full-time now if I could but I keep house since my mum passed away ... my dad's a widower, you see.' In her eagerness to be polite and helpful Olivia had said something that moments later she regretted.

Miss Wallis lifted her carefully coiffed brunette head and her superior expression faded. She grew thoughtful while staring at the attractive girl seated on the other side of the desk. Her eyes darted to the neatly written name and address on the application sheet and she made a worrying connection. 'Miss Bone, are you related to Thomas Bone?'

'He's my father.'

'I see.' Miss Wallis pushed back her chair. 'Just a moment.' She swept from the office, her buttoned boots clacking on the polished parquet and her serge skirt billowing about her ankles. Deborah Wallis was the directors' secretary and had been with the company for seven years. She wasn't about to employ a person who was related to a man who'd been sacked for misconduct. Everybody knew that Lucas Black and Tommy Bone disliked one another and she'd not risk upsetting her gentlemanly boss since she was hopeful of tempting Lucas to ask her out.

Olivia glanced through the glass partition to the office next door. A small fellow with a bald head was looking back at her while pretending to examine files in a steel cabinet. He gave her a wink and to be polite she smiled back before turning her attention to her hands folded in her lap.

She'd not encountered her father's foe when entering the building although she'd hoped to spot him. When the receptionist had enquired after her business Olivia hadn't dared say she'd come to see Lucas Black. Miss Wallis had been summoned to deal with her application for a job. Olivia had cottoned on straight away why the woman had just turned stern-faced on learning she was related to Tommy Bone. She sighed; her father had thought she'd easily get the job. But he should have realised that because he'd left the factory under a cloud it would be nigh on impossible for any of his kids to secure employment at Barratt's.

The idea that her new life might slip through her fingers before she'd had a chance to taste it spurred Olivia to her feet. She wasn't going back to Ward's to be touched up by drunks and she wasn't going back to being nothing but a skivvy for her family either. She wanted this job and she'd accept a trial period if necessary, to prove her worth.

She heard the door open and swung about.

'I told you to come and see me if you wanted a job.' Lucas Black shut the door and leaned back against it.

Olivia noticed the bald fellow next-door sit down quickly at his desk, engrossed in a ledger.

'I ... I didn't like to,' Olivia blurted. 'I know you and my father don't see eye to eye. Thought it might make things difficult between us.'

'No reason why we can't get along.'

'Well ... I'd like to think so.' Olivia glanced past him. Miss Wallis had returned to watch from the corridor. She was pretty, Olivia realised, despite her pursed mouth; probably in her mid-twenties and the sort of smartly dressed businesswoman she envied. A secretary drew a good salary, she guessed, in exchange for doing an interesting job. But Miss Wallis didn't want Olivia to have any job, even one she herself would never contemplate lowering herself to do. It seemed she had been banned from coming back into the room, though. Olivia bit her lip to suppress a small triumphant smile.

Lucas smiled too, understanding what amused her.

'Have I got the job?' she asked.

'Start in the morning, packing department. Eight o'clock sharp.'

'I'd like to start on Monday, please,' Olivia immediately countered. 'I have to tell Mr Ward that I'm handing in my notice at the pie and mash shop and there are arrangements to be made at home with my sisters about taking over chores and so on.'

'You work at Ward's?'

'I do.' Olivia wondered if that admission might have gone against her.

'I've never seen you in there,' he said.

'You like pie and mash and liquor?' Olivia asked, with a glimmer of a smile.

'Every now and then. Why so surprised?' Mr Black enquired, strolling to a window to gaze out.

'Suppose I thought you'd prefer lobster to eel,' she replied cheekily.

'I do ... but every so often something basic is all a man wants.'

Olivia stiffened as he turned about and his deep blue eyes met hers. So he thought her common? Well, she was, and proud of it. And if he was hinting at what she thought he was hinting at then she'd soon tell him to satisfy his basic tastes elsewhere.

'You should probably stick to what you're used to, sir,' she returned lightly. 'Eel might upset your stomach.' She turned for the door. 'Monday?' The single word challenged him to disagree.

'Monday,' he conceded. 'And don't worry about me, Miss Bone. I've got cast-iron guts. And you can call me Lucas in private.'

'I don't think that would be right, sir,' she said, waiting for him to move away from in front of the door.

'Fine ... master and servant it is then, if you prefer,' he drawled, and stood aside so she could pass.

Olivia nodded to Miss Wallis while swiftly passing by but

her legs were trembling by the time she reached the factory gates. She wanted to lean against the brick pillars and take a breather before setting off home. But she didn't, she kept on walking without looking back just in case he was watching her from a window.

She was over-reacting, she told herself; just because she'd found out that Joe Hunter was a nasty piece of work, she shouldn't suspect all fellows who flirted with her of being callous so-and-sos. Lucas Black had been teasing her, she told herself, and his sense of humour was simply too sophisticated for her tastes.

But as Olivia hurried on towards home, she was still unable to shake off the feeling that of the two men Joe Hunter would be the less dangerous.

*

Alfie abandoned his game of football with Ricky Wicks and ran to meet her as she turned into their street.

'You look nice, Livvie,' he said, admiring her dark blue suit with its fitted jacket, and the small hat on her glossy fair hair. As they were nearing home she put up a hand to take off the hat and removed her jacket too, feeling warm. She rotated the hat in her hands, remembering how long it had taken to dust it down and pull the velvet back into shape after Harry Wicks had damaged it. That memory led her to think about her saviour that day and she wondered how Joe could seem like two people: the one she knew and the one his mother had described to her earlier.

Alfie tugged on her sleeve. 'Why're you wearing your best clothes when it's so hot? Where've you been?'

'Had an interview at Barratt's and got a job,' she told him, brightening up. Taking his hand, she pulled him close and they carried on along the pavement arm-in-arm. 'Dad gave me enough money for us all to have roast rabbit on Sunday.'

'Cor!' Alfie said, eyes alight. 'Wish we could have it now. I could eat a horse.'

'Well, can't rustle that up but there's a bit of bacon in the pantry. If you're quick you can put it in a sandwich before Maggie gets home from work and pinches it.' Her sister had started at Kendall's laundry in the High Street after their father had told her to take the job or pack her bags.

'I'll share it,' Alfie offered. 'You and Nancy can have a bit.'

'No.' Olivia ruffled his fair hair. 'There's just enough for you ...' Her voice tailed off as she spotted a short, swarthy fellow dressed like a tramp closing Mrs Cook's gate. 'In you go and get yourself something to eat. I'll pay the rent.'

Mr Silver lifted his battered old hat to her. 'Afternoon to you, Miss Bone.'

'Just get it for you, Mr Silver.' Olivia closed the door in her landlord's face. Mrs Cook might ask him in, but Olivia couldn't be that sort of hypocrite. She didn't like their landlord, knowing him for a pitiless man who was vastly wealthy but, no doubt to wrongfoot people, chose to appear otherwise. What Maisie had said earlier about being threatened with eviction was no exaggeration to gain sympathy. Bernie Silver had made other families homeless for the sake of a few pounds yet Olivia had heard he owned a mansion in Golders Green.

She tipped her coins into his grimy palm and watched him pencil the amount in his book.

'She in up there?' He jerked his head to the upstairs window.

'No ... she's not. Mrs Hunter asked me to give you this.' Olivia handed over three precious florins and a shilling. Silver gave her an odd look but pocketed them.

'Write it down, please,' Olivia said, pointing to his book. 'And

115

I'd like a receipt so she knows I've given it to you. Don't want any misunderstandings.'

His lips twitched. 'There you are, my dear,' he said in his nasal way, patting her hand.

Olivia withdrew from his reach and he tore a receipt from the back of his notebook and gave it to her.

'Let's hope she pays you back, eh?' he said slyly.

Olivia was annoyed that he'd guessed she'd settled Maisie's debt. Pocketing the paper, she went inside. Mr Silver might be a horrible little man but she agreed with him on one thing. She did want the debt settled.

Chapter Ten

Olivia wasn't sure why she'd kept turning up outside the Greengage Caff on Thursdays when she knew in her heart that it wasn't illness or anything of the sort keeping Ruby away. The plain truth was that her cousin didn't want to see her again.

It had been months since Olivia had had a cup of tea and a chat with Ruby on that spring day. She had come back, as arranged, the following Thursday and waited for over an hour, certain that her cousin had been delayed and would soon arrive, breathless and full of apologies.

Now it was high summer and humid, having just started drizzling. Olivia was sheltering beneath her umbrella, feeling damp and depressed and resigned to the fact that any further trips to Chapel Street market would prove fruitless. She'd turned down extra shifts at the caff just so she could spend Thursdays loitering about. But it would be the last time she did so. Next week she started at Barratt's and she'd not be free to come here in the hope of spotting Ruby amongst the market goers even if she wanted to.

She glanced through the window of the Greengage; the place was full of raucous costermongers as it had been when she and Ruby had sat at a table.

Olivia hadn't ventured inside although she could have murdered a cup of tea. She was tempted to enter just to ask the proprietor where Ruby lived. But her cousin wouldn't appreciate being checked up on. Ruby had been friendly enough when they'd sat reminiscing but afterwards she might have considered that things were best left as they were between their two families.

Despite feeling indignant at being rejected a faint hope within Olivia refused to be completely extinguished. There had to be a way to keep in touch with her mother's family. Perhaps she could accidentally bump into Ruby again – but she'd no idea where to head to bring that about. She'd heard Les say to Ruby that anywhere was better than *the Bunk*; from that comment Olivia had gleaned that *the Bunk* must be a haunt of her cousin's.

On impulse Olivia approached a kindly looking woman who had just bought a lettuce and a cucumber and was wedging them into her shopping bag.

'Excuse me . . . I'm not from round here and I want to find the Bunk. Have you heard of it?'

The woman looked mystified, pressing a forefinger against her mouth. 'I'm not exactly from these parts meself, love,' she said. 'Muswell Hill's my neck of the woods.'

'What's that you're after?' Another woman close by had heard and butted in.

'The Bunk . . . d'you know where it is? This young lady here's after finding it,' the Muswell Hill woman said.

'Not *Campbell* Bunk you don't mean, do you?' The second woman looked at Olivia aghast.

'I don't know, perhaps it is,' she said, wishing she'd kept her mouth shut. Others were listening now as well and eyeing her up and down. 'Just heard someone I know might be found at the Bunk,' she muttered, almost apologetically. Her suspicion that the Bunk was a dive was steadily increasing.

'Nice gel like you don't look like you'd have friends down there. Steer clear, is my advice.' The fruit and veg seller joined the onlookers, wagging a finger at her. 'Only tramps and villains seek that place and I can see you ain't either.'

Olivia felt her heart plummet. She accepted that her aunt and cousins might have been forced to take rooms in a rundown area but the Bunk sounded a regular den of iniquity.

'I know where you mean now. It's by Playford Road.' The first woman slapped her thigh. 'Campbell Road! You turn around and go home, love. Even the coppers won't go down the worst street in North London 'less they're mob-handed!' She patted Olivia's arm. 'Best avoid whoever it is you're after.'

Olivia forced a smile. 'Thanks ... right ... I'm off to catch the bus.' She walked quickly away, shielding her face with her umbrella, despite the rain having stopped, because the trio of people stood staring after her.

Having turned the corner she nipped into a shop doorway, her heart thudding and a frown crinkling her forehead. She knew she should heed their warning and forget all about finding Ruby; but she couldn't. Instead of being dissuaded from carrying on her search she was now obsessed with finding out where her cousin was. The Bunk was Campbell Road, by Playford Road, where at number thirty lived Joe Hunter ... with his family, no doubt. And he'd had the cheek to tell her to knock him up there! Had she done so she'd probably have got her eyes scratched out by his wife.

When she saw the coast was clear and her market friends had

dispersed Olivia shut up her umbrella, emerging again onto the street. She walked quickly back to the Greengage Caff and went straight in. She ignored the whistles and went up to the counter to speak to Les.

''Course I remember you, ducks,' he said in answer to her question about whether he recalled treating her and Ruby Wright to a cup of tea.

'I need to find Ruby. Have you seen her lately?'

Les sucked his teeth, eyes soaring ceilingwards. 'Fact is . . . I don't reckon I've spoken to Rube Wright since you 'n' her was in here last.'

'I see. Would she be at the Bunk?'

'More'n likely, ducks,' Les answered with a grimace.

'Where is that?' Olivia's heart began pounding with a mixture of trepidation and exhilaration at the possibility of setting foot in the notorious place.

'You sure you want to go there?' Les cautioned her.

There was just a brief pause before Olivia gave a firm nod. 'I want to speak to her.'

'I'll take you down there if you want to go – I'm heading there meself,' a fellow said. He shoved away his empty teacup and stood up, offering his hand for her to shake. 'Jack Keiver's me name.'

Olivia darted an enquiring look at Les. The fellow appeared to be at least in his mid-thirties, possibly old enough to be her dad. He'd got kind eyes so she guessed he was all right. But after what she'd heard about the Bunk, if he was going there, she knew she should be wary of him.

'I wouldn't let you go off with just any old Tom, Dick or Harry,' Les reassured her. 'Jack's a good sort . . . got daughters, ain't yer, Jack?'

'Yeah.' Jack sighed. 'And don't I know it.'

Les roared with mirth. 'Ain't yer kids you need to worry about, mate, it's that wife of yourn.'

Jack chuckled, leading the way out of the door.

'It's good of you, Mr Keiver, but if you just tell me which way to head, I can find my own way, thanks.' He was roughly dressed – as her father would be for working down the market – but seemed amiable and he hadn't leered at her.

'I know you can do without my help, miss, but I wouldn't let even a grown man go down there without offering to walk by him.' Jack smiled kindly at her. 'Thing is, love, people who live in the Bunk don't like outsiders. And pretty gels like you don't stand much of a chance: the men'll be all over you . . . then the women will too, thinking you're after their husbands.' He shook his head in mock regret. 'Our sort is best left alone to stew in our own juice.' He patted her arm. 'You could just go home, y'know . . . in the end you'll probably wish you had.'

But Olivia had had enough of being patronised and told to go home by well-meaning people. She was sure the peril of walking down a particular street, minding her own business, couldn't be as great as they were making out. She straightened her shoulders. 'I will walk with you if that's all right, just to be on the safe side. I should introduce myself then. I'm Olivia Bone and I'm looking for Ruby Wright. Have you heard of her?'

They had started strolling along, Jack frowning thoughtfully. 'Don't reckon I do know that name. But me wife might. Ain't a soul in the Bunk me wife Matilda don't know. And they know her right enough.' He gave a private guffaw.

'You've got daughters then?' Olivia enquired, feeling awkward as a silence lengthened between them.

'I have, four of the little darlin's.'

Although his voice sounded wry, Jack's face had softened with love and pride as he reflected on his girls. Olivia needed no further proof that she was with a good man, poor or not. She wished she had just once seen that look of pure affection on her father's face when he spoke of his kids. When she'd told him she'd got the job at Barratt's he'd chuckled gleefully but hadn't congratulated her on making a fresh start; his pleasure had been for himself, not for her.

'Are any of your girls my age?' Olivia asked brightly.

Jack looked her over in mild assessment. 'I'd say you're about three years older than my Sophy – she's the big 'un at fourteen and a half. Then Alice is thirteen and Bethany's ten. Lucy's just a baby, not even three yet.'

'You have your hands full then, Mr Keiver.'

He grinned agreement with a rueful lift of his dark brows. 'Here we are then.' He took her elbow to draw her to a halt so she could see what awaited her. 'I've brought you in the top end ... the better end as it's known as. I live down the bottom with the real rogues, close to Seven Sisters Road. You can't see my place from here.'

Another street bisected Campbell Road about halfway down its length, at a point where it bent, and the properties beyond were thus lost from view. Jack had called this the better end yet had pointed to a dismal scene. If there was worse still to come then Olivia feared she should have heeded those warnings and gone home.

'Don't be afraid,' he said gently, noticing her hesitation as two men tumbled out of a house, in a tangle of arms and legs. They carried on fighting and swearing, falling against the iron railings fronting the tenement. 'Nobody's gonna touch you while you're here with me, swear on it.'

Olivia gave a faint smile then, with Jack Keiver at her side, took her first steps into the Bunk. They passed by the grunting brawlers who'd drawn a small crowd of onlookers. A few fellows were sharing a tin of Old Holborn and making roll-ups while shouting support to the combatants. Olivia recognised one of them as Riley McGoogan, the young fellow Ruby had shouted at in the Greengage Café.

A group of shoeless children of both sexes, some naked as the day they were born but for dirty cotton drawers, were squatting on the kerb playing jacks with pebbles. A handled cart of the sort used by street vendors next drew Olivia's startled gaze. Sprawled on top was a dirty-looking man, snoring with his mouth agape and exposing a few broken teeth. Two children were sitting beside him, looking as grimy as their father and chewing on what looked to be cabbage stalks. Olivia found it difficult to determine what age the youngsters might be. Thin and hollow-eyed, they could have been as young as five or as old as eight.

Seeing the direction of her gaze, Jack flipped a coin at the kids. 'Go on, you two, ha'porth of chips each.'

The money was expertly recovered from the cart and the children had fled before their father had roused himself enough to recognise the ping of a penny hitting wood.

'He's overcrowded in there, like most of us.' Jack nodded at the costermonger's doorless house. 'If it's not too chilly outside it's sometimes easier to have a kip on the cart in the street than all squash together in a single room.'

'Have you slept outside on a cart?' Olivia asked.

'In the summer ... plenty of times.'

Olivia walked with him, her eyes darting to and fro, aware of the interest she was arousing. A coarse-featured woman, her stained sleeves shoved back to her elbows and her tattooed forearms on display, looked Olivia up and down then spat in the gutter.

'You mind yer manners!' Jack roared at the woman, making Olivia jump.

But there was little time to fret over the prospect of the tat-tooed woman coming after them; Olivia was yanked to Jack's side to protect her from being bowled over by a fellow sprinting away from a house pursued by his wife swinging a chamber pot.

'You come back 'ere and give me back me money, you thievin' bastard!' the woman bellowed through spittle-flecked lips.

'What's up, Lou?' Jack patted the breathless, red-faced woman on the shoulder to calm her down.

'He's nicked me half-crown, Jack. Come in drunk as a skunk, saying he could take what he liked 'cos he was King of the Castle. I'll give him King of the Castle ... and fucking crown him with this 'n' all!' She shook the chamber pot. 'Who's this then?' Lou tacked onto the end of her impassioned speech, jerking a nod at Olivia.

'This young lady's here on a visit,' he explained.

Lou gave an amused snort. 'You won't want to outstay yer welcome then, love, I can tell you that fer nuthin'.' Having cheered up, she went off with a wave of her hand.

'That's Lou Perkins and the fellow she was after is her husband. He's a bit too fond of a drink is old Vic. Lou's a handy-woman and delivers a lot of the kids in the Bunk. Brought my two youngest gels into the world.'

Olivia turned an astonished look on him, having calculated that he'd been in the Bunk in that case for at least ten years.

'A lot of us have lived here for a very long while.' Jack had interpreted her wide-eyed stare.

'I see ...'

'Some folk come out of desperation 'cos it's a cheap place to live. Others, like us ... well, it's our home. The gels want better. I hear 'em talking sometimes when they're lying in bed at night about growing up and moving off to nice neat houses with pretty flowers in the gardens.'

Olivia smiled, feeling she would like Mr Keiver's daughters. 'All of us girls have our dreams, Mr Keiver.' She was reminded of the conversation she'd had with her cousin in the caff. 'Dreams turn to ashes' Ruby had said, and Olivia could understand her cynicism after being forced to live round here.

They had reached the intersection with Paddington Street and Olivia spotted a knot of men crouched down, gaming on the pavement. One of the players stood up and sauntered over. 'Well, what you up to then, Jackie boy?'

The man was whippet-lithe and good-looking, about five years younger than Jack Keiver, Olivia guessed. Despite his grin Olivia didn't like him or the way his eyes slithered over her.

'Doin' this young lady a good turn,' Jack said. 'Helping her find her friend.'

'I'll take over for you, if yer like,' the man offered wolfishly.

'No need, Jim, I'm doing all right ...'

'Can see that, mate, but if Matilda spots yer? Then you won't be.'

'Oi ... you want yer winnings or not? Coppers are on their way.'

The urgent yell of warning had the fellow called Jim sprinting back to the crossroads to scoop his money off the pavement. Street gaming was illegal and although the coppers hated pounding the beat down this road, they took their job seriously when they spotted mischief.

A pair of policemen were walking up from the bottom end at a smart pace, peering to left and right. Ever since a copper had been sent head first down a storm drain here by a few men who'd objected to his attitude the police only ventured cautiously into Campbell Road, and never alone.

'That's me brother-in-law, Jimmy Wild,' Jack belatedly introduced the man now haring off.

'I see what you mean about an escort being necessary.' Olivia managed a nervous laugh. She might like to think she could give as good as she got but she'd not stand a chance against these folk. Neither, she imagined, would the likes of Harry Wicks and his pals. They might reckon themselves good for a dust up but these Bunk people didn't need to think about violence. She imagined it flowed through their homes and lives as easily as the air they breathed.

Olivia knew she had witnessed just a little of what went on in the Bunk, but from it ascertained that its inhabitants were different from the working-class families she was familiar with. Now she understood why Ruby hadn't come back to meet her. She'd felt ashamed. Their families' positions had been reversed ... but Olivia didn't care a jot about who was now on top. She wanted to repair the rift between them, sure her mum would have approved of that.

Les's comment that anywhere was better than the Bunk had been no exaggeration after all. It was hard to imagine a worse place for people to attempt to rear their children.

The tattooed woman bawled an obscenity from the other side of the street and Jack scowled at her.

'Don't mind her. Me wife's had words with her lately and it weren't Matilda come off worst. But then, she never does.' Jack sounded ruefully proud.

'Yeah ... and your wife will be having words with you 'n' all. Just seen Lou, so don't go denying giving other people's kids money fer chips. Yer own are sitting indoors waiting for their teas and I ain't even got a scrape of marge to put on their bread.'

Jack had been dragged aside by a woman with thick auburn plaits coiled either side of her head. She planted her fists on her sturdy hips. 'You got paid for yer market work? I need something 'cos the tin's empty. And who the fuck is she?' Matilda

Keiver tacked onto the end of her demands, jerking a nod at Olivia.

'You can mind yer manners 'n' all.' Jack shook his wife's arm to chastise her. 'Her name's Olivia Bone, a nice young gel come looking for her friend, and that's all there is to it. And if you think there's more to it then you don't know me. She was asking Les the way to the Bunk so I did the decent thing and brung her.'

'Well, if she's nice she won't have no friends here, will she?' Matilda Keiver retorted, staring hard-eyed at Olivia.

She opened her mouth to endorse Jack's version of events but instinctively grasped she shouldn't take sides or come between the couple. She imagined they might scrap like cat and dog as Lou and her husband did, but Jack and Matilda Keiver would worship one another in their own way. Olivia imagined that they did, just as they undoubtedly loved their girls. What Olivia couldn't have known was that Matilda adored Irish whiskey almost as much – and therein lay a lot of the Keiver family's problems.

Jack scrabbled in his pocket for a few coins and handed them over. 'Get the kids some jam 'n' a bag of broken biscuits from the corner shop for their teas.'

'I'm collecting me guv'nor's rents now. They'll have to wait.' Matilda snatched the cash from her husband's palm then turned her attention back to the young woman accompanying him.

'You heard of a Ruby Wright living in the Bunk, Tilly?' Jack asked.

'Who wants to know?' Matilda eyed Olivia suspiciously. People in the Bunk might rip lumps out of one another but they'd never grass up a neighbour. Campbell Road was a sanctuary to folk fallen on hard times, but prostitutes and thieves populated the tenements as well. For all Matilda knew this young woman could be a copper's nark sent to spy on them; it wouldn't be the first time the police had tried underhand tactics to get information on a crime from the Bunk's close-lipped community.

'I'm looking for my cousin Ruby Wright. I think she and my aunt Sybil and cousin Mickey live here somewhere.' The sun had come out from behind the clouds, making Olivia squint and shield her eyes as she glanced about, feeling overwhelmed by her companions and surroundings. The cacophony of people shouting and children crying was overlaid by a jolly melody being ground out of an organ by an Italian with a monkey on his shoulder. Olivia suddenly wanted to clap her hands over her ears to protect them. She wanted to shield her nose too from the stench of rotting vegetables and unwashed bodies mingling with the odour of decay streaming from sun-drenched brickwork.

'Told you to go home, didn't I?' Jack reminded her with a twinkle in his eye. He'd read her regrets in her face.

'I should have listened to you, Mr Keiver.'

'Jack ... me friends call me Jack.'

'She ain't yer friend.' Tilly shoved her husband's shoulder, sending him in the direction of their home. But she was almost smiling now. 'Go on, get back and see to the kids,' she told him gruffly. 'I'll escort this one off the premises.'

'Give us me coppers back then so I can go to the shop.' Jack held out his palm.

For a moment deadlock ensued between the couple then, reluctantly, Matilda handed over the coins. As her husband walked off she returned her attention to Olivia, cocking her head. The girl stared right back and Matilda gave her a crooked smile. 'Come on then. I'll walk you back up the top end, Miss Olivia Bone.'

'So I don't get set about?' Olivia suggested with a smile.

'Yeah ... you won't get set about if you're with me, that's a fact,' Matilda promised on a chuckle. She glanced at a blonde woman sporting a black eye, jerking her head in some sort of threat. The blonde obviously understood it because she flicked two fingers then sauntered inside a house.

'If she comes back out and sets about you, I'll stick up for you,' Olivia said drolly.

Matilda threw back her head and guffawed. 'Thanks, love, but I can take that one down with one hand tied behind me back. And she knows it.' She smirked. 'Should've blacked both her eyes for her, the cow.'

Matilda's grim expression told Olivia she hadn't been joking; she had bashed the woman up. Curious as Olivia was to know why, she burst out with another question instead because she knew it was high time she went home. 'D'you know my cousin Ruby or not?' She'd sounded rather rude but had soon grasped that being timid or polite wouldn't get you far in this place. Her introduction to the worst street in North London had been brief and blunt but some of its ways had already rubbed off on her. Probably if a person couldn't adapt they couldn't survive here.

'Might do.' Matilda looked her over as they started to walk. 'You want to see her. But does she want to see you? I wonder.'

'She should do. My aunt Sybil is me mum's sister. We're all flesh and blood after all, even if we have had our differences.'

'Family differences, eh?' Matilda grunted a laugh. 'Well, I know all about those,' she muttered sourly. 'Your mum and sister's at loggerheads, are they?'

'My mum passed away years ago. Everything was fine before that only now my dad and her family don't speak, you see. But I'd like to keep in touch with my cousins even if my aunt doesn't want to know me.' Olivia had no idea why she'd just confided in this fiery-haired bruiser of a woman. But, oddly, something about Matilda Keiver inspired her trust.

'I can understand how you feel, so in that case, I'll admit I do know who you mean and I'll show you where they are.'

Olivia caught her lower lip between her teeth. 'Are they well?'

Matilda snorted. 'Well as they'll ever be, living in the Bunk.'

'It's just . . . I arranged to meet Ruby some weeks ago at the Greengage Caff but she didn't show. I wondered if something had happened to her so I came to find out.'

Matilda nodded at Olivia's attractive outfit. Her ruffled summer blouse with its crisp leg-of- mutton sleeves was tucked into a neat blue cotton skirt, and her leather shoes were well polished. 'You're a very pretty gel. So's Ruby . . . but not in the same way as you . . . not any more. She knows it too, so perhaps she don't want no reminders of what's past.' As they came abreast with the fellow curled up on the cart Matilda said, 'That's where they live.' She pointed to the doorless opening. 'Up the stairs then knock on the second door you come to on the first landing.'

Olivia swallowed the nervous lump in her throat. 'Right . . . thanks.' She hoped that Mrs Keiver would go away and allow her a moment to gather the courage to go inside. But Jack's wife stayed where she was, arms crossed over her chest, watching her with a knowing look on her face.

'You ain't one of us, that's the problem, love,' Matilda said quite kindly, understanding the mixture of apprehension and revulsion on Olivia's face at the prospect of entering such a place. 'I'll tell Ruby you was looking for her then, shall I? That way she can make up her own mind on it.'

Olivia frowned. 'Perhaps it'd be best just to say nothing. Perhaps I should go away and let sleeping dogs lie.'

'Yeah.' Matilda sounded a bit sarcastic. ''Course, when you turn yer back, that dog could wake up and bite you on the arse.

But up to you. Tell you this, though: don't come back again on yer own 'cos me 'n' Jack might not be around a second time to see you're all right.'

*

Ruby had been about to buy cigarettes in Smithie's corner shop on Campbell Road when she spotted her cousin with Mrs Keiver. To the disgust of the shopkeeper she clawed back her cash from his palm and abandoned the packet of Weights on the counter. She dashed out to confront Olivia.

'What the bleedin' hell are you doing here?' It was an unnecessary question as she'd already guessed that Olivia had ventured into the Bunk looking for her. 'If Mum sees you she'll go nuts. She chucked a saucepan at me head when I said I'd spoken to you. Told me to stay away from all of your lot.' Ruby stared accusingly at Mrs Keiver. 'What've you told her about us?'

'She's told me nothing,' Olivia quickly said, noting Matilda's lips pursing ominously. She reckoned the woman wouldn't take unfair criticism lightly. And neither would Olivia. A surge of annoyance rose in her. 'If you'd just come and said you didn't want us to meet up again, that would've done for me, Ruby. I thought you might have been under the weather so I kept turning up on Thursdays like an idiot 'cos I didn't want to let you down.'

'Sorry!' Ruby gestured impatiently and tossed her coarse yellow curls. 'Just thought you'd get the message to leave me alone without needing it spelled out.'

'Well, I have got the message now. And I will leave you alone, don't worry about that!' Olivia felt absurd tears prickle behind her eyes as she marched off.

She'd almost made the junction with Lennox Road at the top end of the Bunk when she heard Ruby shout her name. Her cousin trotted up behind her, looking sheepish. For a moment the two young women eyed one another moodily.

'I wanted to come and have a chat again,' Ruby burst out. 'I shouldn't have told Mum I'd seen you. Now she knows about it, she'll keep on about it. You don't know what she's like once she gets a bee in her bonnet over your father. I don't want to upset her, she's got enough on her plate what with Mickey being like he is.'

'What's wrong with your brother?' Olivia asked.

'Got a dodgy foot ... born with it,' Ruby briefly explained. 'Kids tease him a lot over it then he gets into scraps, then Mum goes on the bottle.' She shrugged and blew a sigh as though resigned to it all by now.

'I don't want to upset your mum either,' Olivia said quietly. 'But it would be nice if we could just have a cup of tea together every so often.'

Ruby smiled. 'I know. Got time now?' she burst out spontaneously. 'We could go round the corner to the Orange Caff. Mum's indoors, out of the way, so won't see us if we go the long way round. I've got some money.' Ruby opened her palm to show the coppers she'd snatched back from Smithie's hand.

'I'd like to ... but better not.' Olivia grimaced in disappointment. 'Afternoon's gone and Dad'll be back from work expecting me to have got the kids' teas ready.'

'Still at Barratt's, is he?' Ruby sounded eager to be friendly.

Olivia shook her head. 'He's working down the market most days now. But I'm starting at the factory in the packing department next week.'

'Thought Uncle Tommy wouldn't quit Barratt's till he was ready to retire.'

'Where do that lot work?' Olivia had changed the subject, not wanting her cousin quizzing her over her father's departure from the factory. Besides, she was genuinely curious to know why so many people were milling around in the Bunk during a working day. In her street, men were rarely seen about until the weekends, although the kids were out playing and making the most of the fine weather and the housewives liked a gossip over the fence.

'Most of 'em ain't got proper jobs. If they did they wouldn't be living down there,' Ruby bluntly explained. 'We all do a bit of this and a bit of that to get by.' She avoided Olivia's eye. 'We're a breed apart, so the coppers tell us. If you think about things and decide you don't want to meet up, I'll understand ...'

"Course I want to bloody meet up!' Olivia squeezed her cousin's arm reassuringly. 'I've put meself to some trouble trying to find you, you know.'

'See you next Thursday then?'

'Can't ... doing full-time hours at Barratt's. How about next Saturday outside the Greengage Caff? I'll tell you all about me new job and treat you to a cuppa and a bun out of me first factory wages.'

Ruby nodded eagerly.

'Right ... don't be late.' Olivia wagged a warning finger then set off with a spring in her step towards the bus stop to catch a ride home.

Chapter Eleven

Although she'd passed by the factory gates on umpteen occasions and could have sketched the outside of Barratt's premises with her eyes closed, Olivia had little idea what lay within the factory walls. The office she'd been interviewed in had been uninspiring: just plain wooden furniture and dull painted plaster. The most remarkable thing had been elegant Miss Wallis, looking down her nose at her, Olivia recalled with a private smile.

The main entrance to Barratt's empire appeared to aspire to be the front of a posh mansion, boasting classical columns set at intervals on the façade. It had been given the grand name of Devonshire House, and adding to the illusion was a clock tower and the date carved in stone. Viewed from the side, though, it didn't seem quite so grand with banks of uniform windows betraying its commercial use. A low-lying building abutting it also gave the game away; its function as a wholesale and export warehouse was spelled out under the roofline in white letters.

Other buildings set behind and adjacent were of similar basic construction to the warehouse: rudimentary blocks of brick, some soaring up five storeys high with iron staircases zigzagging up the sides. Olivia guessed that the imposing façade fronting Mayes Road was to impress important customers, who were treated to hospitality in the boardroom. Of course, the business end of things was bound to be quite different.

Taking a look around the boiling room she realised she'd been right to take a pessimistic view; she'd underestimated how violently unpleasant an environment sweet-making could cause. The noise and the heat were oppressive and the inescapable sickly aroma of syrup caught at the back of her throat, making her feel rather queasy.

'Bit overpowering that smell, isn't it?'

'Cor ... not 'alf! Makes you want to throw up. When it's liquorice or aniseed getting thrown into the mix it's even worse.' Cath Mason was a supervisor in the packing department and had been instructed to show Olivia the ropes. In fact Cath felt bilious at work for a reason other than the fumes coming off the caramel. But she wasn't letting on to anybody about that, especially not to her fiancé.

Olivia had turned up early on her first morning, clocking in at a quarter to eight; she'd not seen Lucas Black or Miss Wallis. But she'd been expected. Cath Mason had introduced herself and said she'd been told by the secretary to watch out for Olivia's arrival this morning. Cath seemed a friendly young woman and was only a few years older than Olivia herself.

Cath had led her away, past some vast pieces of machinery, which she explained were the new Lancashire boilers installed a few years ago. Olivia had gazed at everything with a sort of awestruck bewilderment. She was not sure what she'd been expecting but a person under the impression that something

135

as pleasurable as kids' confectionery could be daintily made would be disappointed on touring Barratt's.

The equipment was cumbersome and handled in the main by rough-looking men. The walls above the boilers were criss-crossed with large-bore pipes that twisted to and fro like giant's innards. Rows of dreary industrial benches, lined by women of all ages, stretched away to the far end of the factory floor.

Olivia was brought to a halt by the sight of a young man handling what looked like a giant jellified snake. Olivia had guessed it was a cylinder of syrup even before her companion confirmed it.

'That sugar-pulling ain't a job I'd want to do,' Cath said with a grimace. 'Need muscles like a navvy to handle them heavy boils correctly.' She nodded to the fellow. 'He'll have to work it a good few times to get enough air into the paste to make it ready for rolling.'

'I'm glad I'm just folding up cardboard,' Olivia said, not wholly joking. 'I bet he made sure that'd cooled down before messing around with it.'

She watched a pair of stokers shovelling coke into the furnaces, sweating and wiping their necks with their handkerchiefs. While she was a youngster she'd helped her nan make some blackberry jam. A fleck of the sugar mixture had flown out of the preserving pan and stuck to the back of her hand. Olivia could remember the pain of it and still had a small white scar to show for the scald she'd received.

Barratt's sweet-making seemed as primitive an operation as that undertaken in her nan's small kitchenette . . . just on a larger scale: there were open copper pans containing rolling boils that looked lethal, yet people were stirring the bubbling syrup quite vigorously with ladles gripped in bare hands and just sacking to protect their clothes from any spits.

Glancing about at the ever-present dangers, Olivia wondered

if her father might not have been as clumsy or careless the day he'd been dismissed as she'd imagined. These workers risked getting their fingers trapped or skin burned every time they turned in to do a shift at Barratt's.

Olivia had never let on to her dad that she knew he'd lost his job and not packed it in. There was nothing to be gained from bringing the subject up as far as she could see, either with him or Lucas Black.

Aware he was under observation, the sugar-boiler started to show off. Doubling back on himself, he threw the pliable paste back over the hook on the wall before again tugging on it, without its losing shape or breaking.

'Bloomin' heck!' Olivia breathed, impressed by his skill. 'I'd drop that lot on the floor.'

'You wouldn't if you knew the cost might be docked off your wages 'cos you'd been showing off,' Cath said flatly.

'Like that here, is it?' Olivia said with a frown.

Cath shrugged. 'I'll warn you straight off not to turn in late 'cos they don't tolerate it and you'll be fined. As for the rest ... if they think you've made a mistake it'll depend what sort of mood the guv'nors are in as to what happens next.'

'Lucas Black, you mean?'

Cath nodded, giving a foxy smile. ''Course most of the women ... even them that's married and old enough to know better ... wouldn't mind a spanking off him, if you know what I mean.'

'Yeah, I do,' Olivia said, feeling herself blush. She had imagined that with his virile good looks he'd have female admirers among the staff, and it seemed he had. She believed too that his lazy manner was a sham to conceal a more intense nature and wondered what he had to brood about. He seemed like a fellow with everything worked out.

'Interviewed you himself, I heard.' Cath gave her a sidelong look. 'Bit of all right, ain't he?'

Olivia nodded, adopting a bland expression. She didn't want anybody suspecting there was something between her and Lucas Black because there wasn't . . . apart from a little bit of banter. If all the girls liked him, she reckoned he gave plenty of other women the eye too. Cath was still looking at her as though expecting to hear a better opinion from her on their heartthrob boss. 'Handsome is as handsome does . . . as my nan would say,' Olivia told her jokingly.

'Mine too,' Cath said with a chuckle. 'How come you managed to get preferential treatment? Miss Wallis usually hires the women and he interviews the men.' Cath snorted a laugh. 'Not that long ago, talk went round that he'd had her over the boardroom table. Apparently one of the cleaners saw 'em at it late at night.' Cath pulled a face. 'I reckon Deborah Wallis started that rumour herself. The stuck-up cow certainly wants us all to think she's got her claws into him.'

'I don't think Miss Wallis wanted to take responsibility for hiring me because of me father, so she fetched him to take over.' Sooner or later everybody would know Olivia was related to Tommy Bone. She reckoned she might as well be open about it from the start.

But Cath didn't follow the comment up, being distracted by a whistle from behind.

She waved at the young fellow, who was still forming his rope of sugar. He winked and whistled again but the sound was lost in the clanking of the machinery.

'Keep going, Tony,' Cath yelled out. 'You're getting quite good at it, just need a bit more practice.'

'I'm quite good at using me hands on other things. Show you later if you like . . . don't need no practice in that,' he boasted, setting some male colleagues to guffawing.

'You'd best ask me fiancé about that, mate,' Cath said although they were too far away from the men for them to hear. She settled on communicating with him via a rude gesture. 'Don't mind them. They're all mouth and no trousers.'

'You're getting married?' Olivia picked up on her supervisor's dry comment.

'Yeah . . . sometime never. Can't even get the deposit together for a couple of rooms of our own.' Cath speeded up. 'Come on, better not dawdle any longer. They'll be taking liberties up there if I'm gone too long.' She raised her eyebrows. 'Got a couple of big gobs in packing, like you get in every department.' She glanced at Olivia. 'You're Tommy Bone's daughter, aren't you?'

Olivia nodded, wryly aware of an association being made between big gobs and her father.

'Didn't know your dad that well meself but me uncle does and said he was all right – trying to get a better deal for us workers. Some of the women here went on the march with the factory women south of the water last year. It was all kept quiet though. Management here ain't keen on unions.'

'Don't suppose many factory bosses are,' Olivia remarked.

Cath nodded agreement. 'Can't let the bastards grind you down though, or so my Trevor says. He's me future husband. 'Spect your dad felt much the same way, and good on 'im.'

'He never spoke much about Barratt's once he got home.' Olivia didn't want to let on that Tommy barely said two words to his kids about his work or anything else he did. But if he had fallen out with the management over staff conditions here it made her feel proud of him . . . and that was a rare and pleasant feeling.

'What'll that rope end up as?' Olivia asked curiously as they headed for the exit.

'Seaside rock, I expect,' Cath replied. 'Some of that batch'll get rolled out into a sausage and some'll be coloured red to make the letters that'll spell out Southend or Clacton. The roller-out girls will form it into pieces about a foot long. Need to work fast as you can if you're a roller-out; if the paste cools off and goes hard on you too soon, you're done for 'cos you can't reshape it.

'Right, we go out here and over there.' Cath led the way to another building. 'Up you go ... ' She pointed to the stairs. 'Four floors up we are so you'll need a fit pair of pins on you.' She chuckled. 'Only want the young gels for this job 'cos the old dears would never manage it.'

They entered a large room to hear a buzz of chatter but it soon died away. Olivia knew she was being scrutinised and discussed as some whispering was heard.

'Right, this here is Tommy Bone's daughter. Her name's Olivia and she's joining us lot, so make sure she gets a packer's welcome.' When Cath had bawled out her introduction a cheer rose from the women standing at the benches and a few hands were raised in greeting. Then Cath turned to the newcomer.

'You can work at this bench with me. Nothing to it really. You just load them like this.' With nimble fingers she took cartons of treacle caramel from a wooden pallet then fitted them into the open cardboard box and closed the lid. In all it had taken her under a minute from start to finish.

Olivia gave a nod to indicate she reckoned she'd got the hang of it. It would be boring work, she could see that, but it was a start and it was a proper job and she was ready for it.

By the time it got to her dinner break Olivia's feet were throbbing; unthinkingly, she'd dressed nicely for work, as she always did. She'd put on her good shoes rather than her comfortably stretched old boots. For hours past she'd been dancing from foot to foot to try to ease the cramps in her toes. When she'd been working at Ward's serving dinners she'd run her legs off but being at a virtual standstill felt even worse.

The idea of escaping outside for a brisk walk was inviting and she was longing for the bell to go for the end of the morning shift. It seemed Cath was keen for some fresh air too and thinking along the same lines.

'Fancy a stroll along the High Street dinnertime?'

Olivia nodded. 'Can't wait to stretch me legs. I've only brought a sandwich so it won't take long to eat. What break do we get?'

'Just half an hour,' Cath said grimly. 'That's another bugbear; everyone goes on about wanting longer and having a proper place to sit and eat.'

The room began emptying and Olivia joined the exodus, clattering down the stairs with Cath. Sunshine beckoned them outside and Cath led Olivia towards a low wall set behind a hedge that threw a triangle of shade on them. 'Sit here for a mo and have our eats, shall we?' She pulled a flask from her bag. 'Want a drop o' tea?'

'Thanks.' Olivia glanced up at the cloudless blue sky as she perched on warm brickwork and accepted the cup. She sipped the sweet tea, feeling as mellow as the summer day. She wondered how the kids were getting on at home. She could have nipped back to see them as Ranelagh Road was only a few minutes' walk away but knew if anything was wrong she'd be torn between staying to sort it out and returning to work. And if she didn't come back on time she'd lose her job before she'd done a full day. Nancy and Alfie had been under strict instructions to be on their best behaviour.

She had shown Nancy how to use the washhouse copper, reassuring her she'd help finish the laundry when she got home from work. Washday was a long and tedious part of every

Monday and Nancy had looked panic-stricken at the thought of taking on the task. But she wasn't a little kid, she was eleven, and Olivia had had to do the family's washing when she was younger than that, so she'd not shown too much sympathy.

Maggie had an early start at Kendall's and had walked with Olivia as far as Mayes Road that morning before carrying on towards the laundry. Their father had been up and out first to do his market shift and Olivia had prepared his breakfast as she always did.

Before he'd left the house he'd fixed her with a gimlet stare and said, 'Make sure you give a good impression on your first day. Black'll be watching you.'

'Penny for 'em,' Cath said, having observed her new colleague's faraway expression.

'Oh . . . just hoping me younger sister don't drag the washing on the ground when she's pegging it out in the back yard. Some of the sheets belong to me next-door neighbour.'

'I bloody hate washing. I'm glad me mum still does mine.'

A hooter sounded and they turned to see a motor van pulling in, easing slowly between carts being loaded up so as not to startle the horses. The front entrance yard was busy with traffic and fellows were leading the animals to and from the stables.

'Got a few of those new vans now,' Cath said quite proudly. 'Be good if we could get rid of the stables. With the wind in the right direction you get the pong of horse shit on top of all the rest of the delightful aromas.' She wrinkled her nose.

'You won't turn me off eating sweets,' Olivia quipped.

'Your dad worked in the transport department, didn't he?' Cath took out her packed lunch.

'Believe he did,' Olivia said, unwrapping her cheese sandwich and taking a bite.

'What've you got?' Cath asked, peering mournfully at her own food.

'Cheese,' Olivia said. 'Could do with a bit of chutney to liven it up.'

'Better'n mine.' Cath grimaced on flapping back a crust and looking at the fish paste spread on bread. 'Mum's a daft ha'porth. She's given me Dad's packet by mistake. She knows I don't like potted fish.'

'Does he work here?'

'No, down the railway yard with my Trevor.'

'My dad used to bring in meat and potatoes to eat when he worked here.'

'A lot of folk have a dinner; me uncle's one of 'em. They warm it up by those gas burners in the boiling room then they have to gobble it down before the bell goes to get back to work.' Suddenly Cath stood up and hurried towards the hedge behind them, bending over.

'You all right?' Olivia asked in concern. Although Cath had tried to conceal herself with the bushes Olivia had seen her being sick.

'Yeah ... fine ... just the smell coming off this place turns me stomach sometimes. That fish paste didn't help neither.' She smiled, using her handkerchief on her mouth. 'Don't feel all that hungry anyway. Come on, let's get out of here for a while.'

Olivia packed away her half-eaten sandwich into her bag, having lost her appetite too, and they set off.

As they approached the butcher's shop on the High Street where Harry Wicks worked Olivia glanced in. There was no sign of the nasty bully amongst the few fellows sawing and chopping meat on wooden blocks. Then she saw him come in from the back with a carcass on his beefy shoulder. She turned away and, glancing across the street, spotted somebody else she knew. She called out to Maggie and waved.

'That's me younger sister. She's just started work at Kendall's . . . must be on her break too.'

'Don't fancy laundry work meself,' Cath said sympathetically.

'She's just left school so it's a start for her until she finds something better.'

Maggie waved back but Olivia was disappointed when her sister went back inside the laundry instead of crossing the road to speak to her. Maggie was still sulking over having to take the job but she didn't seem to be making any effort at the weekend to go job hunting to improve her prospects.

'Well, well, look who's over there.'

Olivia had also spotted Lucas Black. He'd just come out of a tobacconist's and was lighting a cigarette, his dark head bent towards a match in his cupped palm. As he glanced up and saw them he started walking their way, hands thrust into his pockets and cigarette dangling from his lips.

'Good job I'm engaged because he's enough to make a girl go weak at the knees,' Cath smirked. 'I bet he's gonna stop to speak to us,' she hissed.

Olivia noticed that half smile tilting his mouth, as though he knew he confused her and it amused him. He took the cigarette from his lips.

'So you turned up then, Miss Bone. Wasn't sure that you would.'

'I said I would, sir, and I'm not given to telling lies.' Olivia was sure he'd already checked to see if she had clocked on.

He smiled but there was a hard glint in his eyes. 'Glad to hear it. You don't look like your father either.'

'What does that mean?'

'It means you're fair whereas Tommy Bone isn't,' he replied silkily before turning to Cath.

'How's our new recruit doing, Miss Mason?'

'Well as can be expected, sir, given the intricate nature of the job.' Cath had unwittingly taken her tone from Olivia, answering ironically; then she felt horrified for having done so. 'She's doing very well, Mr Black,' she garbled out, sounding apologetic. 'Taken to the work like a natural and getting faster all the time.'

'Good.' He fished in his pocket and drew out the packet of Players he'd just bought, offering them the pack.

'Thanks but I don't smoke,' Olivia said.

Cath took a cigarette with a whispered thank-you and let him light it for her.

'Don't be late back,' he said, strolling past.

'We won't be, sir.' Cath puffed furiously on her cigarette. 'Bloody hell,' she coughed. 'He's never said more'n two words to me before in the three years I've been here.' With a nod she indicated a group of women gawping at them from the opposite pavement. 'Put some noses out of joint over there. Given them something to natter about this afternoon as well. They're the roller-out girls.' Cath proudly tilted her chin, linking arms with Olivia. 'They think they're a cut above 'cos they earn a better rate than us packers.' As they started walking again she announced, 'You've caught his eye.' She tilted her head to give Olivia a top to toe summary. 'Can see why 'n' all. When it comes to looks, Olivia Bone, you knock that Deborah Wallis into a cocked hat.' She chuckled. 'Reckon that one's regretting the day she called him in to interview you. And he's right ... I don't think you look like your father either.'

'Take after me mum. She was blonde; Dad was dark-haired before he started going grey.'

'Your mum, she's ...' Cath let the final work hang in the air.

'Yeah, passed away seven years ago.' Olivia glanced over her shoulder and came to a halt. 'Let's get back then, shall we.'

She wasn't obeying their boss's order not to be late; she hadn't needed telling anyway, she was naturally conscientious and had always been on time for shifts at Ward's. She'd just spotted her sister emerge from the laundry again and Harry Wicks had sprinted across the road from the butcher's shop to talk to her. Olivia didn't want Maggie being pestered by the likes of him. He hadn't bothered her again about the broken window he'd paid for months ago, but she didn't trust him. He was a nasty piece of work. If he thought he could bully Maggie into handing over money from her wages now she was working, he wouldn't hesitate to do it.

Chapter Twelve

'You're late!' Ruby pointed gleefully to the clock over the pawn-broker's shop along the street, its hands at just after midday. 'You're lucky I waited for you, seeing as I've got work later.'

'I'm right on time! You're early,' Olivia riposted, trotting the last few yards to give her cousin a hug. 'You managed to slip away then.'

'Oh, Mum'd be after me if she knew I was meeting you, don't worry about that!'

Olivia sighed wistfully. 'Wish she didn't feel that way. I'd really like to see her and Mickey.'

'Perhaps the dust might settle sometime and we'll all have a get-together then.' Ruby attempted to sound optimistic.

They both knew in their hearts that after such a long time it wasn't likely a truce would be called. Sybil Wright and Tommy Bone hated one another because of Aggie, and would probably go to their graves doing so.

As though to compensate for her mother's hostility Ruby tightened her arms about Olivia.

'Mind me hat!' The enthusiastic embrace had tilted the brim over Olivia's eyes. 'The poor thing's already had a squashing.'

'Sat on it, did you?' Ruby crowed.

'No! Had it knocked off me head by a lout down our road.' The reference to Harry Wicks reminded Olivia of the recent conversation she'd had with her sister. Maggie had shrugged off her meeting with Harry in the High Street, saying they couldn't avoid each other being as they only worked yards apart. She'd also said he'd not mentioned a thing about the broken Mission window. Olivia wasn't sure why she'd still felt uneasy after Maggie's reassurance.

'The bleeder! If I see him, I'll knock his head off!' Ruby said, shaking a fist she looked prepared to use.

'You sound like Mrs Keiver,' Olivia chuckled. 'You've been in the Bunk for a while, I can tell that.'

'Too long,' Ruby sighed, the smile fading from her face. 'But not much chance of getting out of there for now.'

Olivia felt desperately sorry for the Wrights, having to live in a slum. Yet something about the Bunk had both attracted and repelled her and the idea of another visit to the worst street in North London was strangely exciting. She even hoped to see the Keivers again, and meet their daughters. She knew she was being daft; with their frantic, hand-to-mouth existence, Jack and Matilda had probably already forgotten about her. Then she felt guilty for being so interested in them; Bunk dwellers weren't circus acts but human beings battling to keep themselves housed and fed.

Olivia had believed that her own family was scraping by in Wood Green. Now she understood that they were doing all right in comparison to people like the Wrights and the Keivers. Tommy Bone had never failed to provide adequate clothes and a daily hot dinner of some sort for his kids, even if it was taken at the school he strictly made them attend.

Which was better? she wondered. Given a choice, would she choose a father like Jack Keiver, who doted on his daughters but reared them in a slum and fed them bread and broken biscuits, or a cold father like hers who did his duty ... but only resentfully and to ease his guilt over his dead wife.

'Perhaps you'll be able to move somewhere better soon,' Olivia said kindly to her cousin.

'Yeah ... perhaps,' Ruby replied glumly. 'Mum has a new job charring in Tufnell Park. Matilda Keiver sorted it out for her.' She sounded more cheerful. 'Silly cow'll need to stay off the bottle, though, or she'll get sacked like she was last time.' Ruby's grimace transformed itself into laughter. 'Her lady come home and found her kipping on her bed.'

'Could've been worse ... might've been the husband stumbled across her.' Olivia was laughing too, finding her cousin's amusement infectious.

'I'd've turned that to me advantage.' Ruby gave her a dirty smirk.

'Aunt Sybil likes a drink then,' Olivia said, smoothing over her cousin's slip about her other job. She had guessed Ruby pulled in money from more than just waitressing. But she hadn't worn much make-up today, and fresh-faced looked so much younger and prettier than on the last couple of occasions that Olivia had seen her.

'Mum's no different from any of them down there, really.' Ruby shrugged. 'The women drink as hard as the men. Matilda can hold hers, and bloody hell, does she sink Irish whiskey! Half a bottle of gin puts Mum flat on her back. Just as well, too, or we wouldn't even afford the rent on that dump if she squandered more.'

'Dad started boozing after Mum died.' Olivia let Ruby know she wasn't the only one with an alcoholic parent to contend with. But she always felt uncomfortable discussing her father, so left it at that. Besides, Aunt Sybil might drink, but if she discovered that Tommy Bone did too, it might give the woman even more reason to hate him.

'Crikey! We're a couple of misery guts, aren't we?' Olivia said. 'Let's talk about something cheerful. Fancy going in there?' She nodded at the Greengage Caff a few yards away. It was so busy the door was wedged open by people queuing across the threshold.

'No fear!' Ruby frowned. 'It'll take ages to get served. If you don't mind a walk we could head to Kenny's Caff in Blackstock Road. I go there a lot 'cos it's not too pricey and he does a decent cuppa, strong enough to stand yer spoon in.'

They set off meandering through the busy market place, zig-zagging from one side of Chapel Street to the other to inspect the merchandise on the stalls. But though they oohed and aahed over the pretty summer clothes, they both kept their purses in their pockets. If she'd been on her own Olivia would have looked for a plain hardwearing skirt for work but she didn't want to treat herself to even something cheap when she guessed that Ruby didn't have more than the price of a cup of tea on her. At the corner they settled in for a good long stroll.

'Tell us about your new job.'

'How's little Mickey?'

They'd spoken together but Olivia made a gesture, inviting her cousin to carry on.

'He's had another fight with a kid at school but that ain't unusual and he soon gets over it. Good money, is it, at Barratt's?' Ruby turned her attention to what really interested her.

'Better than I was getting at the pie and mash shop, but I have to do bloody long hours for it,' Olivia answered. 'Boring work it is too, packing boxes of sweets. My supervisor Cath's been nice and helpful even though she's not felt well all week.'

'If she jacks it in and there's a vacancy, any chance of getting me an interview?' Ruby wheedled. ''Course, couldn't let Mum know you'd got me the job.'

Olivia hesitated over replying. She wanted to help, but just as Ruby wanted to keep her mother in the dark about them being in touch, she needed to keep it secret from her father. Tommy had been in a better mood lately but it wouldn't take much to set him off. At the moment their infrequent meetings were far enough from home to remain undiscovered. It would be a different story if she and Ruby worked together at Barratt's.

'Cath won't be packing it in,' Olivia said. 'She's engaged and saving up like mad for her wedding. She's only got a bit of a dicky tummy making her throw up.'

'Dicky tummy? She's probably had an early wedding night and got knocked up,' Ruby said coarsely. 'Oh, don't worry,' she continued gloomily. 'I know they wouldn't give me the job anyway. Kiss of death it is, saying you live in the Bunk.'

'Is it?' Olivia said, frowning. It hadn't occurred to her that Cath might have morning sickness. Yet she should have recognised the signs. She could recall how ill her mum had been with Alfie during her pregnancy. For months Olivia had fetched Aggie a bowl in the mornings and held her thick blonde locks away from her face while she vomited.

'Can't even get a job working at Ever Ready's battery factory,' Ruby complained. 'Soon as employers know your address is Campbell Road they show you the door.'

'That's not fair!' Olivia exclaimed.

'Got used to it by now.' Ruby's mouth turned down at the

corners. 'Suppose it helped you that yer dad used to work at Barratt's,' she added slyly.

'Reckon it did.' Olivia was aware of her cousin's resentment and that Ruby had a point. She had a feeling that although Miss Wallis had taken against her because Tommy Bone was her father, Lucas Black had taken the opposite view. He might not have shown as much interest in her had she been anybody else's daughter. But since her first day working at the factory when they'd met in the High Street, she'd hardly seen or spoken to her handsome boss. Her father quizzed her regularly about what had gone on at the factory and how she was doing and whether Black had mentioned him. Olivia had cottoned on to Tommy's game. He wanted her to suck up to Lucas Black so that he could apply for his old job back. If a chance arose to do so Olivia would put a word in for her father too. The relatively calm time they'd had with him, when she'd thought quitting Barratt's suited him, was at an end. He seemed increasingly restless, as though he could no longer kid himself or them that he didn't care about losing his job. And when their father was in a mood they were all on edge.

'Yer dad never picked up with another woman then after Auntie Aggie died?'

Ruby's comment jerked Olivia out of brooding about home and into thinking of the time her father had been spotted in Clacton with a woman. Nothing more had come of it and she was sure it must have been a case of mistaken identity. 'Not that I know of,' Olivia said. She didn't want Ruby prying so quickly followed up with, 'How about this one?' She halted outside a caff that looked to have quite a few vacant tables inside.

'Bit pricey in there, that's why it's empty. Kenny's Caff's better,' Ruby said, urging Olivia on. 'It's not far now.'

When they arrived in Blackstock Road the first person they

caught sight of was Matilda Keiver, marching purposefully along on the opposite pavement.

'All right, Mrs K?' Ruby yelled out, and gave her a wave.

'I will be when I've caught up with my Sophy,' Matilda bawled back. She waved her hand to Olivia. 'How're you then, Miss Olivia Bone?'

Olivia felt rather pleased that Matilda had remembered not only her face, but her name too. 'I'm well, thanks,' she called back, wondering if everybody round here conducted conversations at the top of their voice.

'Looks like Matilda's heading to the caff as well,' Ruby said. 'Reckon she's on the warpath. Let's see what Sophy's been up to. She's Matilda's eldest. Sophy and her friends congregate in Kenny's on a Saturday.'

Grabbing Olivia's arm, Ruby pulled her to the kerb. They jogged across the road and on entering the caff saw that Matilda had already started laying down the law. She had a girl of about fourteen gripped by the elbow. Her other hand was palm up under the unfortunate's nose.

'Give it 'ere! Don't want no excuses.'

The red-faced girl dug in her pocket and pulled out some silver to tip into her mother's hand.

'Don't make me come and find you again, miss,' Matilda threatened her eldest daughter with a finger wagging close to her nose. 'You put in the kitty on Friday soon as you get paid, or next time I'll drag yer home and pay you.' With that she barged out of the caff, leaving her embarrassed daughter to slink back down into her chair at the crowded table.

What mildly amused and surprised Olivia was that the fellow behind the counter – who she assumed was Kenny – had carried on buttering buns unperturbed by a woman with wild hair and fiery eyes causing a rumpus on his premises. He

153

was obviously used to Matilda's ways because he'd not even glanced up.

'I hate her! Had enough of her taking all me wages! Never gonna be able to get enough put by to get away from this dump.'

Olivia overheard Sophy's plaintive wail and saw the sympathetic looks directed at her by the girl and boy sitting with her. They all carried on glumly sipping tea.

Olivia felt her heart go out to Sophy Keiver for she knew exactly how it felt. She might not be fourteen or living in the Bunk but she felt just as trapped by her family circumstances as Sophy did. 'Introduce me to the girls, will you?' she said.

'What ... to Matilda's kids?' Ruby sounded surprised by her cousin's request.

'I know they're a few years younger than us but they seem nice.'

Before Ruby could make the introduction, the girl next to Sophy raised a hand and called, 'All right, Ruby? How's Mickey doing? He's been in the wars again, I heard.'

'Yeah ... silly sod got in another scrap but he give as good as he got.' She patted Olivia's shoulder. 'This is me cousin Livvie.'

'Pleased to meet you,' Sophy said, looking as though she'd bucked up after her mother's scolding. 'This is me younger sister Alice.' She pointed at the pretty girl who'd enquired about Mickey Wright and Alice waved hello. 'And this is Geoff, who lives next-door to us.' Sophy nodded at the good-looking youth.

He was a strapping lad, Olivia thought, although probably no more than fifteen. Alice had an elfin face framed by dark wavy hair, and promised to be a real beauty in a year or two.

Olivia pulled out a chair at an adjacent table and sat down. 'I have to do that, you know, and I'm seventeen.' She jerked her head at the door by which Matilda had just left.

'What – hand over all yer wages?' Sophy asked, appalled.

'Give me dad all but ninepence. I save that.'

'When I'm seventeen I'm gonna be long gone from round here,' Geoff added his two penn'orth. 'Going back to Essex where we come from. Wish we'd never landed up in the Bunk.'

'Thanks, Geoff Lovat!' Alice said. "Cos then I wouldn't know you.' She sounded mildly indignant. 'Are you from round here, Livvie?'

'Wood Green.'

'Lucky! I'd like to move over that way. Want a job in Barratt's when I'm older and got enough for me own place. I do factory work making toys at the moment. Can't wait to move to something better, though. Get home every night with me ears ringing from the racket in that place.'

'Livvie's just started at Barratt's,' Ruby piped up, feeling a bit left out of the conversation.

'Money any good?' the Keiver girls chorused.

'Nothing special,' Olivia said. 'I'm only doing packing to start. I'm going to apply for the production line 'cos that pays better.' Olivia had mulled over the idea of a transfer although she'd miss Cath. If she earned better wages and saved extra money, in a year or two she might be able to make a break from her father and set up in a place of her own with her siblings. By then Maggie would be of an age to contribute properly to caring for the younger two. And if she didn't want to put in the kitty then Maggie could sort herself out and Olivia would go it alone with Nancy and Alfie.

After he had ruined their Christmas Day with his vile behaviour Olivia had found it difficult to tolerate being around her father. She knew he regretted what he'd done but like most bullies he was a coward, unable to say he was sorry or even mention the incident at all. It was as though he felt it should all be swept under the carpet. But something had happened that day to loosen the bond of loyalty that previously had kept Olivia tied to him. It hadn't been the pain of the blow, or the loss of their family feast, but something she'd seen in Joe Hunter's eyes when he'd found her picking the remnants of their Christmas dinner off the floor. He'd looked at her with disappointment because she'd been trying to cover up for her father. Not that she cared what he thought now that she knew he was worthy of her contempt. Tommy Bone might be many things but at least he did honest work and didn't pimp off women!

'Suppose I'd better shift.' Geoff put down his empty cup and stood up. 'Gotta go and give Dad a hand packing up,' he explained to the others. 'Me 'n' Danny helped him set up down the market this morning to try and pull in a few extra bob.'

'Fruit 'n' veg?' Olivia asked.

'Bit o' this . . . bit o' that.' Geoff grinned and tapped his nose. 'Whatever we can get hold of.'

He said goodbye and went off.

'You 'n' Danny Lovat walking out then?' Ruby gave Sophy a wink. She'd heard that the girl was sweet on Geoff's brother.

'Might be.' Sophy blushed.

'What about you, Al?' Ruby looked at the younger Keiver girl. 'That Geoff's a bit of all right. If I was a year younger . . .'

'Ain't got time for any o' that.' Alice wrinkled her nose. 'I'm gonna work hard and get some money together and find a nice place first, then I'll start thinking about the rest.'

'Sensible girl,' Olivia said, knowing that she and Alice Keiver were kindred spirits.

'Oh, bleedin' hell! What does she want now!' Sophy had spotted Matilda returning, grim-faced.

'One of yous is gonna have to go back and watch Lucy 'cos your dad's waiting to go out and I'm collecting me guv'nor's rents. Beth's out doing her doorsteps over Tufnell Park.' Matilda gabbled out her message from the doorway before promptly carrying on up the road.

Sophy and Alice scraped back their chairs.

'Finished me tea anyhow.' Alice picked up what was left of her currant bun to take with her. 'You stay if you want,' she said generously to her sister. 'I don't mind looking after little Luce.'

'Got a few things to do at home anyhow.' Sophie gulped down what was left in her cup and followed her younger sister to the door.

'You two young ladies having anything or you just gonna stand around making the place look untidy?' Kenny called out good-naturedly.

'Two teas for starters, please, Kenny,' Ruby told him. 'Let's go and park ourselves by the window, Livvie. There's a clean table over there.'

Once they'd settled Ruby said, 'That walk's given me an appetite. Wouldn't mind a pie. Didn't get no supper last night. The tight-fisted git where I work wouldn't let us girls take home the pies going stale.'

Olivia hadn't been expecting to run to the expense of meat pies. But she knew they'd only see one another occasionally so was happy to treat Ruby to what she wanted. 'I'll pay,' she said when her cousin half-heartedly fished in her pocket to count out coins.

Ruby quickly put away her cash and settled back in the chair. 'Bet you're glad you're not waitressing no more. I hate serving dinners when I'm hungry meself, then poking through the leftovers to find something worth eating.'

Olivia felt shocked to hear her cousin ate scraps from customer's dirty plates. 'My boss never gave me pies cheap either,' she said gamely. 'He never let anything go. He'd swamp the stale ones in extra liquor to soften them up.'

Kenny put down two cups of tea and Olivia saw that the brew did indeed look strong enough to stand a spoon up in.

'Do yer good that will,' he said with a wink, having read her expression.

'Two beef and onion pies, please,' Olivia ordered with a grin. 'And plenty of gravy to take away the taste of the tea.'

'Cheeky you are,' he said.

'I'll have mash with mine,' Ruby said.

'Right ... two pie and mash.' Olivia nodded at Kenny and prayed her cousin wouldn't think of something else she wanted because she'd not have enough on her to pay for it.

'What time d'you start work later, Ruby?' Olivia asked.

'Seven o'clock,' she replied. 'It's a place called Morgan's in Soho.' She wrinkled her nose. 'It's a dive but the hours suit me and they don't care where you live. Wages are poor but you can often make a bit on tips if enough drunks come in. I don't finish until two o'clock in the morning. Works out all right though 'cos when Mum's got weekday work I'm at home and can get Mickey's tea.' She sighed. 'Mum's off to see her friend in Bermondsey. She used to work at the custard factory and keeps in touch with a few of the women there. I'm glad to see the back of her for a while although sometimes she comes back in a worse mood than when she went.'

'Tell me about Nan Wright.' Olivia sat forward and planted her elbows on the table, cupping her sharp little chin in her palms. 'I don't even know where she was buried.'

'She's at White Hart Lane cemetery, with Granddad.'

Their food arrived and immediately Ruby dived in, scooping up her mash with a fork and breaking off bits of her pie to eat with her fingers. 'I'll go with you one day, if you like, and show you where the grave is,' she said through a mouthful of meat and pastry.

Olivia nodded, putting down her knife and fork and handing Ruby a napkin as gravy dribbled down her chin.

'Messy bleeder, ain't I?' she said in challenging way, continuing to eat voraciously.

'I've seen worse,' Olivia said, and she had. The way some of the men had wolfed their food at Ward's had often made her feel sick. But she was disappointed in Ruby's behaviour. The Keiver girls had shown better table manners.

'Gotta get this down me and get home.' Ruby made an excuse for bolting her food. 'Me waitress uniform needs an iron run over it. And I've not rinsed out me stockings yet either. I'll be wearing 'em still wet if I don't hurry up.' Suddenly Ruby dropped the half-eaten pie to her plate, staring out through the window.

'Just seen somebody I know. Won't be a mo . . . need to have a quick word about something important.'

Ruby was on her feet and darting outside before Olivia could swallow her mouthful of food and make a comment. She twisted about to see who it was her cousin needed to speak to so badly and felt her insides somersault.

Joe Hunter was on the opposite pavement with another fellow and Ruby was jogging in his direction. As she came to a halt by his side Joe's friend walked off, leaving the couple on their own.

Although he looked quite relaxed, hands thrust into his pockets and cigarette dangling from between his lips, Ruby appeared to be growing agitated.

Olivia suddenly stiffened; while she'd been concentrating her attention on her cousin Joe had spotted her although she'd attempted to conceal herself behind the menus stuck on the glass. Casually he moved to a better position on the pavement to get an uninterrupted view of her through the caff window.

She whipped her head around; she hadn't seen anything of him since she'd hung off the back of the bus that day, shouting at him to tell her why she should stay away from Ruby Wright.

She no longer needed an answer to that; she knew why. His concern hadn't arisen from any need to protect her from Ruby's bad influence. He'd wanted to keep them apart so she didn't discover that he was her cousin's pimp.

Pushing away the dinner she'd barely touched, Olivia got up and paid Kenny. Then with a deep breath she went outside and across the road to join them.

Chapter Thirteen

'You should've stayed in the caff,' Ruby snapped. 'I'd've been back over in a minute.'

'Sorry, but time's getting on.' Olivia was hurt by her cousin's tone. 'I just thought I'd come and say hello to Mr Hunter before I catch my bus.'

Joe set his mouth in a hard line while Ruby's jaw sagged in astonishment.

'You two know one another?' she demanded.

'Yeah ... we do, but not very well, it seems. Mr Hunter's mother lives upstairs from us. Interesting woman to talk to, she is.'

'You don't want to swallow everything she says,' Joe muttered, then dragged hard on his cigarette. The butt was dropped to the floor and ground out.

'Why's that? Tells lies does she, your mother?' Olivia felt her guts writhing, but her anger was directed at herself as much as at Joe. Even knowing him for a pimp, and married, she still felt a twinge of feeling for him. She couldn't put from her mind how months ago he'd saved her from Harry Wicks then at Christmas given her that box of chocolates.

'Well . . . small world,' Ruby said. 'Livvie's me cousin, on me mum's side. But perhaps you already know that.'

'No, I didn't know that. Wouldn't have taken you two for family.'

'I reckon we're alike.' Ruby's tone held a hint of spite as she watched his eyes linger on her wholesomely pretty cousin.

'You're both blonde but that's about it, I'd say.' Joe's smile was so sour that it made Olivia's hackles rise.

'It doesn't matter what you say.' Olivia turned her back on him, showing loyalty to Ruby although she doubted she'd get any sisterly solidarity in return. Ruby appeared smitten by Joe, gazing at him gooey-eyed, yet she probably also knew he was married.

'I should get back to Wood Green before they all wonder where I've got to.' Olivia gave Ruby a quick hug that lacked the warmth of the one they'd shared earlier by the market place.

'I'll walk back to Chapel Street with you, if you like.'

Olivia knew that Ruby was itching to question her about Joe. But she didn't want to talk about him. She'd made it seem that she'd spoken to his mother recently, but she hadn't because Maisie had taken pains to avoid her ever since, knowing she'd be asked to repay what she owed.

'I'm not going back that way. I'll catch a bus on the corner.' Ruby started to insist on accompanying her so Olivia reminded her, 'Anyway, you've got your waitress uniform to wash and iron before you go to work later.' With a wave she speeded up along Blackstock Road towards the bus stop.

Practically all the way home she brooded on Ruby and Joe and whether they had more than just a business relationship.

Her cousin might fancy him but he'd looked and sounded bored by her.

Olivia almost laughed out loud for even worrying about something as trivial as whether those two were lovers when the consequences of her father finding out she'd been consorting with a tart and a pimp didn't bear thinking of. By the time she'd alighted in Wood Green High Street she had made up her mind to stay away from the vicinity of Campbell Road. She and Ruby were different people now from those friendly kids who years ago spent lovely times together at their nan's house.

She had also made up her mind to concentrate on getting a promotion to a better-paid job at Barratt's. As she set off towards Ranelagh Road at a brisk pace she made a mental note to see snooty Miss Wallis first thing on Monday morning.

A clatter of hooves approaching made Olivia swing about and squint against the early-evening sunlight. A cart shuddered to a halt by her. On its side was written *Merryweather's Haulage*.

The driver jumped lithely down and strode towards her.

'You'd better leave me alone!' Olivia was shocked by his sudden appearance. She'd not expected Joe to follow her back to Wood Green.

'First, you can listen to what I've got to say. After that you won't see me again, if that's what you want.'

Olivia wrenched herself free from his restraining hands.

She stormed off, expecting that he would follow and catch hold of her again, but he didn't. Swinging around, she saw that he'd leaned back against the wagon and was frowning at the ground, his cap pushed far back on his head. She took a step closer. 'Go on then! Explain yourself,' she demanded in a suffocated voice. 'I'd like to know what excuses you've got ready.

You've made some up, haven't you, or you wouldn't have come after me.' She was deadly serious about hearing him out but was conscious too of the danger of being spotted by somebody who knew her father. They were too close to her home for comfort.

As though Joe had read her thoughts he said hoarsely, 'Come for a drive somewhere private ... I swear you'll be safe with me. I want to explain things.' Olivia gasped in disbelief that he might seriously imagine she'd do what he'd suggested.

But he did. He held her gaze with tawny eyes that were unflinching.

'Whose wagon is it? Who's Merryweather?' she demanded.

'It's mine ... Merryweather sold it to me. I'm getting it sign-written with me own name and going into business in haulage. Proper job ... got a start moving coal down the railyard.'

Olivia knew that he was telling her he was going straight. No more pimping. 'Help me up then. But I've only got a few minutes. I have to get home. I'll have been missed.' Olivia knew that her sisters would have made themselves a snack when hungry but they might have forgotten to call Alfie in from playing in the street to feed him. 'And drop me back here. If my dad comes by and sees you in the road, you'll be for it.'

'And so will you, won't you?' Joe's eyes moved from studying the horizon to linger on her face. 'Big, brave man, isn't he, beating up a woman.'

'You're better, are you? How many women have you knocked about in your job?' she flung back at him.

'None ... and that's the honest truth. It was seeing women getting hidings that got me into that shit life in the first place.'

Joe's hands suddenly girdled Olivia's waist and he swung her up, plonking her down unceremoniously on the rough planked seat before jumping up after her and setting the nag to a good trot.

They travelled in silence for a while. Just as Olivia was on the point of asking him to take her back, he started talking.

'What did my mother tell you about me?'

After a brief hesitation Olivia rattled off, 'That I should stay away from you because you're married and you're a pimp. She said you found her clients too. She'd no need to warn me off, though. I'd already decided not to see you again.' She watched his profile harden at the contempt in her voice but he hadn't been fooled. He knew that, but for his mother's interference, she would have gone out with him. 'Why d'you ask anyway?' Olivia demanded. 'Maisie told you'd she'd spoken to me. She said you'd fallen out because of it.'

'Yeah, that's true.'

'So . . . are you going to deny the dreadful things she said?'

'No.' He steered the cart around a corner and pulled the nag to a halt at the kerb. Then he flung down the reins and turned to face her. 'Normally my mother wouldn't admit that any of her family are wrong 'uns. Even the useless bastard she married is still protected by her warped sense of loyalty if people ask after him. So what was it she got from you in return for grassing me up?'

'Rent money,' Olivia answered succinctly. 'She'd got behind and wanted me to keep Mr Silver off her back. And don't go thinking I was prying into your business because I wasn't. Out of the blue one day, while I was hanging the washing up, she told me why I should steer clear of you. She reckoned she did it because I'm a good girl and she wanted to protect me from you. 'Course, how true that was I don't know, 'cos she made it clear I owed her a favour in return.'

Olivia had thought it strange that Maisie had divulged such personal information. Previously when she'd asked the woman an innocent question about going on holiday she'd had her head bitten off.

'Well, she got you right and me wrong. You're a good girl all right, Olivia Bone, but you don't need protecting from me. You can trust me on that.' Joe plunged a hand into his pocket. 'Repaid you, has she?'

'I'll get it off Maisie,' Olivia quickly said, seeing he had pulled out a few ten-shilling notes in his fist. 'I don't want anything off you. It was only seven bob. I'm not waiting on it specially.' That was a fib; she was desperate to have her money returned for she'd very little put by now after treating Ruby and herself to dinners that, infuriatingly, had been wasted.

'She'll be back for another handout if you don't go after her.'

'She won't get any more, and if she thinks I'm interested in hearing anything else she's got to say about you, she's wrong.'

'You interested in listening to what I've got to say?'

For a moment Olivia didn't reply. When she did she sounded distant. 'What else is there? You've admitted everything.'

'What's upsetting you most? That brasses come to me to find them punters or that I was once shacked up with a girl?'

Olivia searched his face as she demanded, 'Shacked up? You mean, you weren't married to her?'

'Good as. Common-law wife or husband is enough for some of us round Campbell Road way. But she's gone now and I'm on me tod.'

Olivia digested that for a moment, suppressing a burgeoning feeling of relief. There was no point in it, though. There was still plenty wrong with Joe Hunter. 'Did you have children with her?'

'None that survived ... thank Christ.'

'What?' Olivia gasped.

'Had a stillborn son a year ago.'

'I'm not surprised she left you,' Olivia said, saddened by his callous attitude to the poor little mite.

166

'Me neither. But then it was no great romance.'

'What a real charmer you are,' Olivia muttered sarcastically.

'You thought so once.'

'You didn't fool me for long!' she insisted fiercely.

'Don't look down your nose at me, Olivia Bone,' he said with a hint of derision. 'Not when you let your father knock you about then cover up for him.' He shook his head in disgust. 'You might think I'm no good, but I think you're weak. I thought you had a backbone. But you're still a kid getting a hiding off her dad.'

'What d'you mean by that?' Olivia cried, incensed. 'What happened at Christmas was an accident! I got in the way, that's all.'

'Who was he meaning to take it out on then, if not his eldest kid?'

Olivia sank her teeth into her lower lip. Whether he'd wanted to or not, Joe had just forced her to face up to how culpable she was in failing to protect her siblings. And more damning even than that . . . she had to acknowledge to herself that the longer she kept their family's dirty secret, the longer the violence would go on.

'The youngest?' Joe guessed. 'That sort of mean bully, is he? I saw the way your little brother was scared of him, the night we got back from the flicks.'

On impulse Olivia slid to the edge of the seat and sprang down to the road, unable to listen to any more of his taunts. She stumbled to her knees but scrambled up and started running towards the corner, her skirts held away from her flying feet. He caught up with her in a few loping strides and she lashed out but he roughly pinned her arms to her sides, jerking her against him. 'You're not so different from me, you know. Forced to live a life you hate because of people in it you can't turn your back on, much as you'd like to.'

'We're not alike!' Olivia shouted. 'None of my family would sink to your level.' She tried to wrench herself free from his grasp. 'You're the lowest of the low!'

'What about your cousin? She's a brass and she's just begged me to take her on. She didn't like it when I said no.'

'What d'you mean?' Olivia could feel the colour rising in her cheeks.

'Don't act the innocent,' he scoffed, loosening his grip on her. 'Ruby wants me to find her clients. I'm not doing it. I've got a proper job now. She'll have to take her chances elsewhere.'

'She's a waitress.' Olivia felt her cheeks fizzing with heat. Of course she knew what Ruby was and had done from the start.

'Yeah . . . but she can't earn enough at it, like most of 'em. They do half and half because they want something else as well. And they want me to help them earn extra money.'

'You think you're a Good Samaritan, do you, rather than a greedy swine?' Olivia scoffed. 'Well, I don't!'

'You've spent too long at home under your father's thumb. You know nothing of what goes on in the world.'

'I'm a factory girl now working full-time, if you must know,' Olivia said proudly. 'And I don't want to know what goes on in *your* world, thanks very much.'

'Stay away from Ruby Wright then . . . 'cos she wants to move into my world, if I'll let her.'

'Ruby wants *me* to get her a job not *you*. She wants to start work at Barratt's.'

'You'll regret it if you help her. I told you to stay away from her.'

'I'd never do what you tell me to.'

'But you'll do what your father tells you to or he'll knock obedience into you,' Joe returned quietly. 'I can stop him doing that, if you'll let me.'

Olivia stared unblinkingly at him, her teeth nipping her lower lip. She knew he was offering to give Tommy Bone a taste of his own medicine and though she knew her father deserved it the idea of the ensuing chaos horrified her. 'Stay away from all of us!'

Olivia felt the grip of his hands soften. He smoothed them gently up and down her arms.

'You're younger than me. Give it a few more years and you'll know what looking out for your family does to you.' He released her suddenly, with a little push. 'Let's start with my lot then: the old man was a pimp, so it's in my blood,' he viciously mocked himself. 'He married Maisie, his favourite girl, because she stuck by him despite the beatings. Then I came along but things didn't change for either of them even though they had a kid. They carried on much as before, my mother tells me. Then she got pregnant again and it all changed.'

Suddenly Olivia wasn't wary of Joe. There was something dreadfully vulnerable about him now, and though she didn't want to admit it, much of what he'd said had resonated with her. He knew her very well. She did hate the life she had and she did feel trapped in it because of those she couldn't turn her back on.

'I didn't want her going back on the game – that's why I got her out of Campbell Road and into Wood Green.' Joe jerked back his head to stare at the sky.

'Maisie lived in the Bunk?'

He gave a single nod.

'You got her clients when she lived there?

'If I hadn't somebody else would've and clumped her into the bargain, just like my father used to.' He gave a bitter laugh. 'Once a woman's on the game she won't get off it, even if you give her a way out. Even if you tell her she's past it and the punters want fresh meat.' He snorted a mirthless laugh. 'All she can remember is the cash in her heyday. For decades my mum would sooner go on the streets and get a black eye than take a decent job charring. I found her those jobs, and to keep me quiet she even did a bit of cleaning here and there. But she'd always go back on the streets.' He paused. 'In the end it was easier to find her a punter myself than let her find her own. So when I was thirteen, that's what I did.' He took out a pack of cigarettes and lit one, drawing smoke deep into his lungs. 'She's done with it now, anyhow. And so am I.'

'All right, Livvie?'

Olivia jumped away from Joe and whipped about on hearing her name called. Walking towards them on the opposite pavement was Cath Mason. She was with an older fellow who seemed familiar to Olivia. As they came closer she recognised him as the kindly man who'd warned her months ago about Joe Hunter, on the day she'd served Joe his pie and mash dinner at Ward's. Olivia hoped they'd not seen Joe's hands on her.

Cath trotted across the road to speak to her, pulling her companion along by the arm. 'Nice to bump into you, Livvie. I can introduce you to me father. I was just telling him that Tommy Bone's daughter's working in packing. He's heard of your dad through me uncle, haven't you, Pop?' She turned to her father, giving him a nudge. 'Told you she was pretty, didn't I? You can see why she's caught the boss's eye.'

'Nice to meet you, Mr Mason.' Olivia politely shook his hand. He avoided looking directly at either her or Joe and she could tell that he wasn't going to say anything about their previous meeting in the caff. For his part, if Joe knew Mr Mason he showed no sign of it.

Cath's expression changed as she realised she might have put her foot in it by mentioning Lucas Black. She gave Olivia an apologetic look while Joe was pulling a cigarette from a packet.

170

'Oh ... this is my cousin's friend, Joe Hunter,' Olivia quickly explained. 'We just bumped into one another by chance as I got off the bus.'

In a mannerly fashion Joe pocketed the cigarettes and offered his hand to the Masons while telling them he had to get going.

And he did. With a nod for them all he strolled back to the cart, smoking the newly lit cigarette, and seconds later the vehicle was on its way down the street.

'Well, I've got to get off home, too. 'Bye now, see you Monday, Cath.' Olivia set off quickly, not wanting to have any questions fired at her. She'd experienced enough drama for one day and her mind was crammed with worrying things. But for now her immediate priority was to find out what had been happening in Ranelagh Road in the hours that she'd been absent.

On glancing over her shoulder at the corner she saw that Joe had disappeared from sight and Cath and her dad were strolling on, deep in conversation.

With a sinking heart, Olivia reckoned she knew what they were talking about.

Chapter Fourteen

'Sorry I'm late back. Where's Maggie?' Olivia asked breathlessly. She had jogged home and entered the parlour to see Alfie and Nancy seated at the parlour table having a late tea. She relaxed on seeing her father hadn't returned early, but she had been expecting Maggie to be indoors.

'She went down the High Street this afternoon,' Alfie answered in between mouthfuls of cheese sandwich. 'We was waiting for her to come in for tea but she didn't so we started anyway.'

'Shops shut hours ago,' Olivia said, feeling a prickle of uneasiness. She'd noticed that Nancy seemed to be avoiding her eye. Unpinning her hat, Olivia combed her fingers through her tangled locks.

'Didn't you buy a skirt after all?'

'Nothing took me fancy.' Olivia suspected Nancy wanted to distract her from asking again about Maggie. She'd caught her sisters whispering together that morning. When she'd asked what it was all about Maggie had responded with a sulky 'Nothing'. She imagined Maggie had got her eye on a boy as she'd started putting rags in her hair every night since leaving school. Previously she'd only curled her hair at the weekends when she was off out with her friends.

'While you was out, that Mrs Hunter from upstairs come and knocked.'

'What did she want?' Olivia *was* distracted now, thinking of the quarrel she'd just had with Joe. She doubted that he would have mentioned their meeting even if he had managed to see Maisie in the short period since they'd parted.

'She gave me this for you. Got money in it.' Nancy retrieved something from her pocket and pushed it across the table. 'She said and make sure to give it to you, too, or she'd be after me.'

'Thanks.' Olivia gratefully took the envelope, sagging at one corner from the weight of the coins in it.

'What's she giving you money for?' Alfie piped up.

'Never you mind about that.' Olivia tapped her nose, giving her brother a teasing smile.

She didn't want word getting back to her father that she'd loaned money to a neighbour. If Tommy thought she had enough of her own to be generous to others he'd tell her to cough up more into the kitty jar. That idea jogged her thoughts towards the Keiver girls and their moans about their mother taking all their wages so they'd nothing left to save. Olivia had liked Alice and Sophy and felt sad that she wouldn't see them again. But there was only trouble for her Islington way.

'Any left in that?' She nodded at the teapot beneath its misshapen woolly cosy. It had been one of the first things she'd made after her mother taught her to knit.

'I'll fetch some water in and make fresh, if you like.' Nancy lifted the lid and peered in.

'Don't use more tea. Grouts'll do me.' She knew the caddy was almost empty and her father liked his strong drink in the morning. 'I'll just go and say thanks to Mrs Hunter while you put the kettle on.'

As Olivia climbed the stairs she realised that it was the first time in all the months Maisie had lived there that she'd knocked on her door.

Maisie opened up just a crack then pulled the door wider on identifying Olivia.

'Sorry I was out when you called. Thanks for this ... ' Olivia tugged the edge of the envelope out of her pocket.

'Sorry it took a while giving it back.'

Olivia shrugged graciously as though she'd never considered ambushing her over it. She glanced past Maisie. There were two large suitcases by the wall. The woman wasn't going away on a short trip this time.

'Moving on then?'

'Yeah ... off for good. Don't worry, I've settled up with the landlord. You won't get no trouble off him on my account.'

A silence ensued and Olivia knew they both had the same person on their minds. 'Are you going back to Islington to stay with Joe?'

Maisie snorted. 'He wouldn't let me through the front door.' Her eyes turned bloodshot and she sniffed. 'He's been a good son to me but he'd be bad trouble for a girl like you. That's just how it is: turned out wrong he did, 'cos of me, but I don't regret letting you know the truth,' she ended gruffly.

'I saw him this afternoon,' Olivia blurted.

'Why d'you go and do that?' Maisie sounded exasperated.

'Wasn't planned ... just bumped into him over Islington.'

'Go there a lot do you?' Maisie sounded dubious.

'I went to Chapel Street market. I don't intend to go back.'

Olivia stepped away then hesitated, thinking it odd that in the long and fraught talk she'd had with Joe about their families he'd not mentioned having a sister. 'You going away to your daughter's, Mrs Hunter?'

Maisie gazed at her with a faraway look in her eyes then said, 'Yeah, I'll be with her for good now.' She bucked up. 'I saw your Maggie earlier. She was up the alley with that lad from over the road. I'd have a word with her if I was you before your father speaks to her with his fists.' With that she closed the door.

Olivia felt her guts lurch. She flew down the stairs and straight out into the street. She marched past the Wickses' house and then stopped to peer into the adjacent alley. It was empty and a glance at the horizon told her that the sun was low, glimmering behind purple clouds. July was coming to a close in heavy sultry weather; thunder was growling in the distance, bringing a premature dusk.

Olivia rushed back to the house and into the parlour. Planting her hands on her hips, she stared fiercely at Nancy. 'If you know where Maggie is and what she's been up to, you'd better tell me.'

Nancy looked sheepish, chewing the inside of her cheek. 'She thumped me and told me not to say.'

'Well, I think you better had, or you'll be in as much trouble as she is. Has she been acting lovey-dovey with Ricky behind my back?' Maggie wouldn't bother trying to conceal an innocent friendship with a boy.

'She's up the alley with him, I expect,' Nancy said evasively.

'She's not, I've just looked.'

That comment brought a frown to Nancy's face and Olivia realised her sister was now as clueless as she was about Maggie's whereabouts.

'She might be by the Mission Hall,' Alfie piped up. 'Sometimes they go over there, where we play football.'

'You two stay indoors, I'll look for her. You'd better hope I find her too before Dad gets back.'

Olivia set off at a fast walk, but as the storm rolled closer and the sky darkened she started to run, cursing her sister under her breath for being stupid.

Ricky had left school at the same time as Maggie. He'd got a job as a delivery boy at the bakery in the High Street. A couple of times Olivia had seen him giving her brother a ride up and down the street on the handlebars of his delivery bike. She'd thought it had been quite nice of him to do that, but perhaps Ricky's ulterior motive in hanging around with a kid half his age was sweetening up Alfie's sister for a seduction.

Behind the Mission Hall was a rectangle of grass where local boys played games of football, ignoring the big sign that said none were allowed. There was also a hut where visitors' bikes could be parked. She imagined if her sister was canoodling with Ricky she'd be in the hut away from prying eyes. It was an open secret that the bike shed was used by courting couples. When at school, Olivia and her pals had giggled on hearing about a school friend getting caught out there with a boy and being dragged home by an irate parent. Now *she* was behaving like an irate parent and she hated Maggie for putting her in that position. But better she went after her sister than their father did!

There was definitely somebody in there, Olivia realised as she gingerly approached. A low laugh and a wisp of greyish smoke wafted her way on stifling evening air. Not wanting to barge in on strangers she hissed: 'Maggie ... you in there? If you are, you'd better show your face this minute.'

The hum of voices was replaced by the sound of scuffling.

'Come to join us? More the merrier ... and very nice to see yer.' Harry Wicks stepped into view, smirking at her behind the cigarette wagging between his lips.

Olivia saw that his shirt was open almost to the waist, exposing tufts of coarse hair, and his trouser belt looked loose too. She rushed forward, pushing past him, and stood at the entrance to the hut. Inside she saw Maggie and Ricky. For a moment she was too stunned to react. Her sister was attempting to do up her gaping chemise and Ricky was looking shifty.

'What in God's name do you think you're doing? Do you know how old she is? She's fourteen!' Olivia turned to Harry with an expression of deepest loathing.

'Don't matter how old she is,' he sneered. 'She's more of a woman than you'll ever be, you frigid bitch.' He hadn't forgotten the humiliation of being knocked down by another man on Christmas Eve on account of Olivia Bone. Harry had kept a look-out for the fellow to try and get his own back, but had never again seen him in the street. He'd come to the conclusion that he'd been a passer-by rather than a friend of Olivia's.

'What have you done to her?' Olivia conquered her shock, knowing she had to do something. 'You tell me what's gone on . . . I'll have the police on you if you've touched her!' Turning to Harry, she grabbed the front of his open shirt, shaking him till the cloth ripped in her fingers.

'Ask me brother what they've been up to.' Harry swiped her away, sending her stumbling. 'Ain't interested in her meself.' He adjusted his neck cloth, wiping his sweaty throat with it. 'Hot night,' he smirked, doing up a few buttons with slow deliberation.

'You liar! You wouldn't be here if you weren't interested in her!' Olivia scrambled to her feet. 'You fucking pervert!' She rarely swore because she knew what she'd get from her father if he heard her. But she couldn't stop now she'd started. She flew at him again, beating at his chest with her fists, cursing and screaming, until he again shoved her aside. Still she went back for more, lashing out with kicks and punches. 'You disgusting, fucking pig!' By the time her sister found her voice Olivia's face was wet with perspiration and tears of rage.

'He hasn't done nothing!' Maggie shrilled in fright and defiance as she saw the paddy her older sister was in. 'We was sheltering from the storm. You should've just left me alone. You should've stayed where you was. I'd've been back soon . . . '

Olivia stared aghast at Maggie, realising why her words sounded so familiar. Ruby had come out with almost exactly the same phrase that afternoon when Olivia had interrupted her with Joe Hunter.

With an angry cry Olivia cracked an open palm across her sister's cheek, wiping the insolence off her face and making her howl. She yanked Maggie closer to her, shaking her by the shoulders.

'You stupid, stupid girl.' With that she turned and marched away, dragging her sister behind by the hand, red-faced and wailing.

By the time they got to the top of their road Maggie had quietened and stopped straining to free herself. Despite fat raindrops starting to fall, cooling her burning face, Olivia jerked her sister to a halt. Important things needed to be brought into the open before they went indoors.

She pushed Maggie back from her as though she couldn't bear to touch her and looked her up and down. 'Straighten yourself up.' She brushed down her sister's rucked up skirt. 'Tidy your hair ... here, wipe your nose and get that rouge off your lips.' She thrust a hanky at Maggie, noticing she was wearing make-up. 'You'd better pray to God that Dad's not home and you can scarper into the back room before he smells cigarettes on you or sees you've been out, all painted up.'

'He won't ever know, will he?' Maggie was starting to look and sound like a frightened child.

'Not from me, he won't. But things get talked about and you couldn't have picked a nastier person to hold your secret. Harry Wicks is an evil brute.'

'He's all right,' Maggie protested. 'You shouldn't have said what you did to him. I went with them 'cos I wanted to, not 'cos he made me. He probably won't speak to me now.'

A loud clap of thunder made Maggie cringe with her hands over her ears. She tried to dart off home but Olivia kept her right where she was.

'I'm gonna pretend I never heard you say that, 'cos I reckon you must be in shock ever to want to be anywhere near that filthy pig again.' Olivia felt like slapping some sense into her sister but she controlled herself, giving Maggie's arm a jerk instead. 'And you can stop that!' she snapped as her sister started to snivel. 'That won't help.' Grabbing Maggie's chin she tilted it up. 'That's not the first time you've been there with them, is it?'

Maggie tried to avoid her eyes in a way that was answer enough.

'What have you been doing with those two?' Olivia's grip tightened as Maggie tried to free her face. A flash of lightning highlighted her sister's scarlet cheeks. 'You'd better tell me so I know what needs to be done about it.'

'You don't need to do nothing about it,' Maggie whined, blinking against the rain. 'Only been in the shed a couple of times. And weren't nothing much to it anyhow. I've just let 'em have a look at me bosom and a touch ... that's all.'

'It *was* both of them, wasn't it?' Olivia felt sick as she said it.

'Harry tried to put me hand down his trousers this time but I wouldn't. Ricky only just watches really. Harry said he'd teach his brother how to do things girls liked.'

Olivia felt her insides writhing at the idea of Harry getting away with what he'd done to Maggie. But she knew she couldn't make any more of a scene; it had to be kept quiet or Maggie's reputation would suffer dreadfully. Everybody in the neighbourhood would be calling her fourteen-year-old sister a slag. Neither could Olivia do what most people would and go home and tell their father about the vile lecher. If Tommy Bone found out a man had been touching up his underage daughter he'd take it out on someone – but it was more likely to be the victim than the perpetrator.

Olivia was about to tell Maggie that she was due a hiding. Instead she groaned, 'Oh, no!' Through the gloom she had spotted a bulky figure swaying from side to side as it proceeded along the pavement. Her father's head was down beneath the steady drizzle, and she prayed he hadn't seen them. She pulled Maggie on at a trot and when inside the house shoved her in the direction of their bedroom.

'Dad's on his way!' she burst out to Alfie and Nancy who were gawping at Maggie's tear-stained face and dishevelment. 'Look sharp! Be best if you're all out of sight when he comes through the door.'

*

'Where's the rest of 'em?'

Tommy's surly greeting was issued before he'd even pulled off his drenched waistcoat. Olivia's spirits sank as he slumped down into an armchair rather than taking himself straight off to bed.

'They've all turned in, Dad.' She felt her heart thundering furiously beneath her bodice. But it wasn't solely her father's untimely appearance getting at her; she couldn't dispel from her mind the sight of her sister buttoning up her clothes over her small bare breasts. Keeping quiet about what Harry Wicks had done was playing into his hands and if that wasn't enough to stick in Olivia's craw it just seemed cowardly and wrong to let him get away with it and do it to somebody else. And he would. He'd tried to force himself on her not so long ago. Olivia wanted to storm into his house and shame him before his parents. They weren't friendly people, Mr and Mrs Wicks kept themselves to themselves, but Olivia was sure they'd be sickened by their eldest son's behaviour.

'D'you want anything to eat before I get meself to bed?' she asked, hoping that he didn't.

'Bit of toast 'n' jam.' Tommy eased off his sodden boots and flexed his toes. 'Got a spud in this sock. Darn it next time you and the gels do the laundry, will you, Livvie?' He frowned at her. 'You been out this evening? Your hair looks wet.' He'd turned to fully face her, eyes narrowed.

'Nipped out the back to the washhouse,' Olivia lied fluently. 'Nancy thought she'd left one of the sheets in the copper. But she hadn't.'

As she sawed a couple of thick slices of bread off a stale loaf she glanced over at her father sinking back in the armchair. He seemed to have accepted her explanation. He only called her Livvie when he wanted something; she knew it wasn't simply having his socks darned that he was after.

'How you getting on at Barratt's then, Livvie? Still keeping yer nose clean. Head down, work hard . . . ' he slurred, nodding to himself.

Olivia could have laughed at that coming from a man who had been sacked for bad behaviour.

'Want to get transferred to a better position,' Olivia told him, opening the range door and holding the toasting fork close to the burning coal. 'I'm going to see about it Monday morning.'

'Good gel,' Tommy praised her then burped, filling the room with beery fumes. 'Go 'n' see Lucas Black soon as you can ... and when you do, don't forget to put in a word for yer ol' dad.' He settled back into the chair. 'Half the year gone already and Christmas's gonna be round again before you know it. Could do with pulling in all we can to pay for a nice time.'

Olivia could have laughed at that too, considering how he'd destroyed last year's festivities.

'Do you want me to ask Mr Black outright if you can have your job back, Dad?' He'd hinted at it enough times.

'He should offer me it without you needing to plead on my behalf,' Tommy snapped. 'If you go about it in the right way, that is.' He glowered at her from beneath his wiry brows. 'Just be nice 'n' polite to him. Could tell he liked you from the start.'

Olivia scraped jam across the toast and found a plate to put it on. She took the kettle off the hob and used a small amount of tea in the pot, pouring in the boiling water and vigorously stirring the leaves. She wanted to hurry up and get to bed even though she knew she'd not sleep until she'd quietened the chaos in her mind.

'I spoke to Mrs Hunter. She's moving out to stay with her daughter,' Olivia blurted, hoping to turn their conversation away from the factory. She'd enough to ponder on without adding her boss to the mix. But one thing she did know: if her father thought a man like Lucas Black would be swayed by a bit of flirtation into doing something he didn't want to do, then he was wrong.

'Maisie's gone, has she? Glad to see the back of her ... miserable cow, she was.' Tommy patted his thigh in tipsy satisfaction. 'You get yer better job and I get me rightful place back in Barratt's, we'll be able to spread out here and have the upstairs again. I'll see Silver and tell him we want first refusal on them rooms.'

'Need to work out if we can afford it first, Dad,' Olivia interrupted quickly. A short while ago her father's suggestion would have been music to her ears, but not now. Now she didn't want to spread out here; she wanted to spread her wings and get her own place, not spend any of her wages on extra rooms in her father's house. She intended to find somewhere safe for her and Alfie and Nancy; Maggie too if that's what she wanted. But, after today, she didn't feel she knew what Maggie wanted.

She picked up her father's tea and toast to give to him.

He was fast asleep, head lolling and mouth agape, feet stuck out in front of him with a big toe poking out of its wet sock. She put down his supper by his chair and went into the bedroom.

'Did he say anything? Does he know I'm in trouble?' As soon as Maggie heard the door open she had nipped out of bed. She plonked her bony backside down beside Olivia on the sagging mattress, her complexion white with anxiety.

For a moment Olivia was struck by just how young and vulnerable her sister looked and tenderness washed over her. In her baggy, patched nightgown, buttoned up to the throat, Maggie didn't even look like an adolescent; she looked like a child, who should still have been in a classroom. Olivia swallowed the reassurance ready to roll off her tongue. Leniency wasn't what Maggie needed or deserved. Her sister was becoming an adult and had to be reminded of the consequences of what she'd done, for her own good. 'If your dad knew what you'd been up to, he'd be in here laying into you with his belt, not in the parlour asleep.'

Maggie cuffed her eyes. 'Won't find out, will he?'

'I hope not,' Olivia said quietly.

With no mother to talk to them about growing up, she knew the task fell to her of explaining to her younger sisters about

183

confusing changes that would affect their minds and bodies as they blossomed into young women. Yet she wondered if she could do a good enough job; she often felt in need of someone to fill in the gaps for her. She'd never had a proper boyfriend, and before she'd met Joe Hunter had never wanted one. She knew she was falling for him despite his villainous ways and was coming to realise how tricky and heart-breaking relationships between men and women could be. She understood that older, more experienced men could find green girls like her and Maggie an opportunity too good to be missed. And then she thought of Lucas Black.

But he wasn't important so she shoved him from her mind, impressing on herself that Joe Hunter and Harry Wicks weren't alike. For all his faults, Joe had always treated her with kindness and respect. He was a gentleman compared to the vile lecher up the road.

'Get to bed, Maggie, it's Sunday tomorrow. You can help me catch up on the mending and ironing to help Nancy out.'

Maggie nodded, eager to please.

As her sister rose from the mattress Olivia caught her hand and hissed quietly, so only Maggie would hear, 'Promise me you'll stay away from the Wickses!'

'I will ... honest.'

Chapter Fifteen

'I'd like a word, please.'

'A word about what, precisely?' Miss Wallis flicked a glance over Olivia's plain work clothes and sturdy shoes. The girl wasn't wearing a scrap of make-up and her hair was simply styled in a workaday bun clipped at her nape. Olivia Bone shouldn't look pretty ... but she did, and that rankled with Deborah who was wearing clothes purchased from the West End and had spent time that morning applying powder and lipstick.

'I'm keen to get on here and would like a transfer to the production line if ...' Olivia was cut off before she could finish her application for a promotion.

'I'm busy now. I'll make you an appointment for another time.'

'Right,' Olivia said. 'When will that be then?'

'I'll send word to your supervisor,' the secretary said stiffly, and disappeared.

Olivia stared at the wooden panels, biting her lip in frustration. If she asked Miss Wallis for anything at all the cow would surely find a reason to deny it to her and close the door in her face.

Sighing, she turned away and headed outside to eat her sandwich. She'd arrived early that morning hoping to speak to Deborah Wallis before her shift started but the secretary's office had been empty. Olivia had clocked in and waited until dinnertime to try her luck. There wasn't much of her precious break left now she'd squandered some of it on a fool's errand.

'Any luck?'

Cath Mason had sprung up from the group of colleagues she'd been sitting with on the wall and trotted over to meet Olivia as she emerged from the factory.

'Don't think I stand much chance.' Olivia shrugged. 'She said she'd make me an appointment. Don't reckon she will though.'

'Well, you know what to do about it, don't you?' Cath said slyly. 'You flutter your eyelashes in *his* direction . . .' She nodded at Lucas Black, who was talking to some men loading up the motor van with pallets of sherbet. 'Reckon any job you want'll be yours . . . even hers.' Cath cackled.

Olivia wasn't so sure about that. Lucas had walked off and got into his car with barely a glance her way.

'Fancy a quick walk, Cath?' Olivia needed to get away from the commotion of the factory for a short while and clear her head. Since her run-in with Harry Wicks she couldn't concentrate on anything other than keeping Maggie away from him. Even her altercation with Joe had been pushed to the back of her mind. That morning Cath had briefly mentioned their meeting at the weekend. Olivia felt reassured that whatever Mr Mason might privately think about Joe Hunter's connection to her family, he'd thankfully kept it to himself because Cath hadn't commented other than to say that she thought Joe nice-looking. Talking to his daughter about a man rumoured to be a pimp was probably something Mr Mason wouldn't do.

As for Maggie, she'd not gone outside the door for the whole of Sunday and had been a good deal of help with the house-work. Nevertheless Olivia still felt anxious enough to want to check that her sister wasn't hanging around outside the laundry to catch Harry's eye.

'You've not had a bite to eat, have you?' Cath remarked. They'd set off at quite a pace, knowing they'd little time before the afternoon shift started.

'Doesn't matter. Don't feel hungry,' Olivia replied.

'Same here.' Cath grimaced then suddenly nudged Olivia. 'Now's your chance to nab him and have a word about your promotion,' she hissed.

Olivia had been occupied peering alternately through the laundry and butcher's shops' windows and hadn't noticed that Lucas Black's car had pulled up a short distance in front of them. She'd spied her sister folding sheets with another girl and Harry had been hooking up strings of sausages at the back of the counter. Both had looked as though butter wouldn't melt . . .

'Loiter about here until he comes out, eh?' Cath suggested. Their boss had raised a hand to acknowledge them before enter-ing the newsagent's shop.

'You all right, Cath?' Olivia asked as her friend suddenly clapped her fingers to her mouth.

'Just thought I was about to burp, that's all.'

Olivia raised an eyebrow dubiously. 'That's a bloody big burp. It's been troubling you for weeks.'

Cath avoided her eye. 'Dicky tummy, that's all,' she muttered defensively.

'Is it?' Olivia said wryly. 'What brought that on then?'

'You know, don't you?' Cath said, defeated.

'I recognise the signs. Me mum was rough for ages when she was carrying Alfie.'

'Don't say nothing, will you?' Cath pleaded. 'I'll lose me job then me 'n' Trev won't manage to save enough to get our own place.'

''Course I won't! We're friends, aren't we? What does Trevor say about it?'

'Nothing . . . he don't know . . . and that's the way it's staying.'

Olivia frowned in surprise. 'But . . . if you're getting married anyway, you could bring the wedding forward, couldn't you?'

'I ain't living with his mum 'n' dad!' Cath said forcefully. 'And I will be if they find out about this.' She knuckled her watering eyes. 'I'll be stuck under the same roof as that bossy old cow for ever, 'cos we'll only have Trevor's wages coming in.'

'Has your mum guessed?' Olivia glanced at her friend's abdomen.

'Staying out of her way as much as I can. Anyhow, she's too wrapped up in herself to notice what goes on. And thankfully Dad's clueless about women's stuff.'

'If you tell them, will they let you live with them?'

'Dad would. But Mum don't hold with being sentimental or helping people out.' Cath snorted in disgust. 'She'll tell me that I've made me bed with a man and can lie on it in me own home.'

'What are you going to do then?' Olivia frowned.

'Get rid of it is what I'm going to do.' Cath sounded adamant.

Olivia tried not to appear shocked. A few years ago she'd heard about a local girl who'd almost died at the hands of a backstreet abortionist. The poor thing had never returned to school and had been seen afterwards looking like death warmed up before the family moved away. 'How far gone are

188

you?' She assessed her friend's figure for any tell-tale signs but Cath's belly appeared reasonably flat.

'Not yet four months, I reckon. But I want it done soon.'

'You don't want to get yourself all messed up inside.' Olivia rubbed her friend's arm in sympathy.

'I've heard about someone,' Cath whispered, glancing about furtively for eavesdroppers. 'Nelly Smith's sister-in-law's a nurse. She lives over Edmonton way and does a bit of moonlighting. But she's not cheap. Wants three quid for her trouble.' She pursed her lips. "Course Nelly's got a bloody big mouth so I can't ask her outright for the woman's address or everyone'll be chinwagging.'

Olivia remembered that name. Ethel Cook had told her that Nelly Smith was the woman involved in the accident that had lost her father his job. And Ethel had found out about it through Nelly's sister-in-law.

Since Olivia had started work at Barratt's her path hadn't closely crossed Nelly's. But she knew who the woman was as Cath had once pointed out a skinny little individual in a group of sugar-boilers. The older women had been having a meeting and Olivia had hung around on the fringes to listen. They'd been discussing going on a Suffragette rally in the East End. The bell had gone for afternoon shift to start before she'd got the full gist of it all.

'My neighbour used to work with Nelly's relative at the hospital.'

'That's worth knowing,' Cath said brightly.

'Why don't you speak to Trevor?' Olivia suggested quickly. She didn't want her friend thinking that Ethel Cook might be in the business of carrying out abortions. 'It's as much his problem as yours and he won't want you to risk getting hurt, Cath.'

'If I have to live with his parents I'll end up swinging from

189

the banisters, so what's the difference?' she answered with bleak humour. 'I'm pulling in a bit extra. I'll have enough in me savings to sort things out soon.'

Cath pressed her lips together, glancing about. Olivia knew her friend was looking for a change of subject.

''Ere ... look, our dreamboat boss is back out of the shop.' Cath nudged Olivia's arm.

While they'd been talking Lucas had got back in his car. He hadn't driven off but had opened a newspaper, spreading it on the steering wheel to read.

'Go on ... dare you to knock on his window and ask him for a job as a roller-out.' Cath gave Olivia a little push along the pavement. 'If I wasn't in this state I'd see if I could get a promotion. I can't rock me boat just yet, though.'

'We'd better turn round or we'll be late back.' It was a valid reason for them to head in the opposite direction. Nevertheless Olivia hesitated; she'd got a prime opportunity to speak to the manager away from her colleagues', and Deborah Wallis's, prying eyes. And she wanted her extra money, and her own place, just as much as Cath and Alice Keiver did.

'He don't look in any rush.' Cath nodded at the stationary vehicle. 'I'll get going. You can follow on when you've had a word. I'll cover for you.' She gave a wave and set off, then hesitated and trotted back to Olivia's side to whisper, 'D'you reckon you could find out off your neighbour where Nelly's sister-in-law lives?'

'I'll try,' Olivia murmured, then she headed for the car and, without allowing herself to think about it, tapped on the window.

He didn't look surprised to see her, she realised as he folded the paper then got out. In fact, she reckoned he'd been waiting for her.

'Sorry to bother you, Mr Black.'

'No bother,' he said with an ironic smile.

'Any chance of a promotion to roller-out?'

His smile deepened. 'Just like that? No chit-chat first?'

'What chit-chat d'you want?' Olivia asked, feeling piqued that he might be laughing at her.

'Oh ... I don't know ... your choice. Perhaps if we meet up this evening it'd give you a chance to think of some.'

'I can't go out, but thanks anyway.' Olivia was unsure if he was joking or not.

'You *can't* go out?' he echoed.

'I've thought of some chit-chat.' Olivia gazed boldly, almost antagonistically, into his deep blue eyes and he watched her closely, equally challenging.

He gestured for her to continue.

'Any vacancies going that'd suit my father?'

Again that sarcastic smile curled a corner of his mouth. 'That's your idea of chit-chat, is it?'

'What's yours?' Olivia retorted. '"Will you sleep with me, Miss Bone?"' She'd startled herself, allowing what was in her head to roll off her tongue.

But he seemed unperturbed ... amused, if anything, by her insolence. 'I'd never say that, not now we're on first-name terms.'

'Are we indeed?' Olivia's tone had lost some of its defiance; she regretted what she'd done, guessing her promotion had just flown out of the window.

'Yes ... we are, Olivia.' There was scant humour in his eyes now, just hard demanding desire.

'It doesn't matter. Sorry I bothered you,' she said hoarsely.

He caught her arm, stopping her from turning away. 'Why can't you go out?'

'I'm the eldest. I've younger ones to look after.'

'And your father can't give you a night off?'

191

She gave a hollow laugh. 'I wouldn't want him to.'

He released her arm and pursed his lips, looking thoughtful. 'He's got you to speak to me about a job, hasn't he?'

'He's too much pride for that,' Olivia retorted. Her father had made it clear that he didn't want his old boss thinking he'd go cap in hand to him.

'Sunday afternoon then. I'll take you to Alexandra Palace. I'll meet you by the factory gates at two o'clock.'

'He won't let me . . . ' Olivia started.

'Of course he will,' Lucas said. 'He'll march you down to meet me himself if he thinks he'll get what he wants out of it.' He brushed a thumb over her parted lips then his hand travelled on, plunging into his pocket. 'Just a stroll on the grass, that's all. D'you want a lift back?' He opened the car door.

'It'll start them all talking.'

He shrugged, looking bored. 'D'you want a lift back?'

It was his way of telling her he didn't give a monkey's who said what.

She was late now and a ride would've been helpful but the idea of rolling up at the factory in the boss's car was unthinkable. Gossip would start about her getting above herself, setting her sights on Lucas Black.

She shook her head. 'Thanks, but I'll walk.'

And she did walk, so fast she was almost running with her skirts in her fists. Her fair hair was falling out of the bun wound at her nape and trailing either side of her hot face in wispy ringlets. When only yards from the factory gates she saw her father striding towards her. She came to an abrupt halt. He looked grim and purposeful and whatever was eating at him she'd sooner find out about it privately. Since he'd been dismissed Tommy had always given Barratt's a wide berth so she knew something important had happened.

'Finished your shift in the market, Dad?' she greeted him breathlessly. 'I'm just on me break and got to get back . . . '

'You can hold on a minute, miss,' he cut across her. 'I hoped I'd catch you to speak about Maggie.'

Olivia felt as though she'd been winded. 'What d'you mean?' She prayed it wasn't what she suspected.

'Just been over Golders Green to see the Jew about the vacant rooms upstairs.' Tommy's lips thinned in disgust. 'Silver reckons Maisie Hunter's gone rather than have him put her out on the street, where she belonged. I knew what he meant, all right. So I had him for letting that sort move in above a decent family.'

Olivia moistened her dry lips. 'What's that to do with Maggie?'

'You answer me that!' Tommy growled, stabbing a thick finger at Olivia's shoulder. 'The Jew told me to look to me own or he'd be putting *us* lot out on the street.' Tommy's face had turned florid as he brooded on the row with his landlord. 'I thought at first Silver was acting snide 'cos I'd made a complaint. But then he said he'd heard about me daughter acting like a tart.' Tommy was grinding his teeth in rage, his fists clenched at his sides. 'I nearly chinned the little maggot. Have you been letting Maggie paint her face again?'

Inwardly Olivia breathed a sigh of relief. Her father suspected Maggie had been wearing make-up outside, and she had. But Olivia doubted that that was what Mr Silver had meant.

'I'll speak to her, Dad, but sounds like somebody's got nothing better to do than cause trouble,' Olivia rattled off, trying to quell her nervousness. She moved closer to the brick pillars by the gate, hoping he would also move out of view of the factory windows. If her father really lost his rag he would make a spectacle of them both.

'If somebody's spreading lies about my family, I'll swing for 'em. Who it is? D'you know?'

'Can't understand why anybody would stoop to it,' Olivia said, truthfully.

But she knew all right who was muck-raking. Silver collected rents from the Wicks family and either he'd overheard Harry and Ricky talking about what had gone on in the bike shed with Maggie or Harry had deliberately started the gossip from spite.

'Shall we talk about it when I get home?' Olivia glanced up at the clock on the front of the factory; she should have been back at her bench over half an hour ago. 'Don't want to get into trouble with them for being late, Dad.'

'You're already in trouble! With me!' he roared. 'We'll have it out now!'

'How have you been, Tommy?'

Lucas Black had strolled out of the factory gates.

A heavy silence ensued during which Olivia wondered if her father was about to be rude and lose any chance of ever getting his job back from the man who'd sacked him.

'I'm well enough ... you?' Tommy jutted his chin, having struggled to control himself.

'I'm well enough too. Let's hope we all stay that way, and nothing comes of this bad business in Belgium.'

'None of our concern. Let 'em sort it out themselves is what I say.'

'Politicians never listen to what the likes of you and I have to say, Tommy. If they did wars wouldn't start.'

Olivia hoped Lucas could read in her eyes her gratitude to him for defusing the situation, even if it had been by turning the conversation to something depressing. The papers had been reporting for weeks the conflict in Europe but it seemed it was

194

worsening and negotiations for peace between the countries were looking increasingly hopeless.

'Get back to work, please, Miss Bone, your break's over.'

Olivia gave a nod. Murmuring a goodbye to her father, she hurried away.

Neither of the men moved; Lucas leaned back against the pillar as though settling in for a talk.

Tommy forgot about Bernie Silver's threats of eviction, concentrating instead on the reason why he'd gone to see the Jew in the first place. He needed some extra space at home and for that he needed extra money and a good job at Barratt's ... plus the sweet perks that would come with it.

'How's me daughter getting on in there?' he asked slyly, jerking his head at the factory.

'She's a good worker.'

'She's a good gel, is my Livvie.'

'I know,' Lucas said. 'I'm taking her out on Sunday to Alexandra Park.'

'Are you now?' Tommy crossed his beefy forearms over his chest and settled his chin low.

'Don't you want me to?' Lucas shifted away from the wall. 'Be good for her if she came along on a day out.'

'I want what's good for *all* of us,' Tommy replied foxily.

'I'll take it you've no objections then,' Lucas said as he walked off.

Deborah Wallis watched from the window as Lucas strode back into the building and Tommy marched off up the road, smiling to himself. She'd seen Olivia, looking attractively dishevelled and pink-cheeked, enter about five minutes earlier. She wondered if the girl had had a romantic assignation ... perhaps with Lucas ... to get her all hot and bothered. Whatever she'd been doing, she'd come back late, and Deborah intended to make sure she was fined for that. No doubt the little hussy would go crying to Lucas about her pay being docked.

He had never before shown an interest in any of the female workers. But then, there were few factory girls who looked as sweet and pretty as Olivia Bone. Deborah guessed that Lucas found a certain piquancy in seducing the innocent daughter of a man he didn't like. Deborah had made it her business to find out about the manager and knew he was a rich playboy whose family had connections to the Barratt's. According to whispers, Lucas had been given a job to try and keep him out of trouble. But for whatever reason he'd taken a directorship at a sweet factory, he was good at what he did and that must have galled some of the old duffers who worked damned hard to get the same results as Lucas effortlessly achieved.

His family moved in elevated circles, socialising with important people. Deborah was a bank clerk's daughter and was eager to climb higher in the pecking order; she wouldn't let the likes of a factory girl stop her from pursuing Lucas when she'd been confident of catching him.

She knew he had a mistress tucked away in Highgate because she'd made it her business to find out. Lucas was handsome and charismatic and attracted women like a magnet so his paramour was no surprise. He'd no serious entanglements for her to worry about as far as she was aware. Deborah imagined that her boss had grown tired of his Highgate floozy and was auditioning the Bone girl to replace her. In Deborah's opinion Olivia would be mad not to jump at the chance of throwing off her sacking apron and becoming a kept woman for a few years. But whoever else he kept wouldn't worry Deborah once she was ensconced in his Hampstead mansion as his wife.

*

The bell went at the end of their shift and Olivia could see that Cath was itching to find out what had gone on with Lucas earlier. But she gave her friend a hurried wave and got going as fast as she could. Catching Maggie on the way home and warning her that their father was on the warpath was Olivia's prime concern.

Thankfully on coming to a breathless halt outside the laundry she could see Maggie still inside, packing a mountain of folded white cotton into a box. Her sister emerged from the shop ten minutes later and scowled on seeing Olivia waiting for her.

'I'm not a bloody kid who needs walking home,' Maggie hissed. 'You don't have to keep checking up on me. I saw you staring through the window at me, dinnertime. I was gonna go and have a look in some shops with Cissy tonight before they close.' The girl loitering behind Maggie was pretending not to listen to the sisters' conversation.

'I've got better things to do, 'n' all,' Olivia retorted. 'But if you don't want to know about Dad coming to the factory to speak to me about you, that's your lookout.'

Maggie's face fell to her boots. She said a quick goodbye to her workmate and hurried back to Olivia to hear the rest. Olivia linked arms with her, pulling her away from the women filing out of the closing laundry so that nobody could eavesdrop. By the time she'd finished her account of what had gone on, Maggie was snivelling. She started making more of a racket when she saw Harry Wicks coming out of the butcher's opposite.

'Ain't ever speaking to him again.' Maggie cuffed her eyes. 'Everybody'll be talking about me now.'

'They won't,' Olivia reassured her, quite confidently. Mr Silver might be a horrible little man in some ways but he was a businessman first and foremost. He wouldn't bother running down teenage girls behind their backs. He might've thought he was doing Tommy Bone a favour by tipping him the wink about the gossip going round. Now they knew about it, they had the chance to nip it in the bud.

Harry had whistled from the opposite pavement, just to jibe at them, Olivia reckoned, but they didn't give him the satisfaction of responding in any way.

'The pig!' Maggie hissed. 'He said he liked me ...'

Olivia hugged her sister to comfort her. 'I told you he was no good. Steer clear of him and Ricky 'cos they're trouble.' Although she hated seeing Maggie's distress, in a way it was a relief. She'd been dubious about whether Maggie would stop seeing Harry. But Olivia reckoned her sister must surely have seen him in his true colours now.

Chapter Sixteen

'I wasn't sure if I'd be wasting my time waiting for you.'

'I don't reckon you often get stood up,' Olivia replied. 'Sorry I'm a few minutes late. I got a lecture off me dad. He wanted to make sure I behaved myself.'

'And will you?'

'Behave myself? Depends,' Olivia said, meeting his eyes squarely. 'I'll be nice and polite ... if you are too.'

Lucas was leaning against the bonnet of his car, smoking a cigarette. He dropped the stub, stepping on it. 'You're expecting a knight in shining armour, are you?'

'Will I be disappointed?' she asked with a sweet smile.

He didn't answer but studied her appearance. 'You look nice.'

Self-consciously, Olivia brushed a speck from her embroidered sleeve. She'd dressed in her Sunday best dark skirt and cream blouse with a summer bonnet tied beneath her chin. She would have done so even if going out with a girlfriend on a lovely sunny afternoon. 'Beats wearing a sacking apron.'

'Please don't tell me you want to discuss staff uniforms.'

'No, I'll leave that for another time,' Olivia replied provocatively. 'I've got a long enough list as it is.'

'Let's get going then, shall we?'

He could be a tailor's model, she thought, watching him saunter towards her. The linen jacket and flannel trousers he had on looked as good on him as his business suits; tall, lithe and handsome, any outfit would suit Lucas Black.

'This all seems different as well on a Sunday.' Olivia put a hand on the crown of her straw hat, tipping back her head to eye the factory. The absence of noise and people gave the range of buildings an oppressive presence.

'Smells the same though,' Lucas said ruefully.

And it did. The aroma of syrup hung heavy and ever-present in the air, even when the boilers were unlit.

He opened the car door for her and she slid onto a firm hide-upholstered seat.

'Can't be out long,' she told him as soon as he got in beside her.

'I guessed as much.'

Olivia darted him a glance although she didn't need to, to know a cynical smile would be slanting his lips.

'Has your father calmed down now?'

Olivia considered her answer. She'd believed that she and Maggie would walk indoors to another commotion that day. But Tommy had been out, and he'd not returned till later in the week. When he did show up it seemed that he'd forgotten about Mr Silver calling his daughter a tart. But ever since then Maggie had taken care to avoid him in case she reminded him of it.

'It was just something going on at home that was getting his goat.' Olivia knew Lucas was waiting for her answer. 'Sorry if he bothered you.'

'Tommy Bone's never bothered me ... although I reckon he could pick a fight with his own shadow.' Lucas started the engine and the Austin started to glide along Mayes Road.

'He does fly off the handle easily,' she admitted, rather sadly.

'It's you that bothers me, Olivia.'

'I'm fine ... no need to worry about me.' Olivia looked out of the side window, feeling the weight of Lucas's blue stare warming her cheek.

'I don't think that's true. I think you could do with getting away from your father's bullying.'

'I didn't say he was a bully – I said he flies off the handle.'

'You haven't betrayed him. I know his character from employing him.'

'You don't know him as well as I do,' Olivia returned sharply, swinging round to face him. 'Me and my brother and sisters, and my father ... we're all well enough, thanks, so there's nothing more to be said.'

'You want me to mind my own business where your family's concerned?'

'That's about the size of it.' She forced some levity into her tone.

'For a girl who wants favours you don't go about it the right way, Olivia Bone.'

'And for a knight in shining armour, neither do you, Lucas Black.' She sighed with genuine regret. 'I think we're going to end up arguing and that won't do any good. Take me back ... no, you needn't bother. If you pull up, I can get out and walk home. It's not far.'

The car had started the climb up Muswell Hill towards Alexandra Palace, the engine purring as it coped easily with the ascent.

'The more you bristle, the easier it is to tell that you're unhappy.'

Lucas carried on driving, ignoring her command to set her down. Olivia decided not to insist he stop the car.

But she wasn't unhappy! Though he was right about something else. She *had* gone about things the wrong way. The week had ended without Miss Wallis calling her for an interview and Olivia regretted now having let the woman ignore her. She should have gone back to the secretary's office and tackled her over it again. She peeked beneath her lashes at Lucas's profile. She'd hoped to dim the memory of Joe Hunter by enjoying going out with another fellow and keeping her father satisfied to boot. But she wasn't sure she would enjoy her boss's company. She still couldn't quite get the hang of when he was joking and when he wasn't. She guessed that was what he wanted ... to keep her guessing.

'Was your pay docked for getting back late from your dinner break?'

'Mmmm ...' Olivia had ducked her face aside, having noticed a girl from packing walking arm-in-arm with a friend. She didn't want to be spotted and bombarded with questions by her workmates on Monday morning.

'I'll see to it.'

'Don't want you to. I *was* late. I don't want special treatment.'

'Is that right?'

She deserved his scorn. Of course she wanted special treatment. That's why she was sitting in his car now, agitated that she might be accused by her colleagues of sucking up to the boss.

'It was my fault. I held you up,' Lucas said soothingly. He drove into the Palace grounds and pulled up by the south slope. The park was crowded with people promenading and picnicking on the grass.

'D'you want to sit or stroll?'

He opened her door, helping her out, and for a moment they stood quietly enjoying the wonderful view over the rooftops of

North London while behind them soared the imposing outline of Alexandra Palace. It never failed to surprise Olivia just how high up these grounds were when appreciating the breadth of scenery below.

'It's odd ... people enjoying themselves, looking carefree ... when just days ago we found out we're going to war.' Olivia had eagerly pounced on the newspaper her father had brought in, reporting the news that Great Britain had declared war on Germany. Even though things had been simmering for a while it had still come as a shock. But everything still seemed the same, as though the threat wasn't real. At the factory the girls in Olivia's department had decided that soon another announcement would be made, calling it all off.

'If the great and the good know what they're talking about it should be a quick victory and over by Christmas.'

'You don't sound convinced,' Olivia said, glancing up at his profile as he stood quite still by her side, gazing far into the distance.

'Those in charge aren't always as great and as good as they think they are ... or people hope they are.'

Olivia wondered if he was referring to himself as well as Whitehall bigwigs but she stopped herself from uttering a smart comment. 'My brother Alfie's already been out playing soldiers with his pals. They march up and down the street with brooms on their shoulders.'

'Let's hope those lads never bear arms for real.' Lucas slanted her a smile. 'Cheer up, shall we, before we bring that storm rolling in?' He nodded to the horizon where a cliff of purple cloud was gathering.

'Yeah.' Olivia grinned agreement. She knew he was right; whatever happened to the world in the future they'd have little control over it, so what point was there in fretting?

A family who'd been occupying a bench close by got up to leave and immediately Olivia set off to claim it before somebody else did. 'Sit down for a while then,' she said with a triumphant smile, settling back. 'Might not get a chance of a seat later.'

'You're not afraid to go after what you want, I see.' Lucas had watched in amusement as she'd nipped forward to beat another couple to the seat.

'It's what people like me do,' Olivia said bluntly. 'We go after what we want before someone else has it instead.'

'I like girls who are ambitious.'

'You think me common.'

'You're not common, you're unique.' Lucas sat down beside her, leaning his elbows on his knees. 'D'you know what that means?'

'I read a lot when I was younger, so I do know what it means even though I left school at fourteen. I even know you're flattering me 'cos there are lots of factory girls want to earn more and better themselves.' She crossed her arms over her chest. 'Not impressed by flattery ... might as well let you know that straight off.'

'What are you impressed by then, Olivia?'

'A knight in shining armour,' she said solemnly, then burst out laughing.

He smiled too but said quite seriously, 'I'm not making any promises on that front.'

'Did you like school?' she asked.

Lucas shook his head. 'Couldn't wait to leave.'

'Don't reckon you were fourteen when you got a job.'

'By the time I came down from Oxford I was twenty.'

Olivia looked wistful. 'You were lucky. I wanted to stay on at school. I bet you learned about a lot of interesting things.'

'I didn't think so at the time. But ... ' He shrugged.

Olivia turned to him. 'But what?'

'I'm more mature now and understand the importance of education, and other things.'

'Is that because you've had to deal with dimwit factory workers?'

'Perhaps.' He slanted her a mordant glance. 'So now we've got all the chips on our shoulders out in the open, you're wondering what I want with you.'

'No, I'm not wondering,' Olivia said quietly, fixing her eyes on the factory chimneys away in the distance. No man before had ever asked her to sleep with him. Even Harry Wicks hadn't had the gall to bluntly come out with that. Yet she was apprehensively awaiting her first proposition from a man whom lots of girls would give their eye-teeth to nab. But not her ... so perhaps she was unique after all.

'I've got a girlfriend,' he said.

'I've got a boyfriend,' Olivia blurted, feeling a fraud. Joe Hunter wasn't her boyfriend ... or even just a friend any more. And she felt melancholy about that and wished she could stop thinking about him.

'Does your father know?'

Olivia frowned. 'I reckon you know the answer to that. Are you going to tell him?'

'Why would I do that?'

'Don't know.' She shrugged, feeling chastened.

'When I said I had a girlfriend – it's nothing serious.'

'You mean, she won't mind if you cheat on her.' Olivia watched children playing with a hoop. One of the little boys had taken a tumble chasing it down the hill and had started howling.

'She might but it's nothing to do with her.'

'But it is to do with me. Best to let you know now, before

205

you say any more, that you should be nicer to your girlfriend because I'm not going to bed with you.'

'Why not? Do you like being a factory girl?' There was no change in his tone; he didn't seem either put out or inclined to persuade her.

'Not sure what you mean … I'll be a factory girl if I do or don't say yes. Got to earn a living after all.' Olivia tilted back her head to read his expression.

'You wouldn't need to work. You certainly couldn't stay at Barratt's.'

A full minute passed before Olivia fully digested what he'd said. 'You're going to *sack* me?' she demanded in outrage and sprang to her feet. She'd not expected him to be mean enough to do that if she turned him down. 'I can see now why you wouldn't promise to be my knight in shining armour. At least you're honest!'

She automatically started to march back towards his car then changed direction and struck off down the hill, expecting that from courtesy at least he'd drive up and offer her a lift back to the factory. But when she glanced over her shoulder she saw Lucas was still lounging on the bench, arms slung along the back of it. He was watching her with narrowed eyes, an unfathomable expression on his face. The idea that she might have to return and tell her father he hadn't got a job, and what's more, she wasn't sure she had either, was making Olivia's heart batter against her ribs.

She came to a halt then slowly turned and walked back to stand in front of him. 'I'm not going to let you make me act like a daft kid over this. You might be a lot older than me and richer than me but you're no better than me. And you won't make me do something I don't want to do.'

He gestured for her to carry on when she fell silent.

'I told you I had a boyfriend ... but I don't.'

'I know.'

'How do you know?' Olivia demanded, indignant.

'You wouldn't dare to in case your father found out, would you?'

'There is somebody I like, though,' she admitted hoarsely.

'Never mind. You'll forget him. Soon you'll like me.'

'You're very conceited.' She'd heard the note of self-mockery in his voice and found herself suppressing a smile. 'So ... it'd be nice to be friends, if that's enough for you. But if you sack me over this then I'll know I've had a lucky escape from even being your friend.'

'I'm not going to sack you.'

Olivia beamed at him. 'I wouldn't have asked you about going as a roller-out at all but Miss Wallis just ignored me when I spoke to her. Also my dad needs a job at the factory 'cos we can't make ends meet with him doing just market work. I know he's done something stupid but he's been loyal to Barratt's and he did have a good record for ages before that. He deserves a second chance, and as you put him off, I reckon you should take him back.' She came to a breathless halt, having poured out her heart.

'We came for a walk on the grass, so let's do that.' Lucas got to his feet suddenly, making her step backwards rather than collide with him. Taking her hand, he rested it on his arm and they set off, strolling between picnickers with tartan rugs, and children dashing to and fro, playing with their toys.

'Tell me about the boy you like,' Lucas said.

'No, I won't.'

'I told you about my girlfriend.'

'No, you didn't! Well, no more than that she sounds like a bloody fool to put up with you,' Olivia muttered.

He laughed. 'You really don't like me, do you? Shame about that.'

'I didn't say so. It's just . . . I don't know or understand you. We're from different worlds.'

'We work at the same place. And I'm offering you a chance to get to know me.'

'No, you're not. You're offering me a way to get into trouble. And you don't want me to know you better.' She gazed up at his profile. 'It's not just me, is it? You don't want anybody to know you. I bet even your girlfriend hasn't got a clue what you're really like.'

'Perhaps, Miss Olivia Bone, you know me better than you think.' He came to a stop and took her hand from his arm, cradling it in his long fingers. He turned up his face to the sky, squinting at the sun peeping from behind a dark cloud as the first fat raindrops fell. 'Time to go back.'

Lucas made for the path and Olivia trotted to keep up with his long stride as all around people started packing away their things and calling to their children. Once seated in the Austin he started the ignition at once, lighting up a cigarette as he drove rather fast, and in silence, towards Wood Green.

Despite Olivia murmuring that it would be better if he let her walk back from the factory as it wasn't raining hard, he took her straight home. She sensed anger beneath his calm exterior so didn't make much of it when he braked outside her door, drawling, 'Who's going to object? Your father?'

Olivia bit her lip at his steely sarcasm. But she wasn't done yet. She'd done nothing wrong although she regretted having lied about having a boyfriend and storming off in the park, making herself seem childish. If it had been an innocent day out instead of one spoiled by underlying tension she knew she would have enjoyed Lucas's company. She would have asked him about his early years and why he'd disliked his schooldays when she had cherished hers as being the best time of her life.

'Would you at least ask your secretary to contact me about changing departments? If there aren't any vacancies at the moment I'll put my name down for one,' Olivia said to him.

'She will speak to you tomorrow.' He got out immediately the car drew up and came round to open her door.

'Right,' Olivia said with a contented sigh. 'And as for my dad . . .'

'And as for him . . . don't push your luck, Olivia Bone,' Lucas interrupted with a dangerous smile before getting back into the driver's seat.

'Thanks . . . 'bye,' she called, wondering if he'd even heard her.

Lucas didn't acknowledge her gratitude although he raised a hand in farewell before driving off.

'Ooh . . . he's nice, Olivia. Friend of yours?'

Ethel Cook had peeked from behind her curtain on hearing a motor outside. Seeing Olivia getting out of a fancy car, accompanied by a handsome fellow, she'd quickly grabbed a broom and emerged from her house despite the light drizzle.

'Just somebody from the factory. He and Dad know one another.' Olivia didn't want her neighbour to think there was any more to it than that.

Ethel approached, busily brushing the path. 'You dad's back at the factory, is he?'

'He's just waiting for a suitable job to turn up,' Olivia replied breezily.

'Good luck to him. What went on with Nelly Smith's accident's all blown over, I expect.'

The mention of Nelly immediately reminded Olivia of the

woman's abortionist relative. Cath had asked her to find out an address for the nurse. Olivia doubted there'd be a better opportunity to dig for clues. Cath was a good friend and Olivia wanted to try and oblige her if she could even though she privately thought it a risky business.

'You know Nelly's sister-in-law, don't you, Mrs Cook?' Olivia blurted, seeing that Ethel had started to push her broom back towards her front door.

'Go back a long way we do.' Ethel leaned on the broom handle, pursing her lips. 'She's a good few years younger than me but we get along all right.'

'Lives close to the hospital, does she?'

'Tottenham way.'

'Tottenham? Thought she was in Edmonton,' Olivia blurted.

'Oh ... so you've heard of Vi Smith, have you?' Mrs Cook said sharply.

'No, not really. A friend at work mentioned her. Said she lived in Edmonton, that's all.'

'Could be classed as Edmonton, I suppose. Lorenco Road's sort of on the border.'

Mrs Cook's gimlet eyes narrowed on Olivia's face before slyly studying her belly. Olivia's pulse quickened. Ethel obviously knew of Vi's illicit sideline, and Olivia didn't want her neighbour jumping to any conclusions after seeing her being brought home by a man.

'Did you know that Mrs Hunter's moved on?' Olivia hoped to distract Ethel. 'She's gone to live with her daughter. Dad wants the upstairs rooms back now they're free.'

'Good riddance!' Mrs Cook spat. 'Never wanted her sort round here. Me daughters said they'd see her off for me. They remembered her all right.'

'Remembered her?' Olivia frowned.

Ethel pursed her lips. 'Maisie Hunter used to pester me husband, God rest him.'

'Did your daughters put that poster up about her?'

Mrs Cook set her chin, looking defensive. 'Well, if they did, I didn't ask 'em to. But I wouldn't blame 'em for doing it, 'cos it did the trick, didn't it? They're good daughters to me ...'

Olivia bit her tongue to stop a blunt comment rolling off it. They were so *good* those daughters that they didn't even bring their mum in a bit of shopping, or help her do her laundry. It seemed all they were good for was showing up a woman their father had paid for sex.

'How's Nancy doing with your washing?' Olivia said pointedly. Whatever Joe's mum was, the woman had been fair to her so Olivia wouldn't run her down behind her back.

'Been meaning to say ... any chance you could take over again?' Ethel patted Olivia's arm. 'Ain't complaining 'cos I know Nancy's still young and learning but me sheets were full of creases this week.'

'I'll speak to her ... better step inside before we get drenched.' Olivia hurried away, hoping she'd given Ethel enough to think about to make the woman forget she'd asked for Vi Smith's whereabouts.

Ethel Cook wasn't the only person who'd seen the car go past. Such sightings were few and far between in Ranelagh Road and Harry Wicks had twitched the parlour curtain aside to get a better look at the Austin roadster. When he saw who got out of it his expression turned savage.

Even when Olivia was still at school he'd fancied her but she'd always turned down his invitations to walk out. Now he understood why that was; she was hanging out for the good life.

Everybody in the street knew that the Bone kids had a hard time with their old man. Harry had thought that Olivia would jump at an offer to get engaged and move away to her own place. Maggie had told him straight out she couldn't wait to leave home. But Harry wasn't giving up yet on getting the sister he *really* wanted.

Maggie had opened up to him and said a few things that had puzzled Harry. He'd known that Maisie Hunter had lived upstairs from the Bones, but he hadn't realised that the woman had a son named Joe who'd showed up once in a blue moon, and once taken Olivia to the flicks and bought her chocolates. Harry had put two and two together and come up with the identity of the bloke who'd beaten him on Christmas Eve. He'd been trying to find Joe Hunter to get his own back. He'd had no luck tracking him down although he had heard a bit about the fellow being a villain. Now Maisie had moved on it was unlikely Hunter would come back ... unless he was after Olivia.

If she had also discovered what Hunter was like she'd have frozen him out; her father would kill her if he knew she'd been knocking about with him. But ... Harry couldn't help but wonder if the fancy man who'd just driven off was a punter Hunter had got for her.

Bitterly, he acknowledged that with her looks she probably could hook herself a nob who'd keep her in style. As the fellow had rolled up to her door bold as brass she might even have found one who'd marry her.

He watched the car pass his window on its way out of the street, getting a good look at the driver's aquiline profile. Harry let the curtain fall and stood grimacing at the floorboards. If the crafty tart had her hands in a rich man's pockets she could afford to give him back his five bob ... and replace the shirt she'd torn defending her slag of a sister.

So, he'd keep a lookout for Olivia Bone and remind her of that.

212

Olivia entered the parlour to find her two sisters gazing at her expectantly.

'How did it go?' Nancy asked dreamily. 'Are you getting engaged?'

Olivia burst out laughing. 'You've been reading too many romance novels.'

'Any chance of asking him if I can have a job at the factory?'

'Not you as well!' Olivia muttered in exasperation.

'Will Dad get his job back?' Alfie's large eyes appealed to his sister to make it true. He knew that the more content his father felt about things, the better it would be for Alfie. He still got sweets occasionally and was coming to trust his father not to hit him for the slightest thing.

'Is Dad in?'

'Yeah ... unfortunately,' Nancy mumbled and pointed her thumb at their father's bedroom.

Tommy had noiselessly appeared in the doorway. His bedroom was situated at the front of the house and when he'd heard the car pull up he'd stirred himself from his inebriated haze. Rolling off the bed, he'd pattered over to peep from behind the curtain. He'd been disappointed to see that the couple parted almost immediately with barely a smile passing between them. He wasn't daft, he knew what the fellow was after. But he knew his Livvie; she was a good girl, sweet and honest, and she'd keep her knees together until a ring was on her finger. Tommy wished Maggie took after her big sister. But Livvie was like her mother, whereas Maggie was like her aunt Sybil – trouble. He knew that Maggie could get herself in bother at any time.

'So ... any news for me?' Tommy saw that Olivia had spotted him in the doorway. 'Did he say I could have a job?'

'He didn't say you couldn't. He's going to get his secretary to speak to me next week,' Olivia said evasively.

Tommy's lips turned down and he scratched his belly over his vest. 'Have to wait and see then.' He eyed her from head to toe. 'You weren't gone long.'

'Started to rain . . . anyway I wanted to get back and help get tea ready.' Olivia started undoing her hat, letting her fair hair loose. 'I'm going to get out of these good things or they'll be ruined.'

Chapter Seventeen

The summer holidays had come to a close with warm sunny September days mocking the children pulling on their drab school uniforms. Nancy and Alfie had set off later than the other kids who'd trooped up the road with books under their arms on the first day of term.

Alfie had wet the bed, making Olivia also late leaving home for the factory. She had been cross with him as she stripped the sheets and bundled them into Nancy's arms for her to dump in the washhouse. They'd need to be rinsed and pegged out to dry as soon as Nancy got in and that had started her sister moaning. Olivia felt guilty for having shouted at Alfie, but she also felt sorry for Nancy, burdened with chores after school. Any disturbance to their routine was greatly felt now that she was working full-time and the housework was irregularly attended to. Alfie had turned eight and he had to learn to wake himself up to use the chamber pot.

Their father seemed to have accepted at first that he'd have to wait a while longer for a job at Barratt's but as the weeks passed by with no news, he'd become impatient. He'd seemed resentful when Olivia had told him that Miss Wallis had interviewed her and given her a job that brought in an extra half a crown a week. Olivia knew it wouldn't take much for Tommy to vent his disappointment on his young son.

As Olivia hurriedly turned the corner into Mayes Road she saw Cath waiting for her at the factory gates. She missed her friend's company during the day now she'd moved to the production line, but they usually met up during their dinner break.

'Got a mo, Livvie?'

''Course,' Olivia said, a trifle breathless from walking so fast.

Cath looked a bit awkward as she linked arms with Olivia and steered her to a spot away from the workers thronging the factory entrance.

'What is it?'

'Got enough saved now. I'm going to see Vi Smith this week.'

Olivia had passed on to her friend Vi's whereabouts. Since then the weeks had rolled on and Olivia hadn't said any more about it, sensing Cath didn't want her to. 'You went to Lorenco Road and made an appointment?' Olivia could tell from the tiny bump inflating her friend's pinafore that Cath couldn't hang on any longer over making a decision.

She nodded. 'Didn't tell her me real name. I'm Mrs Bellamy. She didn't believe me, of course, but said to come back Friday evening and she'll do it.'

'You're really sure . . . ?' Olivia's voice tailed off. She'd aired her thoughts about this plenty of times before.

'No,' Cath said forlornly. 'But I've no choice, have I?'

Olivia smiled sympathetically. Cath was adamant she wanted to keep working and saving for her own place before she got married. Olivia didn't blame her one bit; Cath would be stuck forever living with her in-laws if she had the baby now.

'Vi said to bring somebody with me in case I feel rough afterwards and need helping home.'

"Course I'll come,' Olivia said gently. 'If you're brave enough to go, I wouldn't be much of a friend if I didn't offer to come and hold your hand.'

Cath clasped Olivia to her, smearing tears onto her friend's shoulder. 'Thanks, Livvie,' she snuffled. 'I hate having to ask but there's nobody else I trust or who'd understand.' She wiped her face with a hanky.

'Well, you've got me, and you can trust me, swear on it.' Olivia patted her friend's shoulder. 'Come on then . . . inside or we'll be fined,' she bossed in a jolly way, trying try to cheer Cath up.

*

'You're one of Tommy Bone's gels then, ain't yer? He's got three daughters and a son, so I heard.'

'That's right, I'm the eldest.' Olivia barely glanced up from the pungent paste she was kneading to keep it pliable. As a novice roller-out she'd learned that the work required her fierce concentration. The warm mixture cooled quickly and once it became too hard to be shaped it wasn't fit to be used. And waste was not liked. She'd found it difficult to judge the size of the sweets: shaping aniseed balls speedily by hand to a certain circumference required accuracy and dexterity, and she hadn't yet mastered either. But she'd had it drummed into her that the company needed to keep the cost of materials to a minimum if they were to continue giving their young customers what they wanted – value for money. Without healthy profits being returned they were all at risk of losing their jobs, or at the very least their September share-out. And nobody wanted that.

Olivia was seated at the workbench but she knew that Nelly Smith continued to hover by her shoulder, watching her work. It was just her luck that the woman involved in the incident that had got her father the sack, had been made up to line supervisor. She didn't reckon it had been a coincidence that Nelly had been promoted just days after Olivia was: Deborah Wallis had done it to spite her. Deborah was jealous, believing the other girl had too much influence with their boss. Without a doubt Lucas had helped her get a step up. But his interest in her had cooled since she'd rebuffed him. She'd not spoken to him since their outing and rarely saw him, other than in the distance driving off or striding through the building. She couldn't blame him for ignoring her. She'd made it clear she'd like them to be friends ... but in her heart had known he didn't want or need her in that way. So it seemed he had simply forgotten about her. Olivia felt oddly indignant and sad because of it.

Last week she'd overheard her new colleagues chatting about him meeting clients in the north of the country. She'd been conscious of sly glances slipping her way to gauge her reaction during their discussion. But she kept poker-faced. She never spoke about Lucas Black to anybody other than Cath or her father. Tommy still constantly questioned her over whether Black had yet said there were transport vacancies that'd suit him.

'You'll need to resize them.' Nelly grabbed a handful of aniseed balls Olivia had finished and threw them back into the warming pan. 'Kids want their regular ten fer a penny not seven or eight big 'uns instead. Get it right or I'll have to tell Miss Wallis you're not up to the job.' As Nelly walked away Olivia saw a couple of girls further down the bench smirking at her.

It wasn't as friendly an atmosphere here as in packing but at least Cath had given her a warm welcome to Barratt's. Olivia geed herself up with the thought that she didn't need people to take a shine to her; she just wanted to earn enough to get her own place and take the kids with her. When she got home she'd say sorry for being short with Alfie that morning. She worried incessantly about whether he would do something to attract her father's wrath while she wasn't there. Alfie fretted about it too, even when he was asleep, and that was why he wet the bed. He was a child who even when laughing was never completely free from fear. She had seen him jump up from a game of cards at the sound of footsteps outside in the street, just because they sounded like his father's. He would scurry into the bedroom and stay there even if Tommy didn't materialise in the parlour. It broke her heart that Alfie's young mind would hold such memories of terror throughout his life.

Lucas had said she was unhappy; at the time she'd thought he didn't know what he was talking about . . . but perhaps he did.

'Your dad never spoke much about his family.'

Nelly had come back to lean over Olivia's shoulder, shouting in her ear to be heard over the clang of the machinery in the background. So far, Olivia had managed to avoid being drawn by anybody into a lengthy conversation about her father, and she intended to keep it that way.

'Just want to say, weren't me lost yer dad his job, y'know,' Nelly carried on, undeterred by Olivia's bowed head. 'It was his own silly fault, what happened.'

'All water under the bridge now.' Olivia barely glanced over her shoulder. With Nelly so close to her she'd had to incline closer to the pan full of aniseed mixture and she held her breath to keep the strong smell from attacking the back of her throat.

'Heard Tommy's after coming back,' Nelly said. 'If he does, he'd better make sure he's not so clumsy. Weren't the only accident he caused, y'know. He got off lightly.' She added slyly, "Course, if you've got friends in high places it makes a difference, don't it?'

Olivia swung about to snap at Nelly to spit it out if she'd got something to say, but the bell for dinner break sounded and Nelly immediately trotted off. A supervisor now, perhaps, but the woman wasn't one to surrender a minute of her own time to the company. As Olivia passed Nelly's desk she saw that a knot of women had gathered.

'You coming to the rally?' One of them turned to Olivia but others scowled as though disagreeing with the invitation.

'She's the boss's nark. Don't go telling her nuthin',' called out one of the girls who'd been talking about her earlier.

Olivia ignored the comment. 'What rally?' she asked, moving closer to the friendly woman she believed was named Sal.

'Mrs Pankhurst's giving another speech about the German Peril,' Sal replied.

'I'm right behind her! Should be rounding up all o' them foreigners and putting them behind bars,' a woman yelled.

'They'll be getting our brave boys over there killed.' Another, harsher voice spoke up. 'My Ralph's already been wounded at Mons. I'll go and hand out leaflets ... as many as you like.' The woman shook her fist. 'Need all the Hun put where they can't do no harm or they'll be up telegraph poles, cutting wires, and doin' all the spying and sabotage they can think of, the wicked buggers.'

There was a lot of bad feeling now towards immigrants. The Bavarian butcher by Turnpike Lane had had his windows smashed yet he'd been living locally for over a decade. He'd been naturalised and had declared himself to be against the

Kaiser but still people congregated outside his shop, demanding he and his sons be interned.

'You turning up?' Sal asked Olivia. 'It's Hyde Park on Sunday afternoon.'

'Can't get away ... got housework to catch up on. Thanks anyway.' Olivia gave an apologetic smile and carried on outside to meet Cath. But her thoughts were still with what the women had said. In common with others she'd hoped to remain untouched by the conflict fought on foreign soil. But everybody was feeling more anxious now reports were filtering back about Allied casualties and German victories. The Battle of Mons had been lost and few were now under the illusion that the war was a forgone conclusion, with an Allied victory by Christmas.

Sympathy for the Belgian refugees who'd arrived was already wearing thin. At first they'd been welcomed as poor victims of dreadful atrocities. But attitudes were changing. People with very little themselves were feeling resentful, especially as a lot of the newcomers didn't seem friendly or grateful for the hand-outs they were getting.

'Going to nip home today in me break – got sheets to wash to put on the bed tonight,' Olivia told Cath as they met outside.

Her friend looked surprised but gave her a cheerful smile. Olivia set off walking quickly, confident she'd have time to rinse the linen and get it pegged on the line before afternoon shift started. It would save Nancy the job after school, and on such a lovely day it was likely the washing would soon blow dry. She rubbed together her palms, gritty with sugary mixture that stuck like glue to her skin. She'd need to scrub them before touching the sheets.

Harry Wicks was also on his dinner break and had been about to put his key in his lock and go indoors when he spotted Olivia. In the mornings she and Maggie usually set off together for work so he'd not had an opportunity to catch her on her own and demand the money he felt he was owed. He ducked down behind the hedge, realising he had a perfect opportunity to ambush her.

'Got the sack and been sent home, have yer?' He'd run up silently behind her.

'Get lost,' Olivia snapped, swinging round to face him. 'You're lucky I've not had the law on you.'

'Ain't my fault your sister likes me,' he jeered, pushing his face close to Olivia's. 'Anyhow ... who's showed Maggie them sweet tricks – you?' He crowded her close to the hedge so she'd barely any pavement to walk on. 'Keeping that rich boyfriend of yours happy, I bet ... '

'You shut your mouth about my sister! She's just a kid.' Olivia forced him away, realising he must have seen her weeks ago being dropped off by Lucas to be speaking of a rich boyfriend. Her eyes were blazing as she recalled the row her father had had with Mr Silver. Their landlord had been abrupt every time she'd paid the rent since ... but he'd not made a snide remark about Maggie. And nobody had yet taken Maisie's old rooms upstairs.

'Ain't finished with you yet.' Harry yanked Olivia back as she would have shoved past him. He opened his jacket, displaying his torn shirt. 'You can cough up for that. Eleven bob I want for a new one. And I'm still waiting for me five bob I lent you months ago for that window pane.'

'You're lucky a torn shirt's all you got for what you did. Anyway, haven't got it, and even if I had, I wouldn't give you it.'

'Get it off your fancy man ... or I'll make it me business to find out who he is and tell him a few things about you I'll bet he don't know.' Harry chuckled lewdly. 'Or perhaps he *likes* it that you're mixed up with a ponce ... '

Olivia turned white, staring at the leering face just inches from hers. 'Haven't got a boyfriend and I don't know what you're talking about,' she lied in a hoarse voice.

'I reckon you do know what I'm on about.' Harry sounded triumphant. He'd read in her face that she knew exactly what Joe Hunter did for a living. 'Meet me later in the hut at eight o'clock ... or I'll let everybody know you're a part-time tart with a pimp.'

He made to saunter off, grinning, but Olivia gripped his arm. 'If you've got something to say, you can say it now.'

'Go up the alley then,' he hissed, grabbing her wrist. Quickly he glanced about but the street was quiet. On Monday most of the women were out the back in the washhouses. There was nobody to see what went on.

Olivia wrestled her arm free but went with him because she desperately wanted to know what he thought he knew about her and Joe. 'Can't stop ... me dad's waiting for me.' She implied that Tommy was indoors but Harry just laughed, pushing her back against the wall.

'Ain't got to worry about that, darlin'. Saw your old man go out first thing,' he goaded. 'So let's be cosy. I could get you into big trouble if I wanted.' He grabbed both her hands then pinned them back against the wall by her head. Feeling the sugar on her fingers he leaned closer to lick at it, holding her eyes with his as his long tongue swiped her skin. 'Taste good, don't yer ... aniseed balls ... love 'em.' He moved his tongue to her ear, circling it then whispering, 'Bet you taste good everywhere ... '

'Get off me!' Olivia forced out through her teeth, feeling sick. Despite her disgust she was conscious she must not draw attention to them.

He pounced to kiss her and Olivia kicked his shin, squirming free as his hold loosened. She could tell he'd no intention of talking and there wasn't any point in appealing to his better nature.

Harry Wicks didn't have a decent bone in his body. She made to dart past him, furious with herself for letting him delay her. He moved to stop her and she crashed into him, instinctively swinging a small fist. She caught him on the cheek and Harry reflexively hit back, knocking her down.

'You deserved that, you silly bitch,' he said. But he could see he'd made her bleed and he turned away hurriedly and jogged off.

Olivia dragged herself to her feet, using the wall to support her shaking limbs. Her head was thumping but she managed to keep her face lowered and, thankfully, arrived at her door without having met a soul. Inside, she collapsed onto a chair at the parlour table and cupped her throbbing forehead in her palms. Feeling a warm trickle on her chin she scrubbed at it with her hanky, blinking back tears of pain and frustration.

What a fool she'd been to have allowed that to happen! Harry would have walked on if she hadn't stopped him because she'd wanted to find out what he knew. Probably it was nothing more than that he had discovered the name of the fellow who'd floored him on Christmas Eve. For all his bluster the bully wouldn't spread dirt on her in case it got out that she'd caught him interfering with her fourteen-year-old sister. Harry was counting on her to keep her mouth shut so Maggie stayed out of trouble, and it infuriated Olivia that he was quite right on that score. They were caught in a pact of silence with neither trusting the other not to break it.

Olivia made herself a cup of tea. Almost as soon as the leaves were wet she lifted the pot with shaking hands and poured out a cup, drinking the weak tea in long gulps before it was properly brewed. She rinsed the cup and put it away then went into her bedroom and stared at her reflection in the spotted mirror hanging on the wall. With her bloodied hanky she dabbed gingerly at the torn skin on her lips, soothing the wound with her tongue. It wasn't too bad, she convinced herself. If a bruise did come up it wouldn't be until tomorrow. The injury would have to be explained away as a mishap. Tidying her straggly locks into the hairpins at her nape, she let herself out of the house. She bitterly regretted having come home at all because she'd not helped Maggie with the washing. She'd no time now to do the sheets or she'd be late for afternoon shift and be fined again. If she had stayed with Cath, sitting on the wall in the sunshine and eating her dinner, she'd have avoided Harry Wicks.

Chapter Eighteen

'That's your cousin's friend waiting for you, ain't it?'

Cath had drawn Olivia's attention to a man by the factory gate. As they locked eyes Olivia felt her cheeks burn. She knew for sure Joe wanted to speak to her when he jerked his head.

'Oh ... blast ... I've forgotten me shopping bag. Left it under the bench Better nip back and get it. You carry on. See you tomorrow,' Cath continued.

It wasn't the first time that she had started off home at the end of the day then realised she'd got to go back to collect something. But Olivia had never given it much thought and she didn't now. She was just thankful her friend had disappeared so she could meet Joe alone. He'd crossed the road, stopping at a secluded spot close to where he'd parked his horse and cart. Olivia hurried to catch up with him.

'How've you been?' He'd spoken while his face was lowered to a match cupped in his palm. When he glanced up his eyes immediately focused on her cut lip. 'What's happened to you?' he demanded, blowing smoke from the corner of his mouth.

'Took a tumble earlier today,' she quickly explained, unconsciously touching her injury. 'Clumsy cow I am.' She glanced about but was fairly confident her father wouldn't be in the vicinity.

'You had an accident at work?'

'Did it at home ... out in the washhouse.'

When she'd got back from her dinner break her supervisor's beady eyes had gone straight to the injury. Nelly hadn't been convinced by the lie any more than Joe appeared to be. As for Cath, she'd clucked over her friend so much that Olivia had started to feel guilty that she'd concocted such a convincing tale about having slipped on soapy water, bashing her face on the mangle.

'If you're thinking my father has hit me, he hasn't,' she said to Joe flatly.

'Somebody has.'

'You can't know that for sure,' Olivia retorted. Impatiently she changed the subject. 'How've you been?'

'Better than you by the looks of things. What really happened? Did your father lose his rag again?'

'No! I told you ... '

'Don't lie to me, Livvie. D'you think a man like me doesn't know how to spot a woman who's had a smack in the mouth?'

'It wasn't my dad!' she exclaimed in exasperation.

'Wicks?'

Olivia blinked. She'd hoped he wouldn't mention that name.

'So it was him, was it?' Joe said through his teeth. 'I told you to come and find me if he didn't stop bothering you.'

'I can look after myself ... '

'Yeah ... can see that.'

Olivia ignored his sarcasm. 'I don't want you causing trouble,' she said heatedly. 'My sister's been acting stupid with Harry.' She gestured. 'It won't take much to start him blabbing, then God knows what me dad'll do.'

'What d'you mean ... *acting stupid?'*

She felt flustered but oddly believed that she could confide in him about Maggie's promiscuity. 'She's just started work and is all excited about growing up. She's been playing up to Harry.'

'Likes 'em young, does he?' Joe said.

'Don't seem to matter to that randy pig how old a girl is!'

'You can't let him get away with it. He'll be sniffing around your sister again and walloping you if you try to stop him.'

Olivia had already come to the conclusion that Harry wouldn't leave her alone now he thought he had something to blackmail her with. But she knew if Joe went after him it'd make matters worse.

'Harry'll lose interest in Maggie now she knows not to encourage him.' It was a lame remark and Olivia changed the subject. 'Your mum paid me back before she left to stay with your sister. I miss Maisie now she's gone.' Olivia realised it was true. They hadn't been bosom pals but there had been a promise of friendship between them.

'Want a smoke?' Joe offered the battered pack of Players.

Olivia had noticed a tightness in his features after she'd mentioned his family. 'Don't smoke, thanks. You never mentioned you had a sister.'

He gestured an offhand apology, squinting into the distance.

'Why not?' she asked when it became apparent he'd not elaborate. 'Did the two of you not get on?'

'I loved her,' he said hoarsely. 'She was a sweet kid.'

Olivia silently digested what he'd said and it left her feeling shocked. 'I thought your sister was an adult ... perhaps older than you ... with her own place. When Maisie said she was off to stay with her daughter, that's what I thought,' she murmured.

A small movement of his head indicated that he understood her confusion; he stood grimacing at the pavement as though composing himself. 'She was twelve,' he finally said gruffly. 'She's dead now ... so's my mum. I come over to tell you about Maisie.'

'What?' Olivia burst out after a moment of dumbstruck silence. 'Was there an accident?'

'Sort of ... yeah ... an accident.' Joe pressed his fingers to the bridge of his nose. 'Me sister Annie ... she wasn't well. Always knew she'd not make old bones, but thought she'd get past twelve.' He dragged deeply on the cigarette. 'Mum must've known it was hopeless for the poor little love. She tried to tell me, I think. She came round mine when I was out and put a message through the door saying she wanted to talk to me about Annie. I never got in touch, though ... just thought it was another one of her crafty ways to get me to shell out for her medicine, as she called it. We'd stopped speaking by then.'

'You fell out because of me.' Olivia sounded distraught. 'I asked her if she was going to stay with you when she left Wood Green. She reckoned you wouldn't let her through the door.'

Joe's fingers pinched harder. 'Yeah, we fell out 'cos of you. I wish we hadn't. Stupid of me to cut her out like that.'

'What was wrong with Annie?' Olivia asked hesitantly.

'She was damaged when she was a baby. Last thing the bastard did before he run out on us was hurt her.'

'Your father injured her?' Olivia gasped.

'Herbie Hunter wasn't her father, he's mine. Annie's father was a punter that Herbie brought home, along with all the others.' Joe lit another cigarette from the stub dying between his fingers. 'He thought it was his kid when Maisie first told him;

229

when the baby was born he knew damned well it wasn't being as Annie was dark-skinned. He beat the shit out of me mum because she wanted to keep her daughter.'

Olivia's eyes widened in horror. 'He hurt the baby too?'

'One afternoon, when Mum was out shopping, Annie wouldn't stop crying. He'd had a skinful that dinnertime. He took her out of the pram and threw her at the wall.' Joe's back teeth ground together as he relived memories that were too painful to put into words.

'You were there, watching?' Olivia sounded aghast, touching his arm in comfort.

'I put a poker over his head before he could hurt me little sister again. He went down but not for long then come after me instead. But I was eight and could run. I found me mum and she went for him too. Never heard screaming and shouting like it. All the neighbours joined in. He'd scarpered by the time the police turned up. Ain't clapped eyes on him since, thank the Lord. If I ever do, I'll kill him.'

'I . . . I don't know what to say, Joe,' Olivia mumbled through the lump in her throat.

They stood facing each other in the early-evening sunlight. The road was quiet. While they'd been talking the factory had emptied, leaving them the only visible figures. Olivia realised she should go home. They'd all be wondering where on earth she was. But she couldn't. She felt that Joe needed her as much as her family did. And she wanted to stay and help him, as at times he'd helped her.

'Your mum went away a lot . . . she'd never say where she'd been. I wasn't being nosy asking . . . just thought she'd been on holiday, that's all.'

'Annie was in a sanatorium. Nuns were looking after her in Cambridge. Mum went there as often as she could. The cost of the fares and the guesthouses she stayed in took most of my money. But I didn't begrudge paying for those trips. I went too sometimes. But then ...'

'But then what?' Olivia probed gently.

'Mum started getting ill as well. She was an addict. She'd been giving Annie laudanum from when she was tiny, to soothe her. She started taking it herself. Just small doses at first. But she couldn't stop herself taking more and more and the money she wanted from me was as much for that as the trips to see Annie; she'd sooner have drugs than gin in the end. She always stayed at the same place in Cambridge. The landlord found her dead from laudanum the same day that Annie died.'

'I think she knew what she was going to do.' Olivia's voice quavered with distress. 'Last time I ever spoke to her, she said she'd be staying with her daughter for good.'

'Yeah ... she knew it was the end. Wish I'd been different with her ... kinder ...'

Olivia hugged him as she glimpsed the tears sparkling on his lashes. 'They're at peace together ... I know they are.'

'The fellow from the guesthouse was good enough to turn up at me door to tell me what'd gone on and bring back her things. Me mum'd wrote me a letter and addressed the envelope, you see. She left something for you too.' He dug in a pocket.

Olivia took the envelope, knowing immediately what it contained because she could feel the locket through the paper. She slipped it out of sight. 'It's my mum's locket. I used to wear it on a chain round me neck till I lost it.'

'You're lucky you got it back; she must've pawned it rather than sold it.' Joe paused, his hazel eyes narrowing on a spot behind Olivia. 'Who's that watching us?'

While they'd been embracing a car had driven into the empty courtyard of the factory. The driver had been observing them

231

through the windscreen. He got out of the car and unlocked the building then disappeared inside.

'He's Lucas Black, one of the bosses,' Olivia said hoarsely as she glanced over a shoulder. She turned her attention back to Joe. 'I'm so sorry about what's happened. I wish I could help in some way. It must be horrible for you.'

'You can help, Livvie. Just let me see you, that's all I want. Just being able to talk to you ... look at you ... it's enough.' He sounded diffident.

'I ... I don't know, Joe. What you've been involved in ... if my dad found out ...' she awkwardly explained.

'I don't do that now. I'm no pimp ... never was in my heart. It wasn't what I wanted ... just where life took me, that's all.'

'I don't know enough about you yet.'

'You don't trust me, you mean. What d'you want to know?' He spoke harshly, prowling away from her while lighting another cigarette. 'What got me into it? Easy answer ... I grew up surrounded by half-naked women, and men who'd be undoing their trousers following them up the stairs. One of them was my mother, but strange as it seems, it was better living in that brothel.' He had a faraway look in his eyes but soon snapped himself out of it. 'Then my father took us away from there to a poxy room where he could keep all her earnings for himself. Made me feel nostalgic for the whorehouse, I can tell you.' He barked a bitter laugh. 'Some of those women were all right. I'd run their errands and they'd feed me when she forgot to.' He dropped the half-smoked cigarette and ground it out beneath his boot. 'By the time Herbie Hunter scarpered Mum was getting old and fat. Still she wouldn't quit.' Joe paused. 'Me dad would tell her it was all she was fit for and even after he'd gone she believed it. I left school before I was thirteen and got a job in a warehouse, then in the evenings I'd go out with her and do

me best to keep her safe. I got knocked black and blue at first ...
when I was young.' He slanted a brief look at Olivia. 'Then I
grew bigger and learned to fight. That's why the girls come to
me to look out for them. That's how it started.'

Olivia nodded, rage tearing at her throat and keeping her
quiet as she dwelled on the horribleness of life. But she felt pity
too for Joe although she knew he wouldn't want it. She couldn't
fling her arms around him again because he'd get the wrong
idea ... think she was agreeing to them getting together. She
had her own burdensome family ties and couldn't yet shake
them off, for him or anybody.

Joe laughed grimly and cocked his head at the factory. 'That's
the boss whose eye you've caught, is it?'

Olivia frowned, then flushed as enlightenment dawned. She
recalled Cath having said something similar to her pop when
they'd all met by chance that day.

'Don't worry,' Joe said quietly, shoving his hands into his
pockets. 'Don't blame you ... you keep him looking and get
what you can out of life, Olivia Bone. You deserve it. You
deserve more than me, that's fer sure.'

He strode off towards his cart and much as Olivia wanted to
run after him and tell him it wasn't like that between her and
her boss ... she didn't. She couldn't lie. She had gone out with
Lucas and even though nothing other than an intimate conversation had passed between them, more would have happened
if she'd allowed it to.

She'd warmed to Joe even more now; a pang of tenderness
unfurled in her belly when she dwelled on the hardship he'd
endured as a small boy. But she couldn't promise him anything.
She didn't want to give him false hope. And she was very overdue getting home to her family.

Chapter Nineteen

'What's up with yer, Tom? Christmas'll be here 'fore yer know it. You'll need the extra lolly, won't you?' Bill Morley had shoved his face close to Tommy's bristly cheek as they leaned against the bar in the pub. He'd been trying to persuade Tommy to go for another sortie over the factory wall. But Tommy wasn't having any of it. 'You spooked? You'd better tell me if you've heard summat.'

'Ain't spooked . . . ain't heard nothing. Just looking out for me daughter. Livvie's got her better job now and I don't want her losing it 'cos of me.' Tommy took a swig of beer, wiping his lips with the back of his hand.

'No reason why she should, mate,' Bill soothed him. 'I've kept me eyes and ears open in the factory and nobody suspects a thing.' He tapped his nose. 'Black's not about much lately he's in talks up Birmingham way with a chocolate maker. Anyhow, if anybody do get suspicious, we'll get your gel to sweet-talk him. Everybody knows he's got a soft spot for Livvie Bone . . .'

'What you implying?' Tommy bared his tobacco-stained teeth, grabbing his friend's shoulder.

'Nothing like that, Tom,' Bill protested. 'Just that Black's been spotted talking to her down the High Street. You know he's never been one to show an interest in the factory gels, so people have took notice.' Bill nudged Tommy in the ribs. 'Personally I reckon that Miss Wallis is more his sort. Wouldn't mind a crack at her, eh?'

'She can't hold a candle to my Livvie for looks.' Tommy jutted his chin proudly as he upended his glass into his mouth.

'Yeah, but Miss Wallis is more . . . ' Bill let the description tail away. He knew whatever he said would offend. Tommy Bone was an unpredictable bleeder, and moody. Bill wished now that he'd not felt sorry for him all those months ago when he'd lost his job. He'd thought he'd been doing the man a good turn, bringing him in on the pilfering. He'd given him a way to get back at the management for sacking him because the accident had been as much Nelly's fault. But now Tommy's attitude was that *he* was the one doing the favour. Bill reckoned that things had changed once Olivia started at Barratt's and got cosy with the boss. Now Tommy seemed to think he was sitting pretty. But nobody believed that anything serious was on the cards there. And if it ever got out what sort of company the girl was keeping, Black wouldn't want anything to do with her . . . officially. In fact it was likely she'd be given the sack; Barratt's liked to think they ran a respectable ship.

Tommy had been expecting Bill to conclude his opinion of the secretary so when he remained quiet and sank his face into his tankard, he found his own interpretation. 'You saying my gel's not in the same class as that Miss Wallis?' Tommy snorted. 'My Livvie could work in an office, if she wanted – she's bright as well as pretty.' He shoved his glass over the beer-slopped bar, crooking a finger at the landlord for a refill.

''Course she could, mate,' Bill smarmed.

'So … I ain't getting involved in any more midnight trips down Mayes Road. And as far as I'm concerned I never knew nothing about any of it.' He thumped his friend on the shoulder. 'Wouldn't never grass anybody up over it, though. So you carry on if you want to.' He nodded at Bill's empty glass. 'Same again?'

'*Ain't grassing me up?* That's big of yer!' Bill spat out in a furious, suffocated voice. He reckoned he deserved to be thanked not patronised. He glowered at his pal, undulating his shoulder so Tommy's hand slipped away. He wanted to swipe the smirk off his chops, and he knew a way to do it. Before he could stop himself he blurted, 'Been meaning to say … that Mrs Hunter that lives upstairs to yer, I heard she's a brass, y'know.'

'So what?' Tommy glanced about, wondering what Bill was getting at. 'She's moved on, anyhow.'

'Her son's still about, though.'

'Never saw much of him,' Tommy muttered. Uneasiness was tightening his gut. He sensed Bill was about to bring up something significant, and not to his liking. He recalled that Livvie and Joe Hunter had taken Alfie out to the flicks a long while ago. He'd spotted them coming home and had gone on to make a fool of himself by falling over and knocking himself out instead of chinning Hunter. He'd woken up in bed the next morning and imagined that the fellow had put him there. Feeling embarrassed, Tommy had never again mentioned what had happened and neither had Livvie. He'd not seen Hunter about again, even visiting his mother, so Tommy had let sleeping dogs lie.

'Word to the wise,' Bill drawled. 'Make sure he *do* stay away. He's no good.' He frowned as he leaned closer. 'Wouldn't want that getting round at the factory, would yer? In case Mr Black got wrong ideas about your Olivia keeping company with ponces.'

Tommy grabbed Bill by the lapels, jerking him closer. 'What the fuck you on about? My Olivia wouldn't have nuthin' to do with somebody like that!'

'I'm only warning you for your own good, mate.' Bill wrenched himself free, coughing in air. Tommy's brooding expression had transformed into something more perilous. With a show of camaraderie Bill said, 'Come and sit down over there.' He pointed to a table by the door. 'Don't want no flapping ears picking this up, do we?'

'Just spit it out and quick about it!' Tommy snarled, clamping a hand on Bill's arm as he would have slid off the stool.

Bill wasn't sure that he wanted to say any more but it was too late to backtrack. 'Me brother-in-law's from over Islington originally. He knows some of the villains that way and told me he's seen your Olivia twice now, looking friendly with Joe Hunter ... last time was after she started working with his daughter in packing. He said he wouldn't be happy if it was his Cath knocking about with a bloke like that so reckoned I should put a word in yer ear.' Bill saw Tommy's eyes bulge in disbelief. 'Don't reckon you'd want Lucas Black knowing she's been seen out with a pimp, would yer, Tom?'

Tommy's lips had thinned so much they'd folded back against his teeth.

'Won't have another ... gotta get moving.' Bill hopped off the bar stool. Tommy hadn't commented because he was still digesting what he'd heard but when it all sank in he'd blow his top. Bill wanted to be well away when he did.

After Bill left Tommy sat quite still for some time staring at the empty glass in front of him, his lips writhing as though he were in silent conversation with himself. Slowly he heaved himself off the stool, ignoring the landlord who'd finally ambled over to refill his glass.

He went outside and leaned against the wall, pulling his collar up against a surprising evening chill, considering the warmth of the day. But the autumn evenings had drawn in and twilight was descending. He turned for home, not at a break-neck speed as he'd imagined he would, but slowly, plodding along with his mind picking over what Bill had told him. He knew his pal had been feeling vindictive because Tommy had said he wasn't doing any more thefts. But there was enough in what Bill had come out with for alarm bells to have gone off in Tommy's head. He came to a road junction and instead of crossing stood hanging on a lamppost, feeling tears of rage and frustration spiking his eyes. Without warning he suddenly howled at the misty glow overhead until his breath ran out. He'd pinned his hope on Olivia; he always had ever since Aggie died. Olivia had always been there ... Livvie with her constant sturdy character and warm smile. He knew he could go out every morning safe in the knowledge that Livvie would take care of everything until he returned. How would he cope without her? None of the others interested him or aroused his affection in the way that his sweet Livvie did.

Now he felt empty and frightened by what was left to him. He'd kept secrets because of her ... crept around in shadows so as not to upset her, or have her despise him. He'd always wanted her approval and her love even if sometimes he found it hard to show it. He pushed away from the lamppost and shuffled on, almost as though he was drunk. But he'd had only two pints ... barely enough to fill his hollow tooth he might have said in jovial mood.

He wanted to avoid the confrontation that every step was taking him closer to; but he knew he couldn't. He was yearning for it all to be a misunderstanding and for his Livvie still to be the decent girl he'd thought her that morning when he'd left home. Then he'd be able to take it out on Bill and all the other big mouths, not his darling daughter . . .

'How you doing, Tommy?'

He was so lost in miserable thoughts that he almost jumped as Mrs Cook came out of the off licence, bag jangling with a brace of light ales. 'Yeah . . . all right,' he muttered, keen to get past.

'Heard you're getting back to work at Barratt's,' Ethel said cheerily. She rarely saw this man in the evening sober enough to hold a conversation so thought she might as well make the most of it.

'Who told you that?' Tommy was immediately on his guard. He knew his neighbour was old mates with Nelly Smith's sister-in-law, and he didn't want Nelly finding out any of his business. 'Been speaking to Vi Smith about me, have yer?'

'No . . . it was your Livvie told me, if yer must know.' Mrs Cook sounded affronted. 'She was with a handsome young man . . . friend of yourn she said he was.' Ethel sniffed, about to march on. 'I ain't seen Vi in months. If anybody's been speaking to *her* I reckon it might be your Olivia – she was asking after her address.'

Ethel had been worrying about Olivia. If the girl was in the family way she'd need some support from somebody to see her through it. She doubted she'd get anything off her father other than a right-hander and a kick up the backside to put her outside in the gutter. As she saw Tommy's expression she realised she should have kept her mouth shut; Tommy knew more than she'd expected him to about Vi Smith and she'd just got Olivia into trouble.

Tommy followed his neighbour down the street, his tear-filled eyes fixed on her rigid back. He stood in his porch, head hanging down, while his mind throbbed with two awful facts he couldn't ignore. Livvie had been knocking about with a pimp and had asked Mrs Cook for the address of an abortionist.

He remembered that day she'd been dropped off by Lucas. He knew Ethel wasn't lying about their chat; his Livvie had stood outside in the drizzle talking to the woman for some time. Tommy had watched them from behind his bedroom curtain. There was something else too; a while ago he'd come in one evening and seen her with wet hair as though she'd been out and had just got home. She'd looked uneasy when telling him that she'd just nipped outside to fetch the washing in. He knew she'd been lying but had let it pass. But it was all falling into place. She'd been meeting her fancy man on the sly. And now she was in the family way and needed directions to an abortionist.

*

Olivia cursed beneath her breath when she heard her father's key go in the lock earlier than usual. It was probably not long after half-past eight. The sheets had been rinsed and dried and Nancy had helped her put them back on the bed while Maggie washed up their tea things in the bowl. She'd answered her brother's and sisters' questions in the same way she had everybody else who'd asked about her injured face. They'd seemed to believe her report of coming back at dinnertime to try and get the washing finished early but having to leave it after taking a tumble. Maggie had given her a rather odd look and Alfie had said sorry again for wetting the sheets. But then they had all settled down in the parlour to while away some quiet minutes before turning in.

'Want tea, Dad?' Olivia had automatically gained her feet as she heard him shut the door. She'd hoped to be in bed by the time he got back so he wouldn't get a look at her. He'd ask how she'd hurt herself and she'd use the same excuse of wanting to get ahead with the washing, but leaving out Alfie having wet the bed.

'No, I don't want fucking tea,' he said in a bitter, dreary way.

His four children all turned to look at him; Alfie shifted on his bottom into a corner of the room, his knees drawn up to his chin. Nancy closed her book of ballerinas and Maggie shrank down into her chair. All of them thought they might be the target for his wrath. And they knew he was angry even if his tone of voice had sounded peculiar.

'What's up, Dad?' As always, Olivia attempted to draw attention to herself so he'd overlook the others. But this time she'd no need to do that. His eyes were stone cold yet blazing at her.

'You lot, get to bed,' he growled. 'I need to speak to yer sister alone.'

Unsure which sister he meant they all sat still as statues, just their eyes moving, darting to and fro.

Tommy lunged at his son, jerking him to his feet. 'Do as you're told, you little bleeder. Get to bed.' He cuffed Alfie then stabbed a finger at Maggie and Nancy. 'And you two.' All three scrambled towards the door. Maggie's frightened eyes peeked over her shoulder before she disappeared.

'What's up, Dad?' Olivia repeated herself in a murmur although she had already guessed what had happened. She'd been spotted with Joe Hunter outside the factory and her father had found out. She knew one person had definitely taken notice of their meeting. But Lucas Black surely wouldn't have blabbed to her father. She'd asked him if he'd tell Tommy there was a man she liked and he'd seemed offended that she believed he might.

'You're what's up, miss,' Tommy finally spat out in a voice

that trembled with humiliation and disappointment. The room was quite dim with just a single gas lamp burning on the wall. As he got closer he noticed his daughter's cut lip. Normally he would have felt enraged at the idea of somebody hurting his Livvie's lovely face, so like Aggie's. But this evening it simply seemed further proof that his angel was a whore. He knew that pimps kept their women in line with beatings. There was only one reason a young woman would keep company with a pimp. His Olivia was on the game ... like her cousin Ruby Wright, damn the whole lot of that family. 'Who's done that to yer?' He jerked his chin at her face

'I slipped in the washhouse ...' Olivia couldn't completely keep the quaver from her voice.

Tommy advanced but Olivia held her ground and squarely met his eyes.

'Don't reckon you did. I reckon a man's hit yer.' Tommy felt a little bit of himself die as he saw her wince. 'You're lying to me, ain't yer?'

'Yes,' Olivia whispered.

'So, you sly, deceitful little cow,' he snarled through his teeth, 'I'm gonna ask you some questions about you and Joe Hunter and you'd better tell me the truth. You've been playing me for a fool, pretending to like Lucas Black then getting up to all sorts behind me back with a pimp!'

Olivia took a deep breath, deciding the best thing was to come straight out with an explanation. Any further lies would just backfire on her. 'I did see Joe earlier when I finished work but only because ...'

'What ... *today?*' Tommy roared, and unable to control his anguish he lunged at her, grabbing her hair and jerking back her head so she had to squint up at him. 'You was outside the factory *today?*' He shook her. 'Did Black see yer together?'

Olivia squeezed her eyes shut against the pain in her scalp. 'Joe came to tell me that his mother's dead ... '

'Did Black see yer with him?' News of the tragedy didn't side-track Tommy.

'Yes ... I think he saw us,' she gasped. 'Let me go, Dad, you're hurting me.'

Though her neck was twisted to an odd angle she could see that Alfie had crept back to the door and was watching, tears falling from his huge, misery-filled eyes. With a grimace she tried to comfort him and express that he should go away.

'Know what I reckon?' Tommy said, with a sob in his voice. 'Bernie Silver weren't referring to Maggie when he said me daughter was a tart. He meant you. He knows ... everybody knows ... you've made me a laughing stock.' Tommy let go of Olivia's hair and dragged up her chin with his fingers. His eyes settled on her cut lip as though seeing it for the first time. 'Hunter's done that to yer, has he?'

'He hasn't ... ' Olivia felt like weeping but she wouldn't. She'd not give him the satisfaction of seeing her cowed or pleading with him for leniency. She'd done nothing other than try to protect her sister. If she owned up that Harry Wicks was her attacker then the whole sordid story about him and Maggie would come tumbling out.

'Did Black hit you then? Bet he thinks you've made a laughing stock of him, same as I do.'

''Course not!' Olivia gasped. 'He wouldn't!'

'It was the pimp, weren't it? He's found out you're knocked up, and don't like it. You'd never have met him but for that bitch Maisie Hunter moving in upstairs ... so if she's dead, good riddance.'

Alfie suddenly burst in, yanking on his father's hand as it twisted his sister's hair again, trying with his puny strength to prise Tommy's thick fingers away. 'Wasn't him! He's nice. He took me out. And his mum gave Livvie an envelope with money. They're not bad . . . '

Tommy sent his son crashing into the table. 'Envelopes with money in?' he parroted, staring-eyed. 'You been taking punters' money through her, have yer, and under my roof?' He bent his face closer to his daughter's. 'You've had men in here while I've been at work, ain't yer?'

''Course not!' Olivia burst out. 'I've been at work too, y'know!' She sighed in despair. 'I lent Maisie some money to pay her rent . . . that's all.' With a cry of anguish she punched her father in the chest to try and make him release his hold on her.

He hit her back, knocking her to her knees. 'Raise your hand to me, would you, you little whore?' He started to unbuckle his belt. 'You'll learn a lesson before you leave this house and then you won't ever show yer face round here again.'

A banging on the door was heard. Maggie ran to open it, hoping somebody had sent for the police before her father found out what she'd been up to and turned his belt on her.

'Heard a commotion . . . ' Mrs Cook came into the room hesitantly. She'd regretted immediately having mentioned anything to Tommy about his daughter wanting Vi's address. She'd only blurted it out because he'd snapped at her. Her eyes darted to Olivia crouched on the floor, her face bleeding, and she shook her head in mute apology.

'You can sling yer hook, you nosy bitch,' Tommy growled at her.

'Leave her be now, she's taken her punishment whatever she's done.' Mrs Cook rushed forward, helping Olivia to her feet. She turned on Tommy. 'You quieten down or I'll have the law on yer, see if I don't.'

Olivia smoothed down her dress and tidied her hair although

244

her vision swam with tears and she felt unsteady on her feet. It was the second time in a day that she'd been knocked down by a man and she wasn't allowing it to happen ever again. She blinked at her father, tilting her chin and wiping blood from her cheek. 'I'm going all right and you can't stop me.' She gazed at her stricken sisters who huddled together at the door to their room, knowing that she was leaving them and Alfie at his mercy. But if she stayed she'd be no use to them now. The fragile bond between herself and her father that had kept his violence in check had been broken.

'You *can* go as well, you defiant little slut.' Tommy grabbed her shoulder and hurried her to the door so fast she stumbled.

'Put your sister's things in a bag,' he bawled at Maggie. 'She can take everything with her so she don't ever need to come back.' He swung menacingly towards Mrs Cook. 'You get out of my house or I'll put you out meself.'

'I'll wait for you by the gate, love.' Ethel hurried down the path.

Olivia went into her bedroom and found her small amount of savings then took her carpet bag from Maggie. Swiftly she bent and kissed each of her siblings in turn, stroking their white, wet faces with her trembling fingers. 'I'll not forget about you ... swear,' she said as she hesitated by the street door. She turned to her father. 'Joe Hunter might be a pimp but you're no better than him. You'd've let Lucas Black have me in return for a job at the factory, wouldn't you?'

'You don't talk to me like that!' Tommy started forward but his daughter's next words brought him up short.

'And I know you've got a secret woman. Yet you dare get on your high horse, calling me deceitful and a liar.'

Olivia didn't wait for her father to close his sagging jaw to hear what he had to say about that. She shut the door behind her.

'You can stay with me tonight, love.' Mrs Cook patted her shoulder to comfort her. 'Will your young man see you all right? Tomorrow you'll have to move on, y'know.' Ethel looked uneasy. She liked Olivia but had to admit that Tommy Bone hadn't reacted any differently from any other parent who'd just found out a daughter was in the family way. Not so long ago she'd heard through Vi of a girl over Edmonton who'd bled to death from a miscarriage brought on by her father's savage beating of her after he'd discovered she was pregnant.

Olivia knew what her neighbour was thinking but she felt too lethargic to explain. And she didn't see the point in staying a minute longer. If her father knew she was next-door it would just make matters worse for everybody.

Alfie was looking at her through the window and as he pressed his palm against the glass she saw her father drag him away.

'Gonna get going now,' Olivia said through the lump in her throat. She hugged Mrs Cook, although she'd seen relief flit across the woman's face when she'd heard Olivia was leaving. 'Would you keep an eye and ear open for the others for me?'

Ethel nodded, snuffling. 'Sorry, dear. Didn't mean to cause no trouble by letting it slip about ... you know ... '

'I'm not expecting. But it doesn't matter now. It wasn't just that set him off anyway.'

'I can't see you sleep rough. I can let you have a few shillings to tide you over, if it'll help.' Mrs Cook plunged a hand into her coat pocket.

Olivia shook her head. 'Don't worry about me,' she said as she picked up her carpet bag. 'I've got somewhere to go.'

Chapter Twenty

'Well, Olivia Bone, looks like you are one of us now,' Matilda said with wry gravity. 'Boyfriend or father?' She squinted in the poor light at Olivia's face.

'Me dad,' Olivia replied faintly. 'And before him a swine that lives on our street.'

'Ah ... we got plenty o' them on this street too.' Matilda stepped onto the landing and put her arm round Olivia's shoulders. 'Don't worry, gel. You're safe here.'

The woman's gruff kindness overwhelmed Olivia, who started to weep softly. 'Sorry, Mrs Keiver.' She quickly dabbed away tears as the brine made her cuts smart.

'Nothing to be sorry about. But put this up.' Matilda tapped under Olivia's chin with her grimy, ragged fingernails. 'That's what us women do round here, and you'll have to 'n' all if yer gonna stop a while.' She winked. 'And we take a drop o' something.' She smirked. ''Course, ain't recommendin' you do that being as you might not be old enough to drink.'

'I am. I turn eighteen the day after tomorrow.' Olivia managed a ghost of a smile on remembering that. And what a way to celebrate her birthday: homeless and with no certainty that she'd still have a job at the end of the week. But she wasn't giving Barratt's up lightly, although jawing would start once she turned up for work in the morning in the state she was in.

'Well . . . we'll have a little knees-up on Saturday then, if you're still about.'

Olivia reckoned she *would* still be about, living on the worst street in North London. Where else could she afford to go?

'Sorry to bother you so late, but I remembered you saying you rent out rooms for your guv'nor. Any chance I could have one, please? I've got some money.' Olivia opened her fist to display some silver coins, gleaming in the weak light filtering from the half-open doorway. Olivia could hear a hum of voices within and elsewhere in the tenement building a couple were bawling at one another in bursts of cursing.

'Yeah . . . you can have a room, love.' Matilda jerked her head backwards. 'This one. You kip with us tonight and no arguments about it, then tomorrow we'll sort it all out best we can. In yer come then.'

Olivia didn't want to create trouble for someone else's family. She guessed that the place was barely big enough to house the Keivers, let alone lodgers. 'Perhaps have a word with your husband first?'

'No point . . . I know what he'll say. Anyhow, Jack's fasto. He's got to be up in the early hours to set up down the market.'

Olivia was about to apologise again for being a bother but sensed Matilda didn't want her to. She gratefully stepped over the threshold and into a room of smells and shadows. The square space was crammed with every piece of furniture imaginable and sitting on it, or at it, was the family. But what caught Olivia's attention was the incongruous sight of a polished piano.

Alice jumped up from her chair at the table when she saw her.

'Hello, Livvie. What happened to you?' she asked in concern.

'Been in the wars, ain't she? That's all you lot need to know. She's gonna stop here tonight.'

Sophy turned up the oil lamp on the table so the room brightened and they could see one another clearly. The Keivers always had enough of their own dramas going on yet a visitor was a welcome diversion. Living in two dilapidated rooms was boring and the older girls spent as much time as possible outdoors. 'Put the kettle on, shall I, Mum?' Sophy offered.

'Good idea,' Matilda said.

Pushed into a corner was an iron bedstead and kneeling on it was a toddler. Olivia noticed Jack's dark head on the mattress too; the rest of him was covered with a blanket. He was snoring despite his womenfolk's noise, his face turned to the wall.

Matilda swung her youngest up off the bed, balancing the little girl on her hip. 'This is Lucy. And that there's Beth.' She nodded to her daughter doing her homework. Beth had an exercise book perched on her lap that she was pencilling in. She seemed glad to have a reason to close it and get in on the conversation.

'Fancy a biscuit?' Jumping up from her battered old armchair, Beth reached for a tin on a high shelf. 'Sorry they're all broken.' She began poking inside with a finger to find a whole one.

'I don't mind broken biscuits.' Olivia smiled gingerly to avoid deepening the cut on her mouth and took half a custard cream.

Little Lucy gave Olivia a shy smile and put out her arms.

'She don't do that fer everyone. She's taken a shine to you.' Matilda handed the child over to Olivia then found some teacups as Sophy came back, swinging the kettle she'd filled from the tap on the landing.

Olivia cuddled the little girl, feeling Lucy's warmth through her own night-chilled clothing. She'd come by bus and had got off at Seven Sisters Road, bravely walking in the dark up the Bunk from the bottom end ... the worst end ... because she'd remembered Jack Keiver had said they lived down there, with the villains. A woman loitering under a gas lamp had pointed the way to Matilda's place. She had looked her up and down, doubtless taking Olivia's bashed-up face as proof she was one of them.

'Why didn't you go to your aunt's up the top?' Matilda asked over her shoulder as she dripped milk into cups. 'Ain't complaining, mind. You're welcome to a bed here, like I said.'

'Reckon they've got enough trouble without me adding to it. Aunt Sybil threw a saucepan at Ruby's head when she found out we'd been meeting up.' Despite being apprehensive about her aunt's reception of her, Olivia would have gone to the Wrights if the Keivers had turned her away. And she no longer cared what her father thought about her mingling with her mother's family.

Or ... as a last resort she might have gone round the corner to Playford Road and knocked on Joe Hunter's door. But she knew once she did that, there would be no going back for her.

'Well, can't say that me 'n' yer aunt often see eye to eye, so I understand you not wanting her company. Unpleasant, she is, when she's taken a drop.'

Alice and Sophy exchanged a look that widened their eyes and needed no explanation.

'Just popping next door to see Danny.' Sophy nipped towards the exit while her mother seemed preoccupied gossiping.

But Matilda was especially vigilant where her eldest's sweetheart was concerned. 'No skylarking about with him or I'll be down to drag you indoors.' Matilda pointed a teaspoon at Sophy. 'You're up early fer work in the morning, miss.'

'I've got to get to work at Barratt's in the morning.' Olivia took the focus off Sophy; the girl had blushed at her mother's harsh threat then gladly escaped.

'You turn up looking worse fer wear, you'll give yer colleagues' tongues overtime,' Matilda remarked, turning her attention back to Olivia. 'Might be best to have a day off, love. Give us a chance to have a look round the street and sort you out a place to stay.'

Matilda was dropping a hint that she couldn't lodge with them for long but Olivia took no offence; she could see how overcrowded they were.

'Don't care what they say at Barratt's. Can't lose a shift, I need every penny now.' It was brave talk but Olivia knew that there was a dangerous truth in Matilda's warning; she could get the sack for looking the way she did. Lucy grew restless in her arms and she ruffled the child's wavy dark hair, so like Alice's.

Matilda put her youngest back on the bed by her sleeping father. 'Here ... sit in that armchair and get that down you then I'll have a go at patching you up. Ain't promising to work miracles, though.'

Olivia gratefully took her tea and sank back in the musty, scratchy upholstery that Beth had vacated. But it seemed like the comfiest seat ever, and the tea with its milk on the turn, tasted like nectar.

'You'll have to squash in with the gels in the back room, if that's all right. Me 'n' Jack'll take Lucy in bed with us.'

'Don't mind at all, thank you. You're very generous and kind.'

Matilda flapped a hand but her crinkle-eyed smile showed she was pleased with the praise. Not everybody in the Bunk thought that Matilda Keiver was kind or generous. And with good reason.

Olivia accepted the biscuits that Alice plied her with. She realised she felt shivery and hungry despite having eaten earlier.

It was just a few hours ago that she'd sat with her brother and sisters reading the latest news about the war in yesterday's newspapers. Then her father came home and changed her life for good. She'd wanted a place of her own ... but not like this. Not through violence and estrangement, but perhaps there never would have been another way. She knew she'd fret constantly about the others; as soon as she could afford it she'd find somewhere for them all to be together.

'Let's see to them bruises then.' Matilda had come in from the landing carrying the tin bowl.

She found a cloth and dabbed at Olivia's face with icy water. 'I let it run fer a while. Colder it is, more it'll take down the swelling.' She turned to Alice. 'Nip up to Lou Perkins, Al, and see if she's got any vinegar or arnica. Tell her I'll see her all right tomorrow fer it.'

'I've got some money.' Olivia pulled out her coins. She didn't want the Keivers out of pocket on her account.

'Put it away love. Lou owes me a favour. Won't hurt reminding her of it. That's how we go on round here. So, don't let anybody take liberties with yer 'cos if they get away with it once they'll not stop.'

When the bathing was done, Matilda picked up the lamp and led the way into the back room to show Olivia the sleeping quarters while they waited for Alice to return. It had one large iron bedstead that was strewn with some old coats; Olivia imagined those were used as makeshift blankets. In the corner was a sturdy-looking wardrobe and a tallboy chest of drawers. Her face must have shown that she was impressed by the soundness of those bits of furniture.

'Perks of the job.' Matilda chuckled. 'When one of me guv'nor's rooms goes vacant up the better end, I have a look round then swap me old stuff over if I can.'

'I take it he doesn't mind about that?' Olivia nearly laughed but the ache in her face pulled her up sharp.

'What he don't know, don't hurt him,' Matilda returned with a grin. 'Jack brings back what I want on a cart. Like a lot of the landlords Mr Keane don't show his face in the Bunk other than to collect his rents off me.' Matilda stuck her hands on her hips and glanced about. 'Still ain't no palace ... ' she said ruefully. 'I'm after a couple of nice armchairs next.'

'It's a roof,' Olivia said simply.

'You're getting the hang of it.' Matilda's eyes twinkled. 'Anyhow ... tomorrow your dad might want to say he's sorry.' She glanced at Olivia's belly.

It was a furtive look that she had come to recognise. 'I'm not in the family way. That's not what started him off ... well, not exactly. I've never even had a proper sweetheart.'

'You're a nice-looking gel so I'm surprised at that. You're a decent sort too; makes it all the more surprising that you're kin of the Wrights,' Matilda said bluntly. 'Did yer dad take against you and your cousin getting friendly, like Sybil did?'

'He doesn't know about us seeing one another. He went mad over a stupid misunderstanding. I brought it on meself really, keeping me sister out of trouble.' Without even properly considering what she was doing, Olivia briefly explained how she'd been protecting Maggie. She fell quiet at the end, but it seemed Matilda had guessed there was more and gestured for her to carry on. So she told the tale of how her friend had asked her to get an abortionist's address from the woman next-door, and how that favour had also backfired on her.

'Yer father'll want to beat the living daylights out of that butcher. I know I would. I'll tell your dad what he's done if you're embarrassed to,' Matilda said, in her forthright way.

'I'm not embarrassed but if Dad finds out about it, Maggie'll end up like this.' Olivia pointed to her bruises. 'Harry Wicks knows I'll kill him if he touches her again.'

'Reckon you would too ... girl after me own heart, you are, Olivia. You should put your dad right about not being knocked up, though.'

'My dad's not the sort of person you can put right.' Olivia perched wearily on the edge of the bed. 'He thinks he *is* right.' She glanced at her companion's sympathetic face. 'All I wanted to do was help but it seems I've just made things worse.'

'Well, they say no good deed goes unpunished.' Matilda sat down beside her. 'That'll learn yer.'

*

'Got enough room, Livvie?' The bedsprings twanged beneath Alice's slight weight as she shifted on the lumpy flock mattress.

'I'm comfy, thanks,' Olivia whispered even though she wasn't. She had undressed quickly down to her underclothes then pulled her nightdress out of her carpet bag, slipping it over her head. She'd laid down as close to the edge of the bed as possible to give the others room. She was holding tight to the cold iron bedrail to prevent herself toppling to the floorboards.

Olivia, Sophy and Alice were at the top end of the bed while Beth, being the smallest, had snuggled beneath her father's old coat at the foot. Matilda had found a blanket to go with the ragged garments used as covers. Olivia pulled the itchy fabric to her chin, wrinkling her nose against the mingled odour of damp and boiled cabbage and the sweaty smell of sleep assailing her nostrils. It was a redolence that would haunt her memory, she thought as her eyelids fell and she succumbed to dog tiredness.

'Get yer freezing toes off me,' Sophy grumbled to Beth, who was wriggling to find a comfortable spot between three pairs of legs. Olivia drew her knees up to her chest to try and give poor Beth some space. She started to drowse with her cheek cupped in her palm, realising how lucky she was to have met Jack Keiver all those months ago and to have been introduced to his family.

She'd known Mrs Cook all her life and though the woman had offered to put her up for the night she hadn't done so with the same sincerity as Matilda, a person Olivia had only spoken to a couple of times. In Ranelagh Road she'd had much more ... yet she felt privileged to be given the Keivers' meagre hospitality. Whatever little they had, be it bed or board, she knew they'd share it with her ... and expect the favour returned.

'Danny kiss you, did he?' Alice whispered to Sophy.

'Ain't saying,' came an answering murmur.

'Why not?'

'You'll tell Mum then she'll start on me.'

'I won't. Anyhow s'long as you don't do nothing stupid with him, Mum'll be all right.'

'His friend Peter is talking of joining up.'

'He ain't old enough, is he?' Alice sounded surprised.

'He's sixteen. Danny says he's off down the recruitin' office as well.'

'He's younger than Peter is,' Alice scoffed.

'Not by much, he ain't,' Sophy replied. 'Anyhow he says he'd rather go to war than stick around this dump. He hates it here. He wants to go back to Essex.' Sophy gave a small sigh. 'Hope he don't go and join up. I'll miss him something terrible, and worry meself sick 'case he gets shot.'

Olivia had been sleepily listening to the girls' intimate chat, wistfully wishing she'd had that sort of closeness to Maggie. But there were too many years separating them and she'd always been more of a guardian than a confidante to her fourteen-year-old sister.

'You got a boyfriend, Livvie?' Sophy asked softly.

'No.' Olivia's lashes had fluttered open at the sound of her name.

'You gonna visit your cousin Ruby tomorrow? She'll like it that you've moved into the street,' Alice said.

'Don't know ... got some family differences between us to iron out,' Olivia replied.

'She's sweet on Joe Hunter, round the corner,' Sophy remarked. 'Mum says to stay away from him 'cos he's trouble.'

'Mum says to stay away from Ruby 'n' all 'cos she's a bad influence,' Alice blurted. 'Sorry, Livvie, didn't mean to be rude.'

''S'all right, I know she's a bit racy.' Olivia hadn't wanted a reminder of Joe when so far she'd managed to keep him from her mind. She wondered if he was trying to get to sleep, thinking of her; he'd be livid if he found out that her father had hit her because of her association with him and the misunderstandings that had arisen from their friendship. Joe had only ever showed her consideration and kindness, and in return she'd not given him much at all.

'Good-time gal, Mum calls Ruby.' Alice choked back a giggle.

'Fat chance of a good time round here!' Sophy sounded sour.

'Shut up, you lot,' Beth grumbled. 'Can't get to get sleep with you all yakking. Got a spelling test in the morning and Rotten Rogers told us that anybody who scores less than fifteen out of twenty gets the cane.'

'G'night,' Olivia said, letting them all know she too was ready to nod off ... if she could.

Chapter Twenty-One

'You've been doing a lot o' washing then, ain't yer?' Nelly said sarcastically. 'Taken another tumble on that mangle, I see.'

'Yeah ... that's right.' Olivia, sounding equally caustic, carried on cutting lozenges. She knew that everybody had been staring and muttering behind her back from the moment she walked in the room that morning. Only Sal, the woman who had invited her to the Suffragette rally, had sent her a sympathetic smile. As for the others, she'd not give any of them the satisfaction of rising to their bait. She was just thankful that she'd not bumped into Miss Wallis. That one would have something to say ... not to her, but to her boss.

'Don't look so smug about being the blue-eyed gel now, does she?' Olivia heard the spiteful remark drift along the bench.

'You wait till *he* sees the state of her,' another voice whispered.

Now Lucas was back from his trip to Birmingham she was bound to bump into him at some time. She'd noticed his car parked outside but luckily he'd not been about. She was vain enough not to want him to catch sight of her looking such a mess.

'What on earth's happened to you, Livvie?' Cath gasped as soon as they met up by the factory gate at dinnertime.

'Big bust-up at home,' she answered quietly. 'Fancy a walk? Don't want to hang around here and get gawped at.'

"Course.' Cath linked arms with her.

'Please don't say you got in trouble for asking your neighbour for Vi's address. Did your dad find out about it?' Cath sounded anxious and apologetic.

'It's not your fault, Cath, there was more to it.' Olivia didn't want her friend feeling guilty over what had been just rotten luck and her father's thuggish nature. She gave the bare bones of an explanation for her being kicked out of home. 'I'm stopping with people I know in Islington,' she finished up. 'Very kind they've been to me but I've got to get me own place.'

'D'you reckon your dad'll come up the factory after you and cause a scene?'

'God knows ... I hope not.' Olivia had been fretting all morning about whether he'd be loitering at the gate to catch her on her dinner break, or later on when the factory turned out. She expected no apology from him but he'd want to know what she'd found out about his fancy woman. And the answer, of course, was not much. She no longer felt curious although she was sure now that he did have a woman. She'd seen guilt as well as shock in his face when she'd confronted him over it.

Tommy might let that problem simmer for a while but he wouldn't accept the loss of Olivia's wages so easily. She'd been contributing a good amount to the housekeeping and he'd expect Maggie to give up more to cover the shortfall. Maggie resented giving anything at all.

Olivia just wished her father had got his job back at Barratt's;

she hated the idea of her brother and sisters going short because she was no longer putting in the kitty. She would barely cover her own rent and bills at the Bunk; she didn't earn enough to be able to send money home via Maggie.

'Don't suppose you'll come on Friday now.' Cath didn't relish the idea of having an abortion without a friend by her side.

Olivia had forgotten all about accompanying her to her appointment in Lorenco Road. "Course I'll come,' she answered stoutly. 'I said I would.'

'You in pain?' Cath eyed her friend's injuries.

'Bit sore.' Olivia touched the scab on her top lip. Matilda had done a good job of cleaning her up but she knew it would be days before the damage faded. She steered Cath towards Kendall's then stopped at a distance from the laundry.

'I want to speak to me sister and see how they all are. Would you just stay here, Cath? Maggie won't say much if you're with me.'

Olivia speeded up and peered through the laundry window. Maggie seemed to have been watching out for her because she nodded and a few minutes later came out.

'Bleedin' hell ... surprised you've showed yer face outside looking like that.' Maggie gave her a hug.

'Thanks very much,' Olivia said wryly. 'All of you all right?'

Maggie nodded. 'Dad took himself straight off to bed after the commotion. Alfie wet himself again.'

'You and Nancy have to look after him now. Promise me you will?'

Maggie nodded. 'Where did you go?'

'Somebody I know let me stop with them. Hoping to get a room of me own sorted out this evening.'

'Whereabouts?' Maggie sounded both envious and inquisitive.

'Islington ... but don't tell Dad.' Olivia knew that her father would think she'd bolted to Joe so he could look after her. She wanted her father and everybody else for that matter to know she could look after herself. At the very least she was going to give it a damn' good try.

Olivia could see that her sister was dreaming up more questions so changed the subject. 'Stay away from him, won't you?' Olivia pointed at the butcher's shop.

Maggie turned red. 'I know it was Harry bashed you yesterday before Dad laid into you.'

'Have you spoken to him?' Olivia asked sharply, catching hold of her sister's arm.

'Ricky went home on his break yesterday. He told me he saw you and Harry go up the alley then Harry come out first and you after with yer face bleeding.' Maggie looked sullen, shaking off Olivia's hand. 'Suppose you was having another go at him about me. Why couldn't you just leave things alone? I don't need you poking yer nose in. I can look out fer meself.'

'Well, you're going to have to now.' Olivia felt hurt by her sister's attitude. No sympathy ... no apology, not even a half-hearted mumble from Maggie about telling their father the truth and taking some of the blame; not that Olivia would want her to, but an offer would've been nice. 'Got to get back to Barratt's now,' she said. 'Just look after Alfie and give him and Nancy my love. I'll stop by the laundry later in the week and make sure you're all all right.'

When they reached the factory Olivia spotted Lucas coming out of the building and immediately hung back. She'd not seen him for a while and perhaps absence had made the heart grow fonder because she felt a fluttering in her stomach as her eyes settled on his profile. He looked more debonair than ever, which made her even more inclined to hide her spoiled face. Once his car had driven off into Mayes Road she and Cath hurried through the factory gates.

'What'll you tell him if he comes looking for you and sees the state you're in?' Cath asked.

'Doubt he'll look for me . . . we've not spoken for quite a while now.' As she parted from her friend Olivia realised she'd missed bantering with their boss even if at times she'd found it difficult to know if he was laughing with her, or at her.

Olivia was in the sherbet room for afternoon shift. Ordinarily she liked the delicate smell of sherbet powder and loved the fizzy taste of it on her tongue too. But in the room where it was processed the atmosphere was unpleasantly thick and misty with white dust that clung to clothing and equipment.

She set to work scooping up sherbet from the pan and filling pouches that would later have a liquorice dab added, but her mind was miles away in Campbell Road. Olivia had risen early that morning after a surprisingly sound sleep. They'd all breakfasted on tea and broken biscuits and a small slice of bread and marge each. Afterwards they'd taken turns washing in the tin bowl that was brought into use on every occasion; after their ablutions it had been loaded with used crockery.

Then the room had slowly emptied. Jack had gone off while they were all still sleeping. Sophy was next to go out, hoping to walk with her sweetheart to the Star brush factory where she worked as a general hand. Olivia had set off soon after, desperate not to be late for her shift at Barratt's. She'd marched briskly with Alice and Beth as far as the bus stop before they'd all gone their separate ways. Matilda had followed them down the stairs, carrying Lucy who was to be dropped off at a sister's, living on the floor below. Then Matilda was off out, collecting rents. She'd promised to scour the Bunk to find Olivia a cheap vacant room.

Olivia sighed in something close to contentment; she realised she was looking forward to them all meeting up later in

Campbell Road, and not just to see if Matilda had turned her up an affordable little gem amid the decay. She wanted to hear about their days: how Beth had fared in her spelling test ... whether Sophy's boyfriend had gone to the recruiting office, even though he was barely sixteen ... what sort of day Alice had had making tin toys in a noisy factory that made her ears ring.

'Heard you've left home.'

'Have you now?' Olivia had been startled from her thoughts by Nelly's voice. She hadn't expected news to travel quite so fast. She guessed she had Mrs Cook to thank for that.

'Got far to travel, have you?'

'I'll be in on time, don't worry.' Olivia knew that Nelly was itching to find out where she lived. But she wasn't telling anybody her address.

*

'It's a poky dump but it's cheap. Will it do you, love, till something else turns up?'

'Yes ... thanks, Mrs Keiver.'

'Best to mention that around here a pretty gel living alone and looking like she's taken a right-hander gets the wrong sort of attention. Women, in particular, jump to conclusions and turn nasty.' Matilda shook a fist. ''Course, I'll soon set 'em straight. And if you get any trouble off randy men, you come 'n' tell me and I'll set them straight 'n' all.'

Olivia gave a rueful smile of thanks while looking about at the tiny bedsitting room and trying not to show her deep disappointment. It was a hovel; a slip of a room on the top floor of a tenement that was spitting distance from the Keivers' house. It would barely provide her, let alone her brother and sisters, with a home. There was a tiny hob grate covered in ash and not a kettle or pot in sight atop its pitted surface. The single bed had a stained flock mattress and shoved up against its iron legs was a washstand. A small splintered table embedded with grime had two stickback chairs locking legs underneath. Completing the motley collection of furniture was an armchair losing stuffing and a small wardrobe with a door hanging off a hinge. But Matilda had told her it was the cheapest she could find at three shillings a week or sevenpence a night. And as Olivia's budget was three shillings she'd need to pay up front to secure it at the cheaper rate.

'I'll take it straight away.' Olivia opened a cupboard door to see what was provided in the way of equipment. She didn't have a sheet or a cup and saucer to her name. There was some cracked crockery and mismatched cutlery but not much else.

Matilda wasn't fooled by Olivia's smile. As a house manager on the worst street in North London she was used to seeing sad-eyed people desperately trying to find a place to stay and some work to pay for it. The girl was luckier than most in that she had only herself to shelter, and she had a job. Matilda hoped she wouldn't be given her cards when it go round that her father had kicked her out and she'd settled in a slum. Employers discriminated against Bunk dwellers. Olivia Bone seemed a proud and hardworking young woman, so Matilda would never see her resort to the women's lodging house round in George's Road; that miserable dump made her rooms seem like the Ritz. If it came to it and Olivia couldn't afford the rent, Matilda would offer to squash her back in with them if her aunt wouldn't take her in.

'Your neighbours are nice enough sorts. Mr and Mrs Burton and their three kids live below – they have a tear up every so often but that ain't unusual round here. Across the landing you've got a widower who does a bit of totting. You'll see him carting all sorts up the stairs. Had a stuffed grizzly bear in there once.' Matilda shook her head in amusement. 'Still . . . he's got his uses has Billy. Have a word with him and he'll look out fer anything you want when he's out rag 'n' boning. Meantime, I can lend you some bedding and a saucepan and kettle until you get your own things around you. The tenant before you did a flit, taking some of me guv'nor's belongings.' Matilda winked. 'I told Mr Keane he wouldn't get no more'n half a crown considering the state it were left in. I knew he'd come back wanting a tanner more whatever I said, see.' Matilda stuck her hands on her hips and turned business-like because there was no point in being too sympathetic; Olivia had taken the room so would need to knuckle down to the rules. 'Rent's up front . . . got it, love?'

''Course.' Olivia dug in her pocket and produced the silver, handing it over.

'Let you get settled in then. I'll send Alice over later with the bits and pieces.'

After Matilda left Olivia perched on the edge of the bed then jumped up as she felt a movement. She dragged the mattress up onto its edge then pushed it over, hoping that any livestock had been knocked out onto the floor. But she felt too limp to look for a broom to sweep up any nasties, if indeed the previous tenant had left behind such a useful item. With a sigh she started unpacking her few belongings from her bag.

*

Lorenco Road seemed an unfriendly place. In an attempt to fill the silence Olivia told Vi Smith so as the woman led the way down her dingy brown-painted hallway to a door; it was ajar and emitting weak light.

Moments ago as she and Cath had hurried along in the twilight towards the house where Vi lived, a couple of women wrapped in shawls had spat at them without uttering a word.

'Suspicious lot some of 'em,' Vi responded, ushering the two young women into her back parlour. 'But those two you saw are Russian prossies – this area's known as Little Russia, see. They don't like strange females on the road. Makes 'em think you might be muscling in on their patch. No offence, love, but a lot of me clients are working gels.' Vi turned up the gas mantle on the wall and swung a look between her visitors.

'So you've took my advice and found a friend to bring back with you, Mrs Bellamy.' Vi seemed expectant of an introduction.

'Yeah . . . I did,' Cath said faintly.

'I'm Diane Green.' Olivia protected her identity in case Ethel Cook got to hear of this visit. She didn't want Vi's sister-in-law to find out either. Nelly would relish spreading that sort of scandal about Tommy Bone's daughter and tie it in with her getting a beating.

Vi Smith wasn't bothered about women lying about who they really were, just about getting paid, as her next words proved. 'Got the three quid, love?' She held out a palm.

Cath produced some folded notes, proffering them in a palsied hand.

Vi steadied her fingers, patting them. 'Come on, you'll be fine. Not pleasant but gotta be done, ain't it? Then next time you'll keep yer knees together or get him to wear a johnny, won't you?' She smirked. 'Now you go into the back room and get yer skirt off and your friend can sit and wait here till it's time to take you home.

'Like a nip of brandy, love?' she asked Cath as though the drink came as part of the three-pound deal.

'No.' Cath sounded close to tears; her staring eyes suddenly fixed on the exit as though she were in two minds about bolting. 'This door, is it?' she said in defeat, gesturing at the back parlour.

Vi nodded then turned an enquiring look on Olivia, eyes lingering on her fading bruises. 'How about you, dear? Me husband'll make you a cuppa tea if yer like, while you wait for her.'

On cue, a short stooped fellow with a long greying moustache shuffled out from behind a curtain, leaning on a stick.

'Nothing for me, thanks,' Olivia murmured, feeling suddenly queasy. She perched on the nearest chair and folded her hands on her stomach to quell its rolling.

An array of clocks on Vi's sideboard ticked off the minutes and Olivia was thankful for the quiet in the back room. She wasn't sure what she'd have done if Cath had screamed. She wouldn't have known whether to burst in or stay put. He knew she didn't want his tea, yet the old fellow had remained where he was, staring at her from beneath straggling silver eyebrows.

Olivia wondered if he thought she might steal something. The room was crammed with furniture like the Keivers' home. But these pieces were of better quality, and the crocheted runners on mahogany surfaces held a variety of ornaments, big and small. Olivia knew little about such things but she reckoned some of the figurines might be worth a few bob.

As though he'd read her thoughts the old fellow croaked, 'Some gels come here and ain't got three quid, y'know. Chars, fer example ... they don't earn much but they fetch us up what they can.'

Olivia smiled neutrally. She imagined most of the stuff was 'fetched up' from clients' houses in the way that Mrs Keiver had acquired her new furniture from her guv'nor.

'Can tell you ain't a char.' He turned his head, eyeing her sidelong. 'What d'you do then?'

Olivia bit back the urge to tell him to mind his own business because he gave her the creeps. A sudden loud moan made her jump to her feet.

Mr Smith didn't seem perturbed. 'Almost finished now then,' he said as though it were a signal he recognised, and disappeared back through the curtain.

Vi came out, wiping her red hands on a piece of towel. 'All done. Mrs Bellamy is just straightening herself up.'

Olivia gave a tight smile. She felt angry without knowing why. Vi Smith hadn't forced her services on Cath, the poor cow had sought out the abortionist, yet still Olivia felt like swiping all the pretty ornaments and ticking clocks onto the floor.

She hurried forward as Cath appeared in the doorway, holding onto the frame for support.

'Feel all right?' Olivia whispered, placing gentle hands on her friend's shoulders.

'Yeah ... just got cramps in me belly and I'm woozy.'

'Be right as rain after a good night's sleep,' Vi said in a jolly voice, holding open the parlour door for them to leave. 'Make sure you keep the wadding in place. Bleeding'll stop after about a week. Won't be no worse than a heavy monthly.'

Out in the street it was dark and an autumn mist was damping their faces.

'Lean on me,' Olivia said as Cath swayed and bashed her feet into a low brick wall fronting the houses. 'Come on ... we'll get a cab back on the High Street ... you'll be fine, Cath.' She'd heard her friend gasp a couple of times with the effort of walking and knew the poor cow wouldn't be able to stand around waiting for buses. She anchored an arm about Cath's waist then grabbed her elbow with the other, using her strength to get them along.

Thankfully a vacant hackney cab slowed down and Olivia hailed it then half-lifted Cath on, helping her sit down. The driver eyed them suspiciously as though believing Cath might be drunk and incapable rather than in agony. Olivia gave him a glare and a clipped instruction to take them to Turnpike Lane, turning the fellow's attention back to his horse. They set off at quite a pace and for a while the relief of being on the way home kept them both quiet.

'What a fucking life,' Cath murmured. 'I told Mum me 'n' you was going to the flicks and that's why I'd be back late.'

'I've got nobody to tell or ask anymore,' Olivia said, gazing into darkness as they sped along Tottenham High Street.

'You're bleedin' lucky, Livvie.'

'Don't feel it. It'll get better for you now, Cath.' Olivia put her arm round her friend's shoulders. 'You'll save and get your own place; you and Trevor can get married. In a couple of years' time you'll have a few kids round your ankles . . . ' Olivia fell silent, regretting saying that.

'He never stops talking about the war. All the men down the railway yard are geeing each other up about who's gonna be first to serve King and country. We had a bloomin' great row. I was having second thoughts about the abortion, y'know, till he told me he's joining up. Definitely wasn't risking being a widow with a kid to rear on me own, living me life with his mother.'

Olivia hugged Cath closer, touching their heads together. 'Could still all be over by Christmas. Who's to say it won't?'

'Some of those women that went on the Suffragette rally were handing out white feathers, to blokes over Hyde Park, y'know,' Cath said. 'Anyone gives my Trevor one, I'll go bonkers and have her eyes out.'

'Here we are . . . home.'

The driver was slowing down. Olivia helped Cath to her feet, then onto the pavement, quickly paying the driver.

She saw Cath right up to her door on Hornsey Park Road.

'Get a good sleep and don't come in tomorrow if you don't feel up to it.'

'You clocked in even though you looked like you'd done a few rounds with Kid Lewis.' Cath managed an admiring smile.

'That was a bit different from what you've just been through, Cath.' Olivia sighed. 'Anyhow ... if I don't work, I can't pay me rent.'

'Fuckin' 'orrible life, ain't it?' Cath said with stronger feeling than last time.

'Worse for the poor buggers in France, though.' Olivia realised her friend was feeling wretchedly emotional to be swearing so often. 'Best get going and catch me bus to Islington.' She headed off briskly up the road with tears burning her eyes; she knew if she stayed longer talking to Cath they'd both end up bawling.

Chapter Twenty-Two

'You're late. Weren't sure you'd come.'

'Well, I'm here now, aren't I?'

'What you drinking?' Tommy turned to the landlord, crooking a finger.

'Scotch,' Lucas said, resting back against the bar. He glanced around. This wasn't a pub local to the factory but a classier establishment off Muswell Hill. He guessed Tommy had chosen it as a meeting place to ensure they didn't bump into any factory hands from Barratt's. He'd come out of curiosity, wondering if Tommy wanted to talk about a job or about his daughter. He gave the man credit for possessing enough nous to understand that one wouldn't come without the other.

She might have knocked Lucas back, telling him she'd fallen for somebody else, but even though he'd seen them embracing, he hadn't given up on Olivia; he usually got what he wanted in the end. And he still wanted her despite the complications of conscience and rivals. She fascinated him ... aroused him in the way he'd been horny as a teenager. Too many women throwing themselves at him over the years had left him feeling jaded, then he saw Olivia Bone and everything changed. He knew the fact that she was this man's daughter was giving his obsession a sweeter edge and wasn't sure he'd like himself any more than he would like Tommy when the chase was over and the game played out.

Tommy shoved Lucas's drink in front of him and immediately took a swig of his own beer.

'Are you waiting for me to guess what you want?' Lucas enquired sarcastically after a quiet minute had passed.

'Getting me thoughts in the right order,' Tommy growled. He'd never liked this man: too forthright, too blessed with all the good things in life. But they had something in common in that they'd both been rejected by Livvie in favour of a scumbag who pimped women for a living and who had in all probability left her pregnant.

'Got some bad news about me daughter Livvie, and being as you've taken an interest in her, I thought you might want to hear it.'

Lucas had been about to taste his Scotch but the glass hovered by his mouth then was returned to the bar. 'What's that then?' he asked quietly.

'She's got in with bad company and 'cos I know you've been treating her nice ... I thought it only fair you should know.' Tommy shrugged. 'Not always seen eye to eye, have we? But I don't want you made a fool of, like she's made a fool of her own father.' Tommy shook his head sorrowfully, gulping from his glass.

'Well, you've got my attention,' Lucas said dryly. 'So carry on.'

'She's left home. Gone to live with her fancy man, I reckon, although I've not spoken to her in a while, and don't want to neither. She can't come back home now; she'd be a bad influence on the other kids ... but 'course we miss her wages. I don't mind admitting, I'm struggling.'

'Explain ... *bad company*.'

'He's a wrong 'un ... a ponce, by all accounts.' Tommy cleared his throat. 'Let you come to your own conclusions on that, sir.'

Tommy eyed his companion as Lucas shot Scotch down his throat, turning his thoughts to his own wanton daughter. He wasn't sure what Livvie knew of his secrets but now she'd shamed herself and moved away, there was less likelihood of anything coming out, or of anybody believing what she said if it did. From wanting his daughter working in Barratt's, Tommy now wanted her out ... sacked. And he reckoned Lucas would get rid of her rather than be made to look a prat for having favoured a girl who'd preferred a pimp to him. Tommy also hoped that Lucas would be grateful enough for the tip-off to reward him with a job. Then when he had his foot back in the door ... he'd show them all.

Apart from that Tommy wanted his version of how Livvie came by her bruises to be heard. Once Nelly Smith and her cronies mangled the tale he'd look a villain when all he'd done was chastise his daughter for hobnobbing with low life. Any decent father would've done the same.

Tommy eyed the fellow staring hard into his empty glass with his fingers tightening on it as though they'd crush it. If Livvie *was* a little scrubber she might as well be paid handsomely for staring at ceilings, to Tommy's crafty way of thinking, and Lucas Black could afford to set her up somewhere flash.

'Another?'

Tommy nodded, shoving his empty tankard away. 'Yeah ... I'll take a rum this time, thanks.'

Lucas bought the rum and paid for it.

'Not having one?' Tommy asked in surprise as Lucas started for the door.

'No.'

'There's something else,' Tommy blurted, desperate to ram home his point. He'd no idea if Lucas might turn his back on the lot of them. And he didn't want that.

The other man walked back slowly to join him.

'Could be she's carrying,' Tommy mumbled beneath his breath, making Lucas incline towards him to hear the words. 'Something's been said to make me believe she is, but I ain't gonna elaborate – just think you should know.' He cleared his throat. 'If it's true, I can guess where the blame lies, but not everybody might see it the way I do . . . if you get my drift, sir.'

'I get it,' Lucas said, turning on his heel.

*

There was quite a queue for the bus to Finsbury Park. If Olivia had been in a better frame of mind she might have saved the fare and walked the few miles; there was nobody indoors waiting for her, after all. She could get to bed as late as she liked. It was Saturday tomorrow and she didn't have to be up for work. But the trip to Lorenco Road had taken it out of her, leaving her feeling exhausted. She joined the straggling line of people, plunging her hands into her pockets to protect them from the chilly air. She gazed up at a bright night sky that promised a frost, and as the twinkling stars held her eyes she tried to turn her mind from Vi Smith's gory hands because that memory led to another, far more upsetting image of her mother slowly bleeding to death giving birth to Alfie.

Then she thought of Maisie Hunter, dying alone in a hotel

273

room. Joe now had to lay his family to rest; he'd nobody left to him but a father he despised . . . if indeed Herbie Hunter were still around. Olivia felt a pang of affection for Joe tighten her chest, wanting to be with him, to comfort him through such a sad time. She was determined to make an effort to try and bump into him now they lived quite close to one another, but realised he'd be busy with funeral arrangements . . .

A car went past. It braked then turned round in the middle of the road and came back, stopping with a screech.

Olivia let slip an astonished curse, making a woman in front of her in the queue glance disapprovingly over her shoulder.

By the time Olivia had shaken herself into action Lucas was striding purposefully towards her and there was no possibility of escape.

'You're out late. Where are you off to?'

Olivia didn't answer him immediately because she didn't like his tone of voice, and she couldn't think what to say. Yet oddly she was pleased to see him and the fluttering in her stomach had started up again.

'I've been out with a friend,' she finally replied, keeping her damaged profile turned aside. 'How about you?' It was strange that he was still in Wood Green when she'd heard that he lived in Hampstead.

'Late meeting.'

'With Miss Wallis?' Olivia audaciously enquired, squinting at his car to see if the secretary was getting a lift. The lewd talk of Deborah climbing on the boardroom table for him after hours came into her head. She'd felt embarrassed when Cath told her, at the time believing it to be just factory women's dirty jokes.

'It wasn't a Barratt's matter.'

His clipped answer made Olivia uneasy. She sensed he wanted her to ask where he'd been. So she did.

274

'Drinking in a pub with your father,' he answered.

Olivia's heart jumped then settled to a slow thudding. She started to demand an explanation but then pressed her lips together.

'Don't you want to know what we talked about?' Lucas goaded her.

'There's only one thing he'd want from you and that's a job at the factory.'

'You're right ... but I wasn't expecting the way he went about it.'

It seemed Tommy had tried to befriend his enemy, to worm his way back into Barratt's now he could no longer rely on her to help him. Her father was a proud man so Olivia knew he must be desperate to lower himself this far. From Lucas's attitude she realised her father had wasted his time ... but she asked anyway. 'Will you give him a job?'

'No.'

'Why not?'

'For a number of reasons.'

His silky tone of voice was increasing her uneasiness but she wouldn't let him know it. 'What reasons?' she demanded, cocking her head to a challenging angle.

'Get in the car and I'll tell you somewhere private.'

Their eyes locked in the dusk and finally Olivia realised why he was so cold and angry. But she could hardly credit that her father would betray her to this man of all people. She had accused Tommy of being no better than a pimp, but it seemed he was a Judas as well.

'I'll wait for my bus, thanks. G'night, sir.'

'Get in the car or don't turn up on Monday morning.'

Olivia whipped around, eyes flashing. 'Don't you dare blackmail me!'

He walked off.

Olivia hurried after him, grabbing his arm. 'I told you before . . . don't think you're better than me or can tell me what to do just 'cos you're rich and powerful at the factory.' Her eyes blazed up at him. 'And don't think you're taking my job away . . . 'cos you're not. I need it!'

'I've taken your job away.'

'Why? Because I won't sleep with you?' Olivia sounded incensed.

'I think you overestimate your appeal, my dear. I'm not desperate for you,' he drawled. 'I told you, I've got somebody for sex when I need it. You've lost your job because the factory's no place for pregnant women.'

Olivia winced. Even if her father genuinely believed she was expecting he'd done a terrible thing, telling such an explosive secret to this man of all people. Lucas thought she'd let somebody else have what she wouldn't give him and he was being deliberately harsh because his pride had taken a knock.

But so had hers! Olivia inwardly cried. All the hurt and injustice and frustration she'd suffered recently seemed to be bearing down on her, churning in her stomach. She'd done her damnedest for her father and for Maggie, sticking up for them, and received no loyalty in return. And the final straw was her boss believing everything Tommy had told him without even giving her a chance to defend herself.

'Perhaps your boyfriend can find you some work,' Lucas said with a slight curl to his lip.

Spontaneously Olivia slapped his face with all the force she could muster, knocking his head sideways.

'At least he likes me and treats me with respect! And I'm glad you're over wanting me 'cos I'd never do it with you . . . even if

276

you wore a johnny,' she burst out, though she wasn't sure what a johnny was. But she'd heard Vi telling Cath to make Trevor use one so guessed it stopped a woman getting pregnant. She watched Lucas rub his cheek, shifting his jaw back into alignment; then came his smile but it wasn't pleasant.

'Sorry ... I shouldn't have hit you. But I'm sick of being treated like dirt by some men.' She turned away as the full force of what she'd done sunk in. She'd burned her bridges now, she realised. If she'd just kept her temper ... given her side of the story ... but Lucas had infuriated her, speaking to her like that without first asking her to explain.

'You've moved in with a wrong 'un according to Tommy,' he called after her.

'I live on my own!' Olivia spun about to hiss at him. She felt torn between racing back to beg him to forgive her and taking another swing at him.

He was staring and it was too late to shield her bruise from view by turning her face away.

'He hits you.' Lucas stepped towards her and brushed his thumb over a dark patch of skin on her jaw.

'Who d'you mean?' she asked cagily.

'You tell me.'

'My father shouldn't have said anything. We had a bad argument. He chastised me because he's too pig-headed to ask questions first or believe he could be wrong ... just like you are. It's not true what he's said, although he thinks it is. Anyway, I can't understand why he's told you when it's nothing to do with you.'

'He seems to think it might be ... if you're pregnant.'

Olivia gasped in mortification at the disgusting way her father had behaved.

'Whatever he thinks or says, we both know it sure as hell

can't be mine, don't we?' Lucas sounded sour. 'So put him straight on that.'

Olivia knew her father didn't really believe that she'd let Lucas touch her. They'd only been out at Alexandra Palace for a few hours in broad daylight; he was manipulating things to his own end.

'Where do you live on your own?' Lucas enquired.

'Can't tell you,' she mumbled.

'Why not?'

Olivia gestured weakly.

'The navvy I saw you with outside the factory . . . he's the one your father suspects you're living with, isn't he?'

An almost imperceptible nod answered him.

'You like him?'

'I do like him,' Olivia answered stoutly. 'He's been good to me.'

'I'd've been better.'

'You've just proved that you wouldn't,' Olivia sighed. 'You think a silk dress and a steak dinner's all I want. Shows what you know! I'd rather wear me old clothes and have bread and dripping and me self-respect. Doesn't matter anyway – don't know why we're even talking about it. Whatever my father's said, I'm not living with anybody and I'm not having a baby . . . and I don't care if you believe me or not!' Olivia saw her bus pulling to a halt by the queue of people.

'I'm going home now. See you Monday,' she said with a defiant tilt of her chin.

He raised a quizzical eyebrow, challenging her to go against him. She did; she turned her back on him and dashed to board the bus.

*

278

'My, you've been busy.' Matilda glanced about admiringly at Olivia's home. The bed had been neatly made with the sheet and blanket she'd been loaned and the small table had been scrubbed clean of dirt to reveal its pale pine top. The wardrobe had been repaired too.

Olivia blew a wisp of hair off her perspiring forehead and dropped the washing rag back into the enamel bowl. She'd been trying to make the place a bit more homely with the few resources available to her.

'Billy fix that hinge for you?' Matilda nodded at the wardrobe door, thinking the totter had turned handyman for his pretty new neighbour.

'Did it meself ... found a screwdriver in the drawer. But I had a quick word with Billy. He seems a nice old fellow and promised to get me some decent bits when he goes on his rounds. He's lent me some of his stuff but I really need me own brooms and buckets and so on.'

'Celebrating later?'

Olivia was surprised and pleased that Matilda had remembered her birthday. She shook her head.

'Me 'n' Jack are off down our local this evening. Come along and we'll have a few drinks together.'

It looked as though the woman had started on the razzle already. Matilda's cheeks were flushed and there was a whiff of whiskey on her breath.

'It's kind of you, but I can't afford a night out.' Olivia was determined to preserve every penny she could.

'I'll buy you a drink and I expect me friends'll want to wish you a happy birthday too. Not every day a gel turns eighteen, is it?'

'I'll pop in for just one then ... thank you.'

'Saturday nights we usually have a bit of a singsong round

279

the joeyanna indoors after we get turfed out of the Duke, so you're welcome to come to that 'n' all.' She grinned. 'I'm off down Hornsey baths to have a good soak now.'

Matilda hadn't been gone long when Alice turned up, struggling up the stairs with a box. 'Happy birthday, Livvie.' She dumped the box on the polished table.

Olivia peered in at an assortment of household items that were just what she needed. She lifted the sheet and pillowcase on the top to see cloths and cutlery and a frying pan and basin and plenty more utensils underneath. 'I must give you something for that lot.' Olivia smiled in delight and went to find her purse.

"S'all right ... didn't cost us. Mum would've brought it over but she's been out with her sister and had a couple of dinnertime snifters. I offered to carry it over 'cos I didn't want her dropping it all down the stairs.' Alice pulled a wry face.

'You're very kind.' Olivia felt suddenly overwhelmed and blinked back tears.

Alice grinned on seeing how well the gift had been received. 'Mum got people in the street to put in what they could spare so we could wish you happy birthday, 'specially as you've had a rough time of it lately.' She plonked herself down on the bed. 'Saw your cousin Ruby just now. Didn't stop with her for long. I didn't say you'd moved in ... didn't know whether to.'

'Best if I do it.' Olivia was overjoyed by her new neighbours' unexpected kindness and felt ready for anything – even meeting the aunt her father had banned her from contacting. But she was her own person now. No man was ever again telling her what to do.

Of course, she didn't know how her aunt would take to having her as a neighbour. 'I'll pop up and see them in a short while. I'm here now so they'll have to take it or leave it, family feud or no family feud.'

*

'What are you doing here!'

'Visiting a neighbour.' Olivia gave her cousin a grin.

Ruby's jaw dropped. Quickly she closed the door behind her and came further out onto the landing. 'What?'

'Matilda Keiver found me a room of me own down the other end. I'm living in Campbell Bunk, same as you.'

'You gone nuts or something, Livvie Bone?' Ruby's words emerged in a muffled shriek.

'Most probably,' she ruefully replied. 'Big bust-up at home – got thrown out,' she succinctly explained. 'The Bunk is the only place I can afford to live. I've got a bedsit no bigger than a rabbit hutch.'

'Well ... what a turn-up!' Ruby burst out into astonished laughter.

'Can I have a word with Aunt Sybil?' Olivia looked past her cousin to the door that stood ajar.

'You can if you're brave enough. She's in a right narky mood this morning. I was just on me way out to the caff to escape her.'

'Can't be any worse than my father's moods.'

Ruby stood aside and waved her cousin on with a rueful grimace.

*

'Gawd help us! Does your dad know where you are?' Sybil Wright had recovered from the shock of seeing her niece, and hearing that she'd moved in down the road, by gulping from the bottle of gin wedged down the side of her chair.

Olivia shook her head. 'I didn't tell him where I was heading. I'm sorry I've not spoken to you for so long, Aunt Sybil. It wasn't that I didn't want to know you.'

'It was what yer father wanted. I know he still wants to keep his distance and so do I. You coming here is just brewing more trouble.' Sybil got to her feet with surprising agility considering the hefty gulp of gin she'd just swallowed and started banging around in a cupboard, avoiding looking at her niece.

Olivia remembered feeling amazed by the change in Ruby when she'd first seen her after a long absence. But at least she had recognised her cousin. Her Aunt Sybil could have passed her in the street and Olivia would not have known who she was.

Once you'd never have seen the woman unless she was done up to the nines with her crowning glory nicely primped. Now her hair was neither brown nor grey but a tangled mix of both and her clothes were shabby and needed washing. Stains on her blouse looked weeks old and she wore a bit of fraying blanket round her shoulders as a shawl.

'When you goin' home – soon?' Sybil barked, slamming shut the cupboard door. 'Don't let your father know you've been here. I didn't invite you.'

'I'm never going home. I'm independent now and somehow or other I've got to stay on me own two feet.'

'You'll go home,' Sybil sneered. 'You'll think Tommy's place is a palace once you've had a taste of living round here. I know I would.'

Olivia glanced about at a room that was similar in size to the Keivers' front parlour. Sybil's looked bigger because it had less furniture crammed into it. What there was, was dreary, although the absence of a bed led Olivia to think they had other rooms to use as sleeping quarters, unlike Jack and Matilda who bedded down by the cooking range.

Sybil pointed a grubby finger at Olivia. 'Go on . . . get off with yer. Don't want Tommy knowing we've spoken or he'll kick up. If you've fallen out with yer father it ain't my business.'

A boy suddenly burst into the room, shouting, 'Got a tanner, Mum? Old Smithie said you owe him and he ain't giving me nuthin' on the strap till you've paid up.'

The boy stared curiously at Olivia.

'This is your cousin Olivia, Mickey.' Ruby made the introductions.

'Never heard of you,' he said impishly.

'We'll keep it that way,' his mother said bluntly.

Olivia had noticed Mickey seemed to be walking on the side of his foot. But his disability certainly hadn't slowed him down; he was breathless from tearing up the stairs.

'Well, I've heard of you, young man, and it's lovely to see you again. Last time I clapped eyes on you, you was just this big.' Olivia demonstrated by holding her palms a short distance apart.

'How old was he?' She turned to Sybil, still trying to win the woman over. 'We was all round at Nan's just before Mum passed away when . . . '

'Never mind that,' Sybil snapped. 'What's done's done, ain't got time for reminiscing.' She threw a sixpence at Mickey and he scooped it off the dirty floorboards. 'Give Smithie that and tell the miserable bleeder I'm going down Blackstock Road for me groceries in future. Tight-fisted git.'

'Just off down to see Olivia's place, Mum. Won't be long.' Ruby edged Olivia towards the door.

'Well, you ain't moving in with yer cousin, if that's what you're planning,' Sybil bawled after them. 'You pay rent here, miss, and don't you forget it.'

'Sorry about her being rude like that. Told you talk of Tommy Bone sets her off ranting. Can I move in with you, Livvie?' Ruby asked plaintively as soon as they started down the road.

'It's not big enough to swing a cat,' Olivia protested. She'd like to help her cousin but her brother and sisters were her priority. Her father would be simmering because he couldn't get his job back; sooner or later he would explode. The constant worry about how the younger ones were faring in her absence never left her. 'Mickey looks like Alfie, y'know.' Olivia gave a little chuckle. 'Mum and Sybil used to look alike.'

'She looks a mess now. I'm always going on at her to tidy herself up. Let me bunk with you,' Ruby pleaded. 'She's driving me up the wall.'

'Sorry, you can't.' Olivia knew she had to be hard or Ruby would go on and on about it. 'Soon as I've got enough put by I'm moving out and getting somewhere bigger so Alfie and the girls can live with me.' Olivia returned Alice a wave as she passed by on the opposite side of the road with Geoff. 'Dad's got a nasty streak and it's getting worse. Can't leave them there with him.'

'Sounds like my mother,' Ruby said bitterly.

'Mickey's a nice lad.' Olivia led the way up the stairs to her room, pointing out the place to avoid on the second flight where worm had rotted a tread.

Ruby pivoted on her heel, assessing the bedsit. 'You're right, it is a poky dump.' There was satisfaction in her voice. 'Seen anything of Joe Hunter, have you? I remember you said you 'n' him were acquainted through his mother.'

'Saw him not that long ago,' Olivia replied. She'd had a feeling that Ruby would mention his name at some point. 'He came over to tell us that his mum passed away while she was on a visit to Cambridge.'

'Shame about that,' Ruby said with perfunctory sympathy.

'Not seen much of him meself. Thought he might have gone away.'

'I expect he has. He's got a funeral to arrange,' Olivia pointed out.

'Any jobs going at Barratt's?'

'Not heard of any,' Olivia answered. She could have said that hers might be up for grabs. Anxiety over losing her job was constantly chipping away at her peace of mind. She wondered whether Miss Wallis would send for her on Monday morning and gleefully put her off.

Yesterday, after she'd left Lucas, she'd guessed he might follow the bus to Islington. He could head in that direction to take a long way round to Hampstead.

When she'd got off in Seven Sisters Road he'd made no attempt to hide the fact he was watching her. To let him know she could be as brazen as he was she'd waved and he'd flicked the headlights in response. She'd known he'd be sitting there in the dark, with a sardonic twist to his lips.

But he'd made no further attempt to confront her. Olivia hadn't walked directly into Campbell Road; she'd gone home via Fonthill Mews in the hope he wouldn't think her an inhabitant of the notorious Bunk.

'Mrs Keiver's invited me for a drink later. Fancy coming to the Duke to celebrate my birthday? Your mum can come too if she likes.' Olivia knew that it was unlikely her aunt would accept an invitation as she had virtually told Olivia never again to darken her doorstep.

'Can't ... I'm working at the supper house.' Ruby sounded disappointed, but Olivia, on reflection, felt rather relieved.

Chapter Twenty-Three

'This is me sister, Fran, and her husband Jimmy.' In the pub Matilda had beamed a welcome at Olivia, then introduced her to the people she was with.

Before plucking up the courage to enter the busy place Olivia had stood on tiptoe and bobbed her head to and fro to catch a glimpse of a friendly face through the window. She hadn't fancied walking into the Duke of Edinburgh and finding herself amidst strangers. Luckily she'd spotted Jack and Matilda straight away, so in she'd gone.

Fran seemed nice, Olivia thought, and she resembled Matilda in a wishy-washy way. She'd fine, fair hair, not thick auburn locks, and her features, although attractive, lacked her elder sister's strong definition. Olivia recalled having taken against Fran's husband on the first occasion she'd visited the Bunk, months ago. Jack had told her Jimmy Wild was his brother-in-law when the man had come over to say hello. Moments later he had sprinted off to collect his gambling winnings before the coppers confiscated them. Olivia hadn't liked his over-familiar attitude then, and she'd not changed her view. From the hard looks that Matilda was casting her brother-in-law Olivia reckoned she wasn't keen on him either.

'What you drinkin', love?' Jack asked affably.

'A small port and lemon, please.' Olivia had only had sips of alcohol before at Christmas. But she recalled her mother asking for port and lemon to drink on special occasions so she decided if Aggie had liked it she would too.

'Thanks for my birthday present, Mrs Keiver,' Olivia said with a smile as Jack went to the bar. 'It was a lovely surprise.'

Matilda patted her arm. 'More'n welcome, love. Told you we look out for one another in the street. Poor but loyal, us lot, and I know you'll chip in next time when it's somebody else needs a helpin' hand.'

Olivia knew she'd always remember those battered pots and pans as the best birthday present she'd ever had, just as the Keivers would stay in her mind, no matter where life took her. When Jack returned with her drink she joined in their group's little cry of 'Cheers' before tasting her port.

'And here's to Sophy and Danny and their new life in Essex.' Jack raised his tankard and they all joined in, wishing the young couple well.

Olivia had learned from Alice that her sister's boyfriend hadn't joined up after all. Being keen to do his bit, Danny Lovat had gladly accepted a job on a farm, training horses for the military. The icing on the cake had been that it took him back to his beloved Essex, and the cherry on top was that Sophy had been offered a position as a domestic in the same farmhouse. Needless to say she had jumped at the chance of escaping from the Bunk to work alongside her boyfriend.

'Lot of fellows are joining up,' Jack said sombrely.

'Well, you ain't.' Matilda linked arms with her husband as though to keep him right where he was. 'You've got a family and we need you.' She cast a glance at her brother-in-law. 'You can piss off, though,' she muttered beneath her breath.

Olivia had heard Matilda's sour comment. She'd noticed the fading bruise on Fran's chin and guessed the woman had got it from her husband. She'd felt Fran's gaze linger on her own tell-tale marks ... as had Jimmy's. He was still ogling her over the rim of his glass, so to avoid his eyes she glanced around at her surroundings while Matilda and Jack joined in belting out a rendition of 'It's a Long Way to Tipperary'.

It was Olivia's first time inside a drinking establishment as a proper customer. When she was a child her parents had occasionally taken her and her sisters to a pub. While the adults drank and created a din behind swing doors, their kids had sat in prams in the hall or played chase in the corridors. But her mother hadn't been a big drinker and Aggie hadn't liked her husband carousing too often either. The couple hadn't argued much, but Olivia could recall that Tommy's drinking had been a bone of contention between them. But he'd been different then, with Aggie at his side. He'd been a nicer man ...

'Livvie?'

Olivia twisted round at the sound of that questioning voice, feeling herself bathed in warmth. Joe didn't approach her but stopped where he was, staring at her over the tops of revellers' heads. She eased a path through a throng of people to stand before him, a smile on her face.

'What the ... ?' He shook his head in bewilderment. 'I thought me eyes were deceiving me. What the hell are you doing here? Are you having a drink with Matilda Keiver?'

'I am ... she's a good friend. Dad kicked me out and I'm living in the Bunk now.'

Joe gently touched her cheek. 'I can't believe it. What a wonderful surprise to see you ... but I wish you'd go home. You're too good for the likes of us lot, Livvie.'

'Not according to my dad, I'm not.'

'He found out we'd been seeing one another, didn't he?' Joe's eyes were shadowed with guilt.

She sighed, giving a nod. 'Everything came to a head when I got home after talking to you outside the factory that day.' Olivia gestured in frustration. 'He found out I'd been meeting you, and that I'd lent your mum money, and Maggie acting daft with that oaf up the road only added to the confusion. Dad jumped to stupid conclusions and went mad.'

'He hit you again, didn't he?' Joe turned her chin gently with his finger, inspecting her bruises.

'Got thumped twice in one day.' Olivia tried to make a joke of it but her smile soon faded. 'How have you been?' She could see he looked strained. 'Have you had the funeral? I've been thinking of you, coping with it all alone. You must feel so sad.'

'I've been thinking of you ... all the time.' Again he touched her face tenderly. 'Can't put you from me mind, Livvie, even for a minute,' he said hoarsely. 'Mum and Annie are at peace together in Cambridge. They were laid to rest at the beginning of the week.'

'I'm glad it's over. I know you're grieving but it's a fresh start for you.'

Joe shoved his fingers through his hair. 'I was coming to the factory on Monday to speak to you when you finished work ... say goodbye.'

'What?' Olivia frowned.

'Now I wish I wasn't going. If I'd known about you moving into Campbell Bunk I wouldn't have joined up.'

'You're going to fight?' Olivia felt shivery and tense, fearing for his safety. Allied casualties were mounting all the time and the war was the main topic of conversation now at Barratt's. Posters were springing up everywhere, urging men to do their patriotic duty and visit recruiting offices.

'Things are hotting up over there and I want to do what I can to help. I didn't see anything to stay for, what with Mum and Annie gone and you ...' He hesitated. 'You being so far out of my reach.'

'I never said I was!' Olivia's fingers found his and clasped them, keeping their hands concealed..

'Come outside with me so we can talk somewhere quiet.' Joe tugged her after him.

'I'll just say goodbye to Matilda and Jack. They've bought me a birthday drink 'cos I turned eighteen in the week. I said I'd only stay for the one.' Olivia slipped her fingers free and wove back through the crowd.

'What is it with you two gels and Joe Hunter?' Matilda said when Olivia told her she was off home. She'd spotted the two of them gazing into one another's eyes.

'I know Ruby likes him.' Olivia understood Matilda's comment. 'I take it you don't,' she said bluntly.

Matilda finished her whiskey before giving her a lopsided smile. 'Ain't got nuthin' personal against him. Knew his mother, and his father before Herbie run off. Maisie had a hard time of it and I know her son did too, watching that swine making her suffer.' She shrugged. 'But when all's said and done he's not the sort a mother wants around her daughters. And I've got four gels.'

'He said he's turned over a new leaf. I believe him. He's been good to me,' Olivia said simply.

'Well, reckon that's enough then.' Matilda gave a nod. 'You're nobody's fool, Olivia Bone, and you speak as you find, same as me.' She placed a hand on the girl's shoulder. 'But I'm always gonna be a mother first and your friend after that.'

'I know.'

"Cos I *am* yer friend, I'll tell you that being seen with Joe Hunter will make people think you're out of the same mould as yer cousin Ruby. Now, *I* know that ain't true, but just sayin' . . .'

Olivia nodded. 'Makes no difference to how I feel about him. I understand what's made him who he is. People with too much to say for themselves don't know the bones of it.'

'Right 'n' all, love,' Matilda said. 'You do what you think's right then take the consequences if it ain't. We're alike, you 'n' me.' She glanced contemptuously at her sister, hanging on her husband's arm. 'Just wish Fran had a bit of your backbone.' Matilda jerked her head at the door. 'Go on . . . he's waiting for you.'

'Thanks for the drink.'

'You're welcome. Goodnight to you.'

'Where do you want to go?' Joe asked when Olivia joined him outside.

'Don't know.'

'Come round mine and have a drink, or a cup of tea if you prefer,' Joe suggested. 'Won't try it on, swear. I just want to say goodbye. I'm getting shipped out early next week.'

As they walked arm in arm in the direction of Playford Road, Olivia patted his hand, saying, 'You make sure you look out for yourself over there.'

'Will you write to me?'

"Course! Twice a week.'

'Has your boss taken you out?'

Olivia glanced at him askance at that unexpected change of subject. But he turned away, shielding his expression. 'Just the once, we've been out. Mr Black took me for a walk over

Alexandra Palace. That was a while ago. He's not really interested in me, Joe, it's just a bit of a game to him. I only went along to speak to him about Dad getting his job back at the factory.'

'So your boss thinks he can use you like a toy, does he?'

Joe sounded grim and beneath her fingers Olivia felt the muscles in his arm harden.

'I'll make a few things clear to him before I sail . . . '

Olivia pulled Joe to a halt. 'You will not! He's done nothing wrong. He's never even tried to kiss me. Anyway, I can look out for meself. Always have done and reckon I always will.'

Joe gazed down at her fierce delicate features. 'You've looked out fer yerself, Livvie, but at what cost?' He touched the injury on her face. 'This is what being brave gets you . . . you shouldn't have to do it. You should have a man to care for you. Someone as sweet as you deserves all the good things in life. Would he marry you if you encouraged him?'

'Who? Lucas Black?' Olivia's smile turned into a guffaw; she urged Joe to walk on. 'He doesn't see me as his wife, you daft ha'porth . . . just his factory girl.' She shrugged. 'It's just banter between us. He is quite interesting to talk to. He's clever and well educated so he's probably bored stiff a lot of the time in that office of his, and flirting helps him pass the time. His secretary fancies him, and he's got a girlfriend.'

'Sounds like he needs taking down a peg or two,' Joe said through his teeth.

'He might be posh and arrogant but he's all right,' Olivia said, quite forcefully. 'And I don't want you stirring things up for no reason or you'll get me sacked.' She didn't know why she was sticking up for Lucas Black considering how frostily they'd parted company. She'd slapped him, accused him of being disrespectful, but still she trusted him. She might not know him well but she sensed that he was an honourable man even though in his position he had the opportunity not to be. He wasn't desperate for her, he'd said, and she'd believed him. He wouldn't stoop to force himself on her, or any woman.

'Sorry . . . poking me nose in where it's not wanted, aren't I?'

Olivia hugged his arm closer. 'It's nice that you care.'

Joe led the way to his door and ushered her inside his home.

'Crikey! You're lucky.' Olivia swivelled on the spot, looking around his front room. It was spacious and the absence of a cooking range and bed made her think he had a separate kitchen as well as a bedroom. She was coming to know how to tell from first glance the size and layout of a property. This certainly wasn't a tenement building but it could be that Joe shared it. 'Anybody upstairs?'

He shook his head. 'Got the whole of it.'

'You've taken the *whole* house?'

'I like a bit of room to meself. Mum used to live here with me, and Annie would sometimes come on visits when she was well enough.'

'Did your mum move out when your wife moved in?'

Joe's mouth tilted wryly. 'They didn't get on, that's fer sure. We all muddled along together for a while. But arguments started and Mum wanted her own place. I was glad when she left.'

'Does your wife know you're off to fight?'

'No point in telling her. She's somebody else's wife now . . . proper job . . . church 'n' everything.'

'Sorry,' Olivia said awkwardly.

'No need to be. That was a relief as well . . . when we went our separate ways. Never stopped going at it hammer and tongs after she lost the baby. She wanted another and I didn't. Wouldn't have been right to bring a kid into the world. I knew things had turned sour between us.' Joe pointed to a comfy-looking armchair. 'Sit down. I'll find a bottle of something.'

'Can I have a cup of tea, please?' Olivia chafed her palms. 'It's turned chilly out. Not long till Bonfire Night now, is it?'

'I'll stoke this up.' Joe crouched by the dying embers of the fire and loaded some coal on to it. 'What's your place round the corner like?' he asked over his shoulder as he worked the bellows.

'Like this . . . ' Olivia stretched out her arms. 'Can almost touch the walls each side it's so tiny.' She leaned closer to the fire as the fuel caught and shot flames up the chimney. 'Need to get somewhere for all of us. Miss my Alfie, I do. I know he's missing me. I've not seen him in ages.' Olivia wondered if the port had made her maudlin; tears had dripped from the corners of her eyes to run down her nose while she talked about her little brother. Briskly she wiped them away.

'You can have this place when I go.'

Olivia beamed at Joe to show she was grateful for the offer. 'Thanks, but I can hardly afford the rent on that slip of a room Matilda found me.' She undid her hat, taking it off so she could sit back comfortably in the chair. 'What's the rent on something like this?'

'I don't pay rent. It's mine.'

'What . . . you mean, you *own* it?' Olivia gawped at him. She knew very few people who didn't pay rent to a landlord. In fact, she wasn't sure she knew any.

'Ill-gotten gains,' Joe said mordantly. 'Glad now I sank most of 'em into this place. I kept the money safe from Maisie that way. She'd have had the floorboards up looking for drug money.'

'It must have been a worry for you . . . ' Olivia broke off as Joe strode over and crouched down in front of her chair, gripping her fingers.

'Move in here ... please. I want you to look after the place while I'm away, and in return you can stay rent-free.'

Olivia withdrew her hands. 'I ... I can't, Joe. People know it's your house. They'd think that we'd ... ' She frowned. 'What would I tell my sister? I've been nagging Maggie to behave herself with men, and not let them take liberties. I'd seem a dreadful hypocrite. My dad would think he'd been right about me all along. He called me a whore.'

'Marry me then ... I love you, Livvie. I want you as my wife more than anything. I know you're too good for me and deserve better but I'm selfish where you're concerned.'

Olivia cupped his earnest face between her hands. 'I'd need to think about something as important as that,' she said softly. 'But even if I said yes, my father would never give his consent. And if I lied and told the vicar I was twenty-one, Dad would be bound to find out and get us into trouble.'

'I'll talk to him ... persuade him.' Joe dropped to his knees in front of her. 'I never thought you'd even consider it. I'd've asked you ages ago if I'd realised.' He drew her face closer to sweetly kiss her lips. 'We could elope to Gretna Green this evening. I've got enough saved for the train fare and everything else we need.' He looked boyish when he added, 'Even got you something white and pretty to wear.' He dug in his pocket and pulled out a long, silky white feather. 'Some old gel chucked it at me when I come out of the cemetery in Cambridge.' He eased the quill into Olivia's hatband. 'Didn't have the heart to tell her that I'd already joined up. The poor old soul was ranting about her son getting killed and not even old enough to be in the army.' He paused. 'Let's just go, Livvie, and worry about it all afterwards.'

'Then I *would* lose my job at the factory, swanning off without permission.' Olivia ran thumb and finger along the silky fronds

of the feather adorning her hat. 'And you'd get done for deser-
tion before you've even started in the army.'

'I know,' he said hoarsely. 'Just a joke.' He raised her fingers,
holding them to his warm lips for a long, long while. 'When I
come back on leave . . . you'll tell me yes or no to a trip to Gretna,
won't you? I'm not sure I can wait till you're of age, Livvie, if
your father won't come round to it.'

She nodded and gave him a quick peck on the lips. 'Now, am
I gonna get that cup of tea or are you expecting me to make it
meself?'

Chapter Twenty-Four

Olivia paced up and down outside the laundry, peering in. Her sister was on her break, sitting with her friend sipping a cup of tea. Maggie had spotted her, but for some reason was ignoring her. Olivia planted her hands on her hips and stared boldly through the glass, hoping that she would get the message. If she didn't come out then Olivia was prepared to go in. Her sister's reluctance to be friendly made her wonder if their father had banned Maggie from speaking to her because his meeting with Lucas hadn't turned out the way he'd wanted it to.

'Why are you hanging around?' Maggie had slipped out to barrack her.

'That's a nice hello!' Olivia retorted. 'If you don't like me coming here ... tough. It's not all about you, y'know. I'm interested in hearing how the younger ones are doing too.'

Maggie crossed her arms over her chest and flounced off a yard or so.

Olivia noticed that her sister wouldn't turn fully to meet her eyes. She'd only just stopped favouring one side of her face herself now her injury had healed so recognised that stance. Grabbing Maggie's arm, she swung her around.

'Dad's laid into you.' Olivia's flat words betrayed none of the emotion churning inside her. 'What started him off?'

Maggie gave a sulky shrug.

'I'm going to have it out with him! He shouldn't get away with it anymore!' Olivia blinked away spontaneous tears. 'Has he whacked Alfie?'

'He's always whacking Alfie.'

Olivia turned and marched up the road. She wasn't sure what she was going to do but she'd have to do something or she'd explode.

Maggie pelted after her, cupping her jaw to ease the ache in it as she pounded the pavement. 'Don't accuse Dad of belting me.'

'Why not?'

'"Cos he didn't,' Maggie said sheepishly. 'I told him I bashed me face on the cupboard door when he asked.'

For a moment the sisters stared at one another then Olivia said hoarsely, 'I told you to stay away from that pig.'

'I'm going to now,' Maggie mumbled. 'I'll tell Dad if he does it again.'

'A lot of good that'll do you.' Olivia walked off up the road, shaking her head in despair.

*

Cath hadn't felt up to a trip down the High Street today but she'd not missed a single shift following her abortion. Although she was sore and feeling washed out she'd told Olivia she was glad she'd gone through with it. Trevor had started his training over at Clapham Common and was expected to ship out in a month. As she saw her friend hurry back into the factory looking agitated Cath went to meet her.

'What's up, Livvie?'

'Me sister Maggie's what's up. Gonna swing fer that girl,' Olivia breathed. Yet despite her anger she felt forlorn that her sister should have met up again with Harry Wicks. She knew that he hadn't trapped her into it. Maggie had gone along willingly.

Cath put a comforting arm around her friend's shoulders. 'Bloody families,' she muttered as they entered the building for afternoon shift.

Joe was waiting for Olivia when she finished work. She gladly accepted a lift home on his cart, and as he courteously dusted off the seat then helped her aboard she realised she didn't care who saw them together. She was proud of her association with a man like Joe Hunter.

Lucas hadn't been in and although she'd been curious about his whereabouts she'd not asked about him. She imagined he was again drumming up business for the company. She was grateful that he'd not sent a message via Miss Wallis that she'd lost her job. Perhaps when he'd had a chance to calm down and think about things he'd believed Olivia's version of events.

'What's up, Livvie?' Joe asked as they travelled along Hornsey Lane. He'd noticed her preoccupation. 'Bad day?'

'Sort of.' She gave him a half-smile. 'Not the girls at the factory ... my sister Maggie's driving me bonkers.' She didn't want to burden Joe with any of her worries when they only had a short, precious time left to them before he went overseas.

'A trouble shared is a trouble halved,' he teased, and nudged her arm. 'Come on, spit it out, it'll make you feel better.'

Olivia hesitated only fractionally over doing so; she was

considering Joe's proposal of marriage and believed she already knew what her answer would be. She loved him. But if she felt she should keep secrets from him, then it was a sign she didn't really trust him, and without trust there could be no future for them.

'She's not learned her lesson then,' Joe said when Olivia had finished her tale of woe.

'She said she won't see him again ... but she said that last time.'

'You stay away from Harry Wicks.' Joe turned towards her, frowning fiercely. 'It's your father's job to protect Maggie, not yours.'

'I know. I'm gonna speak to Dad about a few things ... tell him I'm bringing Alfie and the others to live with me, if that's what the kids want. And if you don't mind me taking up your offer to be your housekeeper, that is.'

Joe grinned and fished in his waistcoat pocket to produce a key. 'I don't mind at all. That's a spare ... yours to keep, for as long as you want it.' He put the door key on her lap.

She grabbed his callused fingers, feeling overwhelmed by his generosity. Spontaneously she lifted them to her soft mouth to kiss them before feeling self-conscious and letting them go.

'Right ... that's settled. I can stop worrying about me empty house and put me mind to seeing to the Hun. Now hold onto your hat!' Joe flicked the reins and urged the horse to a fast trot then faster still.

Olivia did hold onto her hat ... and the planked seat while they bumped and rattled along the road. She joined in Joe's whooping with child-like abandon and giddy exhilaration while cool air chafed her rosy cheeks. She felt happiness blotting out all her problems while the cart's wheels sent them spinning wildly towards Islington.

Joe slowed down as they approached Campbell Road and drove sedately into it and right up to her door.

Olivia noticed that Mr Keiver was outside his home talking to his brother-in-law. Jack raised a hand in greeting to them and Jimmy Wild gave them a sly, knowing smile.

'Stay away from him,' Joe said, staring hard-eyed at Jimmy. 'If he troubles you at all when I'm gone, tell Matilda or Jack. They'll sort him out. Matilda does so regular when he turns on her sister.'

'I guessed Matilda doesn't like him,' Olivia said. 'I've hardly spoken to him but he gives me the creeps.'

'Perhaps I'm a fine one to talk, but Jimmy Wild's a wrong 'un, even by Bunk standards.' Joe frowned. 'He treats his wife like dirt, parading his other women in Fran's face, that's why Matilda goes for him.'

Jack entered his tenement and Jimmy departed with such a swagger it was obvious he thought they were watching him.

Olivia turned to Joe. 'Will I see you before you go?'

He shook his head. 'Can't stand last-minute goodbyes,' he said gruffly. 'I'm off tomorrow early, and I've got a few loose ends to tie up this evening. Apart from that I've housework to get on with. Got to leave the place clean and tidy for you.' His cheeky grin faded away. 'I'll write to you as soon as I can . . . let you know me posting. I want them twice-a-week letters you promised me.'

'You'll get them, and you know I said I'd decide about getting married when you come back on leave . . . '

'Yeah, I remember.' He sounded resigned to hearing bad news.

'Don't need to wait. Me answer's yes,' she said simply.

He gazed at her from beneath the brim of his cap as though he couldn't quite believe his luck. 'You'll be my wife . . . proper job?'

'Proper job,' she echoed softly, and leaned in to kiss him on the mouth. She could see the glisten of tears in his eyes and it started her own watering. 'I want you to take this with you and keep it close to your heart as your lucky charm.' She unclasped the silver locket fastened round her neck, letting the chain coil into her palm. Taking his hand, she tipped the silver into it. 'Remind you to think of me, won't it?'

'Don't need anything to help me do that,' he said huskily, but he pocketed the locket. 'I've been thinking of you since I was a kid. I knew one day I'd find you,' he said, quite bashfully. 'As a small boy I'd hide under the bedclothes when Maisie and my father were going at it hammer and tongs. There was some-one . . . a friend, sweet and soft . . . to comfort me in the darkness. I knew you the first time I saw you. That's why I laid into Harry Wicks for touching you.'

Olivia hugged him tightly. 'I knew too that someday I'd meet my soulmate.' She wiped her eyes. 'Right . . . quick march then, Private Hunter,' she croaked, and jumped down from the cart, hurrying towards the tenement entrance. She spun about for a last look at him, knowing he'd be sitting watching her. Slowly she blew him a kiss, then another, before disappearing.

*

'Can't come here again. If me dad finds out what I've been up to, he'll belt me and chuck me out like he did Livvie.'

'Ain't gonna find out, is he?' Harry slid his arm about Maggie's waist to restrain her as she tried to sidle out of the hut.

'He's suspicious already 'cos he didn't believe I bashed me face on a cupboard,' Maggie said in a reproachful voice.

'Know what I reckon? Your nosy cow of a sister's stuck her oar in and turned you against me.' Harry ignored Maggie's reminder that he'd hit her. He jerked up her chin so she had to look at him. 'Livvie's jealous 'cos I prefer you to her.'

Maggie doubted that was true, though she would have liked it to be. All of her life she'd listened to people praising Olivia's prettiness while overlooking Maggie's. Her elder sister had inherited her lovely face and figure from their mother, whereas Maggie's light brown hair and thin frame came from her father. Not that Tommy Bone looked much like the photo they had of him and Aggie in their wedding outfits; that handsome young fellow had now gone grey and grown fat.

Harry started to undo Maggie's blouse, thrusting his hand inside. When she seemed to accept that he shoved her up against the wall of the hut, grabbing the hem of her skirt to lift it.

'Let me go.' Maggie squirmed to get away. She didn't mind him kissing and fondling her but she wasn't getting herself into trouble, and she knew enough about how babies were made to realise that was where she was heading if she let him carry on.

'You leading me on again, you little tease?' Harry panted. He formed a fist, threatening her with it by ramming it against her cheek. 'You come 'n' meet me again and do this and think I won't ... '

'You won't.'

Harry sprang back from Maggie, whipping around at the sound of that menacing voice.

'What the fuck d'you want? You been spying on us?' he snarled, his face turning florid.

'Get home before it turns fully dark.' With a push Joe sent Maggie, gasping in fright, scurrying away into the twilight.

Harry licked his lips, prowling the interior of the hut. He'd recognised Maisie Hunter's son straightaway. He'd been hoping to meet him again at a time and place of his own choosing, so he could creep up on him with a bit of lead pipe. A fair fight

303

wasn't what he'd been counting on and he was keen to get going as well. But he wanted to try a crafty attack first. He tried to saunter past so he could sneak in a rabbit punch but Joe grabbed his arm and shoved him back.

'Quiet word's in order, I reckon, before you get off. You stay away from Maggie Bone and the rest of that family and I won't need to come and find you and teach you some manners, like I did last time.'

'I don't take lessons in manners from a pimp,' Harry sneered, and spat in Joe's face.

'See what I mean? You really do need to learn,' Joe said, cuffing spittle from his cheek. His hand carried on moving to snap back Harry's head with a hard jab to his chin.

Harry staggered against the hut wall, trying to throw a bike at his attacker to keep him away. The vehicle was chained to a stay and clattered sideways onto its handlebars. But it had at least given him time to steady himself on his feet and bring up his fists.

'Ain't leaving till I hear you say you understand that I'll kill you if you lay a finger on Livvie or Maggie Bone ... or any of 'em, fer that matter,' Joe threatened him.

'Who d'you think y'are, giving me orders?' Harry's bared teeth had turned pink from the blood seeping out of his cut lips. 'I'll listen to their old man if he complains. I'll not listen to you. You're just a ponce whose mum's an old brass.'

Joe leaped over the bike and dodged the right Harry threw, landing his own punch deep in his opponent's belly, making him double up, retching. Joe rammed his knee into Harry's sagging chin. 'Stay well clear of 'em all, or next time I won't go so light on yer. Understand?'

He finally removed his boot from Harry's back when he heard the defeated man pant, 'Yeah ... understand.'

Joe left him groaning on the floor. Pulling up his collar, he strode off towards the road where his cart was parked.

'What in the name of the Lord is going on here?' The soft Irish accent brought Harry up on to one elbow but he kept his shoulders hunched and his injured face hidden between them. He was seething that he'd not managed to land a blow on Hunter and wanted to take out his frustration on someone. Being found by one of the nuns, cowering on the floor like a whipped dog, was the last straw for his battered ego. If Maggie had been about he'd have taken it out on her because the throbbing in his groin was bothering him as much as the ache in his face. But Maggie had gone . . .

Sister Clare shook the shoulder of the bulky prone figure she imagined to be a man because she could feel muscle beneath her fingers and smell stale tobacco, though she couldn't see much of him in the dark. 'I heard a noise out here . . . what's gone on?' She tutted as she saw through the gloom the shape of the bike lying on its side. 'Were you trying to steal my bicycle?' She sounded disappointed rather than cross.

Harry knocked her feet from under her so that she collapsed beside him on the concrete floor, with a surprised squeal.

'Shut up,' he growled before ripping at her dark clothing.

*

The next time Olivia went to Kendall's in her dinner break her sister was waiting for her. Maggie burst out of the laundry, dragging her along the road by the arm to a secluded spot.

'Sister Clare got attacked by a man in the Mission Hall hut,' the girl hissed.

'What? Have they arrested him?' Olivia was shocked by that dreadful news but she was also surprised that Maggie wanted to talk about it urgently. Olivia herself had always liked the nun

305

who'd comforted her following her mother's passing and who had been understanding about Alfie accidentally breaking the Mission window.

'Not heard of any arrest. But I know who it was done it,' Maggie squealed.

Olivia's expression hardened and she spat out, 'Harry!'

'Wasn't him. But he knows who did it, and so do I.'

Olivia tilted up her sister's chin so as to examine her face. 'Well, then, you'd better cough up what you know to the police because it sounds very serious.'

'Can't or I'll get in trouble. Joe Hunter did it . . . I know he did 'cos I saw him there.'

Olivia was speechless for a moment then she choked out incredulously, 'You're mistaken. Joe would never do such a thing. Besides he's in France.'

'I was there . . . I saw him!' Maggie shook her sister's sleeve. 'I met Harry in the hut.' She quickly followed that up with, 'Only to tell him I wasn't seeing him no more. Anyway Joe Hunter turned up and saw Harry trying to pull up me skirt, though I told him not to. He sent me home.' She chewed her lip agitatedly. 'I knew a fight was going to happen and it did – Harry's all bashed up. When we found out that Sister Clare had been attacked I went after Harry 'cos I knew we'd been there that night. I asked him not to talk to the coppers 'cos then they'd come round to question me. Everybody would find out what I'd been up to and call me a slag.' Maggie's eyes filled with tears. 'Dad would've found out and killed me.'

'Joe didn't do it,' Olivia said angrily. She now knew what *loose ends* had kept him busy on the evening before he'd left for France. Now he'd gone to war with no idea of the mess he'd left behind him in trying to protect her and her family from Harry Wicks.

'He *did* do it,' Maggie insisted. 'Harry said he's that sort, 'cos he's a pimp. Harry ran off after getting beaten and left Joe in the hut on his own. The nun must've turned up then.'

'Joe's a decent man and I'm glad he whacked Harry. He deserved it. Not only for hitting you and me but for attacking Sister Clare. I know he's to blame. He's tried to force himself on me in the past and I was lucky to get away.'

'Harry said you'd say that. He said you're jealous,' Maggie sniped.

Olivia shook her sister roughly by the shoulders. 'Don't you realise what a lucky escape you've had?' She felt like weeping because of her sister's obstinacy where that brute was concerned. Unable to stomach being with Maggie any longer, she turned away and hurried off up the road.

'You're not going to do anything, are you?' Maggie had caught up with her, smearing away frightened tears. 'I wouldn't have told you if I thought you'd go blabbing.'

'You deserve to get into trouble, you stupid little fool,' Olivia rounded on her sister. 'If you hadn't kept meeting that disgusting swine in the hut none of this would have happened! And poor Sister Clare wouldn't have been hurt. Now you expect me to sort it out for you, don't you? That's the only reason you've owned up to any of it.' Olivia pointed a finger close to her sister's tear-stained cheek. 'Well, I will sort it out but don't blame me if you don't like the way I go about it.'

Chapter Twenty-Five

'I've heard on the grapevine that you've left home.'

'I have,' Olivia answered. 'I've moved to Islington. I'm engaged ... unofficially. We're going to wait until my fiancé comes back from the war before telling people, though.'

'That's grand news,' Sister Clare said, handing her a cup of tea. 'But it's a terrible time, so it is, for all the families waiting for their brave menfolk to return. Let's pray it's over soon.'

'I've heard you've had a terrible time too, Sister Clare.' Olivia gently raised the subject that had brought her to the Mission Hall.

She had known she'd find the nun here, as she would on any Wednesday evening. The young woman wouldn't let something as trivial as one depraved man's lust get in the way of her love for God or her duty to the community. Olivia liked and admired Sister Clare even more for carrying on with her routine and refusing to be Harry Wicks's victim.

'I haven't come to pry, Sister Clare. You've comforted me in the past so I just wanted you to know that I'm sorry ... ' Olivia's voice tailed off. She was unable to find the words to express the mix of anger and sorrow she felt.

'I know,' Sister Clare said with a sweet smile. 'Everybody's been so kind. My colleagues have been a wonderful support although I had to tell Sister Beatrice that going out looking for the brute with a shotgun wasn't at all advisable.' She chuckled. 'Beatrice lived on a farm in the wilds of Peterborough so is quite able to bring down a running stag, let alone a cowardly man. Or so she boasts.' Sister Clare took a sip of tea. 'I was hurt and disillusioned, but not with God ... it hasn't weakened my faith.' She twitched the black fabric of her habit. 'This doesn't shield us from all the evils in mankind, nor should it.' She shrugged. 'We too must bear what other women do.'

'Have the police arrested anybody?' Olivia asked.

'I think they have a suspect but the fellow has disappeared.' Sister Clare sat looking quite serene as she sipped her tea. 'I couldn't give the constable a description. It was dark and he didn't speak other than to mumble a word or two. It was over quickly, thank the Lord, and he just ran off. Didn't even help me up, but I think I managed to give him a scratched face for his deplorable behaviour.' Sister Clare smiled wryly. 'The constable who interviewed me asked if I thought he might be a foreigner. Two women in Edmonton had reported similar attacks and they'd noticed the fellow had a French accent.' Sister Clare shook her head. 'I couldn't say for sure but I did notice an unpleasant smell about him ... like rancid meat. I told the constable that. He said it was helpful because the Belgian refugee they were after had been working in an abattoir until he fled their investigation.' She sighed. 'Whoever it was, I hope they catch him and lock him up so he can reflect on and repent his sins.'

Olivia closed her eyes, feeling overwhelming relief. The nauseating smell of raw beef that clung to Harry Wicks seemed to fill her nostrils. Not for a moment had she suspected Joe had committed such a heinous crime. She'd wanted to speak to Sister Clare to offer condolences, and in the hope the nun might mention a detail that incriminated Harry. And she had. Harry Wicks was a rapist and a liar, who'd blame an innocent man to save his own skin.

'I had better get back and give Sister Maria a hand,' said Sister Clare, putting down her empty teacup. She pulled a face. 'She can get shirty if she believes she's done more than her fair share with the old folk.' Sister Maria was taking Bible study while her younger colleague spared a few minutes to talk to her visitor in a side room.

'You're so wonderfully strong and selfless,' Olivia burst out, getting to her feet to grip the nun's hands. 'I don't know why I worry over having ordinary things like a good wage and a nice home and a decent husband.'

'Get away with you.' Sister Clare fondly cupped Olivia's cheek but her smile showed she appreciated the praise. 'You're no weakling yourself, Miss Olivia Bone, what with caring so long for your father and the younger ones. You were toiling even before you left school, so you were.' She paused. 'How is your da?'

Olivia shrugged. 'Do you remember telling me months ago you thought my father had remarried? I wish it *had* been true,' she said with a wistful sigh. 'He'd benefit from a wife, and so would his kids. I'm sure he'd mellow and be a nicer person ... like when my mum was around.' She paused. 'I think there's someone in his life, but he keeps it all to himself.'

'Sister Maria visited her relatives again in Clacton in August. She didn't spot your father with a lady this time. But she remembered that last year a small boy had been close to them on the pier, staring out to sea through a telescope. Sister Maria said she remembered feeling sorry for the lad; when he ran after them she noticed he had a crippled foot.'

A tap on the door was heard and Sister Maria poked her head about the edge, her eyebrows disappearing into her wimple as she wordlessly conveyed her impatience.

'I'm on my way now, so I am, Sister Maria.'

Sister Clare grimaced an apology. But Olivia was glad of the interruption. Her smile remained on her face until she got outside into the cold November night air. For some time she leaned against the brick wall of the empty hut, wondering why she didn't feel more astonished and emotional to discover that her father and her aunt Sybil had been slyly seeing one another, and Mickey had been taken along too. She'd believed that her mother's sister hated her father and that the feeling was mutual. Such a deception deserved retaliation. But so much had happened recently that her capacity to be shocked or hurt had been blunted. She'd become resigned, she supposed, to coping with sorrows. Yet she wasn't sure she was sad about this, and she wasn't sure why such a lie had been necessary. She expected it was due to the guilt of the people involved, yet it was understandable that a widower and a separated woman, who had known each other for a long while, might find comfort in each other's companionship.

If they felt bad, it should be for reasons other than wanting to ease their loneliness. Her father and her aunt Sybil had had no right to deprive their kids of the support of their extended family. They hadn't after all denied it to themselves. Olivia had always wanted to keep in touch with her mother's relatives. Perhaps neither Tommy nor Sybil would have turned so unpleasant if they'd not been keeping secrets that had now been brought to light despite their creeping about.

311

They'd all missed out on so much ... and for what? Olivia thought as she began to walk slowly in the direction of Ranelagh Road. But there was more than homing instinct taking her that way. She had someone to see before she went back to Islington and her new home in Playford Road.

Joe had left his house clean and tidy for her, as he'd said he would. A vase of Michaelmas daisies had adorned the table in the small kitchenette and against it had been propped a note reminding her that he loved her. Also propped against the vase had been a photo of him in uniform, smiling and looking handsome. That now had pride of place on the mantelshelf.

Olivia slowed down as she turned into her road. Taking a deep breath, she marched up to a door, rapping on it. It was opened just as she was lifting her hand to use the knocker again.

'I need to speak to your brother. Is he in?'

Ricky Wicks had known for ages that Harry fancied Olivia Bone and that she'd always cold-shouldered him. Now here she was on the doorstep asking after him. Ricky was disgusted that Maggie mooned after his elder brother, and that Harry encouraged her; he'd hoped to walk out with her himself.

'Wait there.' Ricky shut the door in Olivia's face.

While some scuffling and low conversation went on behind the door, Olivia glanced across the street to her childhood home. A weak light showed from behind the curtain; she knew Alfie and the girls would be in but whether her father was at home was another matter.

She was tempted to go over and knock and give Alfie a cuddle, but she knew if she did he'd cry and cling to her and beg her to take him with her. She longed to see him, but she wasn't quite ready for another bust-up with her father. After speaking to Sister Clare and hearing such astonishing news she knew a meeting was brewing. But first she had Harry Wicks to deal with.

'What d'you want?' Harry had opened the door. He growled out the query while looking her up and down.

'I need to talk to you about something important. It'd be best if your mum and dad didn't hear, so you'd better come out.'

Harry grabbed his jacket off the peg on the wall and strutted out, shutting the door behind him.

Olivia walked straight into the alley beside the house. She stopped a few feet into it then fixed on Harry eyes that were full of hatred.

'If it's about Maggie, I've already told her to stop hanging around me. Bleedin' embarrassment she is, pestering me all the time.'

'I suppose that's why you hit her, is it? 'Cos she's an embarrassment?' Olivia replied sarcastically. 'I know different. Joe Hunter saw you with her, and gave you a thumping for mauling her even though she'd told you to stop.'

'That pimp of yours raped a nun.' Harry had inclined closer to Olivia, hissing the words through his teeth at her. The gas lamp overhead highlighted two scratches like fingernail marks, running parallel on his left cheek. 'I'll get the law on him fer it.'

'Sister Clare knows who raped her, and so do I. The man who attacked her is the same one who tried to force himself on me. He was a butcher who stank of raw meat. I know what his name is, even if she doesn't . . . yet.'

'What you on about?' Harry shifted uneasily, eyes darting to and fro.

'You raped Sister Clare and she scratched your face.' Olivia nodded at the two red weals visible on his cheek.

Harry licked his lips. 'You're lying. You've not spoken to her. You'd do anything to save Hunter's skin.'

'Could be I would. But I don't need to. You did it.' Olivia put her hand in her pocket and drew out the white feather that

Joe had given her to decorate her hat. 'The recruiting office is open first thing in the morning.' She held it out and, when he refused to take it, deliberately stuck it like a dart into the wool of his donkey jacket. 'It's either that or I'm going to the police and telling them everything I know and everything me and me sister and the nun have suffered because of you.'

'You won't do that,' he scoffed. 'Maggie'd be beaten black 'n' blue by yer father if you did. Don't forget, I've got enough stories of me own about that little tart.'

'Maggie's leaving me dad's house and coming to live with me. He can't touch her there. And where I live in Islington, we don't give a tinker's cuss about gossip.'

That set Harry back; he rubbed at his bristly chin, scowling at Olivia. 'Weren't nuthin' to do with me. But I can see you're set against believing me. What is it you're after, you interfering bitch?'

'You overseas, well away from my sister, that's what I'm after. Or you could go to jail instead if you prefer.' She walked away from him at a brisk pace.

She wasn't absolutely positive that Harry was the culprit following her talk with Sister Clare. If there *was* another rapist about, a foreigner who also worked as a butcher, then there was a slim possibility he had been the attacker.

But to keep her sister safe from Harry she'd take the chance of going to the police and accusing him of the crime if he didn't leave the neighbourhood. With him out of the way, Maggie might at last come to her senses and forget all about him.

Chapter Twenty-Six

'We always keep an eye out for the coppers. They don't like us having bonfires in the Bunk.' Matilda handed Olivia a cone of newspaper containing some roasted chestnuts.

'It is Guy Fawkes Night,' she protested, blowing on a scalding chestnut to peel it before popping it into her mouth.

Matilda grinned, bouncing little Lucy on her hip. 'Don't make a lot of difference to us down here – bonfires get lit any time of the year if we feel like celebrating.'

Mr and Mrs Keiver and their daughters were with Olivia, gathered around an old dustbin that had been piled high with bits of broken wormy furniture and rotting vegetation. Matilda and Jack were washing down their chestnuts with bottles of brown ale while they warmed themselves by the blaze on this chilly November night.

All along the street scattered bonfires were lending a devilish red tint to the decrepit tenement buildings and bangers scattered sparks over the scene. At almost nine o'clock at night

Campbell Road was more crowded with people than it would be during a normal day. Folk from neighbouring streets came, if they were brave enough, Matilda had told Olivia, knowing that the best fun on high days and holidays was to be had in the Bunk. The organ grinders were out and people hawking hot potatoes and pies were criss-crossing the street, bawling out their wares. One old fellow who'd sold his piano to Billy the Totter, and left it by the railings for collection, had lifted the lid and started an impromptu singsong on the pavement. A trio of tipsy girls of about Olivia's age were cavorting and belting out 'Knees Up, Mother Brown'.

Olivia caught a glimpse of a boy darting about a few yards away. 'Just off to have a word with me cousin Mickey,' she told Matilda. As Olivia drew closer she could see that her cousin was being taunted by a couple of lads. He was jumping up and down, trying to get hold of a ball they were keeping out of his reach.

'Clear off, Wrightie, you can't play soccer with that gammy foot of yourn.'

'Give us me ball back then.' Mickey scooted to and fro, trying in vain to reclaim his property from his so-called pals.

Olivia stretched up and neatly intercepted the ball as one of the boys threw it overhand. She secured it against her side.

'These two getting on your wick, are they, Mickey?' she said by way of greeting.

'Nah ... we're just having a lark,' he mumbled, turning his back on the boys.

One of them started catcalling, but they scarpered when Jimmy Wild ambled over, raising his palm to threaten that he'd clip them round the ear.

'Need any help, love?' He gave Olivia his lopsided smile.

'No. I'm fine, thanks.'

'Well, you just let me know if you ever need a man to lend an 'and, now yer boyfriend's gone off and left yer all alone.'

Olivia was about to snap at him but sensed Jimmy Wild would rather receive insults from a woman than be ignored by her. So she turned her attention to her cousin.

'Come and get some chestnuts from Mrs Keiver, Mickey.'

The boy needed no persuading. He gladly accepted the newspaper twist filled with scalding chestnuts, digging in immediately then licking his fingertips to cool them.

'Where's your mum and sister? Are they up the road celebrating Bonfire Night?' Olivia nodded to the far end of the street.

Mickey shook his head. 'Ruby's at work waitressin' and Mum's indoors on her own like she always is.'

'It'd be nice if your mum had a friend to go out with, wouldn't it?'

''S'pose so,' Mickey said, still chewing.

'Has she got a friend?' Olivia felt bad for interrogating the boy like this but the opportunity had unexpectedly arisen for her to find out something about that trip to Clacton. She'd considered confronting her father over it but was still unsure what business of hers it really was if her father and aunt had become lovers. Or perhaps they were just friends . . . but, if so, why hide it? Everybody would benefit from some harmony in the family.

'Mrs Keiver's me mum's friend although sometimes they argue.'

'You'll have a new friend living close by soon. Now I'm living in Playford Road the house is big enough for me brother to come and stay. You'll like Alfie, he's about the same age as you. 'Spect he'll go to the same school too once it's all sorted out.'

'Can he play football?' Mickey seemed to have perked up.

'Plays all the time with his friends out in the street.'

317

Matilda came over with more steaming chestnuts for everybody. 'Me brother-in-law bothering you just now, was he?' she asked, sharing them out.

'No ... it's all right, Joe put me wise to him before he went away.'

'Takes one to know one,' Matilda said bluntly.

Olivia didn't take offence. She'd grown used to Mrs Keiver's ways. Besides there was no denying the truth in her hint that Joe was no angel. 'Joe's asked me to marry him,' Olivia confided.

'And you've said yes,' Matilda replied with a slow grin. 'So *that's* why you've moved round into his place on Playford.' She clapped the girl on the arm. 'Wish you both all the luck in the world. Heard on the grapevine about his mum passing away. Maisie got taken ill while she was visiting little Annie, didn't she? Poor cow ... she had a rough time of it.' Matilda shook her head. 'Remember like it was yesterday when that wicked swine hurt the little girl. If he hadn't scarpered when he did, we'd've strung him up from a lamppost.' Matilda glanced shrewdly at Olivia. 'Ain't come as any surprise to you what happened to his sister, has it? I can see Joe's told you all about it.'

'We don't have secrets from each other,' Olivia said softly. 'We tell each other everything, good and bad.'

'Best way, love, knowing he ain't perfect but taking him all the same. Won't come as such a disappointment then when he does something daft. And he will.'

'D'you have secrets from Jack?'

Matilda cast a fond glance at her husband. 'Now normally I'd tell anybody who asked me that to mind their own business ... or words to that effect. But as we're having a heart to heart and I'm giving advice as an old married woman to a soon-to-be blushing bride, I'll let you in on the secret of me success. A little white lie don't hurt nobody so long as it's nothing serious.'

318

'Such as?'

'Where his baccy money's gone out of the tin.'

'And where has it gone?' Olivia asked, trying not to laugh.

'Down the Duke . . . medicinal purposes . . . settle me nerves.'

'Hear me name, did I?' Jack had come to join them. 'I take me hat off to Joe Hunter for joining up.' He patted Olivia's shoulder comfortingly. 'Now we've come out against the Turks 'n' all, there'll be no let up over there. But your young man's got his head screwed on, love, and will keep it down . . . '

'Well, *you're* still stopping right here, however many countries joins forces with the bleedin' Hun,' Matilda told him.

'Sit over here on the kerb, shall we, Mickey?' Olivia saw that things were getting heated between husband and wife and decided to give them some privacy.

Her cousin followed her to a relatively quiet spot and they sat down, rocking to and fro on their behinds on the hard concrete to get comfortable, legs stretched out in front of them.

'Did you go to the seaside last summer with your mum?' Olivia plunged straight in.

Mickey nodded. 'Somebody Mum knows took us on the pier at Clacton.'

'So your mum has got a friend then, apart from Mrs Keiver.'

Mickey frowned. 'Don't know if they're friends anymore. We never see him much, and they argue.'

'What about?' Olivia asked immediately.

'Dunno. They always stopped talking when I was about. I looked through a telescope at the ships . . . far out to sea they was that day.'

'How about your sister? Does Ruby like your mum's friend?'

'She don't know him. Mum told me not to say where we'd been 'cos it was a secret. She always pretends to Ruby that we're seeing her friends in Bermondsey. But we don't, we see Uncle

Peter. Don't think he's a real uncle, though. She don't always take me. Sometimes she goes on her own and leaves me behind with Ruby.'

'Reckon he is your uncle,' Olivia said hoarsely, ruffling Mickey's fair hair. So Thomas Peter Bone had been conscious enough of his nephew talking about who he'd been with to use his middle name, in case Ruby heard and put two and two together.

'I'm gonna pop up the road and say hello to your mum.' Olivia pushed herself to her feet. 'Why don't you go and ask Mrs Keiver to fill that up for you?' She pointed at the empty paper cone. 'Go on ... she won't bite if you say I sent you.' Determinedly, Olivia headed off. Some of her bravado had faded by the time she reached Sybil's front door but she inhaled deeply then gave a knock.

'Heard you've moved in round Joe Hunter's place,' was Sybil Wright's slurred greeting to her niece, but she left the door ajar so Olivia could follow her inside.

'News travels fast ... well, some of it does,' Olivia added in a mutter. 'Other news seems to take ages to get out.' She sat down on a battered couch before invited to do so.

'Make yerself comfortable, won't yer?' Sybil said sourly, and took the armchair with the gin bottle stuck down the side of the cushion.

'Who told you I'd moved in round Playford – Ruby?' Olivia could tell from Sybil's drooping eyelids that she'd been drinking.

'Yeah, she told me. Do it on purpose, did you, 'cos you knew me daughter fancied him herself?'

'No!' Olivia had been expecting a visit from Ruby but she'd not seen her in a while, so perhaps she was jealous. 'What makes you think I'd do something like that from spite?'

'Take after yer mother, that's why.' Sybil took a swig from the bottle.

Olivia digested this. 'Why d'you say it like that? As though you didn't like Aggie? You were sisters. My mum was a lovely person.'

'Was she now?' Sybil snorted. 'Well, maybe I knew her longer and better than you did.'

'Perhaps you knew her husband longer and better than she did ... is that it?' Olivia felt incensed by her aunt's nasty jibes and had been provoked into making one of her own in defence of her beloved mother.

Sybil had been about to take another swig of gin but instead she turned her pinched features on her niece. 'What's that supposed to mean?'

'Means that I've heard you've been spotted arm-in-arm with my dad in Clacton. And there was all of us, thinking you and him didn't get on. And 'cos you two didn't get on, none of us kids were allowed to either.'

'Who told you that?' Sybil sprang up unsteadily. 'Whoever said it's lyin'! Me 'n' yer father don't have nuthin' to do with one another.'

'Why are *you* lying?' Olivia sounded mystified. 'What difference does it make?' She got up from her chair, standing facing her aunt. 'Do you think that somehow you're betraying Agatha by being friends with him?'

'Ain't betraying her, going with him. *She* betrayed *me*,' Sybil spat. 'Me 'n' Tommy Bone were close before she stuck her claws in him.'

'You 'n' my dad?' Bangers went off outside the house, drowning out Olivia's exclamation of disbelief.

The explosion seemed to jerk Sybil to her senses and she pointed at the door. 'I told you not to bother me last time you come here. Now get going and don't come back here again, you nosy little cow. You want to know anything, speak to your father.' Sybil sneered then, "Course you won't do that, will yer? 'Case he belts you fer speaking out o' turn. Well, sooner you than me,' she muttered.

Olivia stood frozen with distress as memories ran slowly through her mind. She would never forget her uncle Ed fighting in the road with her father on the day her mother had died giving birth to Alfie.

'Uncle Ed left you because you were seeing my dad. You were with one another on the day Mum died. *That's* why I couldn't find him,' Olivia cried. 'I searched everywhere ... all up and down the street and the pubs.' Her voice grew loud with indignation. 'If he'd been around things might have been different. He knew she was near her time ... he could've fetched proper help.'

'Well, I needed help too! I needed help with our crippled baby!' Sybil lurched forward and slapped Olivia's face. 'You shut yer mouth. Say nothing, or it won't be just you gets a taste of his fists. It'll be me and yer brother too. He hates that boy.'

'I know ... and now I know it's your fault. It's always been your fault. How could you do that to your own sister? Alfie's never even known his mum.'

'At least he knows who she was, though!' Sybil roared. 'My kids think their father ran out on 'em when in fact he's still around, just don't want to acknowledge 'em.'

'*What?*'

'You get out of here, you interferin' bitch. You've made me say too much.' Sybil turned pale and swayed as though she might collapse.

'I don't think you've said enough,' Olivia returned quietly. 'You tell me exactly what you mean. I'm not a kid now, I'm gonna be a married woman soon.' She choked back bitter laughter. 'All this time I've been worrying about seeing me cousins when all along there was no need.'

'You still don't get it, do you?' Sybil said bleakly. 'They ain't your cousins … Tommy Bone fathered the lot of you.' She groped down the side of the chair for the bottle. Finding it empty, she hurled it at Olivia, catching her on the forehead.

Olivia staggered, but even the pain and blood on her hand couldn't shock her as much as what she'd just heard. Slowly she turned around and, using the wall for support, left the shabby tenement and made her way back to Playford Road.

*

'If we come out now, we've got a chance of turning the screws and getting all we want.' Nelly stabbed a finger down onto the bench, emphasising her point.

'Not sure about that, Nelly,' Sal called out. 'It don't seem right making use of the war like that.'

'Ain't right we've not been paid the same rate as the men,' Nelly yelled back. 'And I'm sick of dirtying me own clothes 'cos we ain't got no uniform, and eating me dinner off me lap 'cos there's no canteen.'

'What's going on?' Olivia asked. She'd just turned up for her shift to find most of the women grouped around Nelly, raising their voices, rather than sitting at their benches rolling out Southend rock.

'Nelly says we should use the labour shortage to go on strike. She reckons that to keep us sweet they'll give us a rise and perks. Ain't right in my opinion,' Sal said, shaking her head.

'Nor in mine,' Olivia said forcefully, frowning at Nelly. 'I'm not striking,' she impulsively called out. 'Surely the least we can do is show a bit of support for our men overseas. They're not just risking their jobs, they're putting their lives on the line for all of us.'

323

'Hear, hear!' Sal called out. 'Ain't on, Nelly, acting like that.'

Nelly pointed a finger at Olivia. 'Don't reckon she can be Tommy Bone's daughter!' she crowed, starting off some tittering amongst her cronies. 'Tommy would've manipulated things like a shot to get a better deal fer himself, war or no war.'

'You leave my father out of it!' Olivia retorted. 'You don't know what he'd do, and he's not here to defend himself!'

'You ask him if he'd take advantage of the situation . . . or perhaps he don't talk to you now you've shacked up with a wrong 'un and shamed him and yerself.'

Nelly's friends laughed louder this time and it seemed to Olivia that everybody turned to stare at her.

'Wrong 'un, is he?' she burst out. 'Joe's fighting the Germans for the likes of you and me. I'm not ashamed of him or meself. What are you doing to help win this damned war? Nothing! You're just trying to turn our menfolks' sacrifice into money in your pocket. *You* should be ashamed! You're a bloody disgrace, Nelly Smith.'

'I reckon she's right, Nelly. You'd better pipe down.' Sal glowered at the supervisor and followed Olivia towards the bench. Before sitting down, she patted Olivia's shoulder in solidarity.

Olivia worked like an automaton, rolling and shaping and cutting sugar paste, while her mind was far away, overwhelmed by her family's problems. It seemed the harder she tried to decide what to do about the bombshell that her aunt had dropped, the further away the answer shifted. She completely believed what her aunt had told her on Bonfire Night. It hadn't been a confession; Sybil would by now be bitterly regretting letting the secret slip out while she was drunk.

Ever since then Olivia had been feeling dog-tired from lack of sleep. She'd had a thumping headache too. The pain had started after Sybil struck her forehead with the gin bottle. But every night since had been the same. The long dark hours seemed to bring her problems more sharply into focus, keeping her thoughts spinning, and the blood pumping in her ears, while Olivia lay sleepless and aching, yearning for oblivion.

Last night instead of attempting to rest she'd burned the midnight oil at the kitchen table, struggling to write a letter to Joe. But she couldn't concentrate for long enough to come up with any news for him. She wished dearly he was close by so he could comfort her. He was the only person she felt she could confide in over something as shocking as her father's dreadful betrayal of his family. The matter was too sensitive to be put in a letter, and besides she didn't want Joe to spend a moment of his time fretting over her when he should be worrying about dodging bullets.

The notes she'd received from him had been sweetly reassuring, telling her about his new army pals and the larks they'd had. But she could read between the lines, and she could read newspaper reports; battles were ongoing at Ypres where he was stationed with his regiment of fusiliers. Autumn was turning to winter and soon it would be Christmas. She wished he would be back home for that special time but he'd told her in his letter he'd not get leave.

Olivia had considered pouring her heart out to Ruby but had quickly rejected that course of action. Eventually, all of the kids involved should know that they were more closely related than they realised, but it was Sybil's job to break news of such magnitude to Ruby and Mickey.

A showdown with her father was inevitable now, and Olivia no longer feared it. But inwardly she wept for her mother. A daughter's intuition told her that Aggie had probably suspected Sybil held a torch for Tommy, but no more than that. Aggie had been proud as well as beautiful; she would have left her adulterous husband had she known the truth.

Olivia glanced up at the factory clock; it was almost time for dinner break.

'What the hell d'you call that lot?' Nelly had sidled up to peer over Olivia's shoulder at her work. She had felt the woman's spiteful eyes on her at intervals throughout the morning. Nelly picked up some Southend rock. 'Ain't fit to be wrapped. Time you learned this job properly. You need moving back to packing where skill ain't required.'

'There's nothing wrong with it.' Olivia collected some of the sticks of rock, examining them. The red lettering was slightly small but acceptable, considering all the confectionery was hand-shaped, and the red sugar coating was smooth and even. 'You're just finding fault because I spoke me mind earlier,' she fumed.

Nelly inclined her thin body closer. 'Now I'm speaking *my* mind. I'm gonna ask Miss Wallis to transfer you back to packing.'

'She'll go crying to Mr Black,' one of Nelly's pals scoffed.

'She'd better be quick then, hadn't she?' Nelly crossed her arms over her chest. ''Cos he's quit 'n' all. Leaving before the end of the week.'

'What?' Olivia twisted about. 'Mr Black's enlisted?'

'Oh ... ain't he told yer?' Nelly mocked her. 'He's gonna be an officer in the army, according to Deborah Wallis. And she'd know, being as he took her out for dinner to break the news.' Nelly prodded Olivia on the shoulder. 'Seems you're forgotten now, Miss Olivia Bone.'

Chapter Twenty-Seven

'Sorry to bother you,' Olivia began.

'It's no bother.'

Lucas had stood up and beckoned her in, indicating she should take a seat. As she sat down he resumed his place in a large chair behind a huge desk.

She had stared at his brass nameplate on the door for only a second or two before knocking and obeying his summons to enter. She'd not the time to dither, marshalling her thoughts; if his secretary had noticed her, she'd have been sent away. Olivia knew she might only have this one chance to say goodbye and good luck to Lucas. He could go away tomorrow and be one of those unfortunate souls who didn't return.

But she couldn't think of that, only that she'd never forgive herself if she missed an opportunity to wish him all the best wherever his posting took him.

It was the first time Olivia had been inside the well-furnished room with bookcases lining the walls. Behind the leaded glass were hide-bound volumes of varying sizes. But it wasn't all for show; the leather desktop was cluttered with papers and ledgers and a blotter was home to a fountain pen that appeared to have just been discarded. By it was a sheet of notepaper half-filled with black script.

'You seem busy,' she said to break the ice.

'I have things to catch up on.'

Lucas's tone seemed to indicate that he didn't really want a conversation. They'd not spoken since the night he'd told her Tommy Bone had disclosed family secrets over a drink in a pub. In the meantime so much had happened that ages might have passed; yet it was only a couple of months ago that Olivia had given him that ironic wave after he'd followed her home to Islington.

'You've been away a lot recently. Have you had more talks in Birmingham? I love chocolate . . . ' She hoped small talk, or chit-chat as he'd called it on the day he'd asked her out to Alexandra Palace, might lighten his mood.

Lucas opened a drawer and took out a box, spinning towards her an expensive selection of chocolates as though it were a bag of penny chews.

'Keep them, Olivia,' he said soberly, reading her hesitation. 'We both know there's nothing in it. Give them to your sisters and brother if you don't want them yourself. I was given a lot of samples by Cadbury's.'

'Thank you . . . they'll think presents have come early this year.' The box that Joe had given her last Christmas had been smaller but had meant far more than this lavish, idly given gift.

Lucas smiled, watching her over steepled fingers.

'I heard you've enlisted. I just came to wish you luck. That's all, really.' She tucked a stray tendril of fair hair behind her ear, suddenly conscious of her sugar-stained hands and old clothes.

She stood up and approached the door. 'I'll miss you ... take care of yourself.'

That brought a smile to his lips as he, too, got to his feet.

'I'll miss you too. It seems your father was wrong to jump to conclusions about your state of health.' His eyes flitted over her slender figure.

'I told you he was mistaken ... about lots of things.'

'Have you made things up with him?'

'No,' Olivia said hoarsely. 'I've not spoken to him since ... but I must soon.'

'He should apologise.'

'To you as well as to me,' Olivia said pithily. 'But I doubt either of us will ever hear him say sorry. That's how he is.'

'Do you think you know your father well, Olivia?'

'Once I thought I did.' It seemed an odd question. Nevertheless she answered it. 'Now I fear I don't know him at all. Why do you ask?'

He pushed the half-finished letter across the desk towards her. 'I was writing to Tommy when you arrived. Read it.'

'Is it an offer of work?' She'd been ready to pick up the paper but curled her fingers back into her palm. 'It's private ... between the two of you. He wouldn't like me reading it.'

Lucas drew back the paper. 'It's a job offer. It's also a warning.'

'He'll be more careful in future, I'm sure.' Olivia gave Lucas a grateful smile. Whatever she felt about her father's character and morals, if he earned a wage at Barratt's it would benefit the whole family, especially as Christmas was almost upon them.

'I'm sure he will be more careful,' Lucas said dryly. 'Now he knows I'm on to him.' He shoved his hands into his pockets. 'Your father's been thieving from the factory. Did you know about it?' Having watched her expression stiffen he answered his own question. 'I can see you didn't.'

329

'He wouldn't! You're wrong!' Olivia burst out. 'He's never set foot in the factory after he was dismissed. He avoids even walking past.'

'He's had accomplices. His pal Bill Morley and Bill's niece Catherine Mason. Your friend's been hiding the key to the packing room for her uncle. Between them the two men have been getting the boxes away over the wall.'

Despite her disbelief, worrying bits of information drifted into Olivia's mind, compounding an awful suspicion that she'd just been told the truth. She remembered Bill Morley's evening visits. She'd thought it'd been no more than old pals meeting up ... but on reflection it had been odd as her father never socialised at home and they could have met at a pub. As for Cath ... she'd seemed to find an excuse to nip back into the factory on some occasions at the end of shifts. She'd needed extra cash for her abortion and had been desperate to save enough before her condition became obvious.

'Ah ... I see you might've known about it after all,' Lucas said, watching anxiety cloud Olivia's face and the way her eyes dropped.

'Are you going to report him to the police? Why give him a job then?' Olivia felt frustrated and confused by Lucas's attitude.

'I've given him a job because there are vacancies that need to be filled by men of his age, unlikely to enlist. As for the rest, I'm going off to fight a dirty war and the thought of it's put the pilfering of toffees pretty much in its place. I'm guessing you and your younger ones benefited in some way from what he's been doing?'

'He gave Alfie sweets ... we all shared them. And we had a roast dinner on some Sundays just before I left home,' Olivia quietly admitted. Had she known those treats had come from ill-gotten gains she'd not have enjoyed them.

'I'm glad. I'm warning him now to stop because I'm not going to be here to smooth things over if he's caught out, and then you'll suffer. If I come back in six months ... a year ... whenever it might be, and he's still at it, then I'll turn him in for being stupid and greedy.'

'He *is* stupid!' Olivia felt angry tears burn her eyes. 'He's more stupid than you could possibly know.'

'D'you want to explain that?'

She shook her head and turned away. 'Will the others get warnings? You won't sack Cath, will you? She's saving to be married.'

'I'm assuming your father will warn Bill Morley when he gets my letter. In turn Bill will warn his niece. Feel free to pass on to your friend what I've said if you want to do her a good turn.'

'I will. And thank you for what you've done.' Olivia opened the door then pushed it to, turning back to face Lucas. 'Before I go there's something you should know in case *you* want to pass it on. Nelly Smith's agitating for a strike. She's trying to take advantage of the labour shortage to get a rise and perks out of the guv'nors. Me and a few of the others have said we're not coming out and we think it's disgraceful. But she's got some support. And I don't care if she thinks me a snitch for ratting on her!'

'I'll let Mr Barratt know so they can keep tabs on it all.' Lucas gave her a smile of mingled affection and amusement.

'Your girlfriend'll miss you. Reckon Miss Wallis will too,' Olivia blurted out, growing hot beneath his steady blue gaze.

'I've broken up with my girlfriend. It wasn't fair to keep her hanging around waiting. Everything's uncertain now, even life itself.' He shrugged. 'And as for Deborah ... I told her she should find herself a nice man.'

'Perhaps she thinks she has.' Olivia found she couldn't feel sorry for the disappointed secretary.

'How about you? You've found yourself a nice man, have you, Olivia?'

'Yes. I'm getting married when Joe comes back. He's enlisted in the Middlesex Regiment. I had a letter telling me he's been picked out to be an ammunition carrier for the machine gunners. He said his pals are a good lot ... '

'He's a lucky man.'

'He will be if he comes back safe and well,' she said softly. 'And I wish with all my heart that you will too, Lucas,' she added before she left him.

*

As Tommy reached the end of the letter he grimaced. He cursed repeatedly. At last, he'd got his job back, but Lucas Black had got him ... by the balls.

Much to his disgust, Tommy had had to go back, cap in hand, to Bill and say he'd do a bit of thieving again. After he'd kicked Olivia out he'd quickly missed her and for more reasons than that he'd ripped the heart out of his own home. The loss of his eldest daughter's wages had been felt straight away but he'd never let Bernie Silver know he was struggling to find the rent. So he'd signed up for some more midnight trips down Mayes Road.

Tommy knew he should have had more faith in Livvie. He'd not seen her in a while but Bill saw her every day and if she'd been putting on weight the news would have got back to Tommy. She wasn't pregnant after all, and he regretted having jumped to conclusions. In fact, he was trying to think of ways to lure her home, without losing face. If he'd kept his temper he'd not have needed to go back to thieving and Lucas Black would never have got one over on him.

Bill had finally confessed to having another accomplice. Learning it was the man's niece had reassured Tommy ... until now. The girl had been enabling her uncle to get his mitts on the boxes of sweets, but she'd got the breeze up her and didn't want to be involved anymore, she'd said. Now Tommy reckoned he knew why Cath had turned windy: somehow the stupid cow had let the cat out of the bag and in consequence Black had them all over a barrel.

A rat-a-tat on the door brought Tommy to his feet. He wondered if Black had changed his mind about giving only a warning and had decided to act instead. Tommy was expecting to see a copper when he gingerly opened the door, but instead saw an equally unwelcome sight.

'I've told you never to come here!' he burst out.

'Too late fer that,' Sybil said, and marched inside. She'd been expecting to hear from Tommy for a while. Usually if he wanted to see her he'd send her a note giving a time and place for them to meet up. On the rare occasions that he'd treated her to a weekend break they'd meet at the railway station. But for months now she had waited and waited and never received any sort of message. So now, many weeks on from her meeting with Olivia, she'd taken the bull by the horns and come to see him. Sybil had at first regretted blabbing the truth to her niece. But not for long. She'd recognised an opportunity to get what she wanted at last and she was going to use it. If Tommy was ignoring the inconvenient truth or else genuinely didn't know that everything was out in the open ... well, she'd put him straight on a few things, and not before time.

'When did you last speak to Olivia?' Sybil demanded, crossing her arms over her chest.

'Why? What's it to you?' Tommy pocketed the letter he'd left open on the table.

'It's to do with me 'cos she's living round the corner and has made it her business to come and see me. And I'll tell you now that she and Ruby have been pally fer quite some while. Didn't know that, did yer?'

'*What?*' Tommy gawped at her. He knew that Olivia had moved to Islington but had never thought she'd bump into the Wrights, living as they were in a no-go area. Besides after such a long time he'd felt confident his eldest daughter would not recognise, let alone talk to, Sybil or Ruby, especially as he'd banned any such meeting from taking place. 'What've you told her?' he roared.

'The truth!' Sybil bawled back. 'Ain't keeping dirty secrets no more, and ain't hiding away in some slum so you can pretend you're whiter than white to your kids and your pals. I've lost me husband and me decent home, 'cos of you. I've given you the best years of me life, and me looks. And *our* son's getting bullied 'cos of his crippled foot.' She squared her thin shoulders. 'I'm moving in here with Mickey. The boy needs a fresh start, away from the scum living in the Bunk.'

Tommy's jaw sagged further. 'What d'you mean, you've told her the truth?' he whispered, ignoring the rest of Sybil's tirade.

'She has, Dad, and I'm glad.'

Olivia had used her midday break to visit her father. She knew the kids would be at school and Maggie at work, and that her father had taken to having his dinner at home before returning to the market to pack up. She'd hoped they could have a reasonably civil conversation in which she'd tell him that she was taking Alfie to live with her, and that she was settled and engaged to be married. She'd known she had to bring up the subject of his thefts too. On the short walk from the factory to her childhood home there had been many different things spinning round in her mind that she realised she must talk to him about.

On turning the corner she'd seen her aunt Sybil some yards in front of her. The woman had stood stock-still for a minute as though gathering the courage to knock on the door. Olivia had watched from a distance and felt admiration for her aunt when she put her head up and marched on.

Olivia had given them a short while on their own but knew she'd a job to do here before she returned to the factory. As she approached the house she'd been glad to see that the door had been left unlatched.

'You can't believe what she says, Livvie,' Tommy rattled off after a heavy silence. 'She's always been after me, all the time when yer mother was alive she pestered me. Aggie was my life . . . the only one I loved. *She* was what I wanted.'

'So how come I dropped two of yer kids?' Sybil spat, her face red with humiliation. 'You wanted me long before *she* took your fancy. We was sweethearts at school.'

'Shut up!' Tommy thundered, looking appealingly at Olivia.

'It's too late for lies and excuses, Dad. Can't you see, it's not good for any of us to carry on like that?' Olivia held up her hands in a placating gesture. 'I'm not judging you or hating you . . . that was for Mum to do. And knowing her, she would have wanted you to be happy . . . not lonely after she'd gone.' Olivia's green eyes glistened. 'She was lovely like that, wasn't she? She brought out the best in you, Dad, that's for sure, and I've always known that losing her left you bitter. Now I know you've always felt guilty too, and why that was.' The words of heartfelt forgiveness hung in the air. Her father's bloodshot eyes turned redder still and Olivia struggled to speak after a lump formed in her throat. She glanced at her aunt and then her father. 'I'm not getting involved in what you two decide to do,' she resumed huskily. 'But all us kids deserve to know the truth or it'll only store up more trouble. Apart from that, I've just come to tell you about myself, and what I'm doing next now I'm settled in Islington.'

'And what do you think you *are* doing next, miss?' Tommy wiped his eyes and resumed his usual belligerence.

'Well, first, I'm finishing early this afternoon to meet Alfie from school then I'm taking him home with me. After Christmas he can start a new school term in Islington. I've come for his things. But if you won't let me have them, it doesn't matter, I'll get him new stuff.'

Tommy's lips thinned against his teeth. 'You'll do no such thing!'

'Yes, I will, and you know as well as I do that if the authorities find out how you've mistreated him, nobody round here will want to know you, and nor will they at the factory when they hear about it.' Olivia spoke calmly. She knew that her father hated being embarrassed in front of people. 'If the girls want to come, they can, but I think they might choose to stay where they are with you. It's convenient for Nancy to stay at her school with her friends till she leaves in a year or two, and Maggie needs her laundry wages.'

'They can go . . . and welcome!' Sybil interrupted harshly. 'I'm moving in here with Mickey. The boy should know his father . . . Ruby too, though it's high time she got out from under me feet 'n' all.' Sybil jutted out her chin pugnaciously.

'Lucas Black's written to you about a job, hasn't he?' Olivia said, ignoring Sibyl's interference.

'Told you, did he?' Tommy asked, narrowing his eyes.

'Yes . . . he told me. You'd be a fool to go against him, Dad.'

Tommy looked crafty. 'That's why you're settled, is it? Keeping you in style, is he?'

'Lucas has enlisted as an officer in the army. Joe Hunter has joined up too. When *he* returns we're getting married.'

'Hope he doesn't fucking return then!' Tommy roared. "Cos you're too good for the likes of *him*.' His hands clenched angrily. 'You could've had the life of Riley if you'd played yer cards right with Lucas Black.'

'She's been hanging around with people worse'n Joe Hunter,' Sybil jibed. 'The Keivers she likes so much are the lowest of the low, fightin' and drinkin' ...'

Tommy turned a jaundiced eye on his lover. One of the reasons he'd never wanted things to turn permanent with Sybil was her love of gin. He liked a drink himself and one boozer in the family was enough. Aggie had said that to him time and again when he'd tried to persuade her to join him at the pub. It would all have been different if only Alfie hadn't been born ...

'Take the boy with you then,' he snapped at Olivia. 'Don't want to see you again unless it's by chance at the factory. Far as I'm concerned, we're finished. You stick by yer pimp, and good riddance to the pair of yer.'

'If that's how you want it,' Olivia said.

'It is. But remember this before you go thinking badly of *me*, 'cos you're no better, my gel. I ain't the only one who got caught between two people and found it difficult to make a choice.'

Olivia winced as her father's parting shot struck home. She went into the bedroom and collected Alfie's things, putting them into a carpet bag. Then she let herself out into the street mulling over her father's words. To her surprise she realised this was probably one of the truest things Tommy Bone had ever said to her.

*

'What you lot doing here?'

Maggie had emerged from the laundry to find Olivia, Nancy and Alfie standing together outside.

'There's gonna be some big changes at home,' Olivia said. 'I've come to ask you what you want to do.' She drew Alfie close by resting one arm around his shoulders and briefly outlined her reasons for inviting them to live with her in Islington, if they wanted to. Or they could stay put, she said, with their father and his lady friend.

'Dad's got a girlfriend?' Maggie sounded indignant rather than shocked. 'Who is she, and why's she living with us?'

'Best ask him about it all,' Olivia replied diplomatically.

She'd met Nancy and Alfie at the school gates. Both children had been surprised and pleased to see her. Olivia had guessed Nancy might be in two minds about what to do, and she was right. Nancy wanted to find out what Maggie thought about things because she wasn't staying behind on her own with her father and his woman. Olivia had realised that neither of her sisters would remember a lot about their aunt Sybil, if they remembered her at all.

Alfie hadn't hesitated over his decision. He'd beamed and hung on his big sister's arm, nodding repeatedly.

Olivia fancied she knew the answer she'd get from Maggie.

'Might as well stop where I am fer now,' she mumbled. 'Gonna get me own place as soon as I can anyhow.' She crossed her arms over her chest. 'Harry's joined up,' she added moodily.

'Good for him,' Olivia said neutrally.

'He said he wasn't ever going to. Something must've changed his mind.' Maggie shot her an accusing look.

'Perhaps his conscience got the better of him. I for one am glad to see the back of him.' Olivia turned to Nancy. 'Coming with me?'

She shook her head. 'Won't see me friends if I change school. Only got a year left then I reckon Dad'll let me get a job.' She linked arms with Maggie.

'We're going home,' Maggie said.

'Well, take this.' Olivia quickly pencilled her address on a bit of paper whipped from her bag. 'You know where to find me if you need me,' she called out after her two sisters.

Only Nancy turned around and gave her a wave.

Chapter Twenty-Eight

Ypres, Belgium

'Star shell's going up! Heads down, hands down!' Sergeant Dawson bellowed. 'Cover up every inch of that lily-white skin, lads, 'cos if Fritz spots yer he'll give you a *Gute Nacht* all right.' After a moment the brilliant light washed over the wasteland and Dawson's cockney voice bawled, 'Right, take a gander, Private Hunter. See anythin' interestin' out there?'

'To the left there, Sarge,' Joe yelled, peeping carefully over the top of the trench. 'Don't recall nothing layin' by that stump last time I looked.'

Before fading away the flare had illuminated lumps of humanity and vegetation rotting on no-man's-land. The shapes identifiable as corpses were carefully noted and if one less or one more was seen since the last lookout, the discrepancy was checked out. Both German and Allied working parties crept out under cover of darkness to cause as much havoc as possible to their opponent's front line.

'Very light's going up.' The rocket lit the area by the stump and the doggo German took wind and started to haul himself away on his elbows.

'I'll give him a burst then to hurry 'im on 'is way,' Sergeant Dawson cried gleefully, rubbing together palms encrusted with yellow mud. He put down his field glasses and swung the machine-gun muzzle into position.

The Vickers burst into life; when it fell silent after half a magazine had been let loose, three tin hats elevated just enough to allow their owners to peer over the top of the trench.

Joe strained to listen, hoping the poor bugger was dead. He hated hearing the mewling of mortal anguish; it always curdled his guts to hear men slowly dying whichever side they were on. He'd heard cries of *Mutter* and *Maman* and had clapped his hands over his ears because he now understood the word for mother in French and German. He wondered if he too might call for such comfort even though Maisie had provided him with little succour when alive. But perhaps she would be there waiting for him at the Pearly Gates ... Annie too ... when his time came, if he was lucky enough to go up rather than down.

'Buck up, lad!' Sergeant Dawson elbowed Joe in the ribs. 'No daydreamin'. Better 'im than you. He could've been heading this way with a pocket full o' grenades to warm us all up.'

'Could do with something warming me freezin' feet,' Freddie Weedon moaned.

'Can't feel mine at all,' Joe said to his pal. 'Ain't even sure they're still there.' He clasped his hands under his knee to assist him in dragging his left calf out of the mud. As soon as the top of his boot emerged he held onto the leather to prevent it being sucked off and swallowed up.

341

'I reckon me toes are rattling around in me socks.' Freddie sighed mournfully, banging his hand against a puttee that was stiff with clay.

'Right, you lot, pack up and let's go.' Sergeant Dawson had no time or sympathy to waste on grumbling privates. They needed to move the gun in case the enemy had a bearing on its position. The effort expended on toing and froing it up and down the trench was enormous. Moving a few feet in this sludge was laborious, especially where a duckboard had been lost and it was so sticky underfoot that progress was at a snail's pace.

Sergeant Dawson and Freddie dismantled then hoisted the Vickers; Joe grabbed the panniers of ammunition and bag of spare parts, and they made a slow slithering progress along the trench. The winding tunnel was home to soldiers trying to relax or nap in funkholes dug into the trench walls before the whistle sent them hurtling over the top at dawn. The Tommies made room as they bashed into them, edging past, laden down with hardware. The poor sods, jumpy and staring-eyed, for the most part seemed resigned to their fate. They sheltered in dugouts, playing cards or writing home by any feeble light available to them. They knew that the machine-gun teams gave them cover on the dash across no-man's-land so squeezed aside to let them through, mumbling greetings. 'All right, cock?' followed Joe along as a group of Whitechapel pals parted and flattened themselves against trench shuttering to let them through.

The infantry joked that it was a crying shame the Vickers boys could only help them make it far enough to stop a German bullet or bayonet on the other side.

Joe had been drafted on to the machine-gun team due to his predecessor having bought it. The unlucky sod had fallen off the narrow duckboard into a shell hole full of liquid mud. Sergeant Dawson had told them that nothing should be done in those circumstances. Attempting a rescue in the pitch black would only mean more men perishing in a quagmire that could swallow them whole in minutes. Joe had nodded wisely, as though he understood although he didn't. He'd not pass by a drowning man, and if, God help him, it were him in the hole, he'd hope the next fellow in line would feel the same way.

Sergeant Dawson was still teaching him how to strip down the Vickers. Joe had to oil and assemble it, and know how to repair it as fast as possible when under fire. The Vickers was the most important part of the team. It was cosseted and protected far more than the mere humans who lugged it around and fired it.

The duckboard had been reinstated further down the trench, cobbled together with bits of ammo box. They almost jogged along with the equipment banging against their numb bodies then set up again thirty yards away from their previous position. It was as well they had shifted because a crump and an explosion told them the Germans hadn't taken kindly to their boy being spotted.

'I'll take first watch,' Sergeant Dawson volunteered. 'You two get a bit o' shut-eye.'

'Got a fag, mate?' Freddie prodded Joe in the shoulder to stir him. He'd slumped, head to one side, to get what sleep he could before it was his turn on the fire step. He hated the night watches, eyes constantly swerving left to right and up and down until he fancied he saw all manner of man and beast dancing in the darkness. Then he would blink and blink to restore that comforting nothingness that blanked his vision but left his mind free to dwell on memories of Livvie back home in London. If anything made him determined to stay alive it was the sweet promise of her and their future together.

'Gissa fag, mate.' Freddie sounded peeved at his request

being ignored. 'Can let you have one back when I get me post from home. Me sister's promised me fags and a cake in time fer Christmas next week.'

Joe pushed up the brim of his tin hat and fumbled in his breast pocket. 'Only got one left.' He lit the cigarette and he and Freddie shared it, taking equal, lingering drags, exhaling in quiet sighs.

'Hope they have a good Christmas back home.'

'Yeah,' Freddie glumly agreed. 'At least we've got our rum ration to look forward to if me cake don't turn up.'

'Be relieved in a few hours, just in time for rum ration,' Joe said, grinning.

'Right-o, Hunter, your turn to strain yer peepers.' Sergeant Dawson nodded at a pale streak arcing along the horizon. 'Dawn's comin' up.'

'Sleet's comin' down,' Joe said, and turned his face up as the wet mist that had surrounded them separated into droplets that stung his skin. Cold was good in one way. If it froze over, the ground would firm up underfoot.

'Get that gun covered.' Sergeant Dawson whipped off the ground sheet that Joe and Freddie had draped over their shoulders as a makeshift blanket. Quickly the trio shrouded the gun with the cover, protecting it from the wet.

*

'How d'you like it, then?'

Alfie was still gazing at the cosy sitting room with his mouth forming an *'oh'* of delighted surprise. A log fire was set ready for burning in the grate and the table was laid with a cloth and a small vase of greenery cut from the garden in anticipation of Christmas. He spun round on the spot, taking in the neat

344

armchairs and the hearthrug, then ran at his sister, clasping his arms about her waist. 'We really gonna be allowed to stay here, Livvie?'

Olivia ruffled his hair. 'We certainly are.'

'He really don't mind us living with him?'

'No . . . he doesn't mind at all, and when he comes home after this horrible war's won, me and Joe are going to get married. So you'll have a brother-in-law! That'll be good, won't it, to have another man about the house, to help you out?'

'Yeah . . . I like him. But I don't mind it being just us,' Alfie added quietly.

Olivia led him up the stairs and showed him the bedrooms. 'We've got lots of space so you can have your own room now, you know.'

'Can I just stay in with you, Livvie?' Alfie raised solemn eyes to his sister.

'All right . . . just for a little while until you get used to it here. But you can have your own bed now, 'cos we've got lots of them, haven't we?' She began pointing at different doorways off the landing. 'There's two small divans in there and a double one in there.' Olivia knew the best thing was to make her brother independent of her slowly. When Joe came back things would have to be different. She wanted them to have privacy when they were a proper couple . . . and even before they were properly married.

A bang on the door made her turn and peer over the banisters.

'Who's that?' Alfie piped up.

'Don't know. Perhaps Maggie and Nancy have changed their minds.' Olivia wouldn't put it past her sisters to have a taste of life with their father and Aunt Sybil then pack their bags and scarper.

'Happy Christmas.'

The greeting was given in an intentionally sarcastic way, nevertheless Olivia smiled. 'Come in, Ruby ... nice to see you.'

'Is it?'

Olivia led the way into the sitting room and turned to face her visitor. Ruby was glancing about as Alfie had done, but her eyes were filled with undisguised envy, not joyousness.

'Very nice. Fell on yer feet, ain't yer?'

'Don't be like that, Ruby,' Olivia said wearily. 'I didn't mean to fall in love with him, y'know. It just happened.'

'Yeah, I know. Like Aggie just happened to fall in love with my mum's bloke all them years ago.' She snorted a bitter laugh. 'I know all about it now. Mum's told me everything. Had no choice but to, did she, once it all come out? And what a tale, at that!'

She looked Olivia up and down. 'So we're half-sisters ... and I take it this is me half-brother,' she said, glancing at Alfie as he stepped hesitantly into the room.

'Alfie's living with me now. Perhaps the girls will too at some time.' Olivia sounded cool. 'They've decided to give it a go with Dad and Sybil first, though.' She eyed Ruby. 'What are you going to do? Are you joining your mum and Mickey in Wood Green?'

'No fear!' Ruby snorted. 'Anyhow, even if I wanted to, I wouldn't be welcome. Me mum's made that quite clear. And I reckon your two sisters'll be given the same treatment. She only wants her boots and Mickey's under Tommy Bone's table. So if you and Joe Hunter don't work out, you've burned yer bridges for going back there.'

'Have to make sure it works out then, won't I?' Olivia returned.

'It didn't with the other woman he shacked up with. Got her pregnant 'n' all, but he moved the poor cow on pretty sharpish.'

'She's happily married to someone else now,' Olivia said, curbing her annoyance. She changed the subject. 'You're staying in the Bunk on your own, are you?'

'Staying put, but not living on me own. Riley McGoogan's moving in with me.'

Finally Olivia smiled. 'I didn't know you and him were even walking out.'

'We're not. He's not me boyfriend, he's a punter. So the only time we'll be sharing the same bedroom is when he shells out fer the privilege.'

Olivia knew that resentment was making Ruby act more coarse and vulgar than usual. But she wasn't letting her talk like that in front of Alfie and told her so.

'Gonna do us a cup of tea then?' Ruby looked sullen on being reprimanded.

''Fraid not. Me and Alfie are just off up the shops.'

Ruby flounced to the door, saying over her shoulder, 'I hate Tommy Bone, y'know, for what he's done. My dad was a good man and he treated Mum better than she deserved. I know that now. I reckon your dad and my mum deserve one another.'

'So do I,' Olivia said quietly as the door slammed shut on Ruby's departing figure.

'Who's that, Livvie? *Is* she me sister?'

'Yeah. There's more of us kids than we thought – quite nice to be a big family, isn't it?'

'Don't like her.'

'Her brother's nice. Mickey's about your age,' Olivia said with an ache in her throat. It shouldn't be like this, she thought to herself, me trying to find words to explain something he shouldn't have to hear. She felt sad that Alfie probably still wouldn't get to know Mickey and play football with him. And the pity of it was that of all the mixed-up Bones and Wrights, the two young boys probably would have been the only people who genuinely liked and were company for one another.

'Come on, let's go to the shops and have a browse. It's Christmas soon. We'll look for something nice for Maggie and Nancy, shall we?'

Alfie nodded.

'I've sent Joe some cigarettes and chocolate and cake.' Olivia hated thinking of him feeling cold and no doubt hungry too with just rations to eat. 'Hope he gets his parcel in time for Christmas Day.'

*

'Phew ... what's that pong? Those Hun bastards gassin' us?'

'Nah. Their field kitchen's moved up and they're cookin' cabbage. Love it, don't they, them Krauts?'

'I'm so bleedin' hungry I'd fight 'em just for a plate of it,' Freddie said mournfully.

'Had roast pork and plum duff last Christmas,' Joe said, smacking his lips. He could recall exactly what he'd done last Christmas Day. He'd travelled by train to Cambridge to join his mother and Annie. His sister had been well enough to enjoy her Christmas dinner at a hotel. It had been the last time he'd seen her and they'd been happy together as a family.

But what had really stuck in his memory was calling on Olivia to give her a gift before he set off for the railway station. Even when he was with his family in Cambridge his mind had wandered back to London. He'd known that she'd still be feeling hurt and miserable after being hit by her father on Christmas morning. He'd wanted to race back and punish Tommy Bone. But he'd known he couldn't touch the man because, if he did, Olivia would never forgive him, or want to see him again.

'Getting relieved, by the look of things.' Joe jerked the brim of his tin hat at the horizon. 'Won't be sorry neither.' A rumbling noise slowly penetrated Joe's brooding. He interpreted it as marching feet and the accumulated metallic rattle of infantry approaching with their equipment banging about their bodies. Assorted horse-drawn wagons were bringing up the rear of the column snaking closer to them.

From their vantage point on a ridge they had a good view of the convoy.

'Poor bastards don't know what they've let themselves in for,' Freddie said bitterly.

'Never a truer word, mate.' Joe rubbed a hand over his grizzled face. 'If they all knew back home what's really happening, the recruiting offices would be empty.'

'Hope they've brought some post with 'em. I could just do with a bit of cake to go with me rum ration.'

'Yeah, hope they've brought some post,' Joe echoed. Livvie had written to him, just as she'd said she would, twice a week. Sometimes the letters came together if the post had been delayed along the line. He savoured every neatly written word, although he knew that she sweetly made an effort not to worry him about problems at home. And he knew she had some with that family of hers. In turn he wrote that things in France were no more than a bit of a nuisance, when in fact he'd witnessed scenes that gave him nightmares so bad that although he was dog-tired, he was glad that there was scant opportunity to sleep.

'Come on, lads, that's us done.' Dawson stood up, stretching out his bones.

With their watch finished the three men slowly made their way along the trench to find somewhere comfortable to try and get a proper rest.

'Sergeant Dawson!'

They halted and saluted as their commanding officer called out to the sergeant.

'I'd like to introduce you to Lieutenant Black. He's taking over the platoon as I'm returning home for a while.'

Joe had been ferreting to find a dog-end in a pocket but looked up out of politeness. As recognition dawned his eyes narrowed in disbelief. He could see that his new commanding officer was just as aware of the incongruity of this second meeting between them taking place on foreign soil this time instead of outside a sweet factory in North London.

They all acknowledged the newcomer but only Joe detected the ironical light in Lucas Black's deep blue eyes as he accepted their salute.

Chapter Twenty-Nine

'I'm fetching him back.'

'Ain't our job, mate. The stretcher bearers do them runs after dark.' Freddie Weedon grabbed Joe's arm, attempting to restrain him as he leaped onto the ladder. Unauthorised attempts to rescue a wounded comrade from no-man's-land were strictly forbidden. Snipers were always on the lookout for the enemy's heroes, poised ready to shoot them down as dusk descended and they made a dash for their pals.

'I can see him . . . I can hear him calling,' Joe burst out, hands clapped over his ears. 'I know I can reach him.' He swung about, fierce-eyed. 'Never get a better chance than this with our lot running round like blue-arsed flies. Nobody'll know. You can distract Fritz with a burst of machine-gun fire. Keep 'em busy looking the other way for a few minutes. That's all I need. I'll reach him in seconds and drag him back.'

'You might finish the poor sod off, rough-handling him,' Freddie argued.

'I'll ask him if he wants to stay put then, shall I?' Joe snarled sarcastically. Freddie had a point but he knew if it were him he'd sooner perish quickly with a friend than slowly bleed to death while trying to knock off the scavenging rats crawling over him.

Freddie didn't loosen his grip on his pal's arm. 'If Dawson comes back we'll get it in the neck for even talking about it!' he hissed.

'The sarge's got the shits ... he'll be in the latrine fer a good while yet.' Joe wrenched his arm free.

'I'm shitting meself just thinking about the trouble we'll be in.' Freddie shoved his tin hat far back on his head in a show of frustration. 'Ain't right, you dropping me in it like this.'

Joe jumped off the ladder to confront him. 'That lad out there's shitting himself worse'n any of us!' he yelled, pointing up at the barbed wire. 'We've all got the bellyache ... so what! He's prayin' one of us is gonna find the guts to go and get him. If it was me out there, would you do a run? Would yer? I'd do it fer you!'

'Ain't you, though, is it ... or me?' Freddie gestured wildly. 'If it was you, y'know I'd say fuck 'em and go over the top for you.' He pointed along the trench. 'Stretcher bearers'll be with him soon,' he reasoned, not very convincingly. They all knew that the Royal Army Medical Corps boys were run off their pins following the shelling a short while ago. The medics were more concerned with seeing to those within easy reach than making suicidal sorties to men dying on the wasteland.

The other end of the trench had taken a direct hit and the stench of burning flesh and cordite was gut-curdling. But it was the sounds of human suffering that were hardest to bear. Joe had seen the boy go down hours ago, when the whistle went to go over the top. He'd recognised him as being from round Islington way although he didn't know his name. He was a rifleman and looked to be barely seventeen. He'd acted cocksure as all the youngsters did, to hide the fact that they now knew what a grave mistake it had been to risk a life not lived for a cause not understood.

Joe had taken to his mate Freddie Weedon from the moment they had marched onto the troop ship at Dover, shoulder to shoulder. On that long voyage marked by bouts of boredom and anxiety and seasickness, the lad had told him his parents were dead but his elder sister had always looked out for him since he was a nipper.

Joe had said his parents were dead too, because as far as he was concerned they both were even if the evil bastard who'd sired him was still drawing breath somewhere.

'Go on then.' Freddie licked his lips, nervously darting glances to right and left. 'I'll give it a burst skywards.'

The carnage at the east end of the trench had drawn all able-bodied men to help out. But Joe and Freddie had the Vickers to man in readiness for another attack; as Sergeant Dawson was crippled with diarrhoea, the two of them had been left to get on with it.

Joe nodded, adrenaline gleaming in his eyes as he sprang up then disappeared over the top, running at a crouch with the noise of machine-gun fire ringing in his ears.

'Knew it'd be you come fer me,' the boy panted. 'Help me up 'n' I'll run. Just need you to help me up and I'll be all right,' he cried, his shivering hands folded over the guts protruding from his uniform.

Joe pulled himself forward on his elbows until he could cradle the boy's head on his forearm. 'Just wait here a while till I get me breath,' he wheezed, knowing the boy wouldn't be going anywhere. Freddie had been right. Joe let his head fall against the boy's chest while he composed himself, sniffing and gulping, making out he was exhausted. 'So you're out of Queensland Road back home, ain't yer?' he choked, wondering what the hell he was going to do now. He couldn't leave; the lad had hold of his sleeve and was hanging on for dear life, what he'd left of it. 'Seen yer a few times round the Duke pub,' Joe carried on in a croak. 'Don't reckon yer old enough to be drinking, though.'

'Reckon I'm old enough now, eh?' The boy flashed him a grin that finished in a cough.

'Reckon you are, mate, yeah. You'll be back home in no time now. Got a Blighty one there, ain't yer? Have a pint in the Duke for me when yer up on yer pins again.'

'Will 'n' all ... want to go home so bad.' His staring eyes shone with tears. 'Ain't too messy then, is it?' He tried to lift his head and look at his wound. 'Can't see the damage ... getting dark now ...'

'It'll get you home, son. That's all that counts now, ain't it?'

'Yeah,' the boy said, sinking back with a happy, rattling sigh.

From behind Joe heard an angry burst of Vickers spitting into the darkening sky. He knew it was Freddie's way of telling him to hurry up and as the boy suddenly writhed, arching his back and screaming in agony, Joe shifted position, lying over him until he felt him go still.

*

'What the *fuck* was that all about?'

'Machine gun jammed, sir,' Joe and Freddie chorused. They'd had time enough after Joe dropped back down into the trench to get their story straight before their new commanding officer bore down on them. And they knew he would, because they'd seen him coming.

Lucas Black stared at Joe as though searching into his soul then a grim smile touched his mouth. 'Machine gun jammed, did it?'

'Yeah.' Joe's mouth pursed and he stared right back. Freddie had lit a candle and stuck it in the dugout wall. The faint light played on Black's profile and Joe noticed his jaw hardening. If the bastard had something to say, let him say it. Although he kept his thoughts on the tip of his tongue, Joe's belligerent expression spoke for him.

'Cleaning it I was, sir, when it happened,' Freddie piped up. 'Let loose of its own accord. But it's just the ticket now.'

'Well, that's all right then,' Lucas snapped acidly. 'Where's Dawson?'

'On the bog,' the gunners chorused again.

'Looks like you've come a cropper, Private Hunter.' Lucas nodded at Joe's uniform, stained with the boy's blood.

'Not me, sir. I'm fine, sir.' Joe jutted his chin. 'As you can see, sir, I'm just fine.'

'Know what I think?' Lucas paced to and fro on the duckboard, eyes narrowed on the barbed wire lacing the top of the trench.

'Reckon you should tell me, sir.' Joe ignored the warning pinches he was getting from his pal.

'I think you've been in no-man's-land, trying to rescue a young gunner, and your pal here was covering for you.'

'As if I'd go against orders,' Joe gritted out through his teeth.

'But you did because I saw you. I've been watching you, Hunter.'

'And I've been watching you, sir, don't you worry about that. And when we get back home, I'll be watching you even harder.'

Lucas grunted a mirthless laugh.

'What's up, sir?'

Sergeant Dawson's voice broke the deadlock between the men. He came hurrying along the duckboard, giving his subordinates a fierce look.

'Seems you've got a loose cannon on your team, Dawson,' Lucas observed.

He stared so hard at Joe that the other two became aware this simmering hostility was very personal. They darted glances from officer to private, sensing something bad about to erupt.

'I ain't a loose cannon. I'm a man with decent feelings and if I can help some poor kid get back with his family, I'll give it a try.'

'And did you help him?'

'I think so.' In fact Joe felt a mixture of guilt and uselessness for having failed to save the boy's life and get him home. He'd been unable to do anything but put him out of his misery. He didn't regret that and his conscience didn't bother him. He'd felt the lad's whispered thank-you as a warm breath against his coat; seen serenity in those staring eyes before he'd closed them. Then he'd had to leave the lad to rot where he lay.

'It's you lot that's doing all this,' Joe suddenly roared, unable to contain his emotion. 'Toffs with big ideas and big money think you can do what you want and ride roughshod over the rest of us. Them young German soldiers in that trench over there ... ' He jabbed a finger. 'They're no different from us ... none of us count, do we? We're just cheap cannon fodder, whatever language we speak.'

'You know that's treasonable talk, don't you?' Lucas said calmly. 'You've the attitude of an agitator. Just like Tommy Bone. Perhaps that's what she sees in you ... the similarity.'

'You bastard! Don't ever say I'm like him.' Joe leaped forward on the duckboard, fists at the ready.

'It's just his rum talking, sir.' Sergeant Dawson caught Joe by

356

the arms, trying to smooth matters over. He now understood there was more going on here here than just straightforward insubordination. It *was* personal and a woman was involved, and that was always bad news.

'We can sort this out, man to man, if you like,' Joe snarled. ''Less you want to pull rank and get me that way 'cos you ain't got the balls for a fair fight.'

'This is nothing to do with rank . . . it's about military discipline. You could've put more lives at risk acting the hero in a lost cause.' Lucas turned away. 'And if you think I'll brawl with you, you're wrong.'

'Knew you was a cowardly prick. And I weren't *acting* . . . ain't my style, putting it on.' Joe's lip curled. 'That's *your* style, ain't it? Pretending you're charming and using sweet talk when all you want's a quick shag with a factory gel . . . *my* factory gel.'

'Hunter, shut your gob! That's an order!' Dawson hissed in the private's ear.

''S'all right, Sarge,' Joe said. 'I know he'll hide behind you if you'll let him.'

'I don't need to hide, and perhaps a thrashing might work if you're too stupid to understand common sense.' Lucas accepted the challenge, unbuttoning his jacket. 'Just you and me, then . . . right now.'

'Yeah, right now might be the only time we'll get to settle this.' Joe smiled thinly.

'I agree,' Lucas said softly.

A few of the platoon who'd been stationed further along the trench had moved closer, realising something was going on. When they comprehended what was about to happen between an officer and a private they closed ranks, forming a barrier. If the fight was reported to the top brass it could end in a court martial for both men involved . . . or worse . . . and stopping

German bullets was preferable to those from a British firing squad.

The combatants stripped to the waist while mutters about *woman trouble* passed through the men encircling them. What Lucas had in height advantage, Joe made up for in brawn. In skill they were equally matched. Joe had managed to get in a premature punch but his opponent had come back at him quickly after staggering and dropping to one knee. Black was no pushover, Joe realised as he took a right hook that shook his teeth in their sockets.

'Christmas tomorrow, lads,' Dawson burbled to the group of spectators. 'How about we sing a carol then ... '

While the grunting of the circling, jabbing men grew louder, Dawson burst out with 'God Rest Ye Merry, Gentlemen', to muffle the noise, waving his arms as though conducting a choir to urge the others to join in. And they did, and when the voices died away at the end and the fight carried on, Freddie, who'd been on the fire step watching the slugging match while keeping an eye on the opposite trench, yelled, "Ere ... something's going on over there.' He pointed through the barbed wire. 'Can see lights ... the Hun's up to summat.'

Sergeant Dawson had been keeping a beady eye open as well. 'Best finish it up. We're drawing more attention now,' he warned the fighting men in an urgent hiss. Some tunnellers from a South Staffordshire Regiment were heading their way, looking curious. And with them was their commanding officer.

Lucas and Joe exchanged a look and an almost imperceptible nod signalled a truce.

'Let's take a shufti then.' Dawson elbowed Freddie off the fire step to take a look at the German line.

'He's right, sir ... unusual activity over there right enough.' The sergeant frowned over his shoulder at Lucas and got down so his senior officer could use the fire step.

'What's that noise?' Joe had been wiping blood from his split lip when he'd heard something, almost like wind whispering in the leaves on trees. Only there were no leaves and not much left of the trees either.

'Sounds like somebody else is singing.' Freddie took a gulp of his rum ration. Every day the pottery jar was anticipated as though its contents were manna from Heaven, even by those who'd previously considered themselves teetotal. Some men, like Freddie, eked it out till the evening ... others had swallowed the lot almost before the stopper went back in the bottle in the morning.

'It's the Germans havin' a singsong.' Sergeant Dawson was close to laughing. 'I know that tune. It's a carol.'

As they fell quiet and strained their ears to listen, the words *Stille Nacht, Heilige Nacht* ... wafted on the icy night air across no-man's-land.

Joe recognised not one haunting syllable but he knew their meaning was beautiful because the hairs on the nape of his neck prickled. His ragged breathing was steadying and a feeling of serenity started to settle on him, making him want to pull out of his pocket the last letter Olivia had written to him. He'd read it twice already but yearned to sit down somewhere private and quietly savour every word once more. As the melody faded away other voices, singing in English this time, took up the challenge from somewhere along the Allied trench.

'The lights are candles. They've put Christmas candles along the top of their trench,' Lucas said, getting off the fire step and walking away.

From beneath his brows Joe watched him go, buttoning up his jacket, straightening his cap ... doing his duty, despite his bruises. And Joe knew from the throbbing in his own jaw that his opponent hadn't got off lightly but had taken similar heavy blows. Begrudgingly, he admired him ... respected him even. Lieutenant Lucas Black could have had his hide for what Joe had done, a private soldier speaking to an officer like that. But Black was too honourable a man for that, to go down the easy route and use his rank in a personal dispute. Private Hunter had gone against orders, taken a bad risk, but in the end no harm had been done ... that was the way Black would see it, because he was fair, even if he was a toff with a job to do. And even if he did fancy Livvie.

Joe settled down by the candle and took from an inside pocket the chocolate Olivia had sent him. The pack had got squashed and he eased the bar out carefully so it wouldn't crumble and took a bite, savouring the silky sweetness melting on his tongue.

'Come on, lads, join in,' Sergeant Dawson commanded. 'Anything the Hun can do, us lot can do better. '"O, come, all ye faithful ... "' he shouted robustly. As the carol rang out and more voices swelled the sound, sentiment at the special occasion and thoughts of loved ones at home made the harmony even sweeter.

Joe settled further into the funk hole and took out Olivia's letter, unfolding it gently.

*

Christmas morning had broken. The dawn light glinted on a landscape transformed by frost. Even the grotesque woody stumps on no-man's-land were coated with a silver sparkle.

'You'll never believe what I can see.' Joe's voice held mingled amusement and astonishment.

'What?'

'A German's waving at us.'

'I'll wave me revolver back then.' Sergeant Dawson did so, scowling menacingly.

'*Fröhliche Weihnachten . . .* '

'What's that?' Dawson bawled out to his opposite number, inclining an ear in the German's direction.

'Happy Christmas,' came the greeting in accented English.

'Yeah . . . and to you too,' Dawson called back acidly, stroking his ginger moustache. 'Crafty buggers are gonna try and butter us up then shoot us on the sly,' he muttered.

'Don't reckon they are,' Joe said in wonder as he popped his head above the parapet then stood up straight. 'We could shoot them first if we wanted. Look, he's up and out on no-man's-land. Blimey, there's more of 'em coming up 'n' all.'

'Keep yer shooter cocked,' Dawson bellowed as Joe hoisted himself onto the frozen soil above the trench.

He glanced along the line and saw that other Tommies had also clambered up to stand on the lip of the parapet, balancing carefully so they could jump down quickly.

'*Nicht schießen . . .* don't shoot *. . . Fröhliche Weihnachten . . .* '

The words drifted across the shimmering expanse of wasteland.

Joe looked down and laughed incredulously at Sergeant Dawson and Freddie. 'They only fuckin' mean it! They want us to go and join them and say Happy Christmas.'

'They might have some fags. I'll swap 'em a bit of me cake.' Freddie sprang up to stand by his pal. His sister had only sent him two packs of cigarettes and most of those he'd owed back to Joe.

'No fraternising.' Lucas Black picked a meandering path up and down the trench uttering the command he knew he should give, but there was little conviction in his voice. He too had taken a look across at the Germans emerging from their trenches to tread upon the frozen clay. He'd seen his opposite number's field glasses trained on him then the German officer had given him a salute. But whatever he personally felt about this bloody war he had duty and family to live up to ... and a job to do.

'No fraternising!' Lucas bawled it out this time.

Joe swung about at the sound of that authoritative voice. 'It ain't us and them started this war.' He pointed to the young German foot soldiers then swung back to the man who wanted Livvie. Joe had seen the hunger in Black's eyes when he'd watched them embracing outside Barratt's. And whenever they'd met since he'd sensed the rivalry between them ... it was a stare all men understood. The fight yesterday hadn't been the end of it. It had only signalled a break in hostilities until they got safely back home. And the daft thing was that Joe understood now why Livvie had said that her boss was all right. He knew why she liked Lucas Black.

'The truce might hold today but tomorrow they'll make up for it, I can promise you that.' Lucas vaulted onto the fire step then clambered over the top.

Already some British and German soldiers had met midway between the trenches and were shaking hands. Some were exchanging cigarettes for chocolate or candles. The amazing sight held some men spellbound, watching uncertainly; fraternisation could lead to lethal punishment from the top brass. But, slowly, more and more men mingled on the earth separating their trenches. A German private approached them.

'*Wie geht's?*'

'He's asking you how you are,' Lucas interpreted for Joe, who'd taken off his helmet to run his fingers through his hair.

Joe stuck out his hand. 'I'm all right, mate. How about you?'

The German nodded and shook hands. He made to delve

inside his coat and Joe instinctively brought up his gun. The fellow shook his head, indicating that there was no need for alarm. Gingerly he brought out from his breast pocket a bent photograph of a blonde woman seated on a chair with a child on her lap.

'*Meine Frau und Tochter.*'

'His wife and daughter,' Lucas said before he walked on and nodded to the German officer who'd saluted him earlier. The fellow clicked his heels and bowed, very stiffly and politely.

'Where d'you get that?' Joe chuckled delightedly at the sight of Freddie jogging over with a football under his arm.

'Just swapped me sister's cake and half me fags fer it with that fellow over there.' He nodded to a German, chewing happily on a hunk of fruit cake covered in white icing. 'Love football I do. Didn't mind about the cake; it was a bit dry. Needed a swig of rum to get it down. I'll be cadging fags off you, though, till she sends some more.'

Freddie dropped the ball to the ground and immediately Joe got it on the end of his boot and toe-punted it. 'Come on, you Arsenal! Come on, you Gunners!' he sang, chasing after the ball. It was a while before he realised he had a following all trying to get in on the action. He crossed the ball to Freddie who back-heeled it to Dawson. They shouted for a foul as a German hard-tackled the sergeant ... and they got it. After some consultation with his team mates the German shrugged and allowed it.

Lucas watched from a distance, a wry smile on his lips. He would have liked to join in; he'd been good at sport at school. Rugby had been favoured over football but he and his pals would have crafty matches on the playing fields despite the snooty prevalent attitude that soccer was for commoners.

He turned away but didn't return to the trench; instead he

363

walked further onto the hard terrain where the last bodies had fallen. He hunched into his coat, solemnly surveying the human wreckage, then turned around as he heard somebody approaching.

'Any good with a shovel?' Lucas lit a cigarette then offered one to Joe. 'A lot of the dead are ours and they deserve a decent burial; they all deserve a decent burial.' His bleak, encompassing gaze took in those remains clad in grey rags as well as khaki.

'Yeah . . . I know how to handle a shovel. Work down the coal yard, don't I?' Joe wiped his moist forehead. Despite the cold he'd worked up a sweat during the football match.

'A pick would help get into that.' Dawson had come up behind them and was stamping one heel against the solid ground. 'I'll fetch one.'

Joe wandered on to a desolate place he recognised. He hunkered down beside the body of the boy he'd smothered. He was glad he'd closed his eyes yesterday before leaving him so the rats didn't get to them. The emotion he'd felt had gone now. This was just another body to bury. But he searched in the soldier's pockets and took out the letters and photos. He'd hand them to Lieutenant Black and in due course the boy's family would know almost all that had happened to him. Only Joe would know the rest.

Freddie and Sergeant Dawson helped in carrying tools and other soldiers joined in, burying as many of the Allied corpses as they could, almost where they lay.

They finished as daylight was fading and exhaustion was setting in. The wasteland was more or less empty of the living as well as the dead; the Germans had used the ceasefire to lay to rest their fallen too.

Joe shouldered the shovel he'd used and started back as did

the others. 'I've something to ask you.' He addressed Lucas, walking parallel but a yard or so away from him. 'Why d'you try and mess about with Livvie like that? She said you already had a girlfriend.'

'That's right,' Lucas answered, using his field glasses on the opposite trench. He sensed that the truce was petering out and soon fresh bodies would replace those they'd just interred.

'So why then?' Joe demanded.

'Because ...' Lucas swung towards him. 'Because I'm a bloody bastard.' He gestured harshly. 'She loves you. You marry her and cherish her and make sure she stays away from that father of hers.' His lips thinned into a bitter line. 'You'll make her happy and God knows she deserves it after living with him.'

'Well, that's something we agree on,' Joe said.

They carried on in silence and just before Joe jumped down into the trench he asked, 'Would you do that for me?' He jerked his head back to no-man's-land.

'What?'

'If I buy it, would you bury me if you could, stop the rats and dogs getting at me? I'd do it fer you, if I could. I'd make a run fer you. I know Livvie'd want me to. She said you were all right. She didn't want me coming after you back home. And I would've, if she'd let me.'

'Yes, I'd do it for you,' Lucas said, leaping down to land on the duckboard beside his burial party. 'I'd do it for any of you ... if I could.'

'Search me pockets first. I've written a letter to Livvie,' Joe said, and half-pulled an envelope from inside his jacket. 'That's where I keep me letters ... close to me heart.'

Chapter Thirty

'Happy Christmas, Matilda.' Olivia handed over the gift she'd brought round for the Keivers on Christmas evening. It was a bottle of sherry that she guessed Jack and Matilda would appreciate taking a tot from on a winter's night.

'That's mighty nice ... thank you. Wish I'd got something for you now,' Matilda said with a rare blush.

Olivia waved this away. 'You've done more than enough for me and I won't ever forget it.' A rumble of laughter and the scent of booze and tobacco was wafting out onto the landing. 'Won't stop. Sounds like you've got company.'

'Just having a little drink with Fran and Jimmy. You're welcome to one too. I won't take no fer an answer, so in yer come.'

Alfie had been standing shyly behind his sister but Olivia drew him forward. 'This is my brother, Alfie.'

Matilda stuck out a hand for him to shake. 'Good looker like yer sister, ain't yer?' she summed him up.

A chorus of greetings from the assembled family met the newcomers being ushered into the sitting room.

Fran and Jimmy Wild were seated at the table drinking whisky and Jack looked comfortably set upon the piano stool, swigging from a brown ale. The lid was up as though he'd just finished a tune and was taking a breather. He got to his feet, allowing Alice and Geoff to squash together on the seat. They began to make an inharmonious noise, plinking and plonking on the keys, erupting into laughter at the racket they were making.

'Port and lemon, for you, ducks?' Jack said, sorting through some bottles on the table.

'Thanks.' Olivia perched on the arm of the chair Beth was lounging in. 'Alfie's living with me now. In the New Year he'll be going to Pooles Park School. That's where you go, isn't it?'

Beth nodded. 'You can walk to school with me till you get used to it and make some friends,' she kindly offered.

Alfie murmured a self-conscious thank-you.

'Reckon you'd like a glass of pop, wouldn't yer, son?' Matilda held out a tumbler filled with lemonade. 'Got some sweets here somewhere ... ' She opened a drawer and produced a handful of toffees. 'There ... got them off yer aunt Sybil in thanks for a blanket I let her pawn.' Matilda grimaced. 'Want me blanket back at some time. I hope she knows that.'

Olivia recognised the toffees as being the same as those her father had given Alfie. It seemed Sybil and Mickey had also benefited from Tommy's pilfering from Barratt's. Olivia put it all from her mind; this was Christmas Day and she was determined to relax and enjoy it. As for informing Matilda that Sybil had moved away, and why, that could wait too, for God only knew it'd need some explaining.

'There you are, gel, that'll warm the cockles.' Jack handed

over Olivia's port then re-seated himself at the piano and began to belt out a spirited version of 'Pack Up Your Troubles', bashing on the keys.

'Knows how to tickle them ivories, does my Jack.' Matilda looked proudly at her husband. 'Better tone it down though or he'll wake up Lucy.' Matilda jerked her head at the back room. 'She *was* sound asleep,' she added wryly.

Olivia chuckled as the noise soared rather than diminished when others joined in the chorus. 'Did you have a good Christmas Day?'

'We did,' Matilda replied. 'Couldn't stretch to much in the way of a bird but Jack brung us in a nice lot of veg off his guv'nor's market stall to roast with the chicken. Me friend across the road boiled up a batch of plum duffs in her washing copper and sold 'em in the street.' Matilda frowned. 'I've not settled up yet and should give Beattie back her basin fer a tanner off.' She glanced at Olivia. 'How about you? Did you and Alfie have dinner with your dad in Wood Green?'

Olivia shook her head. She'd not heard a word from her father although she'd sent her Christmas wishes to them all via Maggie. She should have felt sad that she and Alfie had spent Christmas Day on their own. But actually it had been nice to be able to relax and eat their festive roast quietly together, knowing that no argument was about to erupt. And Alfie had been in his element having his big sister to himself.

Her father had told her he wanted nothing more to do with her so to avoid a showdown on Christmas Eve Olivia had gone to Kendall's to hand over her sisters' presents, and an ounce of tobacco for her father. She'd not received much back in the way of thanks or good tidings. Olivia knew Maggie's moodiness stemmed more from Harry Wicks's having joined up than the worrying changes taking place in the family. It depressed her that Maggie seemed incapable of forgetting about the brute.

'Your fiancé didn't get no leave then?' Matilda asked.

''Fraid not ... hope he'll get to come home soon.'

'None of those lads'll be getting leave now Fritz is flying over,' Jimmy butted into the conversation. 'The Germans need to be pushed back or they'll be landing at Dover, not dropping bombs on it.'

'Could be right there, Jim.' Jack gave a forlorn shake of the head.

'Right miserable lot we are on Christmas evening!' Matilda pulled Fran, who was sporting a fresh bruise on her chin, to her feet as Jack played another tune. The sisters started to jig in the cramped space, bumping into the furniture.

Jimmy Wild glanced sideways at Olivia as though about to ask her to dance so she started to waltz with her brother. Not to be left out, Geoff put down his bottle of ale and he and Alice joined the crush of swaying bodies.

'I like it here, though it's a bit ... ' Alfie's description of the raucous atmosphere tailed off. Even at his young age he was diplomatic amongst people he knew to be his sister's friends.

'Yeah ... me too. I like it here.' Olivia started spinning him round faster and faster on the spot until they were laughing breathlessly when Jack finally brought the music to a stop.

*

'Told you they'd come back at us damned quick after the cease-fire,' said Lucas, helping the invalids down the cellar steps.

He'd left a second lieutenant in charge of his platoon while he escorted the most seriously injured of his men for treatment at the first-aid post. This was set about half a mile behind the front line in the basement of a village church where there was some protection from the shelling. The bombardment had resumed and had gone on for days before petering out, giving them, and no doubt the enemy, a chance finally to do what they could to attend to the dead and wounded.

They'd been forced into a retreat when the Germans had captured the battered eastern end of their front line. Now they were in the hellish situation of sharing a trench with men they'd only days ago shaken hands with ... exchanged gifts with. But whatever colours they were in, they all knew Christmas was over, and what was required to survive.

'Ain't gonna be much use handling a machine gun now.' Joe had sunk down to sit on the hard brick floor, his head hanging low between his knees. He'd taken a bullet in the hand and was struggling to stay conscious as well as keep his eyes away from the mangled mess of what remained of his fingers.

'Still got your left hand, haven't you? Buck up. In time you'll be sent back down the line to a base hospital. You've got a Blighty one there, you lucky sod.' Lucas jerked cigarettes from his pocket and shook one out of the pack. Once he'd lit it, he stuck it between Joe's pallid lips.

All casualties wanted a Blighty one ... an injury that was serious enough to send them home to recuperate.

Lucas helped more men to seat themselves. One had a gash across his scalp from shrapnel and another had taken a bayonet in the shoulder. A ferocious German had rushed at them out of nowhere while they were cobbling barbed wire and broken boxes into a barrier to keep the Hun to their side of the trench.

'I'm heading back now. You'll be home soon, you lot, and back as you were ... Good luck.' Lucas locked eyes with Joe as he spoke and a nod passed between them before the officer sprinted up the cellar steps.

Joe's head dropped back towards his chest. He knew he wouldn't be home soon, because they wouldn't be relieved soon. They were too isolated for that. Neither would he ever be as he was. You couldn't earn a living shovelling coal with one hand.

He closed his eyes and rested back against the hard wall, dragging deeply on his cigarette to keep himself conscious. A corporal from the Royal Army Medical Corps shook his shoulder to rouse him.

'Let's have a look at you then, lad.' He turned the invalid's bloodied palm in his hand. 'Seen worse today,' he summed up. 'A dressing on that and you'll be back in action in no time.' He sorted through his bandages. 'I'll get an orderly to bring you a cup of tea if you like.'

'Ta,' Joe murmured. He was no fool, he knew his hand was finished. But he was walking wounded and everybody on their feet was needed to hold the line. They'd amputate in the end and he'd let them rather than risk gangrene going up his arm.

Joe raised his head as the dull whine and thud of mortar fire was heard and some plaster flaked from the cellar ceiling to fall like ash in his lap. 'Fritz has got his second wind then,' he said, taking a sip of tea from the mug a fellow had just handed him.

'That's our boys answering them,' his comrade with the head wound replied. With grim humour they all started chuckling as the Allied guns continued chuntering away.

Joe reached inside his jacket with his left hand and pulled out his precious letter, carefully, so as not to get blood on it. He read it over and over again through blurred vision, although he could recite it word for word. When he finally folded it he held the paper briefly to his lips. If he made it home he knew he couldn't put Livvie through the hardship of supporting a cripple for the rest of his days.

371

Chapter Thirty-One

'You're back then, are you?'

'Course I am, Nelly. Barratt's is me second home. Didn't think I'd gone fer good, did you, gel?' Tommy goaded. 'I can see you've missed me . . . so, Happy New Year to you.' He slanted a sly smile at his pal Bill who was listening while licking a Rizla.

Nelly had heard that her old sparring partner had got his job back so had hung about in the courtyard after work, hoping to bump into him and lay down the law. But she could tell that Tommy had returned as bumptious as ever.

Nelly had gained influence while Tommy Bone hadn't been strutting around the factory, acting as though he owned the place. The girls now looked to her to act as their go-between with the guv'nors, not him. She'd had a minor success, with Deborah Wallis's help, in getting them longer lavatory breaks. Nelly knew the secretary only gave her the time of day because they had a mutual antipathy towards Livvie Bone. Livvie didn't seem to care if people liked her or not and always spoke her mind. Brave, strong characters like that grated on Nelly's nerves because they put her to shame. Livvie was the sort of person who was either admired or resented by her colleagues. How she had managed to blossom despite her father's bullying and bad example was nothing short of a miracle in Nelly's opinion.

Tommy should have been proud of his daughter, yet he was one of those who shunned her. It had got round that he had a new woman in his life, who'd caused a lot of friction with Tommy's daughters. Apparently Olivia had bowed out rather than tread on the newcomer's toes. It was the sort of selfless act that Nelly despised. She'd have fought tooth and nail to keep her rightful place in the family.

'Heard from me pals that you've been making sure the staff get their dues while I've been away. Appreciate what you've done in me absence, but you can give it a rest now I'm back, Nelly,' Tommy told her.

'Can I now?' she spat. 'We'll see about that.'

'Yeah ... we will. And none of us are coming out on strike till I say we are.' Tommy had heard from Bill Morley that Nelly was struggling to get support for a walk-out because the majority of the staff didn't like her tactics, using the war as a bargaining tool.

Privately Tommy sided with Nelly, and had he been in charge of things he'd have squeezed every last drop out of the situation, and got the backing needed. But he'd never give Nelly the satisfaction of knowing he approved of her idea.

'You and your gels should just carry on handing out white feathers at the Suffragette rallies,' Tommy added with deliberate condescension before sauntering off with Bill.

Nelly caught up with him, her face boiling with indignation. 'You just might regret coming back and upsetting the applecart, y'know.'

'Ain't upsetting no more carts. I've learned me lesson there, you'll be pleased to hear,' Tommy said drolly, gaining a snort of amusement from Bill.

'Well, if you think you're shop steward, you'd better make sure we're all treated right ... *women* as well as men. We could all up and leave, y'know. The munitions factories are crying out for workers and they're paying better rates than we get here. Could be I'll just take meself and me little gang off soldering hand grenades. Once the guv'nors find out we've all left 'cos *you've* come back, you'll be out on yer ear again and laughing on the other side of yer face, Tommy Bone!'

'We'll have to rub along somehow then, Nelly, won't we?' Tommy said through his teeth. The woman had backed him into a corner and she knew it.

'Yeah ... let's see if we can rub along then,' Nelly said with a triumphant smirk.

'See your dad and Nelly are having a bit of a chinwag,' Cath Mason said.

Olivia had also spotted them together and could tell from their belligerent expressions that it wasn't a happy reunion. Nelly had stalked off and her father was scowling after the woman. He turned her way and just for a moment Olivia thought he might smile, or wave, but he moved on without an acknowledgment. He had all but ignored her since he'd started back at Barratt's and Olivia had sadly accepted that if he wanted to be like that, there was nothing she could do. If he thought she'd beg him to be friendly he was mistaken, just as he was wrong if he expected her to pack in her job because of any bad atmosphere between them. She'd been optimistic that the wounds might eventually heal in this strange, fractured new family that Sybil Wright and Tommy Bone had created, but was coming to realise that it was a vain hope.

'My uncle's got a bloody cheek, y'know, taking that attitude with me,' Cath huffed. Bill Morley had cold-shouldered his niece in the same way Livvie had been ignored by her father.

'I never wanted to be involved in pinching sweets. He put me on the spot until I felt I couldn't say no. It wasn't *me* let the cat out of the bag anyhow. He just thinks it was 'cos I said I wasn't leaving the key out no more.' She grimaced. 'If me mum ever finds out what's gone on, she'll have his guts for garters. She's never liked her brother anyhow.'

Olivia buttoned her coat against the chill January evening, giving Cath an old-fashioned look. 'I reckon you didn't want to leave the key out any more because you'd saved enough for that trip to Lorenco Road.'

'That's true,' Cath conceded on a sigh. 'I wasn't greedy, see. I only did it out of necessity.' She frowned. 'Wonder how Mr Black found out about it?'

'Don't care. I'm just thankful he saw it the way he did or you all might have got arrested.' Olivia prayed her father had learned a lesson; but she wouldn't put it past him to think that because Lucas was out of the way, he and Bill could set up in business again.

'Let's get going, Cath. Got to pick Alfie up and he'll be wanting his tea.' They set off down the road towards the bus stop, keeping their heads lowered against the bitter air. Matilda had said that Alfie could wait at hers after school to save him going home to a freezing cold empty house. Her brother liked his afternoon tea and biscuits in Mrs Keiver's, though Olivia could tell that he wasn't yet quite used to living in Islington or in a strange house.

She urged Cath to increase pace and they huddled together, arm in arm for warmth. Olivia was impatient to get back home to see if the postman had brought her a letter from Joe because she'd not had one for a while.

Chapter Thirty-Two

'Lucas!' Spontaneously Olivia darted out of the house to hug him. Even the dim evening light and his uniform hadn't prevented her from recognising him. 'What a wonderful surprise. Are you home on leave?' She stepped back into the hallway, opening the door wider, conscious of the fresh scent of mist clinging to his clothes. 'Come in ... it's an icy night, isn't it?' Olivia led the way to the sitting room, her heart pounding in her chest with excitement and gladness at his unexpected visit. She'd often thought about him overseas and had prayed that he was keeping safe.

When she'd heard the rap on the door she'd imagined it might be Ruby paying a visit. They'd bumped into one another yesterday when Olivia had been collecting Alfie from Matilda's. Ruby had been hanging on Riley McGoogan's arm, and had seemed friendlier than when they'd last spoken. She'd promised to pop round some time for a chat.

In the sitting room Olivia turned to Lucas, feeling rather

embarrassed to have welcomed her old boss with such heartfelt emotion. What had gone on between them in the past hardly merited such a display, especially as he knew she was now engaged. But she *was* delighted to see him although he hadn't as yet greeted her. In fact, he hadn't uttered a word. He seemed . . . different, and it was odd that he'd even known where to find her.

Lucas had removed his army cap and held it dangling from one hand. Now that his features weren't shadowed by the peak Olivia got a good look at him and her smile faded. He was still handsome even with the wounds on his cheek and forehead that told of the battles he'd been in . . . the ones that doubtless were responsible for digging creases about his blue eyes and thin lips. There was something else too: a gauntness and air of gravity that had matured him more than the furrows etched on his face. There was none of the youthful playboy left in him, she realised with a pang.

'You've been hurt in the fighting,' she said softly.

'I'm lucky . . . one of the lucky ones,' he replied hoarsely.

'I'm sure Joe brushes over the worst of it when he writes. It's dreadful over there, isn't it?'

'Yes,' he answered abruptly, and wiped a hand over his mouth. 'I've brought you something from him. He asked me to.'

He pulled from his pocket Joe's letter and another envelope that looked bumpy to the touch. 'He wanted to make sure you got these.'

'You've seen him?' Olivia breathed. 'How wonderful that you've met up. How is he?' She already knew, though, in her heart. She backed away from his outstretched hand, afraid to take those final things . . . precious memories to be put in a drawer with the photograph that she'd once kept on the mantel.

Lucas dropped his hand and closed his eyes momentarily.

'I'm sorry,' he said huskily, and put the envelopes on the ledge by the picture of Joe, smiling proudly in his khaki uniform. 'Joe was probably the bravest man I shall ever know,' he said, gazing at the photo. 'And he adored you.'

Olivia gripped the back of the armchair to keep herself upright, silent tears dripping from her cheeks on to her blouse, turning the white cotton grey. 'Where is he now? Will he come home?'

'No. He's in the churchyard behind the first-aid post.' Lucas paused, taking a deep breath to steady his voice. 'And when this damned war's done, if you want to go, I'll show you where that is.'

A silence broken only by Olivia's gasping and weeping followed. Unable to bear her distress any longer without trying to ease it, Lucas gathered her into his arms, holding her head against his shoulder until she'd exhausted herself.

'You made sure he was laid to rest? You did that for him?' Olivia took the hanky from her pocket and dried her eyes.

'He would have done the same for me. He told me so. That's how it was between us.'

Olivia went to the mantelpiece and gazed at the envelopes. She'd not open his last letter till she was alone. But she picked at the flap of the misshapen one with palsied fingers. Upending it, she let the silver chain slide cold and silky onto her palm. 'This was my mum's. I dreamed of her last night ... for the first time in ages. She was comforting me like she did when I was little, almost smothering me with warmth and love. I didn't want to wake up.' Olivia turned to Lucas. 'Were you there? Did you see what happened to him?'

Lucas tilted his head back. 'It was pandemonium ... not much chance to see or hear a thing.'

'I want you to tell me.' Olivia smeared fresh tears from her face with the heel of one hand. 'He's nobody else left ... just a brute of a father he hated and never saw. His mum and sister are both dead but Joe cared for them and protected them, from when he was just a boy. Tell me what happened to him so I can grieve for him, and for Maisie and Annie too. I don't mind if it hurts. It should hurt.'

Lucas swallowed. He'd promised himself he wouldn't tell. Not just for her sake but for his own. He didn't want to relive the obscenity of hand-to-hand fighting with knives and bayonets, revolvers too if there was room in the press of arms and legs to use them. The brutality, the stench of men's fear and undressed wounds, the foul cursing and crying when a man knows his life is about to be taken from him. All those horrors he'd locked away, intending to tell Olivia that Joe had received a clean death from a sniper's bullet in the brain, and save them both the pain.

But it hadn't been like that, and he couldn't lie to her now; not when she'd asked for the truth.

So he told her how their line had been cut off and how the relief had come far too late to save them from a lack of food and medicine and frostbite and dysentery and much more that no human being should endure. But blessed help had come at last, strong and accurate. A British reconnaissance plane had flown over to discover what section of the line was still held by C Company. Flares had been sent up to let the pilot know they were holding on. Allied shells had started hitting the German section and the foe had known they must act to keep their advantage.

So they had stormed along the trench and broken down the barrier that kept apart the warring troops.

Her fiancé, Lucas said, had vowed to keep hold of the machine gun that the Germans intended capturing and turning against them. Even one-handed he had fought like a demon for hours during attacks and retreats along that bog-filled tunnel. Morning light had seen a brigade of British infantry start a determined push forward to relieve them and recapture the whole trench, to let the stragglers of their platoon slip away.

Joe and his pal Freddie Weedon were found close to the barrier, having forced the Germans back to the barbed wire. Sergeant Dawson had accompanied the stretcher bearers taking Freddie to the first-aid post. Joe had been past saving. Weak with fatigue, Lucas had carried him on his shoulder, stopping at intervals and laying him on the ground beside him until he could recover strength. The journey done, he'd buried Joe behind the church in a frozen corner of the graveyard and read the Lord's Prayer over him although he no longer believed in God.

'How is Freddie Weedon?' Olivia asked tremulously.

'He has a bad chest wound. He'll go down the line when he's fit enough to be moved and eventually, God willing, come back to England and recuperate.'

'I pray he will.' Olivia covered her face with her hands. 'This filthy war. And there's no end to it in sight. I read about the airship that bombed the coast. They'll come further inland next time, won't they, and drop bombs on our cities?' She inhaled shakily. 'But us here, at home, we've nothing much to fear compared to what all of you brave souls are facing.' She dried her eyes. 'I didn't want him to be a hero, I just wanted him to keep safe and come home so we could be married and have a life together.'

'I know ... I'm sorry.' Lucas said the words, knowing they were inadequate. 'But Joe *was* a hero, Olivia. His bravery has been noted in despatches. He should receive recognition for what he did, holding that barrier.' Lucas closed his mind against an image of a man whose uniform was sodden with blood, wielding gun and knife and even timbers prised from the trench wall to keep the enemy at bay so that his comrades had time to retreat and allow reinforcements to take over. The trench had by then been littered with bloated corpses and the battle had been not only with the foe but with the rats who had been their constant companions for days. In the end Lucas had had to leave all but one of his fallen comrades behind. Only five of his platoon had survived. It might have been six had not Private Hunter shown such suicidal courage.

'I've not offered you anything.' Olivia frowned, remembering to be hospitable. 'Are you hungry? Would you like a cup of tea?'

'I'm not hungry. It's all right. I should go.'

'Not yet ... don't go yet.' She gestured for him to come through into the kitchen. 'I don't want to be on my own. Alfie's in bed. School in the morning for him. Just stay for a cup of tea ... please.'

'Your brother is living with you?'

She nodded, filling the kettle while she explained. 'Big changes have happened at home. There was a dreadful row and some family secrets were unearthed. My father has a woman in his life now and he no longer speaks to me. But don't ask me to explain. I don't want to.'

'I'd hoped giving him a job would make things better between you – easier.'

'I know you did ... and thank you,' Olivia said huskily. 'This business is nothing to do with Barratt's. It's something that goes back a long way, to when my mum was alive.' She gestured weakly. 'It seems silly even to worry about it now. As a family, we'll all survive it and carry on, unlike ... ' She covered her mouth to stifle a sob. 'Joe was only twenty years old ... he had so much yet to do.'

'Children are joining up,' Lucas told her. 'Boys of sixteen

are on the front line. God knows how or why.' He gave a bleak, hollow laugh. 'The world's gone mad.'

Their eyes met in a look of mirrored despair, then Olivia quietly carried on making the tea.

'Please, sit down.' She indicated a chair at the kitchen table and they sat opposite one another, sipping in silence.

'How's things at the factory?' Lucas asked.

'Much the same.' She smiled wanly. 'My father and Nelly Smith are at each other's throats, fighting to be top dog. But thankfully Nelly's talk of a strike has come to nothing, so far.'

'I don't miss the place . . . no, all I miss about it is seeing you.'

'Will you go back there when the fighting's over?' Olivia asked him.

'Don't know.' He met her eyes. 'I think things will be different after the war. I know I can't go back to being the man I was, even if I wanted to. Perhaps you might think that's a good thing.'

Olivia regarded him solemnly. 'You've been kind to me, even if we were from different worlds.'

'Were?' He smiled wryly. 'Are we alike now?'

'You seem different, Lucas, humbler.' She bit her lip, not wanting to sound critical when he'd done so much for her. And she understood what he meant about things changing. She felt too she was on shifting sands and the remnants of her youth were disappearing even now, at this minute, never to be reclaimed.

'When I joined up it wasn't just to do my bit. It was to put you from my mind,' he said. 'You'd become an obsession . . . I'm not sure why. But I know I treated you badly, speaking to you the way I did, about becoming my mistress.'

'I don't hold it against you. You never tried to coerce me and I know you could've . . . because of what you'd found out about my father's thefts.'

Lucas played with the spoon on his saucer, smiling ruefully. 'Joe Hunter was a fine person. If I'm humbler ... nicer, I imagine you mean by that ... then perhaps a little of him has rubbed off on me. I'd heard he had a bad reputation but I saw a man full of bravery and principles. I might not have agreed with all he did or said but I admired him. He spoke his mind and spoke it from the heart.'

'He did. He told me off for not standing up to my father. He made me feel ashamed of having covered up things that should never have been tolerated. He was wise and clever and he made me face up to things I'd rather have ignored because it was easier that way He said I deserved better than him ... but there was no one better than Joe.'

'He told me you were loyal to him despite what people said about him.'

'He had a dreadful early life that forced him to do whatever he could to protect his family, but still he overcame it and turned into a kind and decent man.' Olivia's voice thrummed with pride.

'He turned over a new leaf with your help, I expect,' Lucas said. 'That's why he worshipped you, Olivia. You made him the best he could be.' He stood up. 'I should go now. I have to see my family before I return to Dover to ship out.'

'You're going back so soon?' She sounded disappointed.

'At the end of the week.'

'Will you come and see me before you go?'

'No ... I won't come back. But I'll write to you, if I may.'

'I'd like that.'

He turned at the door and stroked her face for a moment. 'Joe thought he was the luckiest man alive, having you. He wanted you to be proud of him; his valour wasn't just for his comrades.'

'I *am* proud of him . . . I hope that somehow he knows that,' she said, through the tears in her throat.

On the step Lucas put on his cap. 'Tell Tommy I'll be back . . . sooner than he thinks . . . to keep an eye on him.'

Olivia almost smiled. 'How did you find out about him and Bill Morley?'

'Just by chance. I left the factory late one evening and saw two fellows lurking by the wall. I sat in the car and watched. It didn't take me long to put two and two together after I did a stock check.'

'As simple as that?' Olivia said ruefully.

'Yes, as simple as that. And the only reason I left late that night was because I'd sat in my office drinking whisky, wondering if I should call you in the following day and coerce you into bed after all. Seems my conscience got the better of me, or else the whisky did. I was quite drunk when I left Barratt's and had to take the next day off.' He took her hand, briefly raising her small pale fingers to his lips. 'Don't worry . . . I'm different now.'

He walked away into the freezing mist and Olivia watched until his silhouette was no longer visible before she closed the door.

Epilogue

'I feel rotten now, being jealous of you. I'm so sorry, Livvie. Matilda told me about Joe.'

'It's all right . . . we all act like that sometimes.' Olivia patted Ruby's arm to reinforce her words of forgiveness. But her heart still ached when anybody mentioned Joe's name.

'How's your sister settled in? Is Nancy coming to live with you too? Any room round there for me?' Ruby gabbled out her questions.

'I thought you and Riley were liking living together. You looked happy enough the other day.'

'He's a drinker, like me mum, and I've had enough of being stuck with one of them.' Ruby shrugged, pulling a face. 'I'd pay you rent.'

'I can't say yes, Ruby. Now Maggie's moved in, I reckon Nancy'll follow soon. She's only stopped where she is in Wood Green to be with her school friends until she has her certificate. She'll be out working before any of us knows it and then she'll come banging on me door.'

'Yeah. Me mum'll shift her on soon as she can.'

Olivia knew that was true. Maggie had already turned up on her doorstep with a packed bag, saying that their father's fancy piece was a bossy cow who sat on her backside and expected her and Nancy to skivvy for her. She'd also said that their father did nothing to slap Sybil down. Tommy was either at Barratt's or in the pub and it seemed to suit Sybil to have the run of the place.

'So, you're a woman of means now, you lucky cow.'

There'd been envy in Ruby's tone but Olivia knew she'd have felt jealous too if Ruby had been the one to have the good fortune to inherit a property. But she couldn't marry a house ... have children with it or snuggle up with it. There was no comfort or wise advice to be had from bricks and mortar.

'I'd sooner have Joe back,' she said simply. 'There's no good luck for me without him.'

Unbeknown to Olivia, before Joe had gone abroad he had seen a solicitor and made a will leaving everything he owned to her. Olivia had been wondering whether she ought to be packing up to leave on the day she had received an official letter telling her the astonishing news.

She would never again have to worry about finding rent or shelter for her and her brother and sisters. If she wanted to she could sell the house and move elsewhere, to a better area.

But she no longer wanted to do that. She had put down roots that seemed to spread deeper every day into the notorious neighbourhood of the Bunk.

Matilda and Alice had been the first to come and see her when the news got round about Joe's death. After they'd left Olivia had felt brighter although she'd not heard from them any more than blunt advice to keep her chin up and carry on. They were there to help, they'd said. And she knew they meant it. Whatever it was she lacked, be it a shoulder to cry on or a few bob loaned until payday, she knew they'd give it if they could.

'Best get on, Ruby,' Olivia said. 'Alfie's probably clearing out Matilda's biscuit tin. He won't want his tea.'

'Yeah, I'd better shake a leg too. 'Spose I could get me 'n' Riley a bit of fish 'n' chips . . . save me stopping off at the corner shop.' Ruby walked on a pace or two then turned back. 'Coming down the Duke Saturday night, cheer yourself up?'

'Perhaps I will.' Olivia huddled into her coat, stamping her feet against the frosty pavement. She gave her half-sister a wave and started off down the road towards Matilda's.

She felt moisture bead her lashes momentarily but blinked it away and put up her face, letting the icy air dry her tears.

She'd wanted to be independent. She recalled, months ago, telling herself she'd give looking after herself without a man's help a damned good go, even though she hadn't been sure then she could afford to rent just a small room.

Well, now she had the chance to prove to everyone, herself included, that she could succeed in life. The man who'd loved her had freed her from the constant worry of keeping a roof over her head.

And so, when this war was done, she'd let Lucas take her to see Joe, to tell him how she'd managed.

Acknowledgments

Anna Boatman, thanks for your enthusiasm and support for the Bittersweet series.

Juliet Burton, thanks for being a brilliant agent and good friend.

Mark, thanks for all your help with everything.